Praise for Caroline M. Yoachim's
Seven Wonders of a Once and Future World and Other Stories:

"Yoachim's reputation as an exceptional flash fiction stylist is founded on her work for *Daily Science Fiction*. Compiled, some of these brief works initially read as slight. 'Betty and the Squelchy Saurus'—recounting treaty politics with monsters under the bed—works well early on, its context already familiar. Full appreciation of the more science fictional worlds takes time, as Yoachim circles back in successive stories to add layers to major themes: interchangeable or malleable bodies ('Temporary Friends,' 'Stone Wall Truth,' 'Grass Girl'), displaced consciousness ('The Philosophy of Ships,' 'Do Not Count the Withered Ones,' 'Pieces of My Body'), time warps ('Rock, Paper, Scissors, Love, Death,' 'Harmonies of Time,' 'Honeybee'). She's especially successful in skewing hackneyed horror tropes, such as a spore invasion launched by compassionate aliens in 'Five Stages of Grief after the Alien Invasion.' 'Everyone's a Clown' showcases Yoachim's ability to layer multiple themes in a very short space, picking up on the childhood perceptions of 'Betty and the Squelchy Saurus' and refocusing them through the lens of an adult horror chestnut. Her gift for reshaping and polishing dulled old gems makes Yoachim's collection truly noteworthy."
—*Publishers Weekly*, starred review

"An astonishing collection from a writer of boundless imagination—full of heart, intelligence, and sense of wonder."
—John Joseph Adams,
Series Editor of *Best American Science Fiction and Fantasy*

"I've always loved the workings of Caroline M. Yoachim's creative mind. Her stories are full of surprises, both little and large. Tales can be charming and evocative and chilling and disturbing. Caroline perverts technology, crunches math's hard truths, builds intriguing alien worlds, and hides love in odd places. *Seven Wonders of a Once and Future World* gives us lucky readers a chance to enjoy many aspects of her thoughtful imagination."
—Sheila Williams, editor of *Asimov's Science Fiction*

"Caroline M. Yoachim is a master of flash fiction. She has impeccable control of the written word, which is reflected in every world she writes. Her stories transcend their length, with characters that resonate long after the final word has been read."
—Jonathan Laden, coeditor of *Daily Science Fiction*

"I've been reading Caroline's stories for a decade now. The earliest ones had glimpses of something aching and beautiful. Ten years later, the work collected here is a sublime distillation of whimsy and deep melancholic thought, darkness, sorrow, and the occasional ray of laugh-out-loud light, with moments of beauty that will stab you—very, very precisely—so that it hurts the most. This is a bloody good collection that deserves a lot of attention."
—Ian McHugh, Writers of the Future Grand Prize Winner

"Caroline M. Yoachim writes stories that burrow inside you, expanding your mind and touching your heart (and occasionally your funny bone). This collection takes you to a breadth of worlds you'll want to return to again and again."
—Sunil Patel, assistant editor of *Mothership Zeta*

"With beauty and clarity, Yoachim brings these worlds to life. From monsters to aliens to extraordinary humans, her characters explore problems both strange and familiar. Yet every time, we recognize ourselves in their hopes and their choices. These stories are lovely."
—Vylar Kaftan, Nebula Award-winning author

"Touching and sad, revealing and sublime, beautiful and innovative—these are the stories of Caroline M. Yoachim. There's more truth in one of her short stories than in the entire avalanche of cookie-cutter novels which pass for fiction these days. *Seven Wonders of a Once and Future World* will remind you why short stories are still the powerful heart and soul of the speculative fiction genre."
—Jason Sanford, Nebula Award-nominated author

SEVEN WONDERS
OF A ONCE AND
FUTURE WORLD
AND OTHER STORIES

Seven Wonders
of a Once and
Future World
AND OTHER STORIES

Caroline M. Yoachim

FAIRWOOD PRESS
Bonney Lake, WA

SEVEN WONDERS OF A ONCE AND FUTURE WORLD AND OTHER STORIES
A Fairwood Press Book
August 2016
Copyright © 2016 Caroline M. Yoachim

Fairwood Press
21528 104th Street Court East
Bonney Lake, WA 98391
www.fairwoodpress.com

Cover by shichigoro-shingo
Book design by Patrick Swenson

ISBN: 978-1-933846-55-2
First Fairwood Press Edition: August 2016
Printed in the United States of America

For Mom and Dad

CONTENTS

Introduction by Tina Connolly 11

PART 1: OUR WORLD

Five Stages of Grief After the Alien Invasion 19
Betty and the Squelchy Saurus 35
Rock, Paper, Scissors, Love, Death 47
The Philosophy of Ships 63
Temporary Friends 77

INTERLUDE: FLASH FICTION WORLDS

A Million Oysters for Chiyoko 87
Carla at the Off-Planet Tax Return Helpline 90
Do Not Count the Withered Ones 95
Pieces of My Body 98
Everyone's a Clown 101
Harmonies of Time 105

PART 2: FANTASY WORLDS

Stone Wall Truth 111
The Little Mermaid of Innsmouth 132
On the Pages of a Sketchbook Universe 144
Seasons Set in Skin 180
The Carnival Was Eaten, All Except the Clown 192

INTERLUDE: FLASH FICTION WORLDS

Paperclips and Memories and Things That Won't Be Missed 201
Please Approve the Dissertation Research of Angtor 204
Grass Girl 213
One Last Night at the Carnival, Before the Stars Go Out 217
Honeybee 220
Elizabeth's Pirate Army 224

PART 3: ALIEN WORLDS

Mother Ship 229
Four Seasons in the Forest of Your Mind 233
Press Play to Watch It Die 240
Ninety-Five Percent Safe 252
Seven Wonders of a Once and Future World 267

Author Notes 285

INTRODUCTION
by TINA CONNOLLY

Caroline and I first met at Clarion West 2006. In January 2009, we tried co-writing our first story. I had failed at this several times already, but Caroline and I decided to try a new way—we would each write an outline to an entirely different story, and then switch. Ideally, we thought, we would eventually end up with two complete stories. And a key component of this new collaboration? It would be zero-stress, with no deadlines, and no guilt.

This turned out to be lucky, because not long after we exchanged the outlines, Caroline had a baby, and then, a year later, I did. We finished the first story—"Flash Bang Remember," which started with Caroline's outline—in January 2012, three years after we'd first started. Caroline immediately sent it off to *Lightspeed* and as immediately John Joseph Adams bought it. The second story ("We Will Wake Among the Gods, Among the Stars") was completed a couple years after that, and just came out—as I write this—in the January 2016 issue of *Analog*. In between all this we decided really late one night that we'd better conquer all the forms, and we co-wrote a flash story ("Coin Flips") and sold it to *Daily SF*. So we've had a pretty good track record so far—even if it sometimes takes several years between the initial idea and final product. (I'll tell you now that we've just started batting around ideas for a novella—you'll probably see that in 2025.)

So. Ten years out from Clarion West, and we have three jointly written published stories, and we each have another fifty or so published stories out there. (Including flash. We both love flash.) So we were pretty delighted to end up each publishing our first collections at the same time, exactly ten years from the completion of our workshop.

People talk a lot about how going through one of the six-week workshops changes you—Clarion, Clarion West, Odyssey—and it does. We both leveled up in writing—and became fast friends and critique partners along the way.

Caroline got into Clarion West with one of the very first stories she ever wrote. (Go on, be jealous with me. I'll wait.) The first two stories she turned in during the workshop—one about birds who ferry the souls of the dead, the other about art and spiders and dark chocolate—were striking for their lush language and imagery. It had taken me many years of work prior to Clarion West to discover a voice of my own—Caroline seemed to have one already. Her stories were dark and beautiful, full of strong images and feelings.

Caroline went home from the workshop and took those dark and beautiful images, and buckled down to the task of turning them into striking stories. She has a background in child psychology and brain development, and it shows up most clearly in stories like "The Philosophy of Ships" and "Four Seasons in the Forest of Your Mind" (two stories that were written almost a decade apart).

Let me tell you about flash fiction, which is a feature of this collection. I love flash. I love what can be done with the form. The very best flash is like espresso. It is a pure shot of—something, straight to the heart. Caroline is one of the very best people working in flash right now, and some of my all-time favorite flash stories are hers, and are represented in this collection.

I ran a flash fiction podcast (*Toasted Cake*) for a couple years, and I of course immediately knew I wanted some Caroline flash stories. For a while we had been matching each other in flash output—then I started writing novels and Caroline shot past me. *Toasted Cake* ran for 150 episodes—nine of those episodes are stories by Caroline, including the first and last, bookending my podcast. That last one is included here in this book—"A Million Oysters for Chiyoko," which is beautiful.

Another of my all-time favorite flash stories is "Mother Ship," which I ran to close out the first year of *Toasted Cake*. Okay, so at 1,375 words it's maybe a touch longer than most flash. Still. "Mother Ship" is epic. It is vast. It spans time and space and it does it all in less time than it takes a novelist to describe someone having breakfast. Also it will make you cry. (It is a sad thing for a podcaster when they can't get through the story they're narrating without choking up, but I had a heck of a time getting through this one.)

Some of my favorite things flash stories can do: worldbuilding (see "One Last Night at the Carnival, Before the Stars Go Out," which creates a gorgeous universe with a few well-chosen words). The emotional turn at the end of a story where a character makes a choice, where the reader feels the emotional impact (see "Mother Ship"). And pyrotechnics, by which I generally mean doing something inventive with the form or amazing with language. ("Harmonies of Time" is a pyrotechnics story—Caroline plays with time and tenses to convey what the narrator is trying to grasp and explain.)

Caroline is strong in all these, and she is also able to take the concentrated images and worldbuilding that make her flash so powerful and delicately spin them out into longer stories. Several of her stories are quite carefully built out of flash stories. (I keep telling her that I expect to see a novel from her using this trick.) You might wonder if flashmashing stories ends up looking like three kids balancing on top of each other inside a trenchcoat, but the far more apt metaphor here is a lapidary one: a ring or bracelet made of many different gems.

The resulting stories have their own sort of pyrotechnics simply by being so careful with the structure. One of these stories is "Five Stages of Grief." In it, each section of the whole stands on its own, but the five also build up to a stronger story in the end, jumping off a progression we're all familiar with. "Rock, Paper, Scissors, Love, Death" is another one that works within its tight framework, this time to deliver a story of time travel and love.

Caroline regularly plays with time and memory. It's here in the stories "Harmonies of Time" and "Honeybee." But you can also see it in some of her more recent stories that start taking epic jumps into the future. She closes with the title story, "Seven Wonders of a Once and Future World," her story that is the most forward-reaching. Each jump goes ahead into the future—and yet each section is carefully constructed around a familiar conceit to us—the seven wonders of the world. We are familiar with the earthly wonders—and that gives us a basis to understand these alien ones, as she takes us farther and farther out.

Caroline works well within these tight structures, which is something I understand. The structured scaffolding gives a grounding to her vivid imagination; it is a solid jumping off point. As with "Harmonies of Time," she uses structure to good effect with "Press Play to Watch it Die," and "Four Seasons in the Forest of Your Mind." She is representing alien forms of thought; the structure helps rein in the breathtaking worldbuilding; it gives the reader something to hang on to while alien brains grow around her.

Pyrotechnics are fully evident in the worldbuilding of "On the Pages of a Sketchbook Universe"—an engaging conceit that does what it says on the tin. The fun is in watching the characters more or less literally think outside the box to solve their problems. "The Little Mermaid of Innsmouth" follows a different set of conceits—it wraps its Lovecraft story and its Andersen story neatly up together, and comments on both. It is a testament to Caroline's skill that I had never before imagined this particular mash-up, and now I can't think why I hadn't.

Some of my favorite stories of Caroline's are the ones that delicately touch on grief within the family. "Paperclips and Memories and Things That Won't Be Missed," "Mother Ship," and "A Million Oysters for Chiyoko"—three of my favorite stories—all deal with mothers grieving the loss of their child, and figuring out how best to navigate their grief. In "Temporary Friends," a mother debates on how best to explain death and loss to her own child. Loss is inevitable in life, and Caroline's stories are dark but never hopeless. Somewhere, there is a way through—perhaps what you learn can help another.

Caroline's stories still have the strong, dark images I grew to expect at Clarion West. From "Stone Wall Truth," describing the process of opening someone up on the judging wall: "Only the face was still open, facial muscles splayed out in all directions from the woman's skull like an exotic flower in full bloom." That is an image equally beautiful and grotesque, that additionally paints an accurate picture of the event.

(What if you find out you've been doing something terrible all along? Would you risk all to put it right? What would you give up?)

From "Seasons Set in Skin," while mother is tattooing daughter for war: "Around the lines, the skin turned pink and slightly swollen, a temporary effect that made the flowers look three-dimensional and almost real."

(What if you risk everything and fail? Are there any winners in war?)

From "The Carnival Was Eaten, all Except the Clown," an opening both delicious and visceral, that fully evokes the ephemeral and nostalgic air of a carnival: "Overnight, as the magician slept, sugar melted into candy sheets that billowed up into brightly colored tents."

(And, what if you risk everything and succeed?)

They are hopeful stories for being so dark; there is light in Caroline's darkness. The carnival glitters; the clown fights against her fate. After all, she fights to help others—that is a key theme in these stories, again and again. She loses much—she changes—but there is hope for another day.

Tina Connolly
January 2016

PART 1:
OUR WORLD

FIVE STAGES OF GRIEF AFTER THE ALIEN INVASION

DENIAL

Ellie huddled in the corner of her daughter's room. She sang a quiet lullaby and cradled her swaddled infant in her arms. Lexi was four months old, or maybe thirteen months? Ellie shook her head. There hadn't been a birthday party, and thirteen-month-olds didn't need swaddling. She tried to rearrange the swaddling blankets so they didn't cover Lexi's face, but every time she moved the blankets, all she saw underneath was another layer of blankets.

"Oskar?" she called. "Come and hold the baby for a bit, I need to go out and buy formula."

Oskar came in and gave her the same sad look he'd worn all week. Work, she decided, must be going poorly. She wished he would confide in her about it, but he didn't like to burden her with his problems. Lexi's room was dark, and the light switch wasn't working. Ellie opened the blinds, but the window was covered in white paint, making it impossible to see outside.

"Did you paint the windows?" she asked. Their apartment was on the third floor, and it had a lovely view of the treetops. "Lexi will want to see the birds."

"Sporefall killed all the birds," Oskar said, his voice bitter, "and we don't need formula. It's been months, Ellie. I know how hard this is, but I can't do this anymore. The pain is bad enough without reliving it with you every day."

Ellie frowned. "If you're too busy to watch the baby you should say so."

Oskar leaned down and kissed the top of her head. "I'm going, Ellie. There's a caravan heading down to L.A., and I haven't heard a thing from Jessica since sporefall. She didn't even answer the letter I sent about Lexi. I've hired a caretaker to help you get by without me—her name is Marybeth. She lost her wife to the sporefall, so maybe you two can help each other get through your grief."

"A little extra help around the house will be nice," Ellie said. "Tell your sister hello."

Ellie smiled. Jessica was a good influence on Oskar. She'd cheer him right up.

Oskar's eyes were teary when he turned to leave the room. She wondered if his allergies were acting up. He'd said something about spores. When she went to get the formula, she could pick up an antihistamine for him.

Ellie put Lexi in the high chair, still swaddled in blankets, and tried to spoon-feed her pureed peas. It wasn't working very well. Four months was too early for solids and the entire jar ended up on the blankets rather than in the baby. Ellie put the empty jar in the sink.

Someone knocked on the door, unlocked it, and came inside. It wasn't Oskar.

"Your husband gave me a key," the woman said. "I'm Marybeth. You must be Ellie."

Ellie nodded. "This is Lexi. She's a bit of a mess right now." Ellie dabbed at the blankets with a napkin, then added, embarrassed, "She's a bit young for it, but I tried to feed her."

Marybeth smiled sadly. "Lexi died, Ellie. Nine months ago the Eridani seeded the planet with spores. Once they realized the planet was inhabited, they undid the damage as best they could, but they came too late for the elderly and the very young."

"Well, I'm glad they came nine months ago and not now," Ellie said, wiping the tray of the highchair with the food-smeared napkin. "Oskar hired you to watch Lexi? Do you do laundry, too? Her blankets are a mess."

Marybeth carefully unwound Lexi's outermost blanket and put it in the laundry hamper. "It would be better if you could move on, Ellie. This isn't healthy."

Satisfied that Marybeth could take care of Lexi, Ellie went to the bathroom and took a shower. Cold water poured down around her skin, and she scrubbed until she was red to be sure she got rid of all the spores. Oskar was allergic to spores, and she didn't want to make his symptoms any worse. Oh, but the babysitter—she came from outside, she must have been covered in spores.

Ellie ran out from the bathroom, dripping wet and wrapped in a towel. "You came from outside! You've exposed poor Lexi to spores!"

Marybeth put one hand on Ellie's shoulder and gently guided her back to the bathroom. "Hush now, the spores are gone, all grown into plants. We don't have to worry about spores."

Marybeth returned the next day with an old man. Ellie hoped he wasn't sick. He was dressed too warmly for the weather: clunky black boots, several layers of baggy clothes, and a fleece hat with flaps that covered his ears. He was short and stout with ashen skin and a grin too broad for his face. It made him look like a toad, Ellie thought, then pushed the uncharitable thought from her head.

"Come in, come in," Ellie said, then realized that her welcome was too late and Marybeth and her—was the man her father? Maybe her grandfather—were already in the entryway of her apartment.

"I thought it'd be good for you to meet one of the Eridani," Marybeth said. "It might help you come to grips with what happened."

"Nice to meet you, Mr. Eridani," Ellie said. It was time for Lexi's nap. The apartment was warm, good for sleeping, but Ellie could use some fresh air. "Do you sing, Marybeth?"

"Sing?" Marybeth asked. "No, not really."

"What about you, Mr. Eridani?" Ellie turned to the old man. "Will you sing my daughter lullabies? I'd like to go for a walk."

"It might be good for her to get out of the house," Marybeth told her grandfather. "I think Oskar made a mistake in painting the windows." She went over to the kitchen window and pried it open, sending flecks of dried paint flying everywhere.

Ellie turned her back on the kitchen, trying to protect Lexi from the nasty paint dust. "Don't let her breathe the dust, she just got over a terrible cough."

The old man nodded, then held out his arms to take Lexi. He held her gently, and while his mouth was fixed in the same broad smile, his bulging black eyes seemed sad. Ellie wondered if he was longing for grandchildren of his own.

"Don't be sad. Lexi clearly likes you. She didn't even cry." Ellie put on a sweater and opened her apartment door. "I won't be gone long."

The trees along the edge of the sidewalk had oddly purple leaves, and the people that passed looked far too weary for a sunny Saturday afternoon, but as she walked beneath the open windows of her apartment, she could hear the low hum of a lullaby, slow and sweet, sure to soothe her daughter straight to sleep.

ANGER

Amelia was twelve the night the spores fell, and she remembered it vividly. Thousands of meteors burned bright as they fell through the atmosphere. Charred black pods burst open when they crashed to the ground. By dawn, the air was filled with swirling clouds of orange mist, like pollen blowing from the trees. Every person and creature on the planet breathed the spores. The birds were the first to die, but not the last.

"Come away from the window, Sis." Brayden tried to tousle her hair like she was six years old or something. "Dad will be home soon, and you haven't done your homework yet."

"I didn't do my homework because it's stupid to pretend that nothing has changed," Amelia said. "Everyone in my class lost people to the spore. Friends, grandparents ... siblings. Tia's parents got killed in the riots. Zach's older brother died in one of the fires. Then the way they healed us—"

She shuddered. She still had nightmares about the croaker that thinned into some kind of fog and poured itself down her throat, picking the spores out of her lungs and healing the damage the sprouting plants had done. It was that or die when the spores grew, but she'd still thrashed so much that Dad had to hold her down to keep her from hurting herself.

"It was eleven months ago," Brayden said. He stared at the sky for a moment, lost in his own thoughts. "What's the alternative to going back to normal? If you didn't have school, you'd sit home and sulk all day like that guy that came down from Portland."

Their neighbor's brother had showed up on the caravan last week, looking for Jessica, but she'd already left for the space station. She was one of the scientists chosen to help negotiate a treaty with the aliens. The only treaty Amelia wanted to see was 'get off our planet and take your damned purple plants with you.'

"Oskar sits around and sulks all day," Amelia said, "but I would go out and kill croakers."

Brayden shook his head. "You can't kill croakers. People have tried. They can't be poisoned, stabbed, or shot. No matter what you do to them, they recohere, they heal. If you did more of your homework, you might know that."

Unlike the rest of her classes, which she'd given up on, Amelia had paid careful attention to all the details of croaker biology. Despite their solid-seeming forms, croakers were essentially sentient fog. The squat froglike body they used on Earth was a dense gray cloud, thick enough to hold up the clothes they wore, but little else. Projectiles and blades passed right through and did little harm, and poison passed through unabsorbed.

Amelia had a different plan. She would trap a croaker bit by bit in a hundred glass jars. Then she'd throw the jars into a fire, one by one. Would the pain of that death be as bad as the last desperate gasps of her little brother? Gavin was four, and screamed all his last night in pain and fear. Spores made his lungs burn, the doctor said.

Amelia would make a croaker burn.

Croakers wandered the streets like ghosts, occasionally stopping to eat leaves from the purple plants that had grown from the spores. According to the news, the croakers were observing, collecting data so they could repair more of the damage they did at sporefall, but as near as Amelia could tell, the big gray frogs were just making themselves right at home. Amelia waited behind one of their licorice-smelling plants with a cardboard box full of glass jars.

A croaker came to nibble at the leaves, and she jumped out from behind the bush, jar in hand. She scooped out a big section of the croaker's ugly frogface. The croaker was thicker than she expected, like gelatin or pudding, rather than air. The gray goo in the jar was repulsively flesh-like, and her stomach churned as she screwed the lid into place. The croaker let out a high pitched whine. Its face appeared unchanged, despite her jarful of gray goo.

She couldn't do it. She had a boxful of jars, and she wanted the croaker to burn, but she couldn't bring herself to take another scoop of its ashen flesh. It stared at her with round black eyes, still making a high pitched sound, though softer now, a sad keening sound.

"You killed Gavin!" she screamed. "You messed up my whole world and now you stay here like you own it! You should burn for it!"

She hurled the jar of gray goo at the sidewalk. It shattered against the concrete and shards of glass flew everywhere. A cloud of gray swirled up from the shimmering fragments of the jar before drifting back onto the croaker. Into the croaker.

She grabbed another jar from her box and threw it at the croaker. It bounced off the alien's face, and the froglike grin didn't even flinch. "Go back to where you came from!" she shouted and flung jar after jar at the croaker, until her cardboard box was empty and the sidewalk was buried beneath a pile of shattered glass.

The croaker scooped up the broken glass in big webbed hands, mounding it and sculpting it into its own image. Amelia watched, fascinated despite herself. The croaker smoothed the bits of glass as easily as a sculptor might shape clay. It made a statue of a croaker, and in the statue's broad glass hands there was a human child with indistinct features. Not her brother, but a child like him. Perhaps all children like him. Unlike every croaker Amelia had ever seen, there was no froglike grin on the statue's face.

Brayden ran over. "I heard all the noise, and—" He stared at the statue.

"I wanted to set a croaker on fire, but I couldn't do it." Amelia said. "Not even after everything they did."

Perhaps it was a trick of the light, but the statue didn't look empty. Delicate orange flames danced inside the statue of the croaker, complete with thin wisps of gray smoke that reminded her of the swirling cloud when she broke the jar and let the croaker go. It had left a piece of itself inside the statue, to burn inside the glass.

She thought her mind was playing tricks on her, but Brayden saw it too. "They already burn for what they did."

The croaker bowed its head, then turned and walked away.

BARGAINING

The alien standing in front of Jessica was four feet tall, slate gray, and shaped like an oversized toad. It smelled like chalk and made a quiet wheezing noise, barely audible over the hum of the orbital stabilizers. The temperature onboard the station was comfortable for humans, but the alien wore a thick sweater, knitted by one of Jessica's former graduate students as a gesture of goodwill from all humankind. A large round button with the number 17 was pinned to the purple wool. Eridani didn't use names.

Eridani 17 extended a webbed hand. The flesh of its fingers thinned, creating the illusion of wisps of smoke curling up from its palm. The smoke shaped itself into North America, and then a city skyline

"Toronto?" Jessica asked. The city had a distinctive tower. Eridani 17 shook its head.

Negotiating with the Eridani was like a game of Pictionary, except that Jessica was sober and—thank god—didn't have to actually draw anything. Her brother Oskar had always been the artist in the family, excelling at Pictionary even when he was half her age. If his most recent message was any indication, all he ever drew now was pictures of his estranged wife, who lost her mind after sporefall killed their baby.

"Seattle," Jessica said.

The Eridani understood spoken language, but not by translating individual words. According to the best available translation, the Eridani heard ideas in the spaces between the words.

She hoped that this was true. She was not authorized to ask for what she truly wanted, and the sessions were recorded.

Eridani 17 transformed its speaking hand into an image of several Eridani standing between two skyscrapers. As Jessica watched, a giant web appeared between the two buildings, soon followed by several pods filled with what she guessed were baby Eridani.

"Seattle has a substantial human population, but I'm sure we can find an abandoned region that suits your needs," Jessica said. Atlanta, perhaps. It was warmer there, and the sporefall had been particularly dense.

Eridani 17 made no response, and its hand solidified. This meant that an alternate site was acceptable. Jessica would get a list of abandoned and near-abandoned cities to propose in tomorrow's negotiations.

Next on her agenda was a request for additional technology to assist in maintaining and rebuilding the human population in the regions hardest hit by sporefall. Negotiations happened in parallel, with dozens of humans in one-on-one sessions with the Eridani at any given time. She checked her tablet to make sure that nothing from the other sessions had altered her agenda.

"Like many of my people, I lost family members to the spore," Jessica began. She concentrated on her memories of her niece, a tiny baby that she had held only once. "We struggle to rebuild what we once had."

She was supposed to be asking for technological advances in transportation and communications, for new methods of agriculture to help human crops coexist with the invasive purple weeds that grew from the Eridani spores. She was supposed to infuse her spoken words with a plea for these things, so that the aliens would hear their needs in the spaces between her words. Instead, she thought of all the people she had lost in the sporefall and the chaos afterwards—relatives, coworkers, neighbors, friends.

Give them back, she pleaded. The Eridani were so advanced; there had to be something they could do. "Surely there is some technology you have that can help us."

Eridani 17 thinned itself entirely into cloud, leaving the purple sweater in a puddle on the floor. It reformed itself into the shape of Gavin, her neighbor's four-year-old son who had died from the spore. The boy sat cross-legged on the floor and in his lap was a tightly swaddled baby with a drooly grin and dimpled cheeks. Lexi.

The alien had somehow called the children from her mind, but the scene that it created was not a remembered image. Gavin had never met Lexi. And yet, if he had, this was exactly how it might have looked. The boy's expression was a mix of curiosity and wariness, and Lexi—

She very nearly said what she was thinking, that she would give anything to have her back. Her death, and Ellie's breakdown, was destroying Oskar. Each death from the spore cascaded into a thousand unwanted consequences, and all the world was broken now. There must be some way the Eridani could undo time or reshape space and reverse the deaths they'd caused. There had to be a way.

Gavin held Lexi with one arm and raised the other up in front of him. He thinned his fingers, which was disconcerting. Jessica knew the ghosts were really just Eridani 17, but human fingers shouldn't thin the way that Gavin's were thinning.

"You will give us back the ones we've lost in exchange for," Jessica paused to study the map that hovered where Gavin's hand should have been. "The entire West Coast?"

It snapped Jessica back to reality. The Eridani had always shown remorse for what they'd done. They'd claimed to be unaware that the planet was inhabited, that they would not have sent their spore and, later, their colony ships, if they had known otherwise. She hadn't expected them to use her grief to their advantage in negotiations. She could not trade that much territory, not for mere ghosts.

"Not for shadows and memories," Jessica said.

Gavin leaned forward and kissed baby Lexi on the forehead. It was so close to what she wanted, they were almost real. Better than Ellie's empty bundle of blankets. Close enough, perhaps, to pull her sister-in-law back to reality. So close to what she wanted, and yet so

far. And she couldn't trade that much territory even if the Eridani offered to pull the actual children from the past. "I am not authorized
to negotiate concessions of this magnitude."

Gavin and Lexi melted right before her eyes, merged into a puddle, and reformed into the default frogform of Eridani 17. The entire
session was recorded, and back on Earth it was undoubtedly already
being analyzed. They would see the tears in her eyes, and she would be
sent back to the planet in disgrace. Back to Earth, but not back home.
Home was a place that still had those children in it.

DEPRESSION

Oskar got home from a long shift of weeding alien foodplants out
of the avocado grove. His hands were stained purple and smelled
of licorice. He set a 10 pound bag of avocados on the counter. He
should trade some avocados to the neighbor kids for one of the trout
they farmed in the courtyard fountain, but he didn't want to eat. He
shut himself into his sister's guest bedroom and stared at the ceiling,
crushed beneath the weight of his bad choices.

He shouldn't have left Ellie.

The walls were covered in sketches of his wife. Her smile, her eyes,
her slender hands. Cheeks dotted with pale brown freckles. Hair tied
back with a few loose strands to frame her face. She was the one who
left him. She left reality behind and spent all day pretending a bundle
of blankets was their baby girl. No one could blame him for not wanting to relive that kind of pain, day after day. He'd tried for months.
Marybeth was a family friend, and he'd given her everything they had
to take care of his wife.

All of that so Oskar could go and find his sister, Jessica. He'd
been worried that she might need help, but she wasn't sitting helpless
in her apartment. No, she'd gone off to the space station to be one of
Earth's ambassadors. This was supposed to be his big chance to not
be the baby brother anymore, to swoop in and save Jessica from the
post-invasion chaos, and she hadn't needed him at all. She never did.
He had no idea if she'd even gotten the message he'd tried to send.

Someone pounded on the door. Probably the neighbor kids. Brayden liked avocados, and trading with him was a better deal than trying to buy them somewhere.

He opened the door. "Jessica."

"I can't believe you changed my locks." Jessica faked a scowl, then grinned and gave him a big hug. "You look like crap."

Oskar retreated to Jessica's guestroom. His sister hadn't understood how he could come down here and leave Ellie behind, no matter how he tried to explain.

People started pouring in from the east. They moved into abandoned apartments, office buildings, malls. Los Angeles turned back into a bustling city. Jessica said that the government had traded Arizona and New Mexico to the frogs. All the extra people made it harder to get work. His heavy heart made it harder to wake up and face the day.

On his second straight day of refusing to get out of bed, Jessica marched into his room like she was twenty and he was ten, and she could boss him around. "Draw me a bird."

"Go away," he said. There were no birds, and he could see right through his sister's scheme. Birds were from happier times. She thought sketching a picture would pull him out of this funk. She was wrong. Remembering the way things were would only make it worse. "There are no birds. Sporefall killed them all."

"Think of it as rent. It'll do you good to draw something other than Ellie, over and over again. All I'm asking for is one really good picture of a bird." Jessica left without waiting for him to answer.

He only had a few sheets of good thick paper left; he'd used most of it to draw his pictures of Ellie. He got one out. He closed his eyes and tried to picture the stellar jays that had eaten peanuts from the feeder outside his window, back before the sporefall. He remembered blue and black feathers, and the general shape of the head, but the details were fuzzy. There were pictures of birds in books, but he shouldn't need that. He should be able to do this. It had only been a year.

For the first time in weeks, he opened the guestroom blinds. The apartment was on the fourth floor, and the window looked across the alley at a near-identical brick building. He tried to imagine birds flying in the alley, landing on the concrete below to hunt for bugs or seeds, but thoughts of flying set his mind to thinking about soaring out through the window and falling into oblivion.

He closed the blinds.

Two days later Oskar had only one sheet of good paper left, and he had not yet managed a picture of a bird. He ate when Jessica forced him to, and he slept until Jessica made him get out of bed. There was no point to pictures of birds. There was no point to anything, not anymore.

Jessica came in with half an avocado. Did he really have to eat, again? But no, she started eating it herself, spooning the mushy green into her mouth and smiling as though it actually tasted good to eat a plain avocado, again. "This is the last one from the bag, and food rations have been short at the community center, so we can't count on that. We need to decide what to do next. There's a caravan going north, right through Portland."

He didn't want to go back. What if Marybeth had abandoned Ellie, despite all her promises? He couldn't face the chance. "I'm staying here."

Jessica shook her head. "You're not. I'm trading the apartment for passage on the caravan and food for the trip. If you want to stay in L.A., you're on your own."

She left him to consider his options, and his gaze drifted to the window. It would be so easy, so quick. If he never went back to Ellie, he could believe that she was okay, maybe even happy. He wouldn't have to face a world that could never possibly be right again.

He opened the blinds. An alien was walking in the alley, smiling the same damn frog-smile that the aliens always smiled. It saw him in the window, and thinned into a cloud. When it came back together, it was a flock of birds. Not the stellar jays he'd been trying to draw, but pigeons, plump and gray. They fluttered up and landed on windowsills and power lines outside the window. They weren't real, but they were enough to evoke a clear memory in his mind.

Oskar could soar out the window, or he could draw this memory of birds for Jessica and go with her back to Portland.

He calmed his shaking hands and sketched the birds.

ACCEPTANCE

Marybeth walked with Ellie to the clinic. Ellie insisted on bringing 'Lexi,' a bundle of filthy blankets that she refused to believe wasn't actually her dead baby. Marybeth hoped the new treatment would help. Ellie was an amazing woman, able to find joy in all the smallest things. Even now, as they walked along abandoned streets with Eridani foodplants, Ellie chattered to her blanket-bundle baby about how beautiful the orange blossoms were on the lovely purple trees.

Marybeth couldn't appreciate the beauty of the 'blossoms.' They weren't flowers at all, but clusters of tiny spheres, each one full of orange spores. The trees would release spores soon, and despite Eridani assurances that there would be no harm to humans this time, she could not put aside her memories of the last sporefall, and all the death it caused. Yolanda's death.

Very few healthy adults had died in the sporefall, but her wife hadn't been healthy. She'd had alpha-1-antitrypsin deficiency emphysema—a genetic disease that left her with the lungs of a 60-year-old smoker when she was only 32. Even without the sporefall, her condition had been deteriorating. She'd had a complex daily routine of inhalers and pills to try to keep the coughing fits and wheezing in check, and a tank of supplemental oxygen for her worst days.

Yolanda would have seen the beauty in the alien plants, just as Ellie did. Looking at Ellie was like looking into Yolanda's past, back to the early days of their relationship, before her illness sapped away her strength.

Was falling in love with a straight woman any better than carrying around a bundle of filthy blankets?

*

The clinic was an Eridani clinic, one of several that were part of the treaty that had been negotiated with the aliens. They were greeted by a man in a white coat when they entered, and left to wait in a small room with black plastic chairs and battered magazines from before the sporefall.

"Will Oskar meet us here?" Ellie asked. Much as she refused to accept the death of her baby, she continued to believe that Oskar would return.

"He's not here, El. We're going to see one of the Eridani," Marybeth explained. "They have a treatment that might help you."

An alien appeared in the doorway, wearing what looked like a down comforter tied like a toga. It studied them with beady black eyes, then beckoned to Ellie, recognizing that she was the one more in need of treatment.

"I'd like to come too," Marybeth said.

The Eridani doctor nodded its assent.

The treatment was painful to watch. The alien thinned itself into a gray fog, then reformed into images drawn from Ellie's mind—not mindreading, exactly. If Ellie said nothing, the alien could not hear her thoughts. It was only when Ellie spoke about her daughter that the memories came through. Then it was like watching a moving slideshow all in shades of gray:

Oskar holding Lexi in the hospital, the day she was born.

Ellie's struggles with breastfeeding when Lexi wouldn't latch.

Bottles of formula, carefully mixed and warmed at all hours of the night.

So many things that Marybeth had never seen, memories that haunted poor Ellie and made her break from reality. Then came the worst, the sporefall.

Ellie going out to find formula for Lexi, and coming back covered in fine orange dust.

Lexi's pitiful coughing and weak cries.

The days on end where she only slept upright, leaning on Ellie's chest.

Finally, the end, the moment when there were no more breaths, and Oskar took Lexi away. Marybeth cried as the baby disappeared from the three dimensional scene the Eridani recreated from the particles of its own body. She glanced at her friend, hopeful that the therapy had helped. Ellie was crying, but she continued talking. Her baby was dead, but Ellie wasn't finished.

More images appeared, of a Lexi that never was, in a world that no longer existed. Lexi toddling across the living room, Lexi putting on a ridiculously big backpack and going off to kindergarten, Lexi at the park feeding ducks. There were no ducks, and Lexi would never be six, but the Eridani doctor showed the impossible futures right along with the horrifying past.

Lexi's senior prom, her wedding, the birth of Ellie's first grandchild. The scenes skimmed through time and Marybeth could no longer watch, no longer listen to Ellie's words. She simply watched Ellie stare into the images that poured out, and held Ellie's hand as she cried. Since she had turned away from the doctor, it took her a moment to realize that the Eridani had resumed its default frogform. Ellie was no longer speaking, only sobbing softly.

She met Marybeth's eyes, and there was a depth to her gaze that was missing before.

"My Lexi," Ellie said. "My Lexi is gone."

After the treatment, Ellie didn't need a caretaker, but Marybeth had long since abandoned her apartment and they enjoyed each other's company. Ellie often wore the same grim smile that so often graced Yolanda's face when she was sick, and it tugged at Marybeth's heart. She tried to remind herself that Ellie was a different woman, a straight woman, but she could not help but hope that somehow, if enough time passed, things could be different.

Ellie made good progress in embracing reality. Together they dismantled Lexi's crib and set it out on the curb in front of the apartment. It wasn't long before a woman who looked like she might be expecting came and carried it away.

Oskar came back from L.A. Marybeth greeted him at the door,

and had no choice but to let him in, for all that he abandoned Ellie when she needed him most.

"I'm so glad you're both okay," he said. Marybeth shrugged. He could say what he wanted, it wouldn't change what he had done. She only hoped that she wouldn't lose Ellie, now that he was back.

"Hi, Oskar," Ellie said. The sight of him brought her to tears, but Marybeth couldn't tell whether they were tears of joy or pain or anger.

"I'm so sorry," Oskar said. "I didn't want to leave you, but I couldn't stay. I was hurting too."

"I forgive you," Ellie said. "I know it must have been hard."

He smiled and went to embrace her, but she stepped back. "I forgive you, but we can't go back to how things were. I saw what might have been, if the Eridani had never come, and Lexi had lived, and it was beautiful. We could have had an amazing life. But those are impossible futures, and I have to let them go and come back to what is real."

"Is it another man?" Oskar asked, then realized that Marybeth was standing there. "Or another woman?"

Ellie shook her head. "There's no one else. Certainly not Marybeth, though she's a dear friend."

It was nothing that Marybeth did not already know. She had always known that Ellie was straight; there had never been any sign that she was interested. Ellie would never be Yolanda.

Marybeth grabbed her coat and made polite excuses. Ellie and Oskar had a lot to talk about, and Marybeth didn't want to hear it. She went outside and started walking, not caring where she went.

The wind picked up, and an orange cloud blew down from the Eridani foodtrees. The second sporefall had begun, a new cycle of alien life. According to the translators, the initial sporefall had been a different strain, modified to be more aggressive for terraforming, so that the Eridani would be sure to have foodplants when they arrived at their new home. This second sporefall should be as harmless to humans as ordinary pollen.

Marybeth sneezed at the orange air, but she refused to go back inside.

She would not hide from this new world.

BETTY AND THE
SQUELCHY SAURUS

Betty was hanging wet towels on the clothesline when a faded blue Plymouth Roadking came up the drive. Someone had donated the car to the Six Sisters orphanage back in 1952, and Sister Mary Margaret was the only nun who knew how to drive it.

A new girl got out of the car—maybe five years old, with brown hair and lots of freckles. Skittish little thing, probably terrified of monsters. It'd be no problem getting her to follow the rules. Betty hung the last towel and wiped her hands on her skirt.

"Since you're done, you may show Catherine around the orphanage," Sister Mary Margaret said.

"Yes, Sister." Betty grabbed Catherine's hand and pulled her inside. "Come on. You'll be sleeping on the third floor, but you gotta learn the rules first."

"Mary Margaret told me the rules in the car."

"Sister Mary Margaret," Betty corrected the younger girl. "These are different rules. These rules will keep you from being eaten."

Catherine had no answer to that. Betty took her to the second-floor room she shared with Janet. The walls were bare and both beds were neatly made. Betty knocked on the closet door three times, paused, then pulled the door open. Taped to the inside of the door was a sheet of blue-lined paper covered in small slanty handwriting.

"This is the Treaty of the Bathroom Alcove," Betty said. "It keeps you safe from monsters, so pay attention."

The rules had been written in pencil by the Giant Unsquishable Cockroach who lived in the coat closet in the front hall. The treaty had been signed in the bathroom alcove because that was neutral territory—not quite a closet because it had no door, but kind of like a closet because the nuns stored towels in there.

Betty read the treaty out loud:

(1) Closets and under the beds are monster territory. Children may obtain items from the closets during daylight hours, as long as they knock before entering. Items that fall under the bed should be considered lost forever.

(2) Monsters must not be seen during daylight hours. Monsters are free to roam the orphanage at any hour of the day or night, so long as they are not seen.

(3) Monsters may not eat children during daylight hours.

(4) Monsters may eat children at night ONLY if the child (or any portion thereof) leaves the safety of its bed.

(5) Children may ask adults to check for monsters under the bed or inside the closet. However:

(6) Children may not, under any circumstances, request that an adult drag a monster out of its territory to shoot or otherwise kill the monster. Violation of rule #6 will release the monsters from the terms of this treaty.

The treaty was signed by Roach and by Allison Michaels, who lived in Betty's room until last year, when she got adopted. One corner of the paper was missing, and Betty suspected that Squelchy Saurus—the monster that lived in her closet—had eaten it. Squelchy was fond of paper.

"Do you understand the rules?" Betty asked.

Catherine nodded, and Betty sent her upstairs to the big third-floor room where all the younger girls slept.

Squelchy Saurus lived in a closet. It was a nice closet, small and cozy, full of delicious-smelling clothes. With the door closed it was wonderfully dark, and it kept her hidden from the terrifying grownups that sometimes came to make sure the room was clean.

Squelchy wasn't as quick as Stabby Gnome, or as strong as Crushmonster—she wasn't even clever like Gooey-Blob-That-Can-Look-Like-Most-Anything (aka "Bob the Blob"). As monsters went, Squelchy Saurus was disappointingly ordinary. The thing that made her special was where she happened to live—inside the closet of Betty Williams, the oldest girl, and the one who had given the monsters their current names.

Betty had given Squelchy her first name because her skin oozed with clear slime, and her last name because her shape resembled a dinosaur from a book on the shelf above the bed. Squelchy decided to try and get the book. She balanced on her hind legs and bumped the corner of the shelf with her head. If she got the book, she could use it to lure Betty out of bed after dark.

She wasn't sure what she'd do if Betty did leave the bed, but the girl was too smart to fall for any of Squelchy's tricks. The attempts seemed to amuse Betty, and it kept Squelchy entertained, too.

Squelchy heard a sound and darted back to her closet, afraid it might be one of the nuns, but it turned out to be Poison Bitey-Snake. Bitey fit under the bed and seemed to dislike any monster that didn't.

"Hi, Bitey," Squelchy said, creeping back out of the closet.

Bitey hissed. "Those are her namesss. Must you use them?"

"Well, what should I call you?" Squelchy asked. Bitey didn't answer. Monsters were good at many things, but terrible at names.

"So," Bitey said, "have you heard the newsss?"

Squelchy shook her head, sending droplets of slime spraying everywhere. "What news?"

"Theresa Smith was adopted, and before she left, she broke the treaty. All the monsters on the third floor have been shot."

Squelchy felt sad for the poor dead monsters, but Bitey clearly didn't care.

Bitey slithered up one side of Janet's bed and coiled himself around the pillow. "We no longer need to obey the rulesss. Today, we will plan our strategy. Tonight, the children are ours for the taking."

*

Betty finished her chores and went back to her room to read. She was nearly done with *Animal Farm*, and she had just enough time to finish it before dinner. She reached for her book, then noticed that the room was messy—both beds were rumpled, three books had fallen off her shelf, and Janet's pink hair ribbon was on the floor. Sister Mary Joseph was strict about keeping things tidy, and the room was definitely not as Betty had left it.

She knocked three times on the closet door and opened it. Usually the closet smelled musty. Today it didn't.

Squelchy Saurus had gone somewhere.

Betty picked up Janet's pink ribbon and put away her fallen books. One of the covers was slimy, pointing again to Squelchy.

Betty peered under the beds, careful not to let any portion of her body extend into the shadows beneath the mattresses. There was a blue hair ribbon under Janet's bed which, by the rules of the treaty, was now lost forever.

Under her own bed there were two books. One was the copy of *Lolita* that her step-daddy used to read to her, back before the police took him to jail and brought her here. She'd torn the cover off so that the nuns wouldn't recognize it. The other book was *The Velveteen Rabbit*, which she was too old for now, but it was the only thing she had from her real dad. She remembered unwrapping it on her fifth birthday, a couple weeks before he left for Korea to fight in the war. Every time she looked at it, she felt silly for not reaching under the bed and grabbing it, but she couldn't bring herself to break the treaty.

Betty sat on her bed to think. There had been no sign of Poison Bitey-Snake under the beds, but it was daytime, so of course there wouldn't be. Still, something felt wrong, and if the monsters were up to something she'd have to find out what it was.

Squelchy sat at the back of the meeting, her tail looped over a sack of potatoes and her head resting on a basket of onions. Her slime dripped down onto both the onions and the potatoes, making it rather likely that they would go moldy, but there were a lot of monsters at the meeting, and the pantry was crowded. Bitey, unfortunately, was sitting on the shelf above her head. She'd hoped to save that spot for Pink Fluffy Flesheater, who she used to share a closet with.

"All nine monsters living in the attic were killed in last night's tragic shooting," said Bob the Blob. "Crushmonster saw the whole thing. Theresa convinced a grownup to drag each monster out from under the bed, and—with a gun made from his thumb and the first two fingers of his hand—he executed them without mercy. Our brave comrades on the third floor stayed true to the treaty until the end, remaining completely invisible even during the massacre. The children violated the Treaty of the Bathroom Alcove, and the terms are clear. We are free to do as we please."

"Yesss!" Bitey shouted, his voice blending with the cheers of other monsters.

Squelchy said nothing. It seemed unfair to take revenge on the children who were still here. It was only one adopted girl who had disobeyed the treaty. Squelchy tried to remember the girl. She had been timid. Not the sort to cause trouble, and not the heroic type either.

"Strange," Squelchy muttered, "that such a quiet child would cause so much trouble for the others."

Bitey, having heard her, dangled his head down from the shelf to whisper in her ear, "Someone might have given her the idea. Pity about the third-floor monsters, leaving all that nice space underneath the bedsss."

Bitey had never gotten along with the third-floor monsters, but Squelchy never imagined that he would arrange to have them killed. She wondered if anyone would believe her if she told them what he'd done. Probably not. She had a reputation for not being very smart.

The meeting continued all afternoon. They decided to take the children just before dawn, while they slept in their beds. According to Stabby Gnome, the children thought all of the monsters were gone, so they wouldn't expect an attack. They could drag the little girls out of their room through the secret passageway in the back of the cupboard, and feast on tender flesh and lightly roasted bones.

Squelchy went back to her closet. She had no interest in eating

the children, though she did enjoy nibbling on their hair and fingernail clippings, and stray socks and mittens were nice to gnaw on if
they'd been recently worn and smelled of child.

She decided to pretend that the old rules still applied. She hun-
kered down in her closet, back behind the laundry hamper where no
one would see her, and curled up for a nap.

As the oldest girl in the orphanage, Betty usually didn't pay much
attention to the third-floor girls. She taught them the rules when they
arrived, then left them alone. They stared at her when she sat down at
their table at dinner.

"Hi, Betty," one of the girls said. Her name was Elise or Erica or
something. Eliza. That was it. Eliza had been adopted but then "returned" for reasons that were not entirely clear. Rumor was she bit her
adoptive older brother, and if that was true, the boy must have had it
coming because the nuns didn't punish her when she came back.

"Hi, Eliza," Betty said. "I need to know what's going on with the
monsters."

Anna smiled. She was four years old and had dimples that pretty
much guaranteed she'd be adopted. "I can tell you! Teesa's new daddy
came to the attic yesterday and he got all the monsters and he shooted
them—Bang! Bang!"

Anna and the other kids made shooting gestures. Betty had tried
shooting at Bitey-Snake like that once, angling her hand to point
under the bed before squeezing her thumb as the trigger, but it hadn't
worked. Only adults could kill monsters.

Catherine, the new girl, was practically bouncing out of her seat.
"Now we don't have to do all those silly monster rules anymore!"

Poor dumb third-floor kids. They didn't realize the danger they
were in. It didn't matter if you got an adult to get rid of the monsters
you knew about, there were always more. The treaty was the only thing
that kept them safe. Now everyone was in danger of being eaten.

"Theresa's new daddy didn't get all the monsters," Betty informed
the little girls. The monsters from her room had escaped, and she suspected that all the monsters on the main floor had also been spared.

That meant at least a dozen closets worth of monsters, and several of the older girls' beds.

There was no way to get rid of all the monsters, even if they asked the nuns for help. No, she'd have to come up with some way to reinstate the treaty, and for that she'd need something to negotiate with. Prisoners, she decided. They'd need to set traps. She told the other girls her plan. "Get ready for bed, but after Sister Mary Gabriel checks on you, sneak down to the second floor. Come in pairs, and be as quiet as you can."

It was a Monday, and after the children went to bed the nuns watched *I Love Lucy* on the black-and-white TV the Anglethorn family had donated to the orphanage when they brought Eliza back. Their hearing was terrible, so they turned the volume up loud. They'd never notice that the girls were out of bed.

"I'll take care of the rest," Betty said.

Day turned into night, and Squelchy Saurus huddled in the back of her closet. She hadn't heard Betty or Janet come in and go to bed, which was odd. Odder still, there were voices coming from the big common room across the hall. Children's voices.

She strained to hear what the voices in the other room were saying, but slime from her head dripped into her ears, so her hearing wasn't very good. She crept out of the closet and across the room. Suddenly Betty and Janet and several other girls came down the staircase from the third floor.

"The beds are ready," Betty told the younger girls. "Now we wait for the monsters to make their move."

So they waited, the children in the common room, and Squelchy—paralyzed by fear of discovery—just inside the doorway of Betty's room. She chastised herself for being such a pitiful monster. The children should be afraid of her, not the other way around!

Finally, at four o'clock in the morning, the floor above the common room creaked under the weight of a herd of monsters. Led by Betty, the girls poured out of the common room. Thankfully, they hurried past Squelchy without stopping. Squelchy expected them to go upstairs, but instead they went down.

She listened for any sign of the children, and when she didn't hear anything, she crept downstairs. The girls had found the end of the secret passageway—a fireplace in the front sitting room—and they'd covered it with the fireplace grate. They were now pushing furniture up against the grate. The nuns would be furious—the children weren't technically allowed in that room at all.

Squelchy shuddered at the thought of furious nuns, but they were nowhere to be seen. Satisfied that the children were busy blocking the passageway, Squelchy went to the third floor, oozing so much from the effort that her feet made a squelching noise as she climbed.

On one side of the stairwell was the little girls' bedroom, a long narrow room with a window on the far end. The white cupboard with the secret passageway was in the corner, doors wide open. There were two rows of beds, and each one had the enticing odor of a small child. The bleached-white sheets were rumpled, as though recently slept in.

Squelchy knew this was a trap—the beds had not been used tonight, and the children were blocking off the secret passageway. She hovered in the doorway. Under the bed nearest the door, Stabby Gnome clutched a pair of red rubber boots, coated in mud. Not something that would appeal to Squelchy, but Stabby Gnome was fond of boots, and having once been a garden gnome he often spoke wistfully of dirt.

The next bed was covered in colorful candy wrappers. Pink Fluffy Flesheater, lacking any childflesh to eat, was perched atop the headboard, chewing enthusiastically on a mouthful of toffees.

Several of the other beds were carefully arranged to attract monsters. Here a bed with a ragged stuffed animal, there a bed piled high with freshly washed towels. Then she saw it. Her bed. Betty knew her so well. The bed was littered with hair brushes, strands of hair woven all through the tines. She drooled big globs of drool that mixed with her general sliminess before dripping to the floor.

If she was quicker, she could grab the hairbrushes and come back out. If she was cleverer, she could think of some plan to get the brushes without getting trapped. But she wasn't clever or quick or strong, so she backed away from the large bedroom. She heard the children coming up the stairs, so instead of going to Betty's room, she went to the only other room on the third floor—the bathroom.

The children slammed the bedroom door shut. One of the older girls must have stolen the keys from Sister Mary Magdalene, because after the slam Squelchy heard jingling keys and the click of the bolt. Squelchy backed into the bathroom alcove, the worn white towels soaking up her slime.

She heard the children celebrating their victory. She was wondering what she should do next when she heard footsteps in the bathroom.

"I'm coming in, Squelchy," Betty called, "I know you're in there."

Betty left the other girls in charge of guarding the door and went into the bathroom to talk to Squelchy Saurus. As monsters went, she wasn't bad—slimy and oozy and unpleasant to look at, but also kind of shy. She was certainly better than Poison Bitey-Snake, who Betty was afraid of, even though she was too old to be afraid of monsters any more.

Squelchy was in the back of the alcove, sitting on a towel. A washcloth fell onto her back, and slowly slid down toward the pink tile floor, carried by the flow of slime.

"We need a new treaty," Betty said, inching forward until the tips of her shoes were in neutral territory. With all the shelves, there wasn't room for her to get all the way into the alcove, and she didn't want to get too close to Squelchy anyway. She wondered if Allison had gotten all the way in. The Unsquishable Giant Cockroach was smaller than Squelchy, so there might have been room.

Squelchy crept forward and licked one of her shoes.

"Ew."

"Sorry, they smell yummy." Squelchy backed away. "I can't make a treaty. I'm not a leader."

Betty knew she'd rather deal with Squelchy than any other monster, so she went and pounded on the bedroom door. "Okay, prisoners—either you can agree to be bound by whatever treaty I negotiate with Squelchy, or you will still be locked in here when the nuns come up to wake the girls."

Monsters were afraid of grownups, and terrified of nuns. She hoped their fear would keep them from realizing that if the nuns found everyone out of bed, the girls were in worse trouble than the monsters.

The monsters discussed their options.

"We have voted, and we accept Squelchy as our representative," said a raspy voice that probably belonged to Stabby Gnome.

"This is a bad idea," Poison Bitey-Snake hissed. "Ssshe is not a clever monster, and the girl will trick her into thingsss we don't want."

Betty smiled and returned to the Bathroom Towel Alcove.

After an hour of negotiation, Squelchy was ready to sign. Most of the terms of the Second Treaty of the Bathroom Alcove were the same. The monsters kept their territory of under-the-beds and inside-the-closets, and would hide during the day and refrain from kidnapping and eating children so long as they stayed in bed. The children were allowed to get things from inside the closet during the day, and were not allowed to have monsters shot or otherwise killed.

The only thing different about the new treaty was that items under the bed would now be treated in the same way as items inside closets. During daylight hours, children would be allowed to retrieve them as long as the monsters were given ample warning beforehand. This seemed fair to Squelchy. Children had always been allowed into her territory, why shouldn't they be allowed under the beds?

Satisfied with the terms, Squelchy picked up a crayon in her mouth and signed the bottom of the paper. Then she ate the crayon, which was crunchy and waxy and smelled a little bit like Betty.

Betty checked the hallway clock. The treaty was signed, and daytime rules were in effect. She read the treaty to the monsters locked in the bedroom. Janet and some of the other girls went downstairs to unblock the other end of the not-so-secret passageway. When the living room was back in order, Betty told the monsters that she would open the door in thirty seconds.

She counted to thirty. There was rustling on the other side of the door as monsters hurried to find hiding spots.

"I'm coming in," she announced. The room was quiet and empty, and Betty stepped inside to make sure it was safe. Poison Bitey-Snake darted out from behind the door.

"Under the bed is my territory! Things down there are forever lossst!" he hissed, and bit her in the leg.

Squelchy charged into the bedroom when Betty yelped, and other monsters came out from under attic beds. Crushmonster and Pink Fluffy Flesheater subdued Bitey and threw him out the window.

Squelchy went to check on Betty.

"Will you move up here, now that the treaty is signed?" Betty asked, rubbing the spot where Bitey had bitten her. "You've earned the promotion."

Squelchy shook her head. "I like my closet. I've got it all set up the way I like it."

Janet went downstairs in search of Sister Mary Margaret, who was the most likely to help Betty without asking why everyone was out of bed. Squelchy snuck downstairs to her beloved second floor closet.

She hid behind the laundry hamper when two nuns brought Betty in. They cleaned her leg and asked questions about the rat Betty claimed had bitten her. Squelchy waited quietly and hoped the towering figures in their scary black-and-white clothes wouldn't notice that the closet door was ajar. Eventually, the nuns left.

Betty kicked off the covers and examined her leg. The area around the bite was red and irritated, but Poison Bitey-Snake looked (and acted) more poisonous than he actually was.

"I'm getting things from under the bed." Betty announced, even though there weren't any monsters under her bed. No one wanted Bitey's old territory with so many nice third-floor beds available.

By convention, monsters and children weren't supposed to talk to each other, but after retrieving her books Betty said, "I don't need this book any more, I'll toss it in the closet."

The book hit the hamper and dropped to the closet floor. To Squelchy's surprise, it wasn't the children's book that Betty had given up; it was the other one, *Lolita*. Poison Bitey-Snake had spent a lot of time reading that one. He almost never deigned to read the other one, the one about the rabbit that was so well loved that he became real.

Squelchy Saurus wondered if Betty would ever love her that much. It must be a wonderful thing, to be real. Could children love monsters? Squelchy suspected it was rare. But if Betty was leaving snacks for her, they were off to a good start.

ROCK, PAPER, SCISSORS, LOVE, DEATH

ROCK

Rock crushes scissors. Nicole sat on a crowded bus to Spokane, knitting a turquoise scarf. The gray-haired man sitting next to her stared obsessively at his wristwatch. He was travelling with his son, Andrew, who sat across the aisle. She offered to trade seats so they could sit together, but both men refused. The bus wound around the sharp curves of Stevens Pass, and Nicole made good progress on her scarf.

Out of nowhere, Andrew's father grabbed her and shoved her across the aisle, into Andrew's arms. There was a loud crack, and a roar like thunder. A boulder the size of a car slammed into the side of the bus. Nicole stared at the wall of stone that filled the space where her seat had been. The red handles of her scissors stuck out from underneath the rock, the blades crushed underneath. Andrew's father was completely lost beneath the stone.

Love shreds paper. After the accident, Nicole met Andrew for coffee. She returned his father's watch, which had somehow ended up in her jacket pocket, though she couldn't figure out how or when he'd put it there. Andrew gave her a pair of red-handled scissors, identical to the pair she had lost. She invited him for Thanksgiving dinner with her parents, since he had no other family. They took a weekend trip to Spokane, and when the bus reached the site of the accident, they threw handfuls of flower petals out the window.

Andrew was an engineer and a poet. He built her a telescope that folded spacetime so she could see distant exoplanets, and he wrote her scientific love poems. At their wedding, they gave the guests bags of confetti made from shredded strips of his poems, so they could be showered in love.

Rock destroys love. Two years into her marriage, Nicole suspected Andrew was cheating. He stayed late at work, went out late with the guys, took weekend business trips. He was gone more than he was home, and he got angry when Nicole asked him about it. She already knew what she'd see when she followed him out to Beacon Rock, but she had to see it with her own eyes, if only from a distance. She was surprised to see him with an older woman, rather than a younger one. She filed for divorce, and he didn't argue.

Scissors cut paper. A few years after the divorce, Nicole sat in the swing on her front porch and cut love poems and photographs into thin strips. It was her therapy, letting go of the memories she'd kept boxed up after Andrew moved out. There was something satisfying about the snip of the scissors. Words flew everywhere. Eternal. Heart. Devotion. True. Paper piled up on the porch, and a breeze sent a few strips swirling. It reminded her of the confetti at their wedding, and suddenly cutting paper wasn't as satisfying. She hurled her scissors into the front yard.

Death steals scissors. Nicole went out into the yard the next morning to get her scissors. She didn't want to run them over with the lawnmower later, and she wasn't quite ready to let go of the first gift Andrew ever gave her. The poems were gone from her porch, and she couldn't find the scissors in the yard, even after an hour crawling on her hands and knees. The common link between the poems and the scissors was Andrew. Had he taken them? Against her better judgment, she drove to his apartment. The door was open, and there were cops inside. Andrew was missing, and he'd left a note. A suicide note. The body was never found. Neither were her scissors.

Paper covers rock. Nicole visited Andrew's grave on the anniversary of his death, even though she knew there was no one buried beneath the stone that bore his name. A slip of paper covered the top of the tombstone. A poem, taken from her porch and painstakingly taped back together. On the back, a message, in Andrew's careful slanted cursive. *If we had stayed together, you never would have let me go back.*

Love conquers death. Nicole found the time machine in the storage locker Andrew had rented when he moved out. The machine was set for the day she'd taken the bus to Spokane. The day he died, and the day they met. She reset the dial to when their relationship started to fall apart. She was tempted to go further back, to have more time, but she'd only be stealing from herself. Time reversed its course, and Nicole stepped out of the time machine into her own garage, where Andrew waited with open arms.

PAPER

> folded white paper
> contains all eternity
> space-time envelope

Andrew sat at his desk and scribbled haiku into his Moleskine notebook, casting occasional glances out the window to see if the mail had arrived. He wanted to bring the CZT detectors he'd ordered with him on his trip to Spokane. The detectors were the final component for his latest project, a telescope that would bend space-time to generate high resolution images of distant exoplanets. Folding space-time blueshifted visible light, and the CZT detectors would measure the resulting x-rays so that he could convert them back into a visible image. The telescope would give him something to tinker with between meetings at his company's annual 'retreat.'

an icy planet
cast out into empty space
binary no more

He tore the page out of his notebook and crumpled it. It'd been two years since he divorced Liz, and he needed to stop wallowing in loneliness and sorrow. His life was better without all the fighting, and he had more time for his work this way. He willed himself to write a more cheerful haiku, but the words were gone. He stared at the empty page.

A postal worker delivered the mail, and Andrew hurried outside to collect it, pleased to discover a padded yellow envelope in among the other items. He jogged back upstairs to his apartment, unlocked the door, and threw the bills and junk mail onto the counter. He slipped the envelope of CZT detectors into the duffle bag he'd packed for his trip. Then he looked up.

An older man stood in his living room, hands raised so that Andrew could see that they were empty. "When I was fifteen, I cheated on a physics test by writing the entire study guide in Japanese characters on my jeans. I made it look like the fabric was designed that way. No one caught me, which was disappointing. I didn't need to cheat, but I enjoyed the risk of being caught. I was disappointed no one noticed."

Andrew had told that story to a few friends, but never the bit about wanting to get caught. He studied the man. His features were eerily similar to Andrew's, but his skin was wrinkled and his hair was more gray than black.

"You're me," Andrew said, "but from the future?"

His future self lowered his hands and sat down on the couch. "I arrived at 11:47am on November 3rd. Remember that. Write it down somewhere. I have two things to tell you before we go to catch our bus. First, if Nicole asks us to switch seats, we have to refuse. Second, when you build the time machine, you must make it entirely out of things that are in your apartment *right now*. I can't get back to this moment unless all the pieces are here—if the power source, say, is still in some manufacturing plant in China, trying to come to this moment would spread my molecules between here and there, and I'd be too thin to recohere."

"So why are you here?" Andrew asked, a million questions racing through his mind. "Am I really going to build a time machine? What stocks should I buy?"

Future Andrew stubbornly refused to answer any of his questions. In fact, he didn't say another word until they got to the bus station.

"Sometime after we get on the bus, I'm going to hand you some scissors. Hide them, and make sure Nicole doesn't see." He got in the line to board the bus, standing behind a woman with short black hair and a cute vintage dress from the 50s. Andrew stood behind himself, wondering if anyone else would notice that there were two of him in line. An old woman in a matronly pink dress hobbled right by them without giving them a second look, headed for the front of the line. She clearly hadn't noticed that anything was amiss.

Judging by the long line, the bus would be full, so it didn't seem too odd when his future self took the seat next to Nicole. Future Andrew patted the seat across the aisle. "Sit here."

"Are you together?" Nicole asked. "I can move across the aisle if you'd like to sit with your son."

"Oh, no, this is fine." Andrew said, remembering his future self's instructions, and wondering why it was so important.

"We both prefer the aisle," future Andrew added. "More leg room that way."

Andrew pulled out his notebook. He'd intended to work out a few equations for his exoplanet telescope, but instead he found himself casting furtive glances at Nicole and writing poetry.

pairs of particles
in quantum entanglement
giving birth to time

Nicole went to the back of the bus to use the bathroom, and future Andrew passed him the red-handled scissors from her knitting bag. Andrew tucked them into the front pocket of his laptop bag. "What am I supposed to do with these?"

"When the time comes, you'll know," future Andrew said solemnly. Then he laughed. "They're only scissors. Try not to worry about it too much."

His future self held up an identical pair of red-handled scissors, grinned, and then tucked the replacement scissors into Nicole's knitting bag. Andrew wanted to ask why he'd traded one pair of scissors for the other, but Nicole returned to her seat.

His future self glanced at his watch. Without warning, he grabbed Nicole. He ignored her indignant yelling and shoved her across the aisle, practically into Andrew's lap. A deafening crash. A giant rock. The bus careened down the mountain road, screeching against the metal guard rail. A boulder filled one side of the bus, from floor to ceiling. A cold November wind blew in through the hole the rock had torn in the roof. There was no sign of his future self. The red handles of a pair of scissors stuck out from the underneath the boulder.

They were closer to Seattle than Spokane, and Nicole had a friend that worked at one of the local ski resorts. Andrew probably should have gotten on the replacement bus Greyhound sent to take passengers to Spokane, but when Nicole offered him a ride back to Seattle, he accepted. His boss would be angry about him missing the company retreat, but Andrew figured any time you watch yourself die in a bus accident, you got a free pass on work.

The day after the accident, Andrew sketched a preliminary blueprint for his time machine onto the gray-lined paper of his Moleskine notebook. He photographed everything in the apartment with his digital camera, taking special care to document every small appliance and electronic device so he would know which items he could use to scavenge parts. He had nearly finished documenting everything when he remembered the CZT detectors in his duffle bag. He could order another set for his exoplanet telescope, but he was grateful these had arrived in time. There was no way he'd be able to build a time machine without them.

He paused. But why was he so grateful? He'd thrown himself into making the time machine because it was, admittedly, a fascinating challenge and exactly the sort of project he was interested in, but his future self died under a giant rock. He put down his camera. Maybe he'd be better off not building the time machine after all.

The red handles of Nicole's scissors stuck out of his laptop bag. His future self had stolen them and really wanted him to have them. Well, he wanted nothing to do with a future where he died in a freak bus accident. If he was supposed to have the scissors, then he'd get rid of them.

He turned them in his hands.

Nicole had given him her number in case he wanted to talk to someone else who'd been through the accident, stammering that it wasn't really the same because she hadn't lost anyone. She'd shoved the paper into his hand and said an awkward goodbye. From the little he'd gotten to know her on the car ride back to Seattle, she seemed nice. A librarian who spent most of her time buried in books. She even liked poetry.

Maybe he would use the scissors as an excuse to see her again. He wondered if that was his future self's goal all along, and then decided he didn't care. He had no way of knowing which choices led to a heroic but untimely death, and he liked the idea of seeing Nicole again. It had been a long time since he'd had any interest in dating, and it was time to move on. He pulled out the scrap of paper with her number and called her up to see if she wanted to grab some coffee.

SCISSORS

Nicole put her scissors into a compartment at the top of Andrew's latest invention. He'd built it, but she'd come up with the idea—a device that would let them test hypothetical changes to the timeline and calculate the likelihood of various outcomes. The scissors, which would be crushed by the rock that caused the accident, calibrated the device to the appropriate subset of realities.

They had a few hours to run tests before her younger self got back from the library. Nicole was glad there were only a couple more weeks before the weekend at Beacon Rock. It would be easier once the divorce went through and Andrew could spend more time with her.

"Ready for the first test?" she asked.

Andrew nodded. She entered the first test condition.

Death annihilates scissors.

Test: Andrew convinces Nicole to not get onto the bus.

Result: Andrew never builds time machine, cannot go back to warn Nicole.

Probability of timeline collapse: 99.56%

Probability of death, Nicole: 99.56%

Probability of death, Andrew: 99.56%

Exactly what they'd expected. Nicole was pleased that the device was working. Now they could get on with the actual tests.

Death annihilates scissors.

Test: Andrew convinces Nicole not to get onto the bus AND convinces his younger self to build a time machine.

Result: Andrew tries to build the time machine, but fails; cannot go back to warn Nicole.

Probability of timeline collapse: 98.23%

Probability of death, Nicole: 98.23%

Probability of death, Andrew: 98.23%

"Once you know that you need to build the machine, why can't you just build it?" Nicole demanded. "You can obviously do it, because you did it in *this* timeline."

"I got the idea for how to use gravitational lensing from something your mom said at Thanksgiving," Andrew said, "and you only invited me to Thanksgiving dinner because you thought I'd lost my dad on the bus."

"What did she say? We can send that as part of the message to

your past self, when you convince him he needs to build the machine."
Nicole started entering the conditions of the test. "Wait! We could do
even better, we could send the blueprints back."

"It won't—" Andrew began, but Nicole finished entering the conditions and ran the test.

Death annihilates scissors.
Test: Take blueprints for the time machine back in time and give
them to younger Andrew.
Result: Timeline collapse.
Probability of timeline collapse: 99.99%
Probability of death, Nicole: 99.99%
Probability of death, Andrew: 99.99%

"Oh, right. If you build the time machine based on blueprints that
you bring back from the future, then you never actually think up how
to build the time machine." Nicole tried to remember every trick and
twist she'd ever read in a time travel novel, but nothing seemed like
it would work.

They tested several other possibilities, but everything resulted either
in Andrew dying or the timeline collapsing. When it was nearly time
for her younger self to return home, she asked Andrew if she could take
the hypotheticals device to her apartment, so she could keep testing.

"I think we should accept the fact that I have to die, and enjoy the
time we have," Andrew said. "We've always known it would be hard
on you when I go. Your younger self wouldn't have let me do it."

"So why should I? Because I'm older, I should be willing to let
you go? There have to be other solutions." Nicole realized there was
at least one.

Rock crushes scissors.
Test: Andrew doesn't go back in time.
Result: Nicole dies in bus accident.
Probability of timeline collapse: 0.01%
Probability of death, Nicole: 99.78%
Probability of death, Andrew: 0.45%

"This is the one," Nicole said. "It'll be better this way. Neither of us will ever know what we're missing."

"You can't let me go, so you're going to shift that burden to me?" Andrew brushed her cheek with his fingertips. "Not fair."

"Totally fair."

"At least stay until Beacon Rock. We can have one last wonderful trip before we wipe everything we've shared out of existence."

Their life became a series of postponements. She would try to convince him to destroy the time machine and not go back to save her. He would beg for another day, another trip, another kiss, another memory.

She couldn't really blame him. Why shouldn't they enjoy themselves before they wiped their relationship out of existence? She let him stall, let herself enjoy the time she spent with him, and tried not to think about the inevitable end. She allowed herself a year. One beautiful year.

"Four years from today, you go back in time to die," she told him. "Send me to the future."

"What?"

"It's the same problem all over again," Nicole explained. "If I'm here, you won't destroy the time machine. You need to forget about me, move on. Send me to the future, and then all you have to do is destroy the time machine. Any time in the next four years."

"I can't do it," he said. "If I had it in me to let you die, we couldn't be here."

"You just haven't decided yet," Nicole argued. "You can still avoid this loop, find someone else, live a happy normal life. I'll disappear. I was supposed to die that day anyway, and you have more to give to the world than I do."

"That's bullshit and we both know it."

She smiled and thought of the teenagers who'd come into the library for the escape they desperately needed from a terrible reality, the researchers seeking obscure titles or ancient microfiche. Her life touched others, and she had a lot to give. But someone else could step in and give those things. She didn't want to be the damsel in distress, saved by a prince. She wanted to be the hero.

"Send me to the future," Nicole repeated. "It'll be easier for you to decide if I'm not here."

Andrew set the dial on the time machine for 70 years into the future. Nicole took the scissors with her, so he wouldn't be tempted to run any more tests.

LOVE

Nicole stepped out into a condo with huge windows overlooking the ocean. A fire crackled in the fireplace, and classical music played over wall mounted speakers. There was a note, written on a torn-out Moleskine journal page, on the table next to the time machine.

a robot programmed
to prepare for this spring day
our joyous new home

The robot described in the poem was standing in a wall alcove. She wondered if it was a special creation of Andrew's or a standard household appliance. It had a generic humanoid appearance, with facial features that looked like no one in particular. The designers had opted to make it silver, rather than flesh colored. It matched the stainless steel appliances, which she suspected were selected to match the time period she'd left, rather than whatever the modern fashion happened to be.

She heard the soft whir of the time machine behind her, and closed her eyes. Would the shift in the timeline be instantaneous, or would she feel the pain of her death before she dissolved into nothingness? She waited, but the end didn't come.

"Our timeline starts from the assumption that I go back to save you. I can't stop myself, even if you ask me to," Andrew said. "But we can have a little more time together, here in the future, or back somewhere in our past if you'd rather."

Andrew stepped out of the time machine mere moments after she did, but he had aged. He must have stayed in the past years after she'd left, and she still existed. Which meant he hadn't destroyed the time machine, and he probably never would.

He took her hand, an excited grin on his face. "Wait until you see the library I set up in here."

The condo had two bedrooms, and he'd converted one of them into a maze of books. Shelves all around the walls, even up above the door. Rows of shelves in the middle of the room, with barely enough room to walk around them. Shelves underneath the cushioned nook that was built in underneath the window. Every shelf was packed with books.

"Paper fell out of favor," he said, "but I knew you'd miss your friends."

She ran her fingertips over the spines of the books. It was an eclectic collection with a little bit of everything, literary classics, science fiction, mysteries, romance. Nonfiction travel books and assorted science texts. Poetry. It was beautiful.

"Thank you."

They held hands and walked on the beach, watching teenagers fly around recklessly on motorized kites before splash-landing into the ice cold ocean. Nicole worried about them at first, but they all wore protective wetsuits and emerged from the ocean unscathed. Andrew eventually pointed out robots at even intervals along the beach.

"Probably lifeguards," he said.

Robots, it turned out, were everywhere. There were shops manned by robots, shuttle buses that drove themselves, even hospitals and schools with no sign of any humans. Nicole wanted to ask someone about it, but the only people she ever saw were the teenagers on the beach, and they were too busy fly-diving for her to get anywhere near them.

Nicole approached one of the lifeguard robots. "Where are all the people?"

"There are 57 people currently using this section of beach," the robot responded.

"Not here, specifically," Andrew clarified. "Historically, there were people doing tasks that robots do now. Why are there so few people?"

"We are programmed as caretakers for those who remain," the robot explained. "Most people have moved on."

"But are there *any* people left?"

"I only have data for this section of beach," the robot said. "Fifty-five entertainment bodies rented via Central 3, and two independent units."

Nicole figured there'd been some sort of singularity event, like she was always reading about in science fiction novels. After a while, she and Andrew got used to the robots and came to appreciate the privacy. It was a calm, peaceful life, and she was happy. But every morning she looked at the time machine and wondered—was tomorrow the day he would go back? Was today the day she should destroy the machine?

She knew what she needed to do, but she kept putting it off. There was no harm to one more day, a little more time. One more book to read. One more of Andrew's poems. One more walk on the beach.

Then one day it was too late.

She was in the kitchen cooking breakfast, and he stood next to the time machine. "I have to go now, while I'm still strong enough to carry you over the aisle."

And with no more goodbye than that, he stepped into the time machine and disappeared. She had waited too long and missed her chance, and now her paradise would be her prison, and she would be alone with only books and robots until she died.

DEATH

Rock crushes scissors.

Test: Nicole programs the time machine to pull Andrew out of the past before he is crushed.

Result: Unknown.

Probability of timeline collapse: 0.01%

Probability of death, Nicole: 1.48%

Probability of death, Andrew: 50%

An army of helpful robots and a roomful of books went a long way toward solving a time travel problem, but even with all the resources of the future, she couldn't come up with a perfect result. Even odds was the best solution she'd found, and the time had come to try.

The only way she'd come up with to use the time machine remotely was to send a piece of the machine back in time. Andrew had created some kind of bond between all the parts, and the machine would reach out into the past to try to bring itself back together.

Nicole searched for something she could use to hide a piece of the time machine, and eventually she found an antique wristwatch at a pawn shop. After the accident, Andrew had given her a pair of red-handled scissors, and she'd given him a watch that had mysteriously appeared in her jacket pocket. This watch. Their younger selves assumed that Andrew had tucked it into her pocket as he pushed her out of harm's way, but perhaps that wasn't what really happened.

Nicole took the watch home and pried open the back. She removed a case screw from the watch, and replaced it with one of the tiny screws that held the modified CZT detectors to the time machine's circuit board.

With a piece missing, using the time machine would be dangerous. Nicole didn't have to worry about it when she went back, because she'd be wearing the watch. After that, though, anyone attempting to arrive in this section of the timeline might partially recohere on the missing piece, spread too thin across time to ever come back together. It would be dangerous until Andrew came back with the watch, the missing screw.

The watch was loose on her wrist, and she pushed it halfway up her forearm to make sure it wouldn't slip off. At the last moment, she remembered the red-handled scissors. She needed to return them to the past so her younger self could hurl them out into the grass for Andrew to find. She traveled back to when Andrew and both her younger selves were at Beacon Rock. While the house was empty, she snuck the scissors back into their drawer.

Then she went all the way back to the beginning and arrived at

Andrew's apartment a few minutes after the two of him had gone to catch the bus.

Rock crushes love. Nicole arrived at the bus station shortly before it was time to board and cut to the front of the line, determined to be the first person onto the bus. Her age worked to her advantage, because the younger passengers didn't have the heart to tell an old lady to move to the back of the line. Enough time had passed since Andrew left that she was confident he wouldn't recognize her, leaning heavily on her cane and wearing thick glasses. Even so, she had dressed all in pink and worn a wide floppy hat. She hated pink.

She made her way to the back of the bus, ignoring the driver's suggestion that she might be more comfortable in the front. "I like to be close to the ladies' room," she told him. She picked a seat where she'd be able to see the accident.

Out the window, Andrew was talking to his younger self as they stood in line. Young Andrew was listening, but he was clearly distracted by the impossibly young Nicole that was in front of them in line. She could jump across time, but never again would she be that young. It seemed like more than a single lifetime ago that she met Andrew and created this convoluted mess in their timelines.

But maybe she could fix it.

Nicole watched Andrew steal the scissors out of her younger self's knitting bag. She watched him stare at the time on his watch, identical to the one she wore on her own wrist. He had no idea that the watch held a piece of the time machine. He waited for exactly the right moment. He picked Nicole up and pushed her across the aisle into the arms of his youth. That was the moment. She stopped the hands on her watch to record the time.

There was an odd hum from her watch, a vibration that gradually increased in intensity. She worried that the time machine was trying to pull her back into the future, but Andrew was staring at his watch too. He was supposed to take it off and slip it into Nicole's pocket, and his curiosity turned to panic as he realized he had deviated from the plan.

Outside, the boulder broke free. It was oblong and gray and the size of a minivan, and it seemed to hang for a moment, teetering on the face of the cliff before crashing down through the roof of the bus. She stared at the wall of rock where Andrew had been.

When the machine pulled at its missing piece, there was an equal chance that it would pull her back instead of Andrew. Fifty-fifty. Even odds. Two watches, two pieces of the machine, only one chance to get it right.

The crucial moment had passed, and she was still on the bus. She prayed that she'd done everything right, that Andrew was safely in the future, and not crushed underneath the rock.

The younger version of herself embraced the younger Andrew.

In the confusion after the accident, she slipped the watch off her wrist and into her younger self's jacket pocket.

She'd left a note for Andrew in the future, explaining what she'd done. If he lived, he would see it, and maybe he would figure out some way to bring her forward, too. They could join the singularity and transcend together beyond these tangled loops of time.

And if he couldn't find a way to bring her forward? Well, it would take years, but she would wait for the youngest Andrew to build the time machine, and then she could send herself back into their future.

She watched their younger selves get into a car and drive away, and then she felt it, the tug of the future.

Love conquers death.

THE PHILOSOPHY OF SHIPS

Kaimu dug his skis into the snow and forced himself onto the steeper slope along the edge of the run. Michelle was behind him, and there wasn't far to go. He was going to win.

A white-furred creature stirred at the sound of his approach. It rose up from the snow and stared, paralyzed, directly in his path.

The safety mechanism on his skis activated, but it was too late to turn. Instead, the skis treated the creature as though it was a ski jump. Kaimu landed, and the safeties shut off.

Several meters up the mountain, Michelle knelt in the snow. "You hit an Earther."

Impossible. Before he left the *Willflower*, the tourist board had assured him that the glacier-covered Canadian region wasn't populated. All the native Earthers were in a temperate band near the equator.

"*Hominid Class 304. Organic component. . .100 percent.*" Michelle transmitted her initial assessment to the rest of her collective, pausing briefly upon the discovery that the creature had no upgrades. The rest of her transmission was a stream of numbers relating to the creature's condition. All Kaimu gleaned from the numbers was that the creature wasn't dead. Yet. Blood stained its shaggy white coat and seeped into the icy powder. Kaimu stepped off of his skis. Cold seeped through his skisuit and chilled his feet. He trudged up the hill, kicking his toes into the powder.

"Can you save it?" he asked.

"Twenty-eight percent. My training is neurosurgery, and I've never worked on anything 100 percent organic before." Michelle's gaze was locked on the two parallel gashes in the creature's torso, but most of her mind was elsewhere, searching for the knowledge she needed. To her, this was a problem, a challenge. He wondered if she was enjoying it.

Michelle turned away, and Kaimu stepped in for a better look at the injured Earther. Despite its blood-matted fur and diminutive stature, it was undeniably human. She, Kaimu realized from the gentle curve of her hips. *She* was undeniably human. Her fur was downy and short, more silver than white. The coarser, whiter fur that covered much of her body turned out to be clothing, cut from the skin of an animal. He shuddered.

"You're in my way." Michelle nudged him aside. She'd reprogrammed one of her skis to the smallest size, still unwieldy, but small enough to hold in one hand. She drew the sharp edge along the Earther's outer furs, cutting away the clothing. Unable to see, Kaimu extended sensory tendrils, tapping into Michelle's visuals and trying to grasp the severity of the injuries.

"Too distracting," Michelle informed him. She banished his consciousness into a memory cache.

In the memory, there are three consciousnesses in Michelle's body. Michelle, of course, and Jasmine, who isn't so bad. Elliot, however, Kaimu finds deeply disturbing. Not the man himself, but the idea that Michelle is part male. Or that another man is in his girlfriend's head. Kaimu tries to tangle himself with only Michelle, but the three are so intertwined he has no choice but to dissolve into all of them.

Kaimu recognizes the memory. He's on planetside leave on Nova Terra, and it's his first time visiting Michelle at work. She's been easing him into her life. It's a new experience for her, to share herself without drawing him into her collective. It's new for him, too.

Michelle reviews patient data files while she waits for him to arrive. All around her, Hospital617 buzzes with activity. In physical space, the hospital is a cavernous room. One floor, no walls. In headspace, there is more privacy, walls that give the illusion of each patient having a separate room. As part of the staff, Michelle doesn't bother uploading the headspace sensory inputs. Through her eyes, Kaimu can see the entire floor. Specialists of all sorts hover over their patients. Most of the work is upgrades—body reconstruction and routine anti-mortality treatments.

Neurosurgery team 8 to 27-12.

The woman in bed 27-12 is old. Not in the sense that Kaimu is old; his age is from the time dilation caused by his trips between the stars. The woman's skin is wrinkled and blotchy, and her hair has thinned so he can see the top of her scalp. She is frail, her body is giving out.

Kaimu sees himself weaving across the hospital floor. He feels his kiss on Michelle's cheek. Hears himself ask if she's busy. She tells him yes, but stay anyway. So he does.

She goes back to the woman. Elliot crowds his way to the foreground with patient information. Noelani Lai. A flood of datapackets swirl around the name: age, medical history, anything that might be relevant to selecting a treatment. Jasmine dilutes herself into the hospital archives, matching Elliot's patient data to other surgical cases. The mini-collective reconvenes and decides that the woman's body is inoperable. Insufficient regenerative capabilities. Instead, they will re-wire her organics to allow her consciousness to disengage itself. She can be installed into a new body later, if she so desires.

Michelle peels away layers of skin and cuts through Noelani's skull. The tissue beneath is predominantly organic, with traces of ancient wiring. More primitive than Kaimu. As a navigational officer, he's had to upgrade to interface with the *Willflower*.

Michelle blends with Jasmine and Elliot so thoroughly during the surgical procedure that Kaimu can't find Michelle at all. They become Jasmine/Elliot/Michelle. Jem. As the surgery progresses, the sight and smell of Noelani's organics become mildly nauseating. The SmartDust that sterilizes the air leaves behind odor-causing particles because sometimes a strange smell can serve as a diagnostic tool.

Kaimu is relieved when the operation is finished, and he can pick out strands of Michelle again. She doesn't bother to replace the slice of skull she removed, simply folds the skin back down over the wound.

Noelani floats out from her organics and into the vast interconnectivity beyond. Unused to such freedom, she loses cohesiveness, still existing, but commingled with the larger world. Jasmine observes, and notes the response as normal. Twenty-five percent of patients who are absorbed in this way eventually re-cohere. The remainder pursue a less individualized existence. Jem declares the operation a success.

Michelle—the realtime Michelle on the mountain—has shown him what she wants him to see, but now there is something he wants *her* to see. Awkwardly, since he isn't used to manhandling other minds, he takes control of the fractional portion of Michelle that led him here. He binds them to the hospital recording of a young woman. The woman is Noelani's granddaughter, Amy.

She hurries through the maze of hallways, filled with an overwhelming sense of worry. Not for Tutu, but for Mom. She remembers Tutu from her childhood, an energetic woman with long black hair who held her hand in Southside Park while they fed energy chips to the mechanical ducks. They'd gone every time Tutu came to visit, from the time she was two until the time Amy decided she was too old for ducks.

In the pre-op room, Mom is holding Tutu's hand. Mom's eyes are swollen and red, but dry. When she sees Amy, fresh tears roll down her face.

"Tutu," she says. "Tutu, wake up. Amy is here."

Amy puts her hand on Mom's shoulder, half a hug because Mom can't turn away from Tutu. "It's okay, Mom."

"She was awake. An hour ago," Mom says. She pushes gently against Tutu's shoulder. "Your granddaughter is here. Amy."

Amy takes Tutu's hand. It isn't the strong hand that she remembers from her childhood. The surgeons wouldn't fix her body; even Amy could see that Tutu was too old. They would save her by putting her into the collective, and she would be absorbed and lost. Amy can't bring herself to say her goodbyes out loud. The words would be too final, and her voice would fail her. Instead she squeezes Tutu's hand and thinks the word, *goodbye*.

Kaimu withdraws, taking Michelle with him. They drift back to themselves, and the warm hospital air shifts to the biting chill of the mountain. He has to pause and collect himself. Michelle doesn't acknowledge his return.

"That memory meant nothing to you," Kaimu said, disappointed.

"You used my access rights to get a hospital recording of a private individual. Those are only supposed to be used in the event of a malpractice suit." She tried to sound stern, but Kaimu could tell that she was more amused than angry. "Besides, I've seen it before. Outdated minds thinking outdated thoughts."

"Human minds thinking human thoughts," he snapped back.

"I never said the minds weren't human." Her voice was quiet, sad. As though he had missed something, had failed some test. Her sadness diffused his anger, and he let the argument lapse into silence.

The Earther's eyes were open, pale blue like the color of the sky diluted with white snow. They reminded him of his son, Kenji, before he disconnected from his body. He'd been six years old. Kaimu had married and divorced a few women in the centuries since, but he never fathered any more children. Michelle was right, he was outdated. He shook the memory away. The Earther's eyes didn't move except to blink. Her right eye was clouded over by cataracts.

While his mind had been locked away in the past, Michelle had finished work on the lower gash. Now she reprogrammed bits of her skisuit to serve as bandages. She pulled strips of suit from the back of her neck. The thick curls of Michelle's hair would block the icy air.

Michelle buried her hand wrist deep into the upper gash. There shouldn't have been room, the Earther's torso was small. She must have pushed all the organs aside. Orbs of blood dotted the blue-green fabric of her skisuit. The fabric refused to absorb the stain, so the globules floated like crimson buoys on a tropical sea. So much blood.

"Any updates?" he asked. She wasn't transmitting assessments anymore. Maybe more of the collective was in her head now, eliminating the need to broadcast.

"You're not helping," Michelle responded.

*

This time, Michelle sends him to a memory in his own perspective. He recognizes where he is from the functionality of the space. Every inch is utilized, cozy and enclosed, but not cramped. He is cradled in the mind of the *Willflower*, his ship. He's far more comfortable here than he was in the hospital.

At least, he is until he realizes *when* she's sent him.

He is in the aft lounge. A group of passengers is gathered around the bar, downing colorful fruit-and-alcohol concoctions, killing time until they have to get into the stasis tanks. There's an iridescent blue shiproach on the counter, and everyone places wagers on which dimensional coordinates it will take off from. The shiproach scurries about, seemingly uninterested in flight.

Off to Kaimu's right, a section of the wall moves. His brain adjusts to recognize Dahnjii, his least favorite of Michelle's collective. Dahnjii is a collective within the collective, like Jasmine/Elliot/Michelle but with seven minds mashed together. He is trendy and arrogant. His genes are spliced with chameleon or octopus or some other long extinct creature so that he can change color at will. He's been hiding against the wall, and now he ripples with yellow stripes. Aggressive. Nearly all the members of Michelle's collective seek novelty, but Dahnjii goes out of his way to make other people squirm so he can study their reactions.

"Hey precious," he sneers, "want to join my collective?"

Kaimu doesn't know whether he means his mini-collective, or the collective he shares with Michelle. He wants nothing to do with Dahnjii, regardless. "No, thanks."

"You realize how dumb it is, to be with Michelle, and not the rest of us," Dahnjii continues. He's been in the med-ward for several days, and Kaimu isn't thrilled that he's back in circulation. "Like loving an arm."

"An arm isn't conscious, it's not the same."

"Fine, like loving an arm, and the little blob of brain that controls it." Dahnjii turns his head. The left side of his skull is gone, replaced by a clear dome. The surgery he's had done is a brainshaping, purely cosmetic. Instead of the normal folds of gray cortex, his brain has been molded into the form of a dragon.

"I'm getting it colorized tomorrow," he says. Then he lifts the dome that covers the brain. "Want to lick it?"

Kaimu backs away, as though the exposed tissue will leap out and attack him. Dahnjii laughs, sticks his hand into his skull, and pets the dragon with one finger. The lounge has gone silent as all the drinkers admire the unusual design of Dahnjii's brain. Novelty. The shiproach takes off, and Kaimu is the only one to notice.

"Cover that up. Nobody wants to see your little lizard," Kaimu says.

Dahnjii's fist smashes through his face. It is a strange sensation, almost painless despite the sickening crunch as splinters of bone are pushed into his brain.

The safety protocols of the ship lock down his mind. There are several seconds of blackness. The Michelle fragment skips him forward through time.

Kaimu is in his cabin. A few paces away, Michelle studies his most prized possession, a bonsai tree. It is centuries old, with roots that curl around a smooth gray stone before disappearing into a shallow layer of soil. The bonsai comes from a simpler time.

"If you lived in that time, you'd be dead by now. Or horribly disfigured."

Michelle is in his head, monitoring him. He resents the intrusion.

"Okay, okay, I'm out," she says, "I had to make sure the reconstructive surgery was successful."

"That was barbaric," he says. "Bastard could've killed me."

"There's a copy of your consciousness stored in the *Willflower*, so even if the body had been inoperable, I could have generated another manifestation, started from scratch. It would've taken longer, but death wasn't really an issue. Dahnjii doesn't like you, but he's not a monster."

"After what he did to me? How much of my brain did you have to regenerate? How much of my face?" He's practically yelling at Michelle, despite the fact that she probably spent the last several hours putting him back together.

Michelle transmits the surgical data. She's regrown seven percent of his cortex, mostly frontal lobe, and reconstructed his nose and his left eye. This isn't the first time Kaimu has been badly injured. Over the years, almost 45 percent of his brain and body have been replaced. He doesn't feel any different.

"If you have a ship," he says, "and you replace it, one board at a time, and all the while it sails—is it still the same ship?"

The problem is from ancient philosophy, and it takes her a moment to find the appropriate reference. "Sorites. But the ships weren't sentient then. It wouldn't matter."

"It matters to me. Whether it's the same ship, and whether this," he waves his arms up and down his torso, "is the same body, the same brain."

"This attachment to your organics, it's pretty neurotic. You know that, right?" Michelle puts her hand on his cheek. She means it in a caring way, not as an insult. "And while I don't like what Dahnjii did, it's not as vicious as you make it out to be. Not to him. Not really to me either, except that I know how much it bothers you. Dahnjii's just upset that we're here on the *Willflower*, in bodies for the whole trip, rather than going on the *Roving Never* and getting new bodies when we arrive at Earth. He almost left the collective over it. So now he's frustrated and bored—"

"So it's okay that he smashed my face and sent bone shards into my brain. Because he was bored." How could Michelle refuse to understand?

"No. It's okay because it's just organics. Haven't you ever smashed your fist into the ship's interface console when you were frustrated?"

"That hurts my fist and doesn't damage the ship," he counters. "But yes."

"Have you asked the ship how she feels about it?"

"She's a ship."

"And you think *we're* the barbarian."

Something happens, not in the memory, but in realtime. Kaimu can sense it through Michelle's fragment. He tries to go back, but Michelle resists.

*

Kaimu is certain that something is wrong. Michelle is stalling him, keeping him off the mountain. He flings his consciousness forward through the memory cache, against her resistance. She lets him reach the point where they are preparing to ski, early that morning in their temporary lodge at the top of the mountain. The lodge is programmed with red walls adorned with replicas of ancient Japanese art—delicate cherry branches in black and pink, stylized blue tidal waves, bold black characters done in flawless calligraphy.

Michelle doesn't care whose perspective he takes for this memory so he settles into his own mind. He sits on the floor and yanks on the legs of his skisuit, trying to push his toes down into the stiff boot bottoms.

"That's ridiculously antique," Michelle says, "And I have plenty of paint. You're sure you don't want some?"

Michelle is fresh out of the shower, naked and holding a jar of N-body Paint. Her skin is pink from the heat of the shower. The color of cherry blossoms. Sandy-brown freckles splash across her chest, trailing down her arms and up her neck. He loves it when she wears the freckles.

"Well?" she asks, holding up the paint.

"No, I'll wear this," he points to the suit. Uncomfortable as it is, at least his private parts won't flap around while he skis.

"Suit yourself," she says.

Michelle orders up a cushion, and sprawls herself across the squishy blob that emerges from the floor. Comfortable, she opens her jar of paint and applies it to her legs with smooth strokes. Kaimu half-heartedly tugs on his suit, but his attention is focused on Michelle.

She's programmed the nano-fiber paint to a shifting pattern of blues and greens—sunlight filtering through ocean waves. She paints her way down her thigh, coating the indented curve on the back of her knee, the swell of her calf. By the time she gets to her foot, he's dropped his skisuit, and simply stares at her, making no effort to dress himself. She knows he's watching, and takes her time, painting the ticklish arch at the bottom of her foot, then swirling paint around each toe.

He takes the bait and stands up, his legs encased in the suit to mid-thigh, but the rest of the suit dangling down.

"You'll get pretty cold, skiing like that."

"You'll get pretty ravished, teasing me like that."

"I'll get pretty ravished *after skiing*, you mean." She's finished her legs now, and starts painting her way up from her hip. "I'm already painted from the waist down."

"I can think of a few ways to get that stuff off."

"But you won't," she says, "because you're a gentleman, and I enjoy the anticipation."

"You enjoy teasing me all day."

She laughs. "That too."

Kaimu watches himself suit up. The Michelle fragment apologizes, but doesn't explain why.

Kaimu flies down the slopes, his skis skimming over the fluffy snow. Michelle is behind him, taunting him to go faster. Adrenaline pumps through his system and mingles with an urge to impress her. He gives up on turning and points his skis straight down, letting the pines whiz by in the periphery of his vision. Single trunks blur together, their individuality stolen by his speed. He is the wind in air that stands still. Tendrils of his mind reach backwards for Michelle, to share with her this beautiful chaos of falling.

The green wall of treeness to his right closes in, swerves in front of him. Fear replaces excitement and he cannot turn. A single tree separates itself from the others, unmoving despite his speed because it stands directly before him. It looms over him.

Against his volition, his feet shoot upwards and sideways, twisting his body inside the skisuit. He hears the smack of skis on wood. A glancing blow, the safeties on the skis automatically avoiding a harmful collision. His skis reconnect with the snow, back under his control, slowed now, and traveling at an angle to the slope, redirected by the tree. Michelle lets out a whoop behind him, as though he'd skidded off the tree on purpose, a trick to impress her. He slows to a stop, and turns in time to see her mimic his trick, intentionally and far more gracefully. She stops on the hillside above him, spraying him with snow in the process.

"Good trick," she says, smiling.

He relaxes after that, knowing that the skis can rescue him from his own ineptitude. In short order, they reach the bottom of the mountain and cuddle together in the anti-grav chute that propels them back to the top. From above the tree line, he can see mountains in every direction, monuments of ice and rock reaching up to the sky. "Down the other side this time?"

"Race you, meet up at that rock," she says, and dumps the coordinates to his navigation system.

"You win."

"I'll give you a head start."

"Okay, I—"

"Go!" She gives him a little shove, sending him over a ledge and onto a steep mogul-covered slope. The skis recognize his inability to deal with the bumpy conditions, and swerve through the bumps. He gets the hang of it, and the safeties turn off again.

"*Now me!*" Michelle is too far away for speech, so she transmits. Even so, there's no way he'll win with such a tiny lead.

Still, he can at least make it challenging. He bends his knees and tucks down to decrease his wind resistance. A smattering of trees dot the slope as he gets lower, then denser trees close in around the run. He watches them carefully this time, scanning the slope ahead of him so he'll have plenty of time to turn. Avoid the green. Michelle hasn't passed him yet. He risks a glance, and she's farther back than he expected. If he can avoid plowing into the trees, he might even win.

The run curves, and Kaimu turns to follow it. He can see the rock in the distance, and Michelle is still behind him.

Something moves.

He'd have seen it sooner, but it was white and he was watching for green. It's running out across his path. The skis slash sideways.

The safeties on his skis are old, and to avoid overloading them, he'd simplified the obstacle-detection by specifying that he and Michelle were the only humans on the slope. His breath sticks in his chest as the blades tear through fur and flesh. It is worse in memory than in realtime.

Finally, Michelle releases him.

*

The Earther was dead. Her unfocussed eyes reflected the empty sky. Kaimu's freshly relived memories mingled with the realities of the present.

"You should have let me stay," he told Michelle.

"You wouldn't have understood what I was doing," she said. "You don't understand what's happening now. Look." She pointed to the Earther, to the wound that stretched across her chest. Several ribs had been broken away. Her heart and lungs were rearranged, shoved off to the sides to gain access to her spinal cord. Blood pooled in the cavity. Michelle had never tried to save the Earther's body. All along, she'd been working her way down to the spinal cord. Trying to pry the consciousness free before the body died.

"She's completely organic. Why would you even try?" he asked.

"You started organic," she said. "All it takes is time. Time to map the pattern of neuronal connections, time to record the firing patterns."

"But we're on a mountainside, you used a ski to cut her open for godsakes," he said. "You should have operated on her body. How could you possibly record everything you needed to save her consciousness? And even if you could, she'd never make it on the network."

Michelle held up her arm. There was a cut on her wrist. "I reprogrammed some of my peripherals to do the recordings."

He needed to see what she had done, to understand, but she was blocking him out. "It's my fault, not yours," he said. "I'm sure you did all you could."

She still refused to let him in. He'd never experienced this before. Sometimes he had blocked her out, when he wanted privacy, but she had always been open. He missed the closeness of being tangled with her mind. She must have felt this same frustration, when he had closed himself off. From now on, he'd try to be more open to her, less stubborn.

"You don't have to hide from me," he said.

"It worked."

"You put her on the network? And she adapted to that?"

"No." She put her hand on his shoulder. He could barely feel her touch through the stiff fabric of his skisuit. "I started out that way, but I learned something from you. To me, a body is nothing, but to you, or to her . . . I'm sorry."

"You're sorry," he echoed. Then he realized what she'd done. "She's there. With you."

Michelle nodded. "I'm almost done teaching her my body. Her body."

"What about you?"

"I—" she started, but then paused. "We. We are going to merge more fully. Distributed existence was interesting, but it's time for something else now."

"You're leaving me."

"I couldn't bring you, even if you wanted to come," she said. "I'll miss you, even with your strange ideas and your locked off mind. But you aren't ready. And that's okay. Besides, she'll need you."

"But we . . . Stay a little longer."

"And what about her? Leave her trapped in a body she doesn't control?"

He took her hand from his shoulder and brushed her fingertips against his lips. He had always known that she was beyond him, but instead of trying to grow, he tried to force her to come to his level.

Michelle withdrew. He sensed her in the network, mingling with others, dissolving and changing. He felt her brush against the edge of his consciousness, briefly, a goodbye kiss to his mind. Then she was gone.

The Earther stood before him, not moving. The body was unchanged. Michelle's stunning red hair, her long legs, the exposed patch of neck where she'd peeled away her N-body paint. There were freckles there, hiding on the pale skin beneath a curtain of curls. But the woman that stood before him didn't carry herself with Michelle's confidence. Her posture was bad, and her eyes darted in all directions. He was still holding her hand. He let go.

Kaimu waited. He didn't know what to do, whether he should say something. Whether she would understand it if he did.

The Earther looked up at him.
"I am Beyla," she said.

That was all. Nothing that came later was relevant; the jury collective didn't need to see it. Kaimu wouldn't have to relive it, though what came after was less painful than the accident itself and his final moments with Michelle. The jury deliberated for several seconds, unusually long, but for a mind as slow as Kaimu's it wasn't even long enough to worry.

No penalties on any of the charges. The tourist board acknowledges the non-death of the Earther Beyla. You are free to go.

Beyla sat beside him and held his hand, blissfully unaware of most of the proceedings. Out of the corner of his eye, she still reminded him of Michelle, but Beyla wore the body differently. No longer fearful, as she was those first moments on the mountainside, but solemn, because the body was a gift. Was she the same person she was before? Hers was a ship replaced, not board by board, but all at once.

Kaimu sometimes searched for traces of Michelle, but she was gone. She was not a ship at all; she was the ocean, deep and vast, with a form forever changing in waves of green and blue.

TEMPORARY FRIENDS

The second week of kindergarten, Mimi came home with a rabbit. Despite numerous mentions of the Temporary Friends project in the parent newsletter, I wasn't prepared to see my five-year-old girl cuddling a honey-colored fluffball that was genetically engineered to have fatally high cholesterol and die of a heart attack later in the school year.

"I named him Mr. Flufferbottom," Mimi told me. I glared at Great-Grandpa John, who'd been watching her while I finished up my shift at the clinic. He shrugged. My gruff maternal grandfather wasn't my first choice of babysitter, but he needed a place to stay and I needed someone to watch Mimi after school.

"Are you sure it's a good idea to name him, honey?" I knelt down and put my hand on Mimi's shoulder. "He's a completely biological rabbit, and this kind doesn't tend to live very long."

"Teacher said to pick good names for our rabbits," Mimi said. "Besides, you put new parts on people, so if Mr. Flufferbottom breaks you can fix him."

Replacement pet parts were readily available online, and the self-installing models could be put in by anyone who could afford the hefty price tag and follow simple instructions. But replacement parts defeated the purpose of the lesson—research showed that children needed to experience death in order to achieve normal emotional development. Aside from the occasional suicide or tragic accident, there weren't many occasions to deal with loss. Schools were required to incorporate Temporary Friends into their kindergarten curriculum in order to get government funding.

The school couldn't control what parents did, of course, but the parent newsletter strongly discouraged tampering with the damned death pets in any way.

"Mimi, sweetie, that's not how it works this time—I know we get a lot of extra parts for Graycat, but your Temporary Friend is only until . . ." I tried to remember from the newsletter how long the rabbits were engineered to live. Six months? "Only until March, and then we'll say goodbye."

I expected Mimi to put up a big fuss, but she didn't. She took Mr. Flufferbottom to the cage we'd set up in her room and got him some food and water.

Mimi didn't say another word about Mr. Flufferbottom until mid-October.

"Mommy," she said in her most serious voice, "I think we should order parts for Mr. Flufferbottom now, so we'll have them ready when he needs them."

"We talked about this, Mimi. Mr. Flufferbottom is a Temporary Friend. Do you remember what temporary means?"

"It means only for a little while. Like ice cream is temporary because I eat it or sometimes it melts." Mimi frowned. "But Mr. Flufferbottom has lasted a lot longer than ice cream, and I think he should have parts because he is a nice rabbit and I don't want him to die."

"Of course we don't want him to die," I began, not sure how to explain something I rarely dealt with myself, "but death is a thing that just happens sometimes."

"Am I going to die?" Mimi asked.

"Oh honey, not for a long long long time. Great-Grandpa John is still alive, and he is much older than you."

"But he gets parts from the clinic," Mimi said.

"If you need them, you can have parts from the clinic too. You're young now, so your parts are still good."

"So Great-pa John can get parts, and I can get parts, and Graycat can get parts," Mimi said. "Why can't Mr. Flufferbottom have parts?

Don't you think he's a nice rabbit, Mommy?"

Mimi was often persistent, but I wasn't used to seeing her quite this agitated. "Did something happen, Mimi, to make you worried about Mr. Flufferbottom?"

Mimi looked down at the floor. "Lizzy and I were talking to some first graders at recess and they said our bucket bunnies are going to die and then we won't have them anymore."

"But you knew that already, right? We told you at the start that the rabbits don't live very long. That's what it means for them to be temporary."

"I didn't know that I wouldn't have him anymore once he was dead," Mimi said. "I want to have him and have him and keep him forever and ever, like Graycat."

Mimi had never shown much interest in Graycat, who was about 55 years old, and rarely did anything but sleep curled up on top of the living room bookshelves. In his younger days, Graycat had been quite the hunter, but now, despite his extra sensors and state-of-the-art replacement legs, he hadn't pounced on anything for at least a couple decades.

"Graycat is our pet," I told her, for lack of a better explanation. "Mr. Flufferbottom is a lesson."

"Whiskers died today," Mimi told me, without preamble, one January afternoon when I got home from work. "Tommy's parents didn't get him any parts and he died and they burned him in an incinerator and he died again."

"He only died the first time, Mimi. They burned the body." I tried to look at this as a learning opportunity. "Was Tommy sad?"

"Tommy was angry," Mimi said. "He had to go home early for hitting. He did a lot of hitting."

"Well, people react to death in lots of different ways," I said, "but it was wrong of him to hit people, even if he was angry."

Great-pa John came in from the kitchen.

"Of course he was angry. The whole project is ridiculous, giving you kids pets and then telling you not to take care of them properly."

Great-pa had fixed himself a sandwich, but he hadn't gotten used to his new bionic eyes yet, and instead of lettuce he'd used some of the collard greens I was going to cook for dinner.

"The Temporary Friends lesson is supposed to teach kids about—" I started, but Great-pa John interrupted.

"I know what this is all about. Emotional development and learning about loss and yadda yadda whatever. I still have half my original brain in here." Great-pa John tapped his head.

"But not your original eyes," I snapped back, and instantly regretted it when his face fell. It was easy to forget what a proud man he was, and how hard it was for someone his age to adapt to so much technology. He knew death in ways that I never would. When he was young, the replacement parts weren't that good. Sure there were limbs to help amputees walk, and pace makers and cochlear implants and dentures, but you couldn't replace everything that broke. Back then, people died all the time. More than half of everyone Great-pa knew was dead.

"Sorry. I'll go make you a better sandwich," I said, taking the plate from his artificial hands. "You talk to Mimi about how things used to be. Maybe it will help her understand."

To my surprise, I heard him start talking about Great-grandma Arlene, who had died back when the technology for replacement organs was still unreliable. I paused to listen, because I'd never heard the whole story. I'd always had the impression that Great-pa John had convinced Arlene to avoid the new technology because it was too risky.

He stopped talking when he realized I was hovering in the doorway, and I went to make his sandwich. Maybe talking to Mimi would help ease his guilt.

I don't know what Great-pa said to Mimi, exactly, but it did wonders for their relationship. He got used to his new eyes, and together they built a fancy maze for Mr. Flufferbottom so he wouldn't get bored. I questioned the wisdom of building entertainment for a rabbit who was doomed to die sometime in the next few weeks, but Mimi seemed happier to be doing something for her little fluffy companion, so I left them alone. Great-pa made no further mention of his long-departed wife, at least not when I was around, but he seemed more cheerful than I'd seen him for a long time.

Then one afternoon I came home from the clinic after a particularly rough spinal replacement surgery and found the two of them with their heads leaned over Mr. Flufferbottom. Fearing the worst, I rushed over, prepared to swoop a crying Mimi into my arms—but the bucket bunny wasn't dead. He was hopping around the table, sniffing at the placemats.

"Great-pa helped me fix Mr. Flufferbottom," Mimi said. "We ordered him medicines to help with his clestor-all, so he won't have a heart attack after all."

"Cholesterol," I corrected her. "Go run and play while I talk to Great-pa, okay?"

"Can I take Mr. Flufferbottom?" Mimi asked.

"Sure."

She scooped up the rabbit and skipped off to the living room.

"She's supposed to be learning about death," I told Great-pa John firmly. "We already have a pet that doesn't die. We really don't need an immortal rabbit. Besides, the drugs are just stalling the inevitable."

"Are you raising a child or a monster? Do you really think it's good for them to learn that they should sit and watch their rabbits die and not do a damned thing about it?" Great-pa asked. "Some lesson that would be."

Mr. Flufferbottom stopped eating. I couldn't tell if the loss of appetite was a side effect of his medication or some other health problem. Mimi shadowed me every minute I wasn't at work, constantly peppering me with questions about what we could do for her poor rabbit. "Great-pa doesn't know what parts to order, Mommy. You have to help us."

"I don't know either," I told her honestly, "I install parts at the clinic, but I don't do the diagnosis." I didn't mention that I'd had to sign up for extra shifts at the clinic to pay for the cholesterol medicine they'd gotten, which could well be what was making Mr. Flufferbottom sick.

Great-pa John banged around our apartment, starting "home improvement" projects and then abandoning them unfinished. I told him in no uncertain terms not to tinker with the central computer system, but otherwise left him to deal with his anxieties by destroying small sections of our unit.

Mimi went to confer with Great-pa for a minute, then came back. "I want to take Mr. Flufferbottom to the vet clinic that Graycat goes to."

I thought about what Great-pa John had said, about teaching children to passively watch their pets die. I thought about Graycat, who was alive, but was he really the same cat? I even thought about Great-pa John, who by now was mostly artificial sensors and prosthetic limbs and other man-made parts.

I didn't know the answer, and my five-year-old daughter was looking up at me, hopeful that I would save her tiny fluffy friend. Did she really need to learn about death first hand? Would I be doing her a favor or a disservice if I let her sidestep one of life's hardest lessons?

"No," I said, "we can't take him to the vet."

It broke my heart to see the hopeful smile leave her face. I almost changed my mind. But even when the tears started to well up in her eyes, I held my ground. My daughter was supposed to learn the sadness of loss. Both of us would learn from this experience, and it would make us stronger.

The next morning, Mimi ran into my room with tears in her eyes. "Mr. Flufferbottom is dead, he's cold and stiff and he won't eat his breakfast."

"I'm so sorry, honey. I know you loved that rabbit." The words that I had practiced in my head sounded false and empty. I hugged Mimi tight, then we went to her room together to get Mr. Flufferbottom.

Great-pa John was there, standing over the cage. He was clutching something in his hand, an artificial part, I think, although I couldn't see it clearly. He was scowling down at the lifeless rabbit.

"Did you find the right part, Great-pa?" Mimi asked.

He held out the tiny object he was clutching, a self-installing replacement liver. "I don't know if this would have helped, but it's too late now. Even fancy parts won't bring back the dead."

"Can we try? Mr. Flufferbottom didn't eat his breakfast. I don't want him to die hungry."

To my horror, Great-pa put the tiny artificial liver on top of the dead rabbit, and activated the autoinstaller. The tiny organ set to work installing itself, shaving the fur and sterilizing the skin before making an incision and burrowing into the rabbit. We'd have to sell the liver used now, and while they were technically re-usable their value decreased dramatically. More shifts at work, for a rabbit that was already dead.

The liver completed its installation, but immediately began beeping to indicate an error. A few minutes later, it reappeared and clung to the rabbit's skin and waited for further instructions. I picked it up and set it to clean itself for repackaging.

"Sorry, kiddo," Great-pa said. "We did everything we could, right?"

Mimi nodded. "Is he with Great-ma now?"

Great-pa smiled. "She'd have liked that, my Arlene. A cute little fuzzball to keep her company. If there's something after this, maybe they'll find each other."

Amazingly, both my daughter and my grandfather found comfort in that thought. I picked up Mr. Flufferbottom and set him gently in the trash incinerator, along with his uneaten breakfast. We stood in silence while he burned to ashes, and when it had finished, Mimi went to the living room and found, of all things, Graycat.

She picked him up from the bookshelf, and petted his artificial fur. He made a mechanical purring noise. He wasn't her temporary friend, but he was warm and soft and comforting, and he let her bury her face in his fur and cry.

Interlude:
Flash Fiction Worlds

A MILLION OYSTERS FOR CHIYOKO

Nanami was the oldest of the *ama*. A Japanese mermaid, the tourists called her. She dove for oysters, lobsters, sea urchins—most anything edible fetched a good price these days, seafood had become so rare. For decades, Nanami had gone diving for shellfish without any special equipment, but tourists brought more than just money to her sleepy fishing village. They also brought change. Starting today, all the diving girls would wear wetsuits and breathe with fish-gill masks that drew air out of the water. Nanami embraced the new technology, despite her age. It would give her a way to search for the remains of her daughter, Chiyoko.

She plunged into the cool ocean water and resisted the urge to hold her breath. Nanami wondered what Chiyoko would have thought of the fish-gill breathers. She probably would have approved. The girl had always loved the water, diving deeper than Nanami dared, with the adventurous boldness of youth. Her daughter had joked that she would find a million oysters, more than anyone could ever eat, and every single one would have a pearl.

Even all those years ago, the ocean had been too acidic for oysters. Dozens of oysters made a good find, and a million oysters was nothing more than a wistful dream. Now, the shallows were stripped bare, and anything left would lose its shell to the acid sea soon anyway. Now the only dive sites with anything to collect were at the base of the limestone cliffs, and even here the acid ocean left sea urchins with stunted thin spines and thin-shelled oysters and mussels.

This was where she'd taken Chiyoko diving, the day her daughter disappeared.

Today, like that day, the sun was bright and the water was calm, the waves rising and falling in gentle swells on the surface. As Nanami dove deeper, a school of small silver fish swayed back and forth with the current, feeding on the seaweed that grew on the cliffs. She reached the depth where she would have turned back, if she had been holding her breath. It was almost meditative, diving without the time pressure of returning to the surface for air. She spotted an abalone and removed it from the rock with her flat-bladed knife. An auspicious start to the dive. She put it in her collection bag. The abalone would fetch a good price from the tourists back on the docks.

She pushed herself deeper, and felt the tug of a current, flowing into a tunnel that was concealed beneath a ledge of rock. She ducked under the ledge and let the current take her, hoping that it would solve the mystery of her daughter's disappearance, so many years ago. The tunnel opened into a cavern of dark water, lit only by thin bands of light that slanted down from tiny gaps in the rock walls.

The cavern was bursting with life. The floor of the cavern dropped off into the blackness of the deeps, and somewhere down there was another opening to the ocean, letting out the current that flowed in through the tunnel. But all along the sides of the cave the walls were encrusted with shellfish—mussels, clams, abalone . . . and thousands of oysters. Surrounded by limestone, the underwater cave was a haven for creatures that could not bear the acid of the open water. Had her daughter found this place, and seen her million oysters? Nanami swam up to the surface of the water. There was air inside the cave, air that came in through the same small cracks between the rocks that let in bands of light.

Nanami swam to a small ledge and climbed out of the ocean. Water dripped from the ceiling of the cave and into a tiny puddle with a rhythmic plinking sound. Next to the puddle were stacks of oyster shells and her daughter's knife. The air in the cavern was warm, and there was plenty of food. How long had Chiyoko waited here, for a rescue that never came? One large oyster shell sat separated from the rest, a shimmering bowl for a small handful of pearls.

Nanami tucked the pearls into the zippered pocket on the thigh of her wetsuit. There wasn't much more to the cave above the level of the water, and there was no sign of her daughter's body. She returned to the water, focusing her search on the areas closest to the ledge. Then finally she found what she was looking for, below the ledge that held the empty oyster shells. Her daughter's bones, so covered in sea life that Nanami hadn't recognized them for what they were the first time past.

She did not disturb her daughter's bones. Over time, the calcium of her bones would be transformed into the shells of oysters. Nanami swam out through the tunnel, against the current, a long and difficult swim. It would have been impossible without the fish-gill breather, even with her well-trained lungs.

Back in open water, she studied the entrance to the tunnel. It was deeper than most divers went, and mostly hidden by an outcropping of rock. The other *ama* probably wouldn't find it by chance. She decided not to tell anyone about it. It was one thing to collect seafood that was slowly dying in an acid ocean, and another thing entirely to steal from one of the last healthy pockets of sea life. Perhaps someday her daughter's cave would hold a million oysters, each one with a pearl.

CARLA AT THE OFF-PLANET TAX RETURN HELPLINE

T his is Carla at the Off-Planet Tax Return helpline, how can I help you?"

"We are <untranslatable> collective. We file jointly or separately?"

"How many US citizens do you have in your collective?"

"Three hundred fifty-two of us are citizens, yes. Bob is not."

"Are you married, as defined by US law?"

"We are three hundred fifty-two conscious entities melded into one harmonious being for over five thousand years, and also Bob. This is marriage?"

"It is not. You will need to file separate returns for each of your three hundred fifty-two citizens. Bob does not need to file."

"This is unfortunate. Bob will be greatly displeased to be excluded in this way."

"This is Carla at the Off-Planet Tax Return helpline, how can I help you?"

"What form for taxes?"

"The form for filing an off-planet return is Form 9099B. This form is for US citizens currently residing off planet, including those residing on space shuttles, orbital stations, lunar or planetary colonies, and/or inside the intestinal system of Effluvian space worms. If you reside inside an Effluvian space worm that is currently located on Earth, you are allowed to fill out Form 1040."

"No, what form for currency of taxes?"

"The IRS will generally accept foreign currencies in situations where Earth currency cannot reasonably be obtained. To submit your tax payment in a non-Earth currency, fill out Form X-325Z and include your payment with your tax return. In responding to this question, I am required by law to inform you that it is illegal to staple, glue, tape, or otherwise affix sentient currency to your tax return."

"The IRS prefers sentient currency to run loose inside envelope?"

"We have covered everything I know about this topic, is there anything else I can help you with?"

"This is Carla at the Off-Planet Tax Return helpline—"
<untranslatable screaming>
<static>

"This is Carla at—"
"Hi Carla, this is Bob."
"What can I help you with today, Bob?"
"I'm lonely."
"That is beyond the scope of my expertise. Do you have any tax related questions that I can help you with today?"
"You spoke with a different voice of my collective today, and told us that we each must file a separate return. Except me. This makes me lonely."
"Privacy laws do not allow me to discuss conversations I've had with other callers. How did you manage to get my extension? There are over five hundred tax assistants working through this call center, and call assignment is randomized."
"If you marry me, can I file a tax return?"
"I'm sorry, but I need to end this call now."

"This is Carla at the Off-Planet Tax Return helpline, how can I help you?"
"What is FBAR?"

"FBAR stands for Foreign Bank Account Report, but most off-planet residents refer to this form as FUBAR. It is not possible to fill this form out correctly. This form collects basic information on foreign financial accounts controlled by US citizens and is sent to the Treasury Department. It will not impact your tax liability, but does give the Treasury Department direct access to your funds, which will be used in the highly likely event of an audit."

"I have mesh bag of golden snakes, does this require FBAR?"

"FBAR is required for bank accounts, brokerage accounts, mutual funds, and any collection of sentient or non-sentient currency located outside of the United States. There is one exception for live currencies—US citizens may keep up to fifty creatures of any kind as pets. A creature may be considered a pet if it lives in the primary residence of the person filing the return."

"So if snakes stay in house with me, I do not write them onto form?"

"As long as there are less than fifty."

"I will eat the extras. Thank you."

"This is Carla at the Off-Planet Tax Return helpline, how can I help you?"

"Why will you not marry Bob?"

<click>

"This is Carla at the Off-Planet Tax Return helpline, how can I help you?"

"There is a large green creature with many teeth gnawing through the outer dome of my lunar residence."

"Do you owe back taxes?"

"Yes."

"The creature is a Tarmandian Spacemite, trained by the IRS to collect from delinquent off-planet taxpayers. I am legally required to tell you at this point in the conversation that attempting to run from a Tarmandian Spacemite is illegal and will trigger the Spacemite's predatory instincts. Try to remain calm, and let the Spacemite take anything it wants."

"I only owe three hundred dollars in back taxes. It will cost me ten times that much to repair the damage to my dome. Isn't there some way to get the creature to go away?"

"I'm sorry, we have covered everything I know about this topic, is there anything else I can help you with?"

"This is Carla at the Off-Planet Tax Return helpline, how can I help you?"

"Bob is coming for you."

<click>

"This is Carla at the Off-Planet Tax Return helpline, what can I do for you?"

"SCREW YOU IRS I'M NOT GOING TO FILE!"

"I hope you were smart enough to call from an untraceable number. If not, I am legally required to tell you at this point in the conversation that attempting to run from a Tarmandian Spacemite is illegal and will trigger the Spacemite's predatory instincts. Try to remain calm, and let the Spacemite take anything it wants."

"This is Carla—oh my god, there's some kind of alien rampaging through the call center. It looks like a dismembered grizzly bear that didn't get put back together quite right, and it's holding hands with a guy in a tuxedo."

<muffled screaming>

"You help with mine taxes?"

"Please hold while we handle this emergency. The SWAT team is here with tranquilizer guns—"

<gunshots>

<click>

<overly loud '80s music>

"Your call is important to us. Please stay on the line for the next available representative."

<overly loud '80s music>

"Thank you for holding. This is Carla at the Off-Planet Tax Return helpline. I am legally required to inform you that three hundred fifty-two members of the <untranslatable> collective are listening in on this call for training purposes. The IRS requires that they provide fifty-seven thousand, eight hundred twenty-two hours of service at this call center to avoid criminal charges for the destruction of government property. Please do not be distressed by their wailing. They are mourning the liberation of Bob, who has been extradited to his home planet, where he will never again feel lonely. How can I help you?"

DO NOT COUNT
THE WITHERED ONES

Callie kept her heart in the front yard, as people often do. Here, her father's oak, solid and stoic and unchanging. There, her sister's rhododendron, which bloomed with pale pink flowers. One root from each plant grew into her heart, which nourished everything in the yard.

She stepped over the delicate vines of her college roommate's ivy to get to her mother's willow tree. The leaves were dry and brown, and the once supple branches were brittle and fragile. Callie turned on the soaker hose that wound around the base of the tree, knowing it wouldn't help, but wanting to do something, anything, to save her relationship with her mother. As water dripped from the hose, Callie went to the one bough that still bore green leaves on its branches, but even here she spotted leaves with a slight tinge of yellow at the edges.

Callie drove across town to the nursing home. Mom kept her heart in the communal garden, which was a depressing place even under the best of circumstances. The hearts of the elderly were rife with dying plants—friends who passed away, relatives who never came to visit. Her mother's patch was the worst. Her plants were mostly dead, except for Callie's lace leaf maple. The tiny tree had twisted branches and delicate leaves, but it was hardier than it looked. It had outlasted all the other plants, staying green all through her mother's autumn years.

The leaves were not green today. They were yellow, like a caution light, a warning of red leaves to come. Mom, who usually spent all day in the gardens, was in her room.

"You want to go outside, Mom?" Callie opened the blinds to let some sunlight in. The table by the window was cluttered with dead plants—not heartplants but ordinary houseplants.

Mom came over, wary, and peered at Callie's face. "You look familiar."

Yesterday she'd recognized Callie, but that was increasingly rare. "I'm Callie, Mom. Your daughter."

Mom nodded and put on her jacket. "You look a little like my daughter. I have two girls, but they never come to visit. No one ever comes to visit."

Callie steadied Mom's arm as they walked to the communal gardens. Another old woman sat on one of the benches, surrounded by family. She gave Callie a friendly wave. Her patch was greener than most of the others.

The leaves of the lace leaf maple were goldenrod. Had they been more of a lemon yellow earlier? Mom was physically very healthy for her age, but Callie dreaded the thought of visiting, maybe for years, when Mom had no idea who she was. She would come out of love, even when she no longer came out of hope.

Mom stared at the dead and dying plants, and Callie regretted bringing her outside. There was a leafless rhododendron for her sister and a brittle brown primrose bush for Mrs. Denman, who had once been Mom's closest friend. There was dried grass for the nurses and a clump of dead clover, but Callie didn't know who that belonged to. So much lost, and that didn't even count the plants they'd abandoned when Mom moved to the nursing home.

Mom caught Callie looking, and shook her head. "Don't count the withered ones," she said. "They were bright once, and happy. My daughter tends a beautiful garden, and someday she will come and visit me, and fix these broken plants."

She looked at Callie, a silent plea in her eyes. Callie held her hand and together they looked at the lace leaf maple—the one bright plant in her patch. The leaves were vibrant orange, a final burst of flame against the darkness of forgetting.

"Excuse me," Mom said, "Can you find a nurse? I can't remember where my house is."

"I can take you to your room, Mom." Callie waited for her to say, as she always did, that she has two daughters that never come to visit.

"Are you my nurse?" Mom asked instead. She didn't say that Callie looked familiar. As they walked to her room, Callie looked back at the garden.

The leaves on her maple had faded from orange to brown.

When Callie got home she was relieved to see the one green bough of Mom's tree, unchanged. All around that bough were dried up branches, brown leaves that crumbled to dust with the lightest touch. "Don't count the withered ones," she heard Mom's voice remind her. Callie remembered when the whole tree had been healthy and vibrant. She remembered sitting with Mom in the waiting room of the birth center, waiting for her nephew to be born. She remembered Christmas dinner, her first year of college, appreciating home in a way she never had before. She remembered goodnight kisses long after she thought she was too old for such things.

So many things her mother used to be, but wasn't any more. Their relationship had narrowed from a whole tree to a single bough. Callie was the caretaker now, always. Their bond no longer filled the tree of what they'd shared in the past, but it was solid. She touched a delicate green leaf. The tree eased the worry in her heart. She was still a loving daughter, even if Mom didn't remember who she was.

The next time Callie went to the nursing home, Mom didn't recognize her. Callie took her to a garden patch that had green plants. Rhonda, the woman who the patch belonged to, was friendly, and Callie brought her cookies sometimes. After a few visits, the sapling of a lace leaf maple started growing in amongst the other plants.

Mom looked at the maple, and back at Callie, her mind trying to make a connection that wasn't quite there. Rhonda, with a knowing smile, put her hand on Callie's shoulder. "She may not remember why, but she's happiest when you're here."

PIECES OF MY BODY

I gave my left arm to Elizabeth. You've never met her, but she was my dearest childhood friend. After my disembodiment party she went home to London and put it on her end table, hand side down, with a lampshade made of green velvet and children's nightmares. The nightmares gnawed at the nerve endings on my shoulder, or maybe the unpleasant sensation was my longing for Elizabeth. Or perhaps the scab was itchy. The arm was the first part of me to be removed so it was hard to be sure what each sensation meant.

My long-ago first boyfriend Michael was surprisingly squeamish, so I gave him my hair, thinking that it would be bloodless and therefore more appealing. He stuffed it in a plastic bag and took it home to Houston, but then he threw it away. Inside the plastic bag, the hair will never weave itself into the dirt and sing lullabies to earthworms. It will never tangle in a shower drain and capture off-key songs. You know how fond I was of my hair, so you will appreciate how angry I was to see it wasted. Let us never speak of Michael again.

Tim and Jim and Annabel and Nora—did you meet them when we were in college?—have become so close as to be practically a single entity, and they each got a finger from my right hand. They are in San Francisco, which is where I would live if location was an attribute that I could still possess. Tim uses his finger to thumb wrestle with Nora, even though technically it isn't thumb wrestling because he has an index finger. My fingers are happy that they get to be together, although they miss the middle finger, which I mailed to Michael, of whom we are not speaking because he isn't worth the words.

My co-worker Courtney got my right leg, because I couldn't think of anything better and she left my disembodiment party in something of a hurry. She was like that, always dashing off, so maybe an extra leg wasn't such a bad gift after all. Courtney put the leg in a freezer in her Montana basement, nestled in among the ducks and deer she and her husband killed on hunting trips. Ice crystals transform my skin into a delicate lace, which the deer might lick like salt if they could control their frozen tongues.

Lee asked for my heart, which I was saving for you, until I thought of something better. When I gave it to him, he sprinkled it with salt and ate it, raw and bleeding. Then he went back to Germany. It was an interesting experience, being digested on a transatlantic flight. Don't look at me like that, Lee is from when we were separated—it is your own fault for kicking me out.

My brother Andrew got my stomach, with my esophagus still attached. He loves both food and music, so I thought he might fill my stomach with honey or play my upper digestive tract like bagpipes. Instead he put his childhood memories into marbles, and dropped them down my esophagus one by one. The marbles still clink together in my stomach long after all the memories have been absorbed.

I gave my neighbor Deb my teeth, because she likes little things that fit in glass jars. She planted the teeth in her garden, and watered them with root beer. Every night at midnight she puts her nose up to the dirt and looks for any sign of plants. I'm not sure what she thinks will grow, but so far nothing has come of it.

Our daughter Shreya was the most difficult to decide. Nothing seemed to suit her. She clearly shouldn't have a leg, or a shoulder, or a torso. No, definitely something smaller, more delicate. In the end, I gave her my three favorite freckles, which she wore on the back of her hand when she boarded the plane to Bangalore. She shared two of the freckles with our granddaughter, who painted them gold and used them as earrings. The last freckle collapsed into a black hole, a gravitational singularity so small that Shreya accidently dropped it down into the gap between two ceramic floor tiles, where it slowly eats away at the grout.

You didn't come to my disembodiment party to get your piece of me. You cling to your body even as it fails you, dragging you inevitably closer to a final and unending death. I mailed my eyes to you in a package filled with single-serving bags of those potato chips you like to eat, which are better padding than Styrofoam peanuts. I worried that you would throw my eyes away, and the last thing I'd see would be maggots burrowing into my pupils—but instead you strung them like beads on a section of fishing line, and wore them as a necklace.

With eyes no longer mine, I see a forest of rowan and maple, overgrown with moss that weeps with rain. I used to find such things beautiful, but I do not miss this world we shared. I certainly do not miss my body, with its parts scattered around the world. There are some who argue that I no longer feel emotion, but moths eat holes in the fabric of my disembodied consciousness. The goldfish of my past swims in restless circles as it drowns in a bowl of whiskey. I miss you.

If you change your mind before you die, invite me to your disembodiment party. I will take anything—an eyelash or a kidney, your left ear or sixteen neurons from the cortex of your brain. It will be all the body that I have.

EVERYONE'S A CLOWN

When Amelia turned six, I took her to the circus. She'd been a little withdrawn lately, and I wanted to cheer her up. She watched with a grim expression as elephants marched around the ring. "What's the matter?"

"The elephants look unhappy."

I couldn't see anything wrong with the elephants, and the spotlight shifted to a trio of clowns. "Look at the clowns, Meelie, see the big red smiles?"

"You can see their faces? Do you like them?"

"Sure," I said, baffled by her odd response. I stared at the clowns. Amelia mumbled something and touched my arm to get my attention. Her face was painted like a clown—a bright red mouth and paper-white skin, black triangles above and below her eyes.

The woman in the next seat had clown make-up too, and a bright red wig. I scanned the audience. Every single seat was occupied by a clown. Sad clowns, happy clowns, scary clowns, nothing but clowns as far as I could see in the dim light. It had to be a trick, part of the act.

The show continued, and every performer was a clown. Amelia spent more time looking at me than at the stage. I tried to pretend that nothing was wrong so she wouldn't worry.

"Not long after the circus, my daughter turned into a sad clown, with a blue teardrop beneath her left eye," I told the neurologist. Dr. Williams was a silly clown, with a big red nose and high-arched eyebrows. Her rainbow hair framed her face in tight ringlets. I wondered what she looked like to other people.

"I'm amazed you can recognize people," she said.

"Everyone's a clown, but they aren't all the *same* clown."

She studied my MRI results. "There's nothing physically wrong with your fusiform gyrus, or anywhere else on the scan."

"What else can we try?" I asked. I needed to stop seeing clowns. I worried that my break with reality was what made my daughter so sad. We never should have gone to the circus.

"Maybe a psychiatrist?" Dr. Williams suggested. She gave me a referral.

"Midnight was sick all over the carpet," Amelia reported when I got back from my appointment. She had two tears under her left eye. That was a bad sign. People's clown faces didn't change for passing moods.

"I'll clean it up." Midnight's favorite cat pastimes were eating grass and puking on the carpet. I sprinkled a box of baking soda over the befouled area. "Is everything okay at school?"

Amelia nodded.

"Are you worried about something?" I asked. Amelia struggled with putting her feelings into words, as kids often do. Hell, grownups too. But I had to figure out why her clown face was so sad.

"Do you know what your face looks like?" she asked.

My heart sank. It was me, then. I'd been avoiding mirrors, but I didn't want Amelia to worry. In the most cheerful voice I could muster, I said, "Let's go look together at the mirror."

That was a mistake.

My too-big mouth was filled with pointy teeth and my eyes were bloodshot red with black pupils. I searched the face in the mirror for any feature that I recognized, any sign of what I'd looked like before my brain started distorting faces, but all I saw was a terrifying clown. I remembered that Amelia was standing beside me. Thank God she couldn't see what I saw.

"What's the matter with my face?" I asked.

"You used to be such a happy clown, and now you look scary. You look like worry and fear."

I didn't bother with the psychiatrist. If Amelia was seeing clowns, it had to be genetic. Or contagious, but I didn't even want to think about that. We sat down and talked, and she told me that her teacher was a sad clown, and the other kids were happy or silly or sad or scared. I asked her when she started seeing clowns, and she said she'd always seen them, she just hadn't known they were clowns until we went to the circus.

"I see clowns too," I told her, "and I'm worried because your clown looks sad."

"I don't like seeing everybody's inside feelings," Amelia said. "Have you looked at the cat?"

"Midnight?" The cat seemed fine, perched on top of the bookshelf. "She looks okay to me. What do you see?"

"I don't want to share it with you," Amelia said. "I think you don't like seeing the clowns."

"You didn't make me see clowns," I reassured her, "It was something about the circus—"

"No," Amelia said. "It was me. I thought you wanted to see what I saw."

I didn't really believe her, but I didn't want her to feel bad. "Okay, no problem. I see what you see, but not the cat. Let's share that too."

She touched my cheek, and one of her clownface tears faded away. Seeing clowns wasn't so bad. I could deal with a clown-cat if it would make my little girl happier.

I looked up at Midnight.

Perched on the bookshelf was a cat-sized spider, with beady black eyes and hairy legs. I flinched, but managed not to scream. "Has she always looked like that? I mean, to you?"

Amelia shook her head. "I think she's sick."

"We'll take her to the vet."

*

The vet was a tired-looking clown with faded blue hair. The waiting room was full of hideous creatures—dog-sized maggots and featherless birds and a guinea pig that didn't have a face. Amelia was completely unfazed, and sat with our giant spider-cat on her lap.

This was my new world, her world, full of horrifying animals and clown faces.

A happy clown came out of the treatment room with an ordinary-looking dog. I hoped the vet could cure our cat. I hated spiders. I almost wished I hadn't volunteered to see what Amelia saw. Then I saw her contented little clown face. If sharing these nightmarish visions was what it took to make her happy, I wouldn't flinch away.

I stroked one of Midnight's furry legs and tried to pretend the hissing noise was a purr.

HARMONIES OF TIME

You do not know me yet, my love, but I can hear you in my future. You are there from the beginning—at first just a few stray notes, but your presence quickly grows into a beautiful refrain. I wish you could hear time as I do, my love, but this song was never meant to be heard. The future should be *chronobviated*, gathered up in feathery pink fronds with delicate threads that waver in and out of alternate timelines. The past should be *memographed*, absorbed into a sturdy gray tail that stretches back to the beginning of the universe. We humans have neither fronds nor tails, but when the Eternals wanted to talk to us, they found a way to work around that.

The melody of my past is simple.

When I was ten years old, I heard my mother's voice for the first time. The doctors worried that I might be too old to adapt to the change. They told me that the sensation might be overwhelming. They explained that sound wouldn't be the same for me as for a child born with hearing. But none of that mattered. As a ten-year-old child, I saw the procedure as a way to be normal, just like all the other kids, and I jumped at the chance.

When the doctors turned my cochlear implant on for the first time, I was in a quiet room. My mother gave me a moment to adjust to the hum of the lights, and then she spoke to me. She told me that she loved me, signing as she said the words. When I heard her voice, I cried.

I never dreamed that in my lifetime I would gain another sense, but when the Eternals made first contact, they did not ask for politicians or for scientists. They asked for people like me. I had already learned a new sense, and I already had external sensors wired into my nervous system. With my permission, the Eternals altered my cochlear implant, and what they sense as time I hear as music. So much of what they wanted to say to us was contained in the harmonies of the future; they felt they couldn't communicate with us any other way.

It was disorienting at first, far worse than when my cochlear implant had been turned on. That had simply been a cacophony of sound, and the doctors had kept the room quiet to ease my transition. My new sense was a cacophony of time, and not even the Eternals could silence it. Every possible future of the universe echoed in my brain, and it nearly drove me mad. It was you that saved me, my love, even though we have not met. The possibility of you gave me something to hold on to. Something human, something simple, something real.

In the harmonies of my future, we meet today and tomorrow and next year and never. It is impossible to say for sure, but you sound closer now, so I suspect the time is near. I joke and you laugh. This is important, because in the strands of harmony where this doesn't happen, I tend to lose you. We date for weeks and months and years and not at all. I have the advantage of knowing which harmonies end well, so I will take you on the zip line tour that you will love, and avoid that disastrous trip to France.

I propose and you propose and we never speak of marriage. We have a beautiful ceremony in a church and on a beach and at the county courthouse. All our friends come to celebrate with us, or we elope and celebrate alone. We honeymoon in Mexico and Spain and Alaska and sometimes not at all because we can't afford the trip. We buy a house and live with your parents and rent a one bedroom apartment on the twenty-fourth floor of a high-rise.

Sometimes we have children and sometimes not. Either way is

fine with me, love, but there are things I can't control, even with everything I know. We have two girls and one boy and no children even though we try. We lose children before they are born and from sickness I can not prevent and as a soldiers in a foreign war. There are strands in the harmony where you resent me for failing to stop these things. There are strands where I hate myself. But there are other strands with so much joy. Yes, either way is fine with me. The happiness is worth the risk.

We grow old together and alone, but the aging is inevitable—avoided only by death. We get glasses and you get a hearing aid, and the harmonies of time start to slip away from me. I prefer the strands where you are at my side when I die, but sometimes you pass first and I am there with you.

The Eternals warned us of a catastrophe that will and won't happen, two million years from now. They believed their message was urgent. They failed to comprehend the timescale of our lives, even after we explained. Once they had given their warning, they left in search of others who could not foresee the coming danger.

I kept my implant, even after the Eternals moved on. I am changed forever by this sense of what has been and what may someday be. Even when the song threatens to overwhelm me, I must listen. I would not cut out my eyes because light is too bright; I would not cut out my tongue after tasting something bitter. I cling to the song of time even though it makes me doubt my connection to humanity. I am different, yes. But I still cry when I think of my mother's voice, cracking with emotion as she tells me that she loves me, the first time I ever heard her. The memory helps me remember who I am, no matter how disconnected I may feel. That memory is the next best thing to having you.

The harmonies of when we meet collapse into a single note, and we are meeting now. I tell a joke, and wait for you to laugh. Oh, I hope you laugh. Please, please laugh. It would be so hard to lose you, now that you are here.

For an agonizing moment I wait, and the harmonies of our future waver. Then you laugh, a sound as sweet as the first time I heard my mother's voice. A sound that bodes well for our future.

In ninety-eight percent of all the harmonies I hear, I love you.

PART 2:
FANTASY WORLDS

STONE WALL TRUTH

Njeri sewed the woman together with hairs from a zebra tail. Her deer-bone needle dipped under the woman's skin and bobbed back out. The contrast of the white seams against her dark skin was striking.

"The center seam makes a straight line," Njeri told her apprentice, "but the others flow with the natural curves of the body, just as the Enshai River follows the curve of the landscape."

Odion leaned in to examine her work, his breath warm on the back of her neck. Foolish boy, wasting his attention on her. Njeri set her needle on the table and stood up to stretch. The job was nearly done—she'd repositioned the woman's organs, reconstructed her muscles, sewn her body back together. Only the face was still open, facial muscles splayed out in all directions from the woman's skull like an exotic flower in full bloom.

"Why sew them back together, after the wall?" Odion asked. "Why not let them die?"

Njeri sighed. The boy had steady hands and a sharp mind, but his heart was unforgiving. He had been eager to learn about the cutting, about the delicate art of preparing a patient to hang from the wall. What he questioned was the sewing, the part of the work that had drawn Njeri to this calling. She studied the woman on the table—the last surviving grandchild of Radmalende, who had been king when the country was ruled by kings instead of warlords. The two of them had come of age the same spring, and had taken their adulthood rites together. That had been many years ago, but it was hard for Njeri not to think of her childhood friend by name. "You think I should leave her to die?"

"Her bones were black as obsidian." He traced the center seam with his finger.

Njeri said nothing. She admired the woman for her strength; she hadn't cried or protested or made excuses. Few women were put on the wall, but this one had faced it as bravely as any man, braver than some. And her shadowself had been like nothing Njeri had ever seen. Dark, of course, but a tightly controlled blackness, an army of ants marching out from her heart and along her bones. A constantly shifting shadow that never rested too long in any one place.

"She made a play for the throne. Killed six Maiwatu guardsmen in the process. Her attack has opened the way for the Upyatu. I heard a rumor today the capitol is still under siege." Odion masked the worry in his voice, but Njeri knew he was concerned. He had many friends in the upper echelons of the ruling class—it was how he came to be apprenticed to the highest ranking surgeon at the longest stretch of wall.

"There is always unrest in the capitol." Njeri didn't add that this woman had a stronger claim to the citrine throne than most. "Besides, it's not our place to say what people deserve. General Bahtir pays us to take people apart and put them back together, not to judge them."

Njeri nudged Odion aside. She settled back into her stool, and he went outside to set some water boiling for tea. He didn't appreciate being pushed away, didn't understand why she didn't want him the way he wanted her. She wanted to tell the boy to find someone his own age, someone who *liked* boys, but Odion wouldn't listen. Njeri returned to her work. The woman's jawbone hung slack below her skull, but her mouth still closed around the clear stone that held her mind while Njeri patched her body together. The woman's eyes stared up at the thatched straw roof, empty, with nothing but bone surrounding them. Flayed open, everyone looked wide-eyed and afraid. Njeri visualized how her muscles should fit together to recreate her strong chin and high cheekbones.

"Ever wonder what you'd look like on the wall?"

Njeri tensed at the interruption, then relaxed. Odion knew better than to startle her while she sewed, but she hadn't taken up the needle yet. The boy was certainly persistent in seeking her attention. She considered his question. The work she did was good, healing those who came off the wall, but she had her share of secrets, her share of shame. Life demanded dark things sometimes, she didn't need the wall to tell her that. What would her balance be? She hoped the good in her would be enough to cancel out the darkness, but she could not say for sure.

"I do," Odion said, finally. "Wonder, I mean. I've never seen anyone clean—not on the smaller wall in Zwibe, and not here."

"True, that." Njeri picked up her needle, ending the conversation, and began to reconnect the muscles of the woman's mouth. She stitched the entire face together without taking a break, though by the end her fingers ached.

When the sewing was finished, Njeri made Odion examine her work. It served two purposes. First, it was good for the boy to learn the ritual of checking and rechecking before the patient was restored to consciousness. Ripping out seams already sewn was a tedious process, but a mistake caught now could be corrected. After the mind-stone was removed, however, mistakes meant pain and often death. She had to train the boy to be observant, to notice the slightest error. Second, of course, was that Odion's eyes and hands were fresh—he was more likely to catch a mistake if she'd made one.

Odion ran his fingertips up the seam of the woman's left arm, then down the seam of her right. His touch was firm enough to feel both the surface seam and the muscles underneath, allowing him to test the depth of the stitches. He tested the woman's legs, her chest, and finally her face. He didn't speak as he worked.

"Flawless," he said. "You never make mistakes."

"I'm well-practiced now," Njeri answered. "I made my mistakes before your time."

She laid her fingers on the cool flesh at the base of the woman's neck. Odion might be more likely to catch a mistake, but that did not relieve Njeri of her obligation to check her own work. She pressed her fingers along the center seam, sliding her hand between the woman's breasts and over the gentle rounding of her belly. Her body was softer than Njeri's, an alluring contrast to the fierceness she had shown in facing the wall. Where Njeri was lean and angular, this woman was feminine and curved. Njeri lost her place and had to backtrack her pattern along the seams.

"Did I miss something?" Odion asked, frowning. He placed his hand over Njeri's.

"No," Njeri said. She moved her hand away and finished tracing the seams.

Confident that she had made no errors, Njeri slipped her thumb and index finger into the woman's mouth, which was dry and cool, preserved in a state of half life. She grasped the mindstone and pulled it free. The woman's muscles tensed, then relaxed.

Odion held out a cup of hibiscus mint tea, but Njeri waved it away. Too soon. The woman's eyes were closed, she wasn't ready to face the world. She remained motionless, as though the stone was still in her mouth. Even her breath was shallow, as though she begrudged the rising and falling of her chest.

Odion shifted his weight from foot to foot, refusing to be still. Patience was not a virtue he possessed. Perhaps the young were never patient. Njeri had not been, when she was Odion's age. Noticing her attention, Odion thrust the cup forward again. Njeri took it.

The woman's eyes opened, clear and dark.

"The light of the wall shines upon us and reveals our shadows," Njeri said. "Its light is the gift of a race long gone from this earth. You have faced the wall and returned. Speak your name and you may go."

These were the ritual words that Talib had taught her, when she was in training. There was a falseness to them, for no patient was ever ready to leave so soon after being awakened, and none saw their ordeal as a gift. But the speaking of names was good, for it confirmed that the mind had returned from the stone. A name provided continuity between time before the wall and time afterwards.

"Kanika." Her voice was breathy and weak. Odion pulled her shoulders up and pushed a wedge of bundled straw behind her back so she could sit. Njeri tipped the cup against Kanika's lips, slowly pouring tea into her mouth. For every sip she swallowed, two spilled down her neck and over her chest. Njeri gave the empty cup to Odion to refill it.

"My son?" Kanika asked. "Bahtir's men came for my son."

General Bahtir put only his most powerful enemies on the wall, for fear that if he killed them they would curse him from the Valley of the Dead. A child, even one with royal ancestry, did not pose enough of a threat to be spared.

Odion returned with more tea. "Drink," he said, pressing the cup into Kanika's hands. Njeri reached to take it from her, but she clutched the carved wood in her fingers and drained the cup.

"I remember," she said, "I feel myself open on the wall. Like looking in from the outside."

Her hands shook. Had there been any tea left, it would have sloshed over the sides. "So much darkness I never knew was there, and my son is dead by now, because I couldn't protect him. I failed him. You should have killed me. There's nothing left of me worth saving."

Njeri took the cup. She wanted to cradle Kanika in her arms and comfort her, but she had to act as a surgeon, not as a friend. She searched for something she could do to ease Kanika's pain. The stone that had held Kanika's mind still sat beside her on the table. Rainbows swirled beneath the clear surface of the smooth stone. It was a relic of the Ancients, made from the same glassy material as the wall.

"Here." Njeri picked up the mindstone and pressed it into Kanika's hand. "To remind you that there is light inside you too. The colors in this stone are the echoes of your mind."

"There are not so many stones that we can give them freely," Odion said. He scowled at Njeri. "You're treating her differently because she's a woman, because you knew her before the wall."

There was truth to that, but Njeri did not retract her offer. Kanika stared into the stone. "So pretty. Light without shadows. I could swallow it, and drift away from my pain."

"You would have no way to return, if you changed your mind," Njeri said.

Kanika smiled, but her eyes were sad. "I speak of escape, but that has never been my way, you know that. Holding life at such a distance would be like not living at all, too big a price to pay."

Odion reached for the mindstone, to take it from her, but she closed her fingers over it.

"I may not be able to use the stone," she told him, "but I cannot give it up. It is my light, and I carry much darkness."

Heat rose from the cracked-mud earth. The stars winked in and out of existence at the edge of Njeri's senses, their light distorted by miles of wavering sky. Beyond the thatched rooftops of the village, rolling hills of dry grass stretched into the darkness. Kanika leaned against Njeri as they walked across the village to the healer's hut.

"I wish I could go home," Kanika said. "I want to pull into myself and sleep. I feel like I could sleep forever."

"Your punishment is ended. You could leave for home tomorrow, if you wished," Njeri said, but she hoped that Kanika would stay.

"Ended? The wall was the worst, Njeri, but my punishment will last until I die. Anyone who sees my skin will know that I hung on the wall. Do you think people will forgive me? Embrace me into their lives?"

"Any man worth having would want you still," Njeri said. "Or any woman."

Njeri couldn't read Kanika's expression. Was there interest there?

"You don't know what it's like to be up on the wall. The things I saw . . ." Kanika brought her hand to her heart, digging her fingers into the fabric of her shirt to press against the seams in her skin.

"Dreams from the mindstone. Many of my patients have spoken of such visions."

"No. There is only truth on the wall," Kanika said. "I thought, before I went on the wall, that I wouldn't have shadows. But I was only adding self-deception and arrogance to the list of my flaws." Her words came in a steady stream, with only the barest pauses for breath. "No one can understand me, not with these scars. Not because of how I look, but because I know my shadowself."

Kanika fell silent as they approached a cluster of Bahtir's guardsmen. Normally they patrolled the periphery of the village in pairs, so it was unusual to see them gathered in the road. Several men shook their shields, zebraskins stretched taut over oval frames. Strands of human teeth hung below and rattled as the shields moved. One man ran his fingers over the tigers-eye clasp that held his threadbare orange cloak closed, and another tapped the butt of his spear against the dirt. The guardsmen were on edge tonight.

One of the men stepped forward to stop the women, then recognized Njeri and saw Kanika's scars. He signaled to the others, and the entire group turned and headed back towards the guardhouse, a large clay-brick building at the outskirts of the village. When they had gone, Kanika pulled out her mindstone. In the moonlight there were no rainbows, only swirls of a silvery blue. "This is what I thought I was. I was so foolish."

"That is as much a part of you as the shadows are," Njeri said.

"We all have darkness," Kanika said.

Njeri had heard this from many of her patients. It was a source of great comfort for them to think that they were not alone in having shadows. Sometimes Njeri wondered if there was truth in their assertion. There was no way to know; the innocent weren't sentenced to hang on the wall. "You've lived your life well, despite your darkness. Doesn't that give you some comfort?"

"No, don't you see? We all have darkness. *All* of us," Kanika pulled away. "The wall is pointless. You torture people for no purpose."

Kanika took a few steps, then stumbled. Njeri caught her. Her skin was moist with sweat—heat and exertion were taking their toll. "The wall is about revealing a person's darkest truth. If they see their darkness, they can fight it. The knowledge can heal them."

"It destroys them. It destroys me. And you condemn people to this torture."

"I am the hands that do the work," Njeri said. "I don't decide who faces the wall."

Kanika tried to pull away a second time, but she was too weak. "You pass judgment every time you open someone onto the wall. Don't pass the responsibility to someone else. We all judge, and we all mete out our punishments. You saw how all the guardsmen fled at the sight of me."

"Superstitious fools," Njeri said.

They walked in silence to Durratse's door. Njeri knew the old healer well, for he had cared for her for several months after her mother died. She watched carefully for his reaction when he opened his door. He hid his revulsion well, but she could see the slight flare of his nostrils, the falseness in his smile. She wondered how she'd failed to notice it with the other patients she'd brought him. Or perhaps he'd been more forgiving of the men.

"We all judge," Kanika repeated.

Durratse led Kanika inside. It was late, so he did not invite Njeri in. He simply nodded his head and closed the door.

The roughly hewn wood of the door had shrunk with weather and age, and she could still see them through the gaps in the wood. She wanted to argue with Kanika, to defend herself. Kanika insisted on focusing on the worst of the wall, the worst of her, the cutting. Like Odion, she paid no mind to the important work of sewing. She healed people, just as Durratse did, and her patients needed more healing than anyone.

When Njeri went out to stoke her cooking fire shortly after sunrise, the village was bustling with unfamiliar guardsmen. The new arrivals were Upyatu—a tall people, with broad flat feet. She watched them as she boiled plantains for breakfast. They were more boisterous than Bahtir's men; they spoke in loud voices punctuated with barking laughter. Their heads were covered with elaborate beaded headdresses, and their shields were round and crimson. It could mean only one thing. The capitol had fallen.

Njeri pounded the boiled plantains into mash. It made little difference to her, the struggle for power. One general was replaced by another, but they all wanted the same work done. She wished for peace not out of support for any current ruler, but because in times of war she had to put more people to the wall. She took her mash back to the hut, where Odion was waiting.

"The new general brought two prisoners for the wall," he said, speaking quickly. "He wants to hang them together."

Njeri divided the mash into two bowls and topped each one with slices of green mango. How could Odion be excited about such a thing? The Maiwatu were his people. Besides, to put criminals on the wall was one thing, but to leave one there for the time it took to flay a second was cruel. Dissecting them simultaneously, but slowly, would be no better. "Cruelty. Already I dislike the man."

Odion stirred his mash. "I thought, with two men, I might be charged with opening one of them."

"We have but one obsidian blade," Njeri said, "and the new general will want the services of a surgeon, not an apprentice. I will open them, and you will assist, as we have always done."

A guardsman came to fetch them before they'd finished their morning meal. He was paler even than Odion, with a reddish tint to his skin, like dry dusty earth. Shorter, too, than most Upyatu warriors, and injured. Njeri could just make out the outlines of a bandage beneath the guardsman's tightly fitted leather tunic.

"General Yafeu commands your presence." The guardsman's voice was nasal, and far higher pitched than Njeri expected. Not a man at all, but a woman with her breasts bound. The warrior laughed at Njeri's surprise. "Call me Zola, and a woman. Bahtir would not allow women in the fight, he wanted them only for his bed. Yafeu is better. With him I can show my strength in both places."

Zola grinned at Odion, exposing teeth sharpened into points. Her stare had an animal quality to it, something almost predatory. Judging from his reluctance to meet the woman's stare, Odion did not find her aggression appealing. Njeri didn't like it either; Zola had a showiness about her that was distinctly off-putting. Not like Kanika's understated strength.

Njeri took up her obsidian blade, protected in its leather sheath. "The general will set us to work immediately then?"

"In a land where power shifts like flowing water, there is no later. Everything worth doing is worth doing now." Zola glanced again at Odion, but again he gave her no response. She shrugged and led them to the guardhouse. A pair of goats were tethered outside, undoubtedly part of her payment for serving the new general.

Before they entered, Zola tapped the door three times with one end of her bow, announcing their arrival to those inside. The guardhouse looked the same as it always had. Sleeping bunks lined the walls, and supplies were stacked in neat piles beneath and around the beds. Only the occupants had changed, the Maiwatu guardsmen replaced by the Upyatu.

General Yafeu sat atop a makeshift throne at the back of the room. He was a young man, barely older than Odion, and he had surrounded himself with female guardsmen. His guards were in full uniform, but the general's chest was bare except for a piece of vibrant yellow citrine that hung on a leather cord. It was carved into the shape of a lion's head, reminiscent of the decorations on the citrine throne in the capitol. Two other stones hung from his belt, Bahtir's tiger-eye and the rose quartz of Bahtir's predecessor. At the base of Yafeu's throne were two men, bound and gagged. Njeri was unsurprised to see that Bahtir was one of the prisoners. The other was a man she did not recognize.

Zola stood to left side of the general's throne and whispered something into his ear.

"So you are the Surgeon of Stonewall," Yafeu said.

"Yes," she replied, "and this is my apprentice." She did not bother with her name, or Odion's, for Yafeu had the look of a man who cared not about such things.

"And the wall will show these men for the evil creatures they are?" Yafeu asked, gesturing at his prisoners and curling his lips as though the very thought of them repulsed him.

"The wall reveals the innermost secrets of our nature," Njeri replied. "Those placed on the wall can hide nothing."

Odion stepped forward. "If they have shadow in them, the wall will expose it."

Njeri resisted the urge to rebuke her apprentice, but only because she didn't wish to fight in front of the general. It was not his place to speak in this situation, and it diminished Njeri that he would misbehave like this.

General Yafeu laughed. "I like this apprentice of yours. He shows spirit, and a willingness to please."

Njeri forced herself to nod and smile, even as Yafeu let his gaze linger on her apprentice. The general's words held the promise of intimacy that Odion had long sought with Njeri, and the boy was lonely enough that he might be swayed by the man's attention. She would have to be careful.

A guardsman entered without knocking and knelt, with his head bowed, in the center of the room. He was coated in sweat and dirt, and panted as though he had run the entire way from the capitol.

"Go." Yafeu waved them away. "I will send you the prisoners when I'm finished here, and you can begin your work."

The wall was three times as tall as Njeri, and thicker than the length of her arm. It stretched twice the length of the village, winding east into the hills like a crystal snake. The morning sun glinted bright off the stones, if they could really be called stones. The wall was made from blocks as clear as glass, irregularly shaped but fit together so seamlessly that there was no need for mortar. According to Talib, the wall had once enclosed the entire nation of the Ancients. The fragments that remained were laid roughly in a circle, with the capitol in the center.

"The stone wall," Yafeu said. "It's more impressive than the pitiful fragment in Zwibe. Though neither looks anything like stone."

Odion showed no reaction to the mention of his home village. Instead, he answered the unasked question in Yafeu's comment. "They call it the stone wall because people used to throw stones at the condemned while they hung. You can see the cracks where rocks flew wide of their targets."

"The practice was discarded centuries ago," Njeri added, before Yafeu got any ideas. "You can see how damaging it was to the wall."

Njeri did not mention that it also damaged the people that hung on the wall, making it impossible to sew them back together. General Yafeu shrugged, then waved his hand at the guardsmen. The two prisoners were marched out to stand before the wall. Njeri pressed her palm to the forehead of each man in a silent blessing. It was ironic that Bahtir, who had once feared the ghosts of the valley, now received a blessing that asked those same ghosts to protect him.

"Don't do this," Bahtir pleaded. She had heard such pleas before, many times, but never from a man who had ordered others onto the wall. The former general had always seemed so brave, but that had been an illusion of his power. Now that he had no power, he had no courage.

Njeri brushed her fingertips against the icy surface of the two mindstones in her pocket. She wondered if she would be brave, in Bahtir's place. She liked to think that she would be, knowing that the wall revealed only the truth—nothing more and nothing less. Kanika had been brave. The thought of her called back her assertion that Njeri had been wrong to put people on the wall. Did these men deserve such punishment? It wasn't her place to decide, it couldn't be. Her job was to cut and to sew.

Odion paced in the periphery of her vision.

She put a mindstone into the mouth of the older man first, and left him on the ground at the base of the wall. She moved on to Bahtir. Two guardsmen held him in place, one gripping each of his arms. She slid the glassy stone between his lips, and the life flowed out of his body. The guardsmen held him against the wall, and she pinned him there, driving shards of amethyst through the nine sacred points—palms and feet, hips and shoulders, and the final point through the nook at the base of his throat. The amethyst penetrated through his flesh, just until the tips touched the wall, and yet the attraction between the lavender shards and the clear stone held Bahtir firmly. His head drooped as though he bowed it in remorse, but once he was opened, smaller amethyst pins would hold the muscles of his face, and his head would no longer hang.

Odion handed her the obsidian blade. Like the wall itself, the blade came from an older time. Mbenu, who made tools for the village, could knap a blade from obsidian, but his tools did not have the power of the Ancients in them. This blade slipped between the cells, and Njeri had learned through many years of training to trace the exact paths that would peel a man open without spilling a drop of blood.

Her first cut sliced only skin, beginning at the top of Bahtir's forehead and moving down the midline, over his nose, and to his lips. There she paused and traced the outline of his mouth with the blade before picking up the midline once more. Chin neck, chest, groin, all without a drop of blood. The only loss was a strand of his hair that grew exactly on the midline. Sliced away by her blade, it fell to the base of the wall.

She sliced down the inner edge of each leg to the ankle, then drew the blade around to the front of each foot and into a gentle curve to the tip of the middle toe, completing the first vertical sequence. After that came a series of horizontal lines, branching out from the center. One cut along each arm, branching into five lines at the fingers. Evenly spaced cuts along the torso and legs so the skin would lie flat against the wall. Last, a series of lines radiating out from the center of his face, so that it would open like an exploding sun.

Light streamed through his skin. Any darkness on his surface was artificial, a trick of the eyes and not an indication of his being. On the wall, skin of every color let the same amount of light pass through. Njeri passed her blade to Odion and wiped the sweat from her face.

When she looked up, she saw Kanika, standing on the hillside, one face among many watchers. She stood near the top of the hill with the people of Stonewall, all of them staying as far from the wall as possible. The villagers had seen this many times, and attended now only because the general demanded it. A foolish demand, Njeri realized, for even if no one watched, the shame of these men would be forever sewn onto the surface of their skin. No army would follow a sewn general.

Everyone on the hill judged these men. All except Kanika. She was there to judge Njeri, and simply by having begun the flaying, she had failed. Standing at her side, Odion held the obsidian blade lightly, as though it was made of air from the night sky. When she took it from him the weight of it pulled her down towards the earth. She had to ease the burden on her heart; she had to prove that Bahtir deserved this punishment. Instead of moving on to the next man, Njeri stayed with the former general, peeling away the muscles to get down to his bones.

She placed the tip of the blade on Bahtir's breastbone, and leaned into it with all her weight. His breastbone split in two. She pried his ribcage open and revealed his shadows. They crawled like slugs from the core of his being, leaving trails of black slime behind them. This was her vindication, her proof that the punishment was just—but it was a hollow victory.

Njeri could feel the eyes of every man, woman, and child on the hillside, boring into the back of her neck. They looked at Bahtir, not at her, but she felt as though she was the one whose heart was exposed. She wanted to throw down her blade, or smash it to slivers against the wall.

The sunlight that passed through the wall cast no shadows. Even the stones that were flawed with a spiderweb pattern of cracks—scars from poorly aimed rocks of generations past—even those stones contained no darkness. Those imperfections on the wall simply broke the light into rainbows. It was a mockery of mankind. A mockery of Bahtir, whose shadowed heart was exposed for all to see.

Judging from the sun, it was mid-afternoon now, and a plate of untouched food sat behind her. Odion must have offered it, but she did not remember waving it off. The boy stepped forward and sprinkled water on Bahtir's body to keep the tissue from drying out. When he finished, he came to her and put his hand on her shoulder. He could see that she was suffering, and Njeri knew he would gladly take over her task.

The second man lay unconscious in the dirt, his mind still locked away in stone. He was older, his hair a pale gray, almost white in the bright glare of the wall. Njeri could see the outline of his bones; he was underfed, or ill, or both.Njeri didn't know the man's name.

Two guardsmen held his limp body against the wall and Njeri pinned him into place. She raised her blade, holding it at the man's head, at the starting point for the series of incisions she had made a hundred times before. It didn't matter that the man was old. It didn't matter that she didn't know who he was or what he had done. She had opened Kanika, she could do this.

"Do you tire?" Odion whispered when the pause grew too long. "I can bear this burden for you."

Njeri could not pass the blade to her apprentice, not at this moment, not in this way. Not even if the boy was ready, which Njeri doubted. This was a decision she had to make, to cut or not to cut. If she couldn't open this man, it meant that Kanika had been right—

that in thinking it was not her place to pass judgment, she had been judging just the same. The blade quivered in her hand, and a droplet of blood appeared on the man's forehead.

"Give me the blade," Odion said, holding out his hand.

"No," Njeri said. This was her duty, and had been for many years. She could not escape from this, not now, not ever. To fail in her duty would be an act against General Yafeu. She could feel his gaze boring into her from the hillside, waiting, judging, finding her wanting.

"What is the delay?" General Yafeu called out. "Your task is not yet finished, woman."

"Who is this man?" Njeri asked. "What is his crime?"

"That is no business of yours." Yafeu's voice held amusement. He found this entertaining. Like a circus act, or a play. This was the man who Njeri had trusted to pass judgment. If she had believed herself unfit to decide the fate of others, surely this man was worse. Which made Njeri worse for having accepted his orders.

Njeri couldn't do it. She couldn't open this man that she didn't even know. She tore an amethyst pin out of his hand and reached for the one in his shoulder. Guardsmen rushed in to restrain her, and she put up no fight. The obsidian blade was taken from her.

"Open him," Yafeu said, speaking to Odion.

"No!" Njeri cried. "Please, let him go."

"At last, a statement with conviction." Yafeu smiled. "Will you take his place, then? Do you believe so strongly in this man that you would face the wall instead of him?"

Njeri knew her motives weren't pure. She wanted to save the man, yes, but not for his sake. She wanted to save him to make up for all the times she'd cut people open blindly. She wanted to make amends for opening Kanika without even asking of her crime. But surely it was better to do the right thing for the wrong reason than to not do it at all.

Odion stood before her. His eyes brimmed with tears. He had wanted to prove himself today, but not this way. Even with all his impatience and ambition, he still loved her. There was hope for him yet.

"Yes," Njeri said. "I will take the man's place."

"Pin her up," the general ordered. "Boy, you can gut them both."

Njeri managed two steps toward Yafeu before the guardsmen closed in and restrained her. "It could kill him. Especially at the hands of the inexperienced."

"You had your chance to do it, and if the boy kills him, the ghost will curse him, not me," Yafeu said. "I can't let an enemy go free."

Njeri turned to Odion. "Open me first. I can stand to lose a few drops of blood, and you will do better with the old man if your hands are practiced with the blade."

"I don't have a mindstone," he said. His whole body shook, and he reeked with the sweat of fear. "We only brought two mindstones."

The general would not be pleased. She wondered if he would order her opened without the stone. That way would surely mean death.

"Take this one." It was Kanika, her voice soft and close. In her hand was the mindstone that had held her mind, the one Njeri had given her to keep. The guardsmen moved to encircle her, but backed away at the sight of her scars. She was a ghost, a curse, a plague. Njeri couldn't believe she hadn't noticed it before, the punishment that continued after the wall.

"I will be there when you wake. We can face the world together," Kanika said. She brushed her hand against Njeri's cheek.

"Touching," General Yafeu said, "but it's time for you to go back to the hill. Unless you'd like another turn on the wall? I don't think anyone has ever faced it twice."

Kanika kissed Njeri's forehead, exactly on the spot that Odion would begin the first incision. She lingered a moment more, then walked past General Yafeau and up to the top of the hill. Odion stepped forward. It hurt the boy to see Njeri with someone else, sharing the intimacy that he himself longed for.

"You and I will share a different bond, Odion," she told him.

He nodded, and his jaw clenched as he prepared for what he must do. For a moment she feared he would refuse this duty, as she had done. It would anger Yafeu if he had to take his second prisoner to a lesser fragment of wall, and it would mean death for her and Odion—they had no claim to the citrine throne, their blood wasn't powerful enough for Yafeu to fear their ghosts. She held her mouth open and waited.

Odion pressed the mindstone between her lips, and she closed her eyes and swallowed herself.

The stone became her body. She sensed its boundaries, smooth and round. Her mind swirled restlessly inside. It felt like something was missing. She was indigo-blue. Perhaps green was missing? She searched and found flickering flecks of green, like emerald rain in her river of blue. She found red and yellow and purple. All her colors were here, but something was fundamentally wrong with this existence.

She pressed against the boundaries of her stone, and discovered thousands of tiny windows. Speckles of color were stuck to the edges of each opening. She tasted one of the windows, and the flavor of otherness repulsed her. She withdrew to the center of her stone, checking her threads of red and yellow, her flecks of green, her river of blue. She was intact.

Her churning nature sent her out to her boundaries once more, and she tasted each of the windows in turn. She began to develop favorite spots, flavors she returned to again and again. Her extremities oozed out through those windows, the ones that tasted best, and her strands of rainbow-self brought images from beyond the stone.

The first was Odion. The boy held the obsidian blade in his right hand, and a bundle of muscle tissue in his left. The tissue belonged to Njeri. The name came without the sense of self that she knew ought to accompany it. Njeri was a painting of a memory, hanging on the wall. Njeri was the body, and she was the stone, and yet they were the same.

Odion flayed Njeri open. Tiny beads of blood leaked out from misplaced seams and poorly detached muscles. The tip of the blade tore into her and isolated every thread of her being. Odion cut Njeri's body apart, and every slice he made burned her in the space between her colors.

Odion plunged the blade into Njeri's breastbone and pried her ribcage open. She burned like a white-hot flame, a blaze too strong for her river of blue to extinguish. Ragged black canyons stretched out from Njeri's heart like festering wounds. Her colors recoiled from the darkness. Odion misted the body with water. The searing fire of pain died to glowing embers. He was finished, and he disappeared from her senses.

She stretched her colors towards the darkness. That was what was missing inside the stone. Her colors dimmed with the setting sun, but even as her red and yellow shifted into lavender and silver, there was no shadow. She reached into the dark canyons and tried to latch onto them, to pull the blackness out. Instead, the shadow pulled her inward, down through the center of Njeri's heart, and into the wall itself.

Bahtir was beside her. The cuts she had inflicted on his flesh drew her further out of herself, closer to her patient and deeper into the wall. Echoes of Bahtir's shadowself seeped out from his body and writhed in the cracks between the giant stones of the wall. She felt his flesh, still hanging, but he stayed inside his mindstone.

Someone new appeared. She recognized the woman by her shadow. Kanika. Tendrils of red and gold and green seeped out from Kanika's mindstone, but they wandered aimlessly, without direction or purpose. Kanika had stretched out from her stone and seen visions on the wall, just as she had claimed, but the wall did not guide Kanika backwards. The wall did not pull everyone as it pulled her. She wanted to stay with Kanika, but the wall carried her away.

She moved backwards through time. She felt every cut of every man and every woman she'd ever flayed open, and still the torture did not end. Talib's final patients were next, the ones that she had watched to learn his trade. Then people she didn't know, stretching back before she was born, before Talib was born. The knowledge that passed from teacher to student across the generations bound them all together as surely as if they'd shared blood. She was tied to the surgeons, and that bound her to their patients.

An infant appeared on the wall. Black threads grew out from his heart like mold, and covered the insides of his ribs. His blackness barely moved, it was a constant, steady thing. She did not know if it was greed or fear or rage. Perhaps it was something she had no name for, because a shadow grew within her people before they had the words to name it. She felt the infant's agony twice over—the searing heat of the blade that cut him open, and the anguish in her heart at learning that even the innocent held shadows.

Soon after that, she came to the earliest days of her people, when watchers threw stones at those who hung helpless on the wall. Each blow crushed her colors, smashing them together into a muddy brown.

Then, nothing.

She had seen all that the wall had to show her. She waited for Odion to return, to take her down. She sensed that in her distant present, Odion was taking the men down from the wall. The men, but not Njeri. He could not bear to heal her, after having seen her darkness.

The wall rebuilt itself.

Tiny fragments merged together to form a perfect ring of glassy stone. It happened so fast that she had no way to know what had destroyed the wall. All she knew was that it was whole now. The vastness of it made her feel small, a tiny raindrop of color in an ocean of stone and light.

Two Ancients touched the wall, and she felt them as though they touched her skin. It was the end of their time, and the knowledge of that fact filled them with sadness. She waited for the surgeon, the last true surgeon, but then she realized that each of the Ancients that touched the wall also held an obsidian blade. Moving in perfect synchrony, each Ancient sliced open the other. They controlled the blades in a way she did not understand, and even after they were opened, they continued to cut each other. The surgeon and the patient, the judger and the judged—in the time of the Ancients, both went together to the wall.

Like them, she knew both ends of the obsidian blade.

Odion appeared before her.

Not yet, she pleaded. They were almost done. She wanted to see the Ancients, to see if they had blackness. Odion began to take her down, removing the amethyst pins one by one as guardsmen held her in place. Her colors pulled back into her heart and towards her mindstone. With just one hand still pinned against the wall, she could not see the Ancients, but she could feel them, and what they did here was not punishment, it was not judgment. For them, the wall was love. The Ancients did not hide their shadows—not from each other and not from the wall. And in the moment of their union, when they lay open to each other, they drew knowledge from the wall. They absorbed the history of their people, the wisdom of countless generations.

She caught fleeting images of cities a thousand times larger than the capitol, and weapons that could scar the earth itself, and ships of glassy stone that sailed not on water but in space. Her river of blue wept in undulating strands of turquoise at the beauty and the horror of their past.

Njeri's hand came free of the wall, and the connection was broken.

She watched from the mindstone as two guardsmen placed Njeri on a stretcher. They moved the body to a table, and Odion spent hours stitching it together, stopping once to sleep. The boy made two mistakes, and had to tear out the seams and start again. It didn't matter. It didn't matter how long it took, or even if he never woke Njeri at all. She had been wrong about the wall, wrong about the blackness. They had taken something beautiful, and sullied it with their imperfections.

Odion checked every seam seven times, then reached into Njeri's mouth. His touch shattered the boundaries of the stone. Her colors whirled outward, searching for structure. She dissipated into the space around her, traveling down her tendrils into Njeri's body—her body—the form she had lived in all her life. The shape of the body was wrong, like a shell that was too big.

Her eyes wouldn't open. Her body was desiccated and weak, and she couldn't stretch tendrils into the world beyond. She longed for her colors, for the fullness of history within the wall, for the knowledge of the ancients. After such vivid truth, the drab reality of life seemed false.

Strong hands pressed against her back, and her body bent at the waist. She felt so brittle she feared the action would snap her in two. Something warm pressed against her lips. The world was out there, acting on her, shaping her body, inflicting this warmth. The heat spread down from her lips, over her skin and down her throat. It smelled of mint. Tea. Odion was giving her tea.

She wished she could open her eyes.

"The light of the wall shines upon us and reveals our shadows," Odion said. "Its light is a gift, from a race long gone from this earth. You have faced the wall and returned. Speak your name . . ."

Njeri heard the words. She heard the boy falter, and waited for the rest. *And you may go,* she thought, prompting him to finish. But she found comfort in the pause. Comfort in knowing that Odion still did not want to let her go.

"Speak your name, and you may go," Odion whispered.

Njeri opened her mouth, but no words came.

"Oh, Njeri," Odion said, breaking with tradition and speaking her name before she had spoken it herself. "I would have sewed you sooner but the general forbade it. He insisted I start with Bahtir. But I didn't check him. Not a single seam. I was too impatient to get to you. Then, after Bahtir died, a soldier stood guard while I sewed the second man, watching work she didn't even understand to make sure I didn't unleash another vengeful ghost . . . Oh, please don't die. Please come back."

She heard the desperation in his voice, but how could she go back to the world, after what she had done? She had ruined so many lives, on a wall that wasn't meant to be used that way at all. Time passed, and more tea flowed over her. She passed through several cycles, the warmth of the tea followed each time by Odion's words. She could not speak.

Kanika's voice came from across the room. "You can't hide forever, Njeri. Speak your name and come back to us."

She was right. Njeri couldn't hide. She had seen what no one else knew, the true nature of the wall. If she did not wake, no one would know what she had discovered, and the wrong would continue. The Ancients did not hide their shadows, they learned from both their darkness and their light.

Njeri opened her eyes and spoke her name.

THE LITTLE MERMAID OF INNSMOUTH

Tomiko knelt at the table with her back straight and her webbed hands folded in her lap. She hoped the formal posture would make her father take her seriously, but he barely looked at her as he ate his breakfast of rice and *nattō*, fermented soybeans with a pungent smell that overpowered the fishy odor of his scaly skin.

"You are nearly seventeen, and it's time to consider your future." The words were calm, but Father was angry. Tomiko could see it in the way his veins bulged out beneath the gray-green skin of his forehead, and in the tension of his tightly-closed gills.

She stood her ground. "I don't want to join the Esoteric Order of Dagon."

"Everyone who lives in Innsmouth joins the Order."

"Not Mom." Tomiko stared defiantly at her father's bulging black eyes. Mom was forty-nine years old and still fully human. She was spending the summer in San Francisco, visiting her brother, Yuji. Tomiko had begged to go along, but Mom insisted that she'd be better off here, where she fit in. Mom was massively overprotective.

"Natsumi bore seven daughters for Dagon, and if she wishes to decline the honor of unending life in the watery deep, well . . ." Father trailed off. Tomiko often heard him arguing with Mom about it, but everyone else in town left her alone. She'd done her duty.

"I want to go live in San Francisco with Uncle Yuji. My English is good, and I could work as a waitress in his restaurant." Tomiko dreamed of streetcars and brightly painted row houses like the ones on the postcards Mom sent.

"None of your sisters gave me so much trouble."

"They wanted to have fish-froggy families and be rewarded with gold trinkets. I don't. That's not me."

"You can't live in the human world, my little *ningyo*. The deep ones are in your blood, even if you haven't pledged. You're already starting the transformation."

"Don't call me *ningyo*. I'm not a mermaid!" Tomiko looked at her arms, covered in scabs from where she'd used Mom's tweezers to pluck out her scales. The affliction was becoming ever harder to conceal—she had to wear scarves to hide the gills forming on her neck, and thin webs of skin gave her hands and feet a batrachian appearance . . . She would need surgery, and that would cost money she didn't have. Getting a job in San Francisco would be the perfect solution, if only she could convince her parents.

Father slapped his webbed hand against the table. "Maybe you can't see it, but I want what is best for you. I want you to embrace who you really are."

"You have no idea who I really am."

Father had nothing to say to that, and they finished their breakfast in silence. Tomiko ate her rice not with the stinky *nattō* that her father was fond of, but with a fried egg and pickled vegetables. If Mom had been home, there would have been miso soup to go with the breakfast, and fewer arguments from Father. It was so unfair that Mom would leave for San Francisco and abandon Tomiko here.

Webbed hands or no, she would find a way to get out of Innsmouth. She grabbed her bento lunch, but instead of going to school she walked to the bus station, arriving just as the decrepit gray motorcoach pulled in. It was empty save for the driver, Joe Hashimoto, and a single passenger. The passenger was clearly an outsider, with none of the classic Innsmouth look—his eyes were sunken, and his nose was sharply pointed, almost like the beak of a bird.

Tomiko watched him get off the bus, intrigued by his pale skin and sand-colored hair. He noticed her and recoiled in disgust. Had he seen her webbed hands, the scars on her skin? She was not as far transformed as Father, but she clearly couldn't pass as human even if she did manage to get herself out of Innsmouth.

"Skipping school to spend the day in Santa Cruz?" Joe asked, smiling. She'd cut school once to go to the beach with her friends, a couple years ago when she'd looked more fully human, and Joe hadn't breathed a word to her parents. He wasn't far out of school himself.

Tomiko shook her head. That'd been her plan—to ride with Joe to Santa Cruz and then take the train north to San Francisco—but she'd clearly have to work on her appearance first. She was too far along in her transformation to pass as human. She waved her hand in the direction the man had gone. "What's *he* doing coming here?"

Joe frowned. "He spent most of the ride rambling on about research of some sort or another. Came up from Los Angeles and saw the gold tiaras at the museum in Monterey, piqued his curiosity."

"He say what his name was?" Tomiko asked.

"Robert Homestead? Olmstead? Something like that." Joe give her a stern look. "Nothing but trouble there, though. Your father finds out you're talking to outsiders he won't be happy."

While she was talking to Joe, Mr. Olmstead disappeared into the grocery, perhaps looking for breakfast. Tomiko trailed behind, not wanting to go to school, but not sure what else to do. She didn't want to attract the man's attention by following him inside, so she sat on the curb and watched the gulls circling above the fish refinery.

Mr. Olmstead came out with a bottle of some kind, mostly wrapped in a brown paper bag, with only the top of the bottle protruding from its wrapping. It was well before noon, and she wouldn't have pegged him for a drinker, so she followed him with renewed curiosity as he headed toward the pier.

Joanne Hoag was there, and the pieces suddenly fit together. Joanne was an elderly white woman with frizzy gray hair who'd come to Innsmouth from Fresno after her husband died. She was the only outsider to join the Esoteric Order of Dagon, and also the only person Tomiko could think of who had ever escaped it. She decided Mr. Olmstead must be a reporter or a historian of some sort, trying to learn about Innsmouth by getting gossip from the town drunk. Joanne was always good for a tale after a few shots of liquor, so Tomiko found a nearby bench and settled in to listen.

Mr. Olmstead noticed her again and frowned, but made no

comment. He spoke to Joanne softly, but when Joanne didn't appear to hear him he raised his voice. "So how is it that you live in Innsmouth, but you don't have the Innsmouth look about you?" Joanne squinted at him, studying his face. "I don't like you."

"I brought some whiskey," he said, holding out the bottle.

Joanne snatched it, and poured herself a flaskful. "I still don't like you."

"I've heard there's another Innsmouth out on the East Coast," he said, trying to lure her into conversation.

"There's a Portland out there too," Joanne snapped. "What of it?"

They sat for a while, Joanne drinking from her flask and Mr. Olmstead occasionally taking a small sip from the bottle. He shifted his tactics and started with a safer topic. "You follow baseball? The Yankees are looking good to make the series again this year."

"Don't keep up much on baseball, but my cousin met Babe Ruth once, a few years ago. He came to Fresno and played with a team of Japanese players. Towered over them like a giant. My cousin invited me to visit, but . . ." Joanne trailed off, then took a swig of whiskey from her flask.

"Well, you missed Ruth, but I'd imagine you've seen some pretty interesting things in your life," Mr. Olmstead said.

Joanne stared off at the horizon. "There's creatures, out in the deep water. When I was a young widow, fresh out of Fresno, the deep ones courted me. Promised me a longer life and golden trinkets. I was stupid then, and joined their esoteric order."

Tomiko strained to listen. Mr. Olmstead strung Joanne along skillfully, leading her to the story he wanted to hear.

". . . and when the gills started to bulge in my neck, I panicked. I swam out to the reefs, you can see them just there—" Joanne pointed. "I begged the deep ones to let me make a deal with Dagon. I wanted desperately to regain my human form, to go back to the life I lived before I stumbled upon this cursed seaside town."

"And what price did Dagon demand?"

But this question Joanne would not answer. She drank deeply from her flask and tears streamed down her face. "I don't like you. I knew I didn't like you."

Mr. Olmstead asked several more questions, but the only answer he got was quiet sobs.

Twenty minutes before the evening bus to Santa Cruz, Tomiko followed Mr. Olmstead back to the bus stop. The motor-coach rolled in from Monterey, unloading a few native residents of Innsmouth. Mr. Olmstead stepped up to the bus, but Joe stopped him.

"Sorry, engine trouble," Joe said. "No way to get it fixed before tomorrow, maybe longer. You'll have to ask at the inn, unless you got someone to stay with."

Mr. Olmstead shook his head. He seemed unsettled at the thought of remaining in Innsmouth at night. Tomiko felt sorry for him. She didn't like it here, and she was part of the community. To be stuck here as an outsider must be even worse. She almost stepped up and asked him if he wanted to stay at her place, but the thought of her father's reaction held her back.

Tomiko waited until Mr. Olmstead had disappeared into the inn. "Anything wrong with the engine?"

"Nah, I'm just tired from driving all day." Joe smiled. "If anybody local wanted to make the trip, I'd do it, but for him? He can wait until morning. Besides, this gives the Order a chance to scope him out—"

Joe stopped suddenly, realizing that despite her features, Tomiko technically wasn't part of the Order. He'd said enough for her to figure out what was going on, though. She smiled reassuringly. "I've lived here long enough to know a few things. Gibbous moon tonight, hungry deep ones, that sort of thing."

Joe chuckled. "Yeah, I forgot you aren't pledged yet."

"My father's been on my case about it," Tomiko admitted. "Especially now, with Mom spending the summer in San Francisco."

"She's quite the woman, your mother," Joe said. He rubbed his hands over his back, sore from a long day driving. "Well, you better run home, young lady. It's almost dark and the streets are no place to be tonight, even for you."

Tomiko nodded and started walking home. When she was out of sight, she stopped and doubled back, keeping to the side streets and eventually hiding in an alley across from the inn.

When the sun went down, members of the Esoteric Order of Dagon began to congregate on the street—older men and women with bald heads and flattened faces, people who mostly hid indoors during the day, because the sun dried out their fish-frog skin. They spoke in a mix of Japanese and another, older language, chanting prayers to the deep ones that were not well suited to human tongues. Tomiko cowered in the darkness of the alley. No one noticed her. They were too intent on other prey.

The moon was waning, not quite full but still bright in the night sky, illuminating the streets with silver-blue light. The townsfolk made their way into the inn. For a time, the streets were quiet.

A window creaked open on the uppermost floor of the inn, and Mr. Olmstead climbed out. It seemed a stupid thing to do, to leave the relative safety of his locked room to chance the dark streets of Innsmouth. He scrabbled across the roof of the inn and leapt onto the neighboring building before slowly climbing down.

He took off to the north, toward the highway to Santa Cruz. Moments later, Tomiko saw her father emerge from the inn with several members of the Order. They chased after Mr. Olmstead, and a morbid curiosity compelled Tomiko to follow the angry mob.

Mr. Olmstead led them on a winding chase through the streets of Innsmouth, weaving through the buildings with a hint of evasive strategy at first, but growing ever more careless as he failed to shake his pursuers. In a fit of panic, he ran to the outskirts of town, where there were precious few places to hide.

It was in this poor position and state of panic that Tomiko approached him, and he scurried away from her in terror, stumbling off the side of the road and backwards into a ditch. Tomiko climbed down carefully, and ascertained that he was breathing, though not conscious. Whether he had struck his head upon a rock or merely fainted she couldn't say.

If she didn't do something, the members of the Order would find him and sacrifice him to the deep ones. She didn't know the man, but he was trapped here unwillingly, just as she was. Tomiko had heard about the sacrifices that sometimes happened in the middle of the night, but she had never actually seen one of the victims. It made the horror of it real. This was not some abstract sacrifice but a human life, and she felt compelled to save him.

She emerged from the ditch, and when the mob arrived, she pointed them to the pier. Her father scowled and yelled for her to go back home, but he didn't stay to make sure that she complied. Tomiko glanced down at Mr. Olmstead, passed out in the ditch. She wondered whether he would be grateful, and whether that gratitude might compel him to help her escape Innsmouth.

It seemed the perfect opportunity, if only she could make herself more human.

The deep ones always swam closest to the surface when the moon was bright. It must have been on a night like this that Joanne Hoag had made her deal with Dagon to become fully human. Tomiko ran after the mob, joining them as they gathered at the end of the pier. The call of the sea was strong, and several of the town elders dove into the salty water. Tomiko kicked off her shoes and plunged in after them. She paused to remove the heavy skirt of her school uniform, then swam hard against the current, all the way out to Devil's Reef. All around her the sea was full of town elders and deep ones. Even her sisters were here, with their golden tiaras glistening in the moonlight.

Tomiko struggled against the churning waves in the shallow water above the reef. She sliced her foot on an outcropping of coral, and deep ones swarmed around her like sharks. A dark cloud of blood drifted through the water.

Dagon emerged from the depths, a hideous creature of vaguely human shape, but with the face of a fish and a mouth filled with pointed yellow teeth. "You are not the sacrifice I was expecting."

Tomiko shouted against the howling wind, "Make me human!"

"You are one of mine, little *ningyo*," Dagon answered. "They will not accept you."

"Make me human," Tomiko repeated.

"Foolish child." Dagon stared at her with unblinking black eyes. "Very well. I will make you human, and we will see if you can pass for one. If you win the love of a man, you may stay human until you die a natural death. If you fail, you will be tomorrow's sacrifice."

It was too much risk, for too little reward. "One day isn't enough time to win someone's love."

"One day," Dagon insisted.

"You will make me beautiful, like my mother?"

"Yes."

Tomiko considered the offer. It would have to be Mr. Olmstead, for there were no other human men close enough. Robert, she corrected herself. If he was going to kiss her, she must start using the more familiar form of address. He had been repulsed by her before, but Dagon would make her attractive, and perhaps she could draw him out with conversation about the history of the town. "How will I know if I have won his love? Perhaps a different goal would be more easily measured—a kiss. Surely if I can coax a human into kissing me, I will have proven my ability to pass as one of them."

"It is . . . sufficient. Do you accept?"

"Yes." As soon as the word left her lips, pain shot through the webbing in her toes and fingers, a sensation like the cut of a knife, but without the release of blood. Her gills were absorbed back into the flesh of her neck and each breath was like inhaling fire. She struggled to swim through her pain, and would have drowned but for the webbed hands that reached out to her. Three of her sisters, with golden tiaras upon their bald fishy heads, held her up and helped her swim back to the pier.

"You should not have made this deal," they told her in rasping voices. "You should have been content to transform and live with us in the sea."

"I want more from my life than that."

Her sisters shook their heads and helped Tomiko haul herself back up onto the pier. Dagon had not given her much time, but after staying up all night, she could barely keep her eyes open. Robert was likely sleeping, anyway. She went home, and with her webbed feet cut into dainty toes, each step felt like walking on shards of broken glass.

Tomiko woke before sunrise and put on her nicest outfit, a flowing red dress with delicate floral print that Mom had brought back the last time she'd gone to San Francisco. Tomiko's hands and feet ached with the pain of her transformation, but her skin was a flawless golden brown, and her hair—once stringy—was full and black and permed in a fashionable wave. For the first time she could remember, she felt beautiful.

She tiptoed past her parents' room, where her father snored loudly, and she slipped outside. The streets were deserted as Tomiko hurried to the bus station. It was two hours before the morning bus was scheduled to depart, and Robert was nowhere to be seen. There was no sign of Joe either, so Tomiko rummaged beneath the hood of the motor-coach. She tore out belts and anything else she could pry free.

It would take a while for Joe to fix the damage, so there would be no way for anyone to get out of town before evening. Sabotage completed, Tomiko went back to the ditch where she'd left Robert. He wasn't there, but thankfully he hadn't gone far. She found him walking on the road that led to the highway. She called out to him, and he regarded her with suspicion.

"Come with me back to town, and I'll tell you the history of Innsmouth. You can take the evening bus to Santa Cruz, and it'll be faster than trying to walk."

He stood, obviously torn between wanting to flee the horrors of Innsmouth and wanting to hear more about its history. "The creatures," he said softly, "are they gone?"

"Asleep," Tomiko assured him. "The town will be no worse than it was when you first arrived. Look, the sun is rising, see the pink glow above the hills?"

She led him back to town, where they bought breakfast from the grocer. Tomiko got *onigiri*—rice balls wrapped in seaweed and filled with pickled plums and salted salmon. She encouraged Robert to do the same, but he insisted on more Western fare, though the stale rolls he purchased hardly looked appealing.

They ate their breakfast on the front stairs of the inn. Tomiko positioned herself carefully, not too close, but leaning in suggestively, her hair blowing gently in the seaside breeze. Robert hardly noticed her in his eagerness to get more information about the residents of Innsmouth.

So Tomiko changed her tactics, and tried to court him with her knowledge rather than her appearance. "Innsmouth is run down now, but it used to be a prosperous town, almost a city. The main industry was abalone. Ryuunosuke Kodama brought divers and harvesting techniques with him from his home in Chiba, Japan."

"Wait, I've heard that name. Kodama is the founder of the town, right? And the source of the—" Robert paused and his face flushed red, but then he continued, "the Innsmouth look."

Tomiko laughed, as though completely unbothered by his disgust for the fish-frog residents of the town. True, she had been cursed with the Innsmouth look, but she was human now. What did it matter if Robert found the fishy features of the other townspeople offputting? She herself had hated it, when she was afflicted. Still, she could not reveal the true nature of the transformation without explaining the Esoteric Order, and she felt it would be unwise to share such information with an outsider. So she skirted the subject by saying only, "Many of the residents of Innsmouth are descended from Kodama in some manner. He had six children, all of whom stayed here to run the family business."

They talked at length about the town. Several times throughout the day Robert attempted to make excuses and take his leave, but always she regained his attention by meting out historical facts, anecdotes, even idol gossip about the residents of the town. But by late afternoon she was no closer to winning his affections than she had been in the morning, and her time was running short. When once again he tried to make excuses, she made a desperate suggestion, "but first come out to the pier and I can tell you the story of Devil Reef. Joanne has always been an outsider, and the tale she tells is but a fraction of the town's true history."

To her relief, this was enough to recapture his attention. She had hoped the pier at sunset would be a romantic setting, but the tide was low and the breeze coming in off the water bore an unpleasant stench of rotting fish. Tomiko could see the shadowy forms of deep ones not far from the end of the pier. The sun was low, and her time was nearly done. If she did not win her kiss soon, she would be their sacrifice, a feast for Dagon.

Robert's attention was focused on the reef, and a whisper floated up from the water beneath the pier. Tomiko knelt, and saw her sister, Amaya. Her stringy black hair was plastered to her gray-green face and her gills flapped gently in the open air. Her golden tiara was gone.

"We've made a deal for you," her sister whispered. She held up a knife carved from the shell of some large sea creature. It had an opalescent sheen as it caught the rays of the setting sun. "Sacrifice the human, and you can transform into one of us, and live your immortal life beneath the waves."

Tomiko took the blade. Robert had no part in her deal with Dagon, save for being the only human who happened to be in town. She wasn't sure she could take his life for hers. She held the blade behind her back, hoping he wouldn't see it.

"Robert," she said, calling his attention away from the pier. She was a beautiful woman, a human woman, and she would be bold and take this opportunity to live the life she wanted. She looked at him with deep brown eyes catching the merest hint of gold from the setting sun, and whispered, "kiss me."

Robert pushed her away. "I will not defile myself with some perverted mockery of the human race, some horrifying creature of the Yellow Peril. Your eyes are hideous, bulging and nearly lidless with their epicanthic folds. You smell of the fish you are always eating, and your skin is a color better suited to simians than to men. I was curious as to the history of this town, but I want no part of you with your Innsmouth look."

"I saved you! I could have told them where you were, but I protected you. And this is how you repay me?" Tomiko held up her knife and called to her sisters. They dragged themselves out of the water and stood beside her to lend their support against the unspeakable horror of his xenophobic hatred.

Tomiko stepped closer. Her sisters formed a wall behind her, making it impossible for him to escape. She pressed the tip of her blade against his chest, and red blood bloomed like a flower against the white of his shirt. His pale eyes widened with terror at her attack, and he hurried backwards, careless of the slick boards at the end of the pier, where the waves had splashed up and soaked the wood.

He screamed as he fell into the water. Dark shapes beneath the surface pulled him down, and his screams transformed into incoherent burbling as his head disappeared beneath the waves. Tomiko hurled her knife at the spot where Robert had disappeared. The deep ones had their sacrifice for Dagon, and they swam back to the reef, content.

The sun set.

Tomiko's skin burned as though the last rays of the sun had lit her on fire. Her face melted into itself, and the red lines of gills sliced into her neck. Human skin fell away to reveal a scaly back and a slimy white belly. Her hair fell to the pier, leaving her completely bald. She had lost her deal with Dagon, and she was human no more.

But the love of her sisters had saved her from being a sacrifice. She didn't have the human form she wanted, but she was determined to live her life. She dove with her sisters into the cool ocean water, and together they swam out past the reef. Her sisters returned to their underwater city, but Tomiko swam north along the coastline, to San Francisco.

Mom would be furious, but maybe there was a place for a fish-frog waitress at Uncle Yuji's restaurant.

ON THE PAGES OF A
SKETCHBOOK UNIVERSE

The First Page of the Sketchbook

In a sketchbook of pure white paper, a watercolor king met a pencil queen.

The king was made of sixteen shades of watercolor paint, with colors pressed together in thin diagonal stripes. His fingertips were brushes and his heart was a jar of water that had no lid. He dipped the end of his pinky-finger brush into his heartwater and loaded the brush with yellow paint from the stripe that ran down his neck.

He touched his brush to the blankness of the white, leaving a tiny dot of yellow that spread into a circle as it seeped into the page.

Nothing happened.

The queen was stiff and straight, made of wooden pencils with graphite cores. Her joints were erasers and her heart was a steel blade. She pulled one fingertip across her heartblade until the graphite core came to a delicate point, and tiny curls of wood dropped down to the page. She scooped them up and offered them to the king, but he shook his head. He had no use for them. It seemed wrong to discard little bits of herself, so the queen held the shavings with one hand and used the sharpened finger of her other hand to draw a box.

She drew an outline in delicate straight lines, but nothing happened.

The king came to examine her sketch, and when he reached out to touch it a smear of yellow stained one corner of the box. As the paint dried, the corner began to jut out from the paper, as solid and real as the queen and king.

The queen sketched the king's yellow circle into a sun, which rose above them and lit the page in a glorious warm light. The king painted the rest of the box, and the queen put her pencilself shavings inside. Together they created a forest of deep green pines and a sparkling blue lake. The queen sketched distant mountains and a handful of clouds to diffuse the light of the yellow sun. Everything she sketched, the king painted, and together they created a beautiful realm.

The clouds darkened, and rain began to fall. Water ran down the king's face and pulled his paint down to the paper, leaving murky brown puddles of mud on the once-white ground. He ran and hid beneath the branches of a dark green pine, horrified that the clouds they had created could turn against him so thoroughly.

In this, his first moment of need, the queen abandoned him, disappearing into the vast undrawn white. He huddled against the tree and waited for the rain to stop.

The pencil queen had come to love the watercolor king, for his colors were beautiful. The box he'd painted for her pencilself shavings fit neatly into her chest, nestling up against the blade of her heart. When the rain drove him into hiding, she decided to sketch him a castle, a place where he could be safe.

A castle required an empty expanse of paper, so she left the forest and walked toward the center of the page. As she traveled, most of the page was pure and blank and white, but halfway between the upper bindings and the unbound lower edge, there was a great rift, a tear in the paper. She detoured to walk the length of the tear. It ran a great distance, starting at the leftmost edge of the page and running nearly to the center. On the right side of the page, there was a second tear, a mirror-image of the first. She sketched a large stone at the end of each tear, in hopes that the weight of the rocks would keep the rifts from spreading. When she finished sketching the king's castle, she would ask him to paint the rocks real.

The queen continued on past the rifts, and found a wide expanse of blank paper. She sharpened all her fingers to make the work go faster and placed her shavings into their box. White paper gave way to sketched-stone walls—storerooms and apartments and a cavernous great hall, all connected with covered walkways so that the king would never need to face the weather. At each corner, she drew a tall tower, so that he could look out over the realm in all directions. In the center of the castle she sketched an even taller tower, so that she and her king could sleep close to the heavens.

By the time she had finished, the rain had stopped, so she returned to the forest and found the watercolor king.

"Did it honestly take you this long to realize you can't make anything real without me?" the king asked. His diagonal stripes were smeared from the rain, and all around him were formless blobs of paint where he had tried to make—something—in her absence.

"I was drawing a surprise for you," she said, but her excitement about the castle was dampened by her guilt at leaving him to suffer the rain alone.

It was many days' work to paint the castle, and by the time it was finished the king had forgiven the queen for abandoning him in the rain. He fell in love with her angles and her strength, and he admired the delicate lines that she drew. He painted the rocks she had sketched to stop the page from tearing, and admired her foresight and ingenuity.

The queen drew birds and beasts and fish to live in their beautiful realm, and he brought them to life with his colors. He painted the night sky black, and she sketched a moon and stars. He painted the celestial bodies in whites and yellows and tossed them into the sky.

"Let's make ourselves a child," the king said. It was the right time. From his tower window, he could see reflections of moonlight dancing on the lake. "We've made a beautiful world, and all it needs is a child for us to share it with."

They'd left one wall of their tower bedroom blank with the original page, intended for just such a purpose. The queen began to sketch a pencil child.

"I thought," the king said, "that we could have a watercolor child."

"The eldest will be heir to the realm. Clearly a pencil princess is the better choice. When she is finished, she can sketch herself a prince that is to her liking."

"It is no more your realm than it is mine," the king answered. "If not for my paint, your sketches wouldn't even be real. A watercolor prince would make a fine heir."

"And then what? He would paint a formless princess for me to sketch?" The queen kept drawing her straight-lined wooden child, with a sharp-blade heart and eraser joints. "I'm not going to sketch you a prince."

"And I'm not going to paint you a princess," the king said.

So the royal couple remained childless, and the heir was nothing but a sketch, abandoned in the highest tower of the castle.

Strange art crept in from beyond the edge of the realm, giant lizards that flew and breathed fire. The king named the creatures dragons. They gathered on the white page beyond the proper boundary of the realm, up near the bindings of the page. Periodically, they fought amongst themselves, soaring high above the page and spewing jets of fire from their mouths.

"The fire is too dangerous. We must fight the dragons," the queen said, "before they destroy the realm."

"They have done nothing to attack us," the king said, "and they only breathe their fire when they are in the sky, well away from the paper."

"This is our page of the sketchbook, and we have to defend it. The beasts have been flying wide circles over the realm, scouting. It is only a matter of time before the dragons attack the castle, and everything we've worked so hard to create will be destroyed."

"We should have someone to tend the realm if we fail," the king said, choosing his words carefully. "Perhaps instead of one heir, we could have two, a prince and a princess—"

The queen didn't let him finish. Her mind was as rigid as the pencils that formed her body, and she lacked the flexibility for compromise. She believed the realm had to be controlled by someone who could sketch. She led the king up to their tower and pointed to her sketch of the pencil princess. "Here. This is your heir. Paint her and be done with it."

She left without waiting for the king to reply.

The king considered the drawing. It had the form of a princess, true, but that didn't mean he had to paint the child as pencils. He dipped a red fingertip into his heartwater and painted the core of one pencil red. He did the outside of the pencil in red paint, too, all but the bit of wood where the pencil had been drawn already sharpened. That detail was a credit to the queen—the heir would not begin with blunted fingers, as she had, but would begin life ready to create art.

He stepped back to admire his work. A red pencil with a core of watercolor paint. He set to work on the rest of the sketch, giving the heir watercolor pencils in all his sixteen shades, and four ordinary graphite pencils as a token to the queen.

It was not quite the prince he had envisioned, but he would have to do.

The queen was furious at the king's trick. She refused to speak to him, and instead spent hours sketching an army of soldiers to lead into battle against the dragons. The soldiers were not pencils or watercolors—not artists at all—though they had limbs and faces. They would have no purpose but defending the realm, and she sketched hundreds of them to be her army, each one identical to all the others. When her sketches were finished, she sent the king to paint them so that she could have a private audience with her heir.

The princess was a mess of bright colors, but the king had given her *some* true pencils. The queen set up several easels around the room. She would teach the princess how to be a proper heir for the realm. "Begin by sketching spheres."

The heir approached the first easel and touched it tentatively with a purple-pencil finger.

"No," the queen corrected. "Sketch in pencil, in black."

Under the queen's watchful eye, the heir drew a circle onto each of the easels. "Now may I have water, so that I can paint them into spheres?"

The queen smiled. The king had painted her princess in colors, but he couldn't change her heartblade into a jar. Without water, the heir could not paint, and therefore she truly was a princess. "The sketches are not finished. A sphere is too simple. You must imagine something grander, and draw in the details. A sphere can become anything—a planet, an orange, the eye of a spider—all it takes is the right details. With enough practice, you will be a lovely queen." The heir looked at the easels. "I'd like to paint. If I finish these sketches, will you let me paint them?"

"A princess doesn't paint," the queen said.

"I'm not a princess." The heir slashed at one of the easels with all ten fingers, leaving angry scribbles in a cacophony of colors.

"I drew you to be a princess. It doesn't matter what your colors are, at your core you are designed to sketch." She left the heir in the tower and locked the door behind her.

There was no water in the tower room, nothing but easels with black circles. If the heir drew them full of detail, would the queen let him paint? There was nothing else for him to do, and perhaps if he tried to sketch the queen would relent. He stared at the brightly colored scribbles on the easel before him, and idly sketched outlines around the lines of color. They looked like worms or snakes, and he sketched them with gaping round mouths of pointy teeth, monsters of rage. It would not please the queen, he was sure of it.

He turned the sheet of paper over, putting the art of his anger out of sight. On the blank white side, he drew a circle. A planet, the queen had said. He would sketch another realm, a world of watercolor pencil citizens that could sketch and paint as they pleased. For hearts, he gave some of the citizens blades and others jars.

He drew castles made of gemstones but with organic shapes, like trees. The towers of the castles twisted together to create a vast interconnected city. All around the city, he drew a jungle of trees and vines. He drew rivers and lakes, an abundance of water for those who had heartblades. Still the queen did not return. The heir didn't want to face another blank sphere, so he continued sketching his planet, adding birds and beasts and fish in every shape and size. He drew more citizens, more gemstone cities, and thousands of trees.

"Better," the queen said, when she finally returned, "but a bit cluttered. I left you plenty of paper, why didn't you move to another easel?"

Despite himself, the heir basked in the queen's approval. He chose his words carefully, for he did not want to anger her again. "You said to practice details, so I did a lot of details."

"A planet with this much detail should be drawn onto the primary paper of the true page, not onto secondary paper that was drawn into creation. This is practice paper, best for simpler things."

The heir looked sadly at his planet, at the work he'd done, wasted because he'd used the wrong sort of paper.

"You will learn, with time, what can be drawn where." The queen studied the easel for a moment, then shrugged. "It is a fine practice sketch. The king has finished painting my army, and I will lead them on a scouting expedition, to see what the dragons are doing at the edge of our realm. Keep up your practice while I am away."

She turned to leave, and the heir resisted the urge to ask again for water. His restraint was rewarded—when the queen left, she closed the door but didn't lock it, leaving him free to explore the castle. He watched at his window as the queen led her army away from the castle, between the two great rocks that marked the edges of the twin tears, and into the first forest. Only when the army was completely hidden by the trees did he open his door.

The king stood outside, holding a bowl of water.

"She wanted me to be like her," the heir said. "I suppose you want me to be like you?"

It was entirely the wrong thing to say. He wanted to paint, he needed water, and the king was at his door with a bowl of water.

"You're already like me. And also like her. You have her heart, but no water to even try to paint." The king held out the bowl. "A jar would be better, but she refused to sketch one. This was the best I could find of the things we had already created."

The heir took the bowl with shaking hands. Finally he would paint.

*

The heir studied the planet he had sketched. The queen had cautioned against painting a planet drawn on inferior paper, but with watercolor pencil fingers, the heir painted differently than the king did. He shaded the trees purple and blue with delicate cross-hatch strokes of his still-dry fingers, and made green fish that glowed bright in the black water of the rivers. He created a dark planet illuminated by a distant blue sun, everything shifted away from the warmth of red and orange.

Only after the first layers of shading were already applied did he dip his fingertips in the bowl of water and begin to blend the colors together. The planet was so large and detailed that he had to re-wet the areas that were finished to keep them from becoming real before the entire project was done. The tower room was large, but it wasn't capable of holding a planet. The extra water—or perhaps the inferior paper—made the paint bleed beyond the lines of the sketch, tangling the branches of the trees and blurring the edges of the watercolor-pencil citizens that crowded together in the cities.

Worse, the water soaked through and dampened the scribbles of rage that he had slashed across the back side of the paper. The heir did not like to think what those would do, if they were let loose upon the realm.

The paint began to dry, and the planet expanded, bulging up from the surface of the paper. With both hands, the heir pulled everything off the easel, the planet and the paper and squiggles of rage, and he hurled it all out the window into the night sky. His creation receded into the darkness, and soon it was no more than another pale dot, dimmer than the bright stars. Then even the dot vanished, for he had thrown the paper with such force that it had flown off the edge of the page and into the sketchbook beyond.

The king knocked, and then entered. "I caught a glimpse of your creation, as you sent it into the sky. Did you like the painting?"

"I did," the heir admitted. "Have you come to gloat?"

The king shook his head. "The queen has returned from her

scouting expedition. She has asked me to go with her to the edge of the page. I wanted to give you this, something to entertain you while I am gone." He held out an odd bit of paper, a loop with half a twist.

"What is it?"

"A Möbius strip. The queen set me to playing with paper, to try to come up with a way to defeat the dragons. I don't see a use for this yet, but it is interesting, is it not?"

The heir took the strange loop. Paper had two sides, but this, because of the way it was twisted, had but a single surface. "What will you do at the edge of the realm? Some other trick of paper?"

"We will bend back the corner of our page and draw on the other side."

The king went with the queen to the corner of the realm farthest from where the dragons gathered. Together they walked across the thin border of white to the place where the paper ended. Unlike the bound upper edge of the page, which curved steeply downward into the binding of the sketchbook, here the paper stopped abruptly in a clearly defined line.

The king told the queen, "We are lucky that the dragons are on the bound edge, leaving this corner free for us to use. We will not even have to cut the page before we bend it."

The queen knelt near the edge of the paper. "What if there is nothing on the other side of the page?"

"Then we'll put the corner back as it was and come up with a new plan," the king answered, "but I think there must be paper on the other side."

He knelt beside the queen, and together they grasped the corner and pulled, bending the page in towards themselves. The back of the page was a pure and pristine white. The king held the corner and the queen sketched. She drew a copy of herself, and a copy of the king. Then she held the corner while the king painted them real.

"No tricks this time," she said. "Paint them true, and they will be our allies in the fight against the dragons."

The king painted the newly sketched couple to be a perfect match to himself and the queen. The drying paint pulled at the corner of the page, and as the copy of the royal couple became real, the queen lost her grip and the page snapped back to flatness.

"Quick, we must pull it back again," the queen said. "We have not warned them of the dragons, and they will not know how to draw their realm in preparation for the war."

With greater effort, they pulled the corner up once more, but their copies were gone. All that remained were scuffs of paint and pencil, tracks leading off toward the center of the page.

"Should we try to follow them?" the king asked.

"It would leave our realm unprotected, vulnerable to the dragons," the queen said. "but we could try again, and draw another couple."

She let go of the page to sharpen her fingers, and the corner slipped out from the king's grasp and snapped back into place.

"I don't have the strength to hold it alone. The page is heavier now that it has been drawn on both sides."

Far across the page, a plume of fire and smoke rose high above the realm.

"Your paper trick was a good idea," the queen said, "but we've run out of time. We must make what soldiers we can and face the dragons ourselves."

While the king and queen were at the edge of the realm, the heir remained in the tower. The Möbius strip the king had given him was interesting. The heir drew a tiny copy of himself onto the loop, near the spot where the former edges of the paper were joined together. Drawn so small, it reminded him of the queen's soldiers, though much smaller. A toy soldier, marching on a thin strip of paper. As the toy soldier made its way around the loop, it drew simple spheres and geometric shapes on the paper. Eventually it came around to where it had started, and something strange happened. It was not only the paper that looped, but time itself, for the page at the start of the loop was once again blank. The toy soldier used the last of its graphite and paint to draw a copy of itself at the start of the loop, and the copy marched around the paper, drawing geometric shapes.

The first tiny soldier, the one the heir had drawn, stood at the boundary between the two pages, unsure of what to do next. Tentatively, it crossed over the line. Nothing happened. The toy soldier was all used up, with not enough of itself left to make even the simple shapes it had once created. The heir regretted making the soldier as a copy of himself. He had thought the loop of paper a mere toy, but to the tiny soldiers, it was a world, and they believed themselves to be artists. They were certainly more artistic than the queen's soldiers, for unlike true soldiers, the heir's tiny creations could draw.

But what could he do, now that he had made them? Destroy them and end their misery? Certainly he could not let the loop continue, for if each tiny artist drew a copy of itself the strip would soon be full of used-up artists. The heir cut the loop with his heartblade and laid it on the tower floor, placing it so the side that held the two tiny artists was facing upward.

Outside the tower window, a pillar of flame and smoke rose in the distance. The heir wondered what the dragons were burning. His royal parents had gone in the other direction, to the unbound edge of the page, so he assumed that they were safe. Were the creatures truly a threat to the realm, as the queen claimed? Fire was dangerous, but no more so than many things.

He stared at the horizon, searching for more smoke and fire, but whatever had provoked the dragons, it did not happen again.

The king returned to the castle. "Our first plan didn't work, so we must fight the dragons on our own. The queen will need more soldiers, and you must help draw them."

"I don't want to sketch soldiers."

"I would let you paint some, too," the king promised.

"If she wants soldiers, she should sketch them herself. I think we should leave the creatures at the edge of the realm alone."

"We must defend the realm," the king insisted. "The dragons breathe fire that could burn away the very paper of the sketchbook, and us with it."

"You created this world, so you think you can control everything that happens. The queen wants to drive the dragons off the page because she didn't draw them. She wants me to sketch, like a good little princess. You want me to paint, like a good little prince."

"But you want to paint," the king argued. "We want the same thing."

"No! I want to be left alone."

"Then be alone," the king said, "but draw soldiers while you are alone. If you don't sketch, the queen will come back to find out why, and she will be angry. Perhaps I was wrong to paint you as I did. We might all be happier if you were a pencil princess."

And with that, the king left.

"I don't care what either of you want," the heir said, even though there was no one to hear. "I'm not a princess or a prince, and I will have no part in this senseless war."

He was like the tiny artists on the cut-apart Möbius strip, trapped in the realm his parents had created. The heir turned the strip over and studied the back. That side of the strip was not as cluttered, for there were no artists there to fill the paper with art. Did the true page also have a back? It must. But how could he get there?

On the tiny strip of paper, the heir drew a door. But clearly that was not enough, for there were doors in the castle and they led to other rooms, not to other pages. What he needed was a way to go through the page. He used his heartblade to cut around the edges of the tiny door he'd drawn. The door opened, and the tiny artists stepped through.

The cut-edge door went from one page to the next.

One wall of the tower was still white with the original paper of the page, for the king and queen had originally planned to make themselves more children, back before the heir had turned out to be such a challenge. There was plenty of space for a door.

The heir sketched a sturdy oak door and painted it into reality. He sliced around the edges of the door with his heartblade, cutting his way to the next page. Then he stepped through the door and sealed the cut edges with paint to be sure no one would follow.

The Second Page of the Sketchbook

I assumed, when I drew my door into the next page of the sketchbook, that it would be a blank white page, waiting for whatever world I cared to draw onto it. Instead, I found myself in a maze of buildings that stretched to the sky, each one made of mirrored glass that sent reflections scattered everywhere. My door, a sturdy wooden door of oak planks like the ones in my parents' castle, was decidedly out of place.

I'd left the easels and my bowl of water in my parents' realm, so my first order of business was to find a blank bit of page and some water. Once I had those, I could draw myself any new supplies I might require. The water would be easy enough. There were puddles on the sidewalk from a recent rain, but the world was so fully drawn and painted that finding some blank page might prove to be a problem. My parents hid sections of the page behind curtains and tapestries, and the castle had an abundance of white paper on easels to create sketches of needed things.

This world didn't have curtains or castles or easels, at least, not that I could see.

Three black birds flew lazy circles above me in the sky. Another flew down between two buildings, and landed on the sidewalk at my feet. It sipped water from a puddle, then hopped over to the door I had arrived through. More birds arrived, and landed on the door. They swished their black tail feathers, and with so many birds working together, they quickly erased the door, exposing a line of white page where the door had met the sidewalk.

I stepped forward, thinking I might be able to use the blank page to make the tools I wanted. The birds let out a loud screech, then used their beaks to paint the sidewalk back into place. The only trace remaining of my door were the barely visible slits in the paper where I had cut it with my heartblade. The birds patched the cut with long strips of a clear film that I had never seen before. Several more birds flew down to the sidewalk. They stared at me and fanned their tail feathers.

I jogged around the base of one of the mirror-glass buildings, looking for a way in. Birds continued to gather on the sidewalk, watching me in eerie silence. It wasn't until the second trip around that I noticed the door, which was made of the same reflective glass as the rest of the building. This seemed a fussy sort of world to draw, and everything was so entirely unfamiliar that I hated to go inside and leave behind the sky, and the abundant water of the puddles.

The birds, though, I would be happy to get away from.

I reached out to open the door, but it slid aside before I could mar it with my colors. The inside of the building was as intricate as the outside, with patterned rugs covering any blank white that might have been on the floor, and swirling paisley wallpaper plastered over all the walls. I pulled up the corner of the rug, and was disappointed to find some sort of gray stone underneath.

I had to find some paper. I did not want to meet whoever made this world entirely unprepared. There was no reason to believe that whoever had filled this page would be hostile, but there was also no reason to believe that they wouldn't.

At the opposite end of a long hallway, silver doors slid open, and two figures approached, one made of watercolor and the other of pencils. They had used a lot of themselves to create this world, and they were smaller than my parents, their bodies painted and sharpened away.

"Is this your page?" I asked.

"What an odd creature you are, neither watercolor man nor pencil woman, but a bit of both," the watercolor man said. "Can you do both sides of art?"

It seemed a rather intrusive question for someone who I'd only just met. I wasn't sure I wanted to reveal what I could do, here in a strange realm without even enough blank paper for me to draw myself an exit. On the other hand, it would be rather rude not to answer at all, and I didn't want to offend them. "I mostly paint."

The pencil woman studied me carefully. Before she could ask any questions, I changed the subject. "Your artworld is lovely, very detailed and complex."

"Thank you," the watercolor man answered. "We created dozens of artists, and they made most of the art by making subtle variations of our original work."

"The black birds did this?" I asked.

"No." The pencil woman laughed. "The birds maintain the city. They can use the mirrors to make copies of existing art, but they aren't artists."

"Shall we take her to meet the artists?" the watercolor man asked, grinning at the pencil woman.

"Him," I corrected. "I'm more for painting than sketching, despite my pencil shape."

The watercolor man waved away my complaint. "Painter, sketcher, it makes little difference in the grand scheme of things what you call yourself."

I thought back to my mother's insistence that I was a princess, and her demand that I learn to sketch despite my painty nature. "It matters to me."

The watercolor man stepped forward, but before he could say anything further the pencil woman interrupted. "The artists are drawing new residents for our city today, in the garden district. We could take him there."

On our way to the garden district, we passed a section of page that had been torn, like the twin rifts of my parents' realm. Shockingly similar actually, both in the length of the rifts and in their position on the page. These weren't similar rifts—they were the same rifts as seen from below. On this side of the page, there were no giant boulders to mark the ends of the torn page. Instead, the entire rift was patched with strips of clear film like the ones the birds had used to repair the slits I had cut along the edges of my door.

The pencil woman caught me looking. "The page has always been torn. Even in the beginning, when all the page was white and empty, the tears were there."

"What is the film that you have used to repair the rifts?" I asked.

"Tape."

We left the rifts behind, and soon found ourselves in a field of colorful wildflowers. I liked the garden district better than the city, for it reminded me more of my parents' realm. There was a maze of rose bushes, a grassy lawn, even a little creek. Beside the creek, on a wide expanse of flat gray stone, an artist had set up an easel. Like me, the artist was both watercolors and pencils. Unlike me, the division was sharp—the artist was all pencils on one side, and all paint on the other. As though someone had chopped mother and father in half, and pasted one side of each together.

On the easel was a picture of a creature, the same height as the artist, with two arms and two legs and all the same features. But it wasn't made of pencils or paint. It reminded me of my mother's soldiers, although this one did not look as fierce. It stepped away from the page.

"Hello," it said. It wore brightly-colored clothes, which reminded me of my father, but its skin did not have diagonal lines of color, and when it turned back to touch the blank page, its fingertips left no mark.

"Aren't they lovely?" the watercolor man gushed. "Residents for the city. We'll have thousands, and each will be unique."

I looked out across the garden district. There were several artists here, all identical, all standing before their easels and creating subtle variations on the form of the resident. Tall residents and short ones, thin ones and fat ones. Many of the newly made residents touched the blank pages they were drawn from, but of course they left no mark. "How sad that they will never make art."

The watercolor man laughed. "A tree doesn't make art. How is this any different?"

The city bustled with residents, intricate pieces of art that harvested food from the gardens and lived in the mirror-glass buildings. I watched them for hours, and what the watercolor man had claimed was true—there were no two that were the same. The residents were individuals, just as artists were. They sang and danced and paired off into couples.

I studied them, but I didn't draw any of my own. It seemed wrong somehow, to create such lifelike things and yet not give them access to any tiny sliver of creation. I petitioned the first couple for a blank white apartment, which they granted me, and I sketch-painted it into stone walls and tapestries.

I had hated home while I was there, but now that I was here I was homesick. I drew a door to go back and sliced the page with my heartblade. I didn't open the door. Not yet. But I found it comforting to know it was there.

One of the residents that lived in my building asked me to draw a rocking chair. It seemed a reasonable enough request, so I sketched the design and painted it in dark wood tones, a fine chair for a lazy summer afternoon. A while later the resident returned, asking this time for a tiny bed, a crib. I made this, too, and offered to help carry it back, curious to see what it was for.

The resident's apartment was decorated in the standard style with patterned-rug floors and paisley walls. The preferred designs of the first couple were standard in every non-artist apartment, as were the furnishings. It must have been tedious to paint so many identical rooms, and I wondered how the artists had managed it. Perhaps this was what the pencil woman had meant when she said the birds could use mirrors to copy art.

We set the crib next to a larger bed. Another resident was there now, despite it being the middle of the day, a time when residents generally went about their business in the city. The bedridden resident was malformed, stretched out of shape in the middle.

The resident who had come for the crib caught my stare and pulled me aside. "She's pregnant. The little bed is for the child."

I heard the words, but it didn't make any sense. I smiled and nodded, and went back to my apartment. Residents, being art, clearly did not understand how children were made. Like any creation, children come into the world full-sized and perfectly formed. They do not misshape the mothers, or make them ill. Something had clearly gone wrong with the art, and I went to find the first couple.

I found them in the building that the residents had designated as a hospital, surrounded by a flock of black birds. The pencil woman came over to greet me, but the watercolor man stayed focused on the work he was doing.

"Something is happening to the residents that live in the apartment next to mine," I told her. "They've gone a little mad."

"Ah, so you know. I'll give you some birds and you can help us mop up."

I slowly approached the watercolor man, barely listening to the pencil woman's words. He stood over one of the hospital beds, where a resident slept. In a smaller bed was an odd bit of art, like a resident, but small and pudgy. "Did the resident make that? Is it art?"

The watercolor man scowled. "It definitely isn't art, and it's ruining my vision." With a wave of his hand the birds flocked down and erased both the resident and the misshapen little thing that it had made. I was sad to see it go. The tiny resident didn't suit the city, but it had been interesting to look at.

"I told him he could have some birds," the pencil woman said. "Help us fix the problem before it gets out of hand."

The watercolor man had moved on to the next hospital room. "Fine," he called out. "They mostly come here, but sometimes they make these little messes at home. He can clean out his building."

The pencil woman led me back outside. She screeched and a hundred black birds landed at our feet. They fanned their tails and bowed their heads. "Do as the artist bids you," she told them. All at once the birds turned and stared at me with beady black eyes. The pencil woman went back inside the hospital.

"Follow me home," I told the birds. Then, remembering what the birds had done to the resident and its tiny creation, I added, "but not too close."

It didn't seem right to wipe away the neighbors, even when the misshapen resident painted the bed with a mess of blood and made one of the odd little residents. It looked much the same as the one I'd seen in the hospital. Perhaps residents weren't very creative. This one spent a lot of time screaming, but it stopped when the residents rocked it in the lovely chair I'd made.

I didn't erase the tiny resident. It wasn't right to destroy something simply because it didn't turn out the way you intended. The residents were only doing what their nature compelled them to do.

"Don't take the new resident out where the first couple might see it," I warned them. "They don't think the little ones are art, and they don't fit with the aesthetic of the city."

They did their best to keep the little one inside, but the constant noise was irritating to their neighbors. It wouldn't be long before someone complained and the first couple came, and they would be angry that I hadn't used my birds to clear this smudge away from their artistic vision.

I looked at the door that led back to my parents' realm. I didn't think the residents would be any better there. They were not soldiers, and the queen would force them to fight if I brought them to the realm. But if I could draw my way to a blank page, I could make them a safer world.

I sharpened all my fingers and tossed the shavings out the window. The delicate curls of wood drifted down to the sidewalk. Birds fluttered down to erase them; tiny discarded pieces of me did not belong in such an orderly world as this. With newly shortened fingers, I drew myself a heartglass full of water, narrow enough to fit next to my heartblade. I sketched a scroll of white paper with a strap that let me wear it across my back.

I wasn't ready to go back home, not yet, but we could go to the next page of the sketchbook. I took two sheets of paper and used a strip of clear tape to bind them together along one edge. To go from the first page to the second page, I had cut through the page, but looking at my makeshift model of the sketchbook, I saw that it would not work to cut a door to the third page. Instead, we needed to leap across the binding, or draw ourselves a bridge.

I called the neighbor-family over, and they followed me to the bound edge of the page. I drew a long plank of wood and tipped it until one end fell beyond the edge of the page. It didn't slide down into the gap, so the far end of the plank must have landed on the next page.

I walked across the bridge, and the residents followed.

The Third Page of the Sketchbook

Scribbles. Angry frustrated tangles of rage with gaping mouths full of pointy teeth. It is not safe here. Draw a door. Paint it quickly. Cut through the page. Escape.

The Fourth Page of the Sketchbook

Trio watched with two heads as a door appeared on the far wall of the laboratory, a door drawn by an artist they could not yet see. Their third head did not look up from their work, a delicate dissection they were conducting for the Multitude. Art often had unseen layers, inner workings that were only revealed through careful scientific study. Trio used their two heartblades to flay the pet open, and with two hands sketched each layer of anatomy onto a writing stone. These were things that should not be applied to paper, the gruesome and incomplete innards of an art-worthy whole.

Only when the door swung open did Trio pause in their work.

A singleton hurried through, followed by a pair of unchained pets. They slammed the door behind them. The singleton gave no commands to their pets and made no apology for their abrupt and unwelcome appearance. Something squirmed in the arms of one of the pets, and the Trio realized it was a third, smaller, pet. Intriguing.

"The nature of your arrival is unusual," Trio noted, speaking with all three voices in unison to emphasize their relatively greater status.

The singleton stared at the partially dissected pet on the table, then gawked out the window, which boasted a sweeping view of the bluetree forest and the black-water river. Finally, the singleton spoke. "Are all of you in threes? I didn't mean for you to stick together like that."

"*You* didn't mean?" Trio laughed. "We are made in the image of the creator, mostly in twos and threes, but sometimes less and sometimes more. Our creator is not some lowly singleton, but an artist of infinite identities, a being that is vast beyond our comprehension."

"No," the singleton insisted, "I drew this world—I painted the trees and the black river and the gemstone cities and the bright green fish." The singleton crossed the room to stand before an easel and sharpened their fingers on their heartblade, leaving the shavings to clutter the laboratory floor. They drew a seedling bluetree, and it was in the same style as the world had been drawn.

"A good imitation, for a singleton. But copying the work of the creator will not teach us the workings of the world. For that we must have science."

"Science?" one of the pets asked.

Trio stared at the pet in surprise. "Your pet can speak."

"They are residents," the singleton answered, "not pets."

Trio shrugged. The singleton could believe as they wished. They would not be the first to treat pets as though they were artists. "In any case, I do not think I have ever seen one with a mouth before. How very curious. May I dissect them?"

The singleton considered the proposal. "Can you put it back together again afterwards?"

Trio laughed and shook all three heads. "No, of course not. But I would give you paper to draw a replacement."

The pets, agitated by the conversation, edged back toward the door. "We don't want to be dissected."

"But it is the will of the Creator that we study the internal workings of our art!" Trio insisted. "The Multitude has declared this truth!"

The pets opened the door, and a raging beast came through, red and angry.

It thrashed around the laboratory, knocking over equipment and absorbing art into itself through its gaping mouth. It latched onto the partially dissected pet like a leech and swallowed it off the page, and then it consumed the writing stone, covered in scientific notes. Trio was well studied in the sciences, but they had never heard of a creature such as this.

Trio fled. The singleton and their pets followed.

The heir followed the odd trio of artists through a winding maze of alleys, but the residents fell behind and the heir was reluctant to leave them alone in a place where someone might come along and cut them open. They quickly became lost. The heir had drawn the city, but they had done so from a distant vantage point. This new perspective was unfamiliar.

The buildings were interspersed with trees that stretched impossibly high into a cloudless blue sky, a triumph of art or a failure of scale. Perhaps both. The trunks and branches were a pale silver-blue, and high above them broad purple leaves blocked the sun. Up in the canopy, the trees blurred together, with silvery branches linking one tree to the next and leaves forming a subtle quilt in shades of purple.

The buildings were shaped like trees, too, smooth curves of ruby and sapphire, topaz and emerald, all spiraling around each other and stretching into the sky. The upper levels were connected by a maze of bridges. At the base of the buildings were doors decorated with delicate opal branches, woven together with swirling patterns of jade leaves.

The city was densely populated with artists. As the trio had said, most of them were in twos and threes. Eventually, the heir found a singleton, patching a broken section of the city. It was simple work, demeaning for an artist—on the second page, the birds had done it.

The singleton noticed the heir and smiled. "We don't see a lot of other singles."

"Where I come from, everyone is single," the heir said, "and some artists are only pencils or only paint."

"Not even whole," the singleton said, amazed "How do they make art?"

"They work together in pairs."

The singleton stopped smiling. "It is the creator's way, we suppose, that art should be made by the many, and not by the one."

After so much repair work, the singleton was in terrible shape. The erasers at the heir's wrists and elbows were pink and unused, but the singleton had barely any joints left. Artists weren't meant to spend their lives only repairing the work of others.

"Come with us," the heir said. "I am looking for a safe place for my residents."

"Residents?"

The heir looked behind themself. The residents were gone.

The heir searched the city, and the singleton helped. The tiny resident was so loud, it did not take long to find where they had gone. They were in a courtyard surrounded by duos and trios of artists.

"What are they doing?" the heir asked the singleton.

"They are bidding," the singleton answered. "Pets are very popular, and the small one is interesting. Did you make them?"

"No, but I brought them with me to this page."

A vast artist came into the courtyard, stepping forward with dozens of colored pencil limbs and at least five heads that the heir could see. Many of the limbs were sharpened down to stubs. The heir called out, "Stop! Those pets belong to me!"

The heir did not truly feel ownership for the residents, but they felt they had to at least try to help the poor creatures.

"Bow before the Multitude," the singleton whispered.

The heir bowed their head.

"Lower than that," the singleton urged. "Flat on the ground because you're a singleton, like us."

The heir deepened their bow slightly, but did not get down onto the ground. This world was their own creation, after all, and they were the equal of any number of artists.

"This trio tells me that you have opened a door and let monsters onto our page," the Multitude said.

"The page before this one is filled with art-sucking leeches, and when I cut a door into this page, one of the monsters came through."

The Multitude scowled. "The words you speak are blasphemous. This is the first of all possible pages, brought into existence by our vast creator. The monsters on the page *after* this one are guarding the bliss of beyond, where our creator will reward us by drawing us into the infinity of all creation."

The heir quickly changed the subject, not wishing to anger the Multitude. "Please, those residents—you call them pets—will you return them to me?"

The Multitude made a brief gesture with several hands, and a duo collected the residents and brought them to the heir. The heir, surprised, bowed. "Thank you."

"We do not have time to study your pets, interesting though the little one might be. The page is full of the unintended consequences of our art, and we have more pressing things to do than dissect pets. We must find a way to defeat the monster that has invaded our realm."

"There was something from the page of my youth that may be helpful," the heir said. "There were creatures—large lizards that flew and breathed fire. I have never seen them, but perhaps your artists could draw something of that description."

The heir was impressed with the quality of the artists' work. Duos and trios worked tirelessly on the blank paper at the edge of the page, creating enormous lizards with leathery wings and sharp claws. On command, they could send forth jets of fire. They hunted down the giant leech that had come onto the fourth page through the heir's door, and burned it to ashes. The remains of the monster looked like tiny flakes of the paper from which it was drawn. Paper to paper, white to white.

The Multitude was grateful. "For a singleton, you have an uncommon creativity."

It was high praise, but the heir wanted more than words. "Let me take the fire lizards to the third page. There are more monsters there, and I worry that they will escape to the page on the other side, and lay waste to the earlier pages of the sketchbook."

"To the *later* pages of the sketchbook," the Multitude corrected, but gently. "If we give you these fire lizards it would leave our page unprotected," the Multitude said. "What do we care what happens to pages besides our own?"

"With your fire lizards, I can get rid of all the monsters, ensuring the safety of your realm in the future."

"You are a singleton, we are the Multitude. For what you have done for us, you may have one fire lizard, and we will keep the rest."

The heir bowed. It was not ideal, but it would have to do. They climbed upon the back of their fire lizard, and beckoned for the residents to climb aboard after them.

The Third Page of the Sketchbook

Blank white paper. No monsters here. Hurry to the bound edge of the page, before it is too late. Find the bridge. Run.

The Second Page of the Sketchbook

The page I returned to was nothing like the one I remembered. The orderly rows of buildings were gone, and the ground was covered in sparkling mirror shards. Black birds flew across the sky in swarms, sometimes descending on piles of debris to try and erase the mess, but it was beyond them. I told myself that the monsters of the third page might have found their way here even without my bridge, but it didn't ease my guilt.

In among the broken bits of art were chunks of watercolor paint, edges smoothed by rain and colors smeared together. Here and there were splinters of wood, bits of pink eraser, and even a heartblade, slightly rusted from exposure to the elements. One of the residents picked up a chunk of watercolor paint and a section of pencil. It sharpened the pencil on the rusty heartblade, letting the shavings fall among the debris.

Was this what death would bring for me, someday? I shaved a curl of wood from my shortest finger, an offering to the dead artists. The resident tucked the paint and pencil into its clothing, which struck me as odd. No worse than leaving the artist's body to deteriorate in the rain, I suppose. I wondered whether the pieces scattered here were from the first couple or the artists they had made. Or perhaps all of them, their pieces mixed together, like the vast multitude the fourth page artists believed was the endpoint for us all.

There were no monsters here, but the destruction was surely the aftermath of their passing. I commanded the fire lizard to kneel and climbed onto its back. The residents climbed up after me, their expressions grim. "Away from the bridge, it may be better," I told them.

Further down the page, birds were trying to paint the buildings back into existence. Misshapen buildings rose from the rubble, tipsy spindly shacks with oddly-colored walls and lopsided roofs. The birds were meant for tedious copying and simple patchwork. Their attempts at original art were unstable. From the fire lizard's back, I reached over and gently touched one of the walls. It quivered at my touch, trembling as though afraid it would fall, a valid fear if so light a touch could make the building shake. The birds, displeased at my interference, began to cluster at my feet, their tail feathers fanned in a threat of erasure.

We rode onward, leaving the bird-made city behind us. We passed the pair of rifts, and I saw that tape no longer covered the torn area. The art-sucking leeches had eaten the tape, and the wildflowers, and the maze of rose bushes. They had even consumed the creek that once ran through the garden district.

Near the unbound edge of the page, we came to an area that was less thoroughly destroyed. Great walls of mirror-glass rose up from the ground, not entire buildings, but a few of the mirrors were big enough to use for copywork. I slid down from the fire lizard's back. I unrolled the paper I carried on my back, but it was shorter than a fire lizard, too small for what I wanted. So I drew myself a bigger roll of paper, shading and blurring the far edge in the illusion of distance, a hint of scale. The paint dried, and the new roll of paper was the proper size.

I unrolled a section as tall as a fire lizard and several times as long. This was third iteration paper—paper drawn onto paper that had been drawn on the original page. It was thinner and smoother and tore easily at the edges, but there was too much debris here to uncover the blank page, so we had no other options. I whistled to the birds, hoping that the flock the pencil woman had assigned to me would respond.

Only one bird answered my summons. It landed at my feet and bowed its head. Then it fixed its beady eyes on the fire lizard, an almost hungry expression on its face. It recognized the creature as alien, drawn in a style that was not consistent with this page.

"We need more birds," I told it. "We need copies of the fire lizard."

The bird whistled, a call that seemed indistinguishable from mine.
But the flocks in the sky could clearly tell the difference. Birds that
had ignored my summons now dove down from the sky and landed
on every available surface.

"We haven't seen a single monster," one of the residents said. "If
the monsters have moved on, why do we need more fire lizards?"

"Those leeches suck up the art that others have created. They left
because there is nothing here for them to feed on. They need fresh art.
We came from the third page, and they were not there. So they must
have gone on to my parents' realm. If we rebuild this world, the new
art would just draw the leeches back here, and they would destroy the
page again. Instead, we have to find a way to destroy them."

I led the fire lizard up next to a large mirror and set the birds to
painting—tracing the reflection on the mirror as they were trained
to do. I tore a sheet of paper from the roll and pressed it over the
wet-paint reflection, but the sheet was too small, which left the newly
painted copy with a somewhat shortened tail. Birds flew to the paper
and sketched the outlines of the painting, not altering the shape in
any way, even the stunted tail. The deformity did not seem to hamper
the copied fire lizard, for as the paint dried the beast rose from the
whiteness and let out a fiery belch. Our one fire lizard had become
two, in far less time than it took for the artists on the fourth page to
draw one from scratch.

It occurred to me that while the original was truly a fire lizard,
an alien creature drawn by the artists of another page, the copy was
something rather different. It was like an echo of a fire lizard, or the
memory of a memory, like a creature of legend or myth. I remembered
the name my father had given the creatures, or rather the name that
he would give them, when we somehow got back to the first page—
dragons.

We stood our dragon next to a mirror, and now two teams of
birds could work in parallel, each flock painting a new dragon. Two
dragons became four, and four became eight. Eight became sixteen,
and then our progress slowed. For one thing, we didn't have enough

mirrors for another doubling. For another, even with the residents helping, it was difficult to keep up with the birds. Each time they finished a painting, someone—either myself or a resident—had to press a paper to the mirror to capture the art into reality.

For hours, we made dragons in sets of eight. They were not perfect copies. The first couple would have cringed to see them, missing bits of tail, or with oddly textured scales because the paper was of such low quality. They were smudged and blurred in places, sometimes even missing a foot or the tip of a wing. But they were every bit as fierce as the fire-breathing lizards from the planet on the fourth page, and I would somehow take them back to the beginning of all things, and save my parents' realm from the art-sucking leeches of my rage.

Packed so close together, and with nothing else to do, several of the dragons launched into the air. One let out a jet of flame, and the others folded their wings and dove back to the page, narrowly avoiding the fire. The birds, unnerved by the fire, scattered. I did not call them back. We had seventy-two dragons. Surely that would be enough to defend my parents' realm.

"So now you draw a door to the first page?" one of the residents asked.

"No. If we use a door we will arrive too late. The leeches have already gone through the cut-out door in my old apartment, or perhaps through the torn-page rifts. Somehow we must go back to the start of the first page, and arrive before the leeches. I know we can do it because the dragons came to the first realm before I left."

A resident tore a scrap of paper from the roll we'd used to make the dragons. "A page is like a piece of paper?"

"Yes," I said, "but the paper is better quality than this."

The resident turned the paper over in its hands. The paper had come off of the roll, so instead of being flat it had a bit of curl to it. The resident rolled the paper so the edges met. "Perhaps like this?"

I shook my head, but it reminded me of the thin strip of paper my father had used to make the Möbius loop. A loop with a half twist would get us back to the beginning, not the start of the second page, but the start of the first. I took the rectangle of paper from the resident and tried to make the loop with a half twist that I remembered from the page of my youth. The paper was too wide, and not long enough, and I couldn't make the loop without crumpling the paper.

Or tearing it.

I carefully tore the paper, once on each side, a matching pair of rifts like the ones that marred the first and second pages of the sketchbook. It decreased the width of the paper enough to form the Möbius loop. I showed the loop to the residents. "I think we can do this with the page, and go back to the very start of the sketchbook." I studied the residents who had followed me dutifully across the pages. "You can stay here, if you'd rather."

The residents looked at one another. The tiny resident cooed. "We will stay. Someone has to rebuild this world." The resident took out a broken piece of pencil and a chunk of paint, and tore a sheet from the roll of paper I had drawn.

For a moment I was appalled that she would presume to make art from the broken pieces of a dead artist. But no, this was fitting. The true end of an artist came when all the wood was sharpened away and their graphite and paint was spread across the page.

I looked at my own hands, my watercolor-pencil fingers nearly gone. The pencil woman of this page had drawn her hands clean away, cut off her eraser-wrists and sharpened the pencils of her arms to continue her art. Soon, it would come time for me to do the same. I was not as young as I once was. I had left my mark upon the pages, for good or for ill.

"Stay well away from the rifts," I warned the residents. "I don't know exactly what will happen when I try to twist the page and loop it back around."

I took my army of dragons to the unbound edge of the page and climbed aboard the back of the original fire lizard. I commanded them to grab the edge of the page in their mouths. They pulled. The page began to warp, curving inward so the tips of the few remaining trees leaned in toward each other, rather than reaching straight up into the sky. It was just as well, perhaps, that the leeches had destroyed the mirrorglass city, because it seemed unlikely that such fragile structures would have survived even the gentle curving of the page, much less the twist that was still to come.

The underside of the page was white. The dragons continued to pull, and when they neared the bound edge of the page they flew around each other and upside down to create the half twist that folded space and time into a loop. A Möbius sketchbook page, with the world of the second page below us, and the pure white paper of the untouched first page stretching up above us and disappearing into the sky.

The first page was new and fresh and blank. I knew that the dragons arrived after my parents, so I waited, staring at the white page and waiting for them to appear. The dragons began to tremble from the strain of holding the page. Where were the watercolor king and the pencil queen? This was the beginning, why did the world not start?

I thought back to the Möbius strip I had played with on the first page. In the beginning, I myself had drawn the tiny artist onto the paper, but the second time around, it had been the tiny artist that had restarted the cycle. There were no other artists here but me.

I reached up to the paper and began to sketch. I was tempted to draw some other kind of artist—someone like me, or the half-and-half artists from the second page, or the Multitude from the fourth. What would happen to the cycle if I changed it, redrew the world to suit my own desires? I wished that there was time to run a test, but the dragons were nearing the end of their endurance. If I hadn't been angry at my parents, I wouldn't have created the third page, but I also wouldn't have created the fourth. There was beauty all throughout the sketchbook, beauty that would never exist if I did not begin at the proper beginning.

I sketched my parents as I remembered them, and painted them true even knowing what would come of it. These sketchbook pages weren't perfect, but they were salvageable, and I would save them. King and queen and all.

I watched my parents draw the beginnings of their realm, and when they vanished beyond the paper that I could see from where I stood, I stepped from the second page back to the first, to the beginning of the sketchbook, and called my dragons to join me.

The First Page of the Sketchbook

The pencil queen surveyed her army, several dozen soldiers, wearing suits and helms of silvery metal and armed with swords. The soldiers had made their camp between the giant boulders that stopped the great rifts from tearing the page in two.

The army was woefully inadequate. The soldiers were smaller than the dragons, and they only outnumbered their enemy two to one. Even with the heir to help her, it would take quite some time to draw enough soldiers to defeat the dragons, and they'd have to wait for the king to paint them.

She saw the king approaching. "You're supposed to stay at the castle and paint soldiers after the heir sketches them."

"The heir has vanished," the king replied. "Drew a door onto the blank-page wall and cut through to the second page."

"My princess," the queen said sadly. "If these dragons hadn't invaded our realm, I could have stayed with her, and she would not have left us. We must redouble our efforts, and banish these dragons. Then we can search for our heir and bring her home."

The queen stood before one of her many easels and began to sketch, using the last nubs of her fingers. The time had come for her to slice off the erasers of her wrist joints and draw with the pencils of her forearms.

"Perhaps we should try to find the heir first. What if he's in trouble?" the king asked. He saw the queen bring her wrist up to her heartblade, and he looked down, unable to watch her cut so much of herself away. He heard the soft thud of her eraser wrist as it fell to the ground.

"The realm must come first. We can draw another heir when the war is done, if we survive the battle. A true princess, not some bizarre creation of watercolor pencils."

The king shook his head. Even now, having seen what the heir could do, the queen could not appreciate the child they had created. Was it his fault, for making their child something other than what she intended? The heir had diverged from their vision, grown in ways they had not expected, and in the end, abandoned them. But was that not the way of art, to begin to change from the very moment it left the artist's hands?

The queen's hands were gone, her pencil fingers all used up and the erasers of her wrists now sat useless on the ground. The king's arms were smaller too, but being paint his limbs simply grew thinner with time, without the dramatic change of chopping off portions of his limbs at the joint. He bent down and picked up the queen's erasers. They were too large to fit into the box of her pencilself shavings, and she did not seem to want them anyway. She had already set to the task of sharpening the pencils of her forearms, and these shavings she carefully collected into the box he'd made real for her, so many paintings ago, when the page was blank and white.

He put the erasers into his heart jar, where they bobbed and floated in the water. A shadow passed over them. He peered at the sky, expecting a dark cloud. What he saw was a dragon. The soldiers started shouting and pointing at the sky. The dragons had left the border of the realm, and they were flying in circles above the soldiers.

The heir scanned the realm from the back of a flying dragon. The leeches would arrive soon, and the best hope for the realm was for the dragons to incinerate the art-suckers before they could do too much damage. A single leech on the fourth page had destroyed a building, and a horde of leeches had destroyed the entire second page. The heir didn't know whether the leeches would come through the old door or through the torn rifts, but the rifts were by far the more dangerous entry point because they were large enough for all of the leeches to pass through at the same time.

Besides, the heir wanted the dragons close enough to protect the king and queen, and their soldiers, all of whom were in the narrow strip of page between the rifts. The soldiers shouted and pointed, but were powerless to stop the dragons in the sky. With their attention directed upwards, the soldiers did not see the true danger. On both sides of the queen's army, leeches squirmed through the great tears, wriggling up like giant worms before bending their round mouths back down to the page to consume the art on either side of the rifts.

The heir ordered the dragons to attack, and they swooped low over the rifts and let loose their flame, lighting the leeches on fire. Leeches kept pouring out of the rifts, far more leeches than the heir had drawn. They had found a way to multiply, just as the residents had done. The dragons split into teams and flew at the leeches in waves. Each team dove down to breathe flame onto the leeches, then flew in a wide slow circle to get back into position, giving the dragons a moment of relative rest while the other teams attacked.

On the fourth page, there had been one leech, and several dragons had burned it fast and hot until it was nothing but ash. Here there were more leeches than dragons, and though the leeches caught on fire, they did not burn instantly to ash. Flames were everywhere, and if the page itself caught fire, all would be lost.

The heir landed near the pencil queen. "You must have the soldiers control the fires. Tell them to stay clear of the leeches, and douse the flames that spread beyond the torn rifts."

"What do you care about the fires you started?" the queen demanded. "Afraid of burning the realm you seek to conquer?"

"You do not know me, for I have traveled a longer path than you did to get here, so I am older than you expect. But I am your heir, and I am here to save this realm."

All around them, the battle continued to rage. A dragon dove too close to the rift, and a leech bit into its wing with sharply pointed teeth and started to suck the art away. The leech grew, and the wing shattered, leaving the dragon with only one wing, desperately flapping as it crashed to the ground. The next wave of dragons torched the leech.

The queen stood and stared at the heir. "I do not take orders from you, or from anyone. I am the queen of this realm. I sketched this world, it is my creation, and you have destroyed my vision with your dragons and your fire."

"The page itself will burn," the heir said. "Are you really willing to let the entire page burn to maintain the illusion of control?"

"Control? I have no control! All I wanted was to make this realm and keep it safe, but you have all betrayed me, siding with the dragons!" The queen began to laugh hysterically. "Perhaps fire is what the page needs, a cleansing flame to burn the sketchbook clean, that we may begin again and be born in pure white ash!"

The queen turned her back on the heir and sketched flames onto her easel, ignoring the chaos that surrounded her.

"I will save our realm for you," the king said softly, but the queen made no sign that she heard. He turned to the army, and raised his voice. "Soldiers, listen, for I have painted you into reality and I am your king. Use your helmets as buckets, and put out any fire that is not burning a monster."

And so the dragons fought the leeches, and the soldiers fought the fires, and—despite the queen—the realm was saved.

Up in the tallest tower of the castle, the heir looked out over the realm. Here and there, black plumes of smoke rose from the burning corpses of leeches. The smoke was worst along the edges of the rifts, but even there the soldiers had the fire under control. Dragons flew high above the castle, looping and diving, playful now that the battle was done.

In the castle courtyard, the queen stood before an easel, filling sheet after sheet of paper with sketches of fire. The king, of course, did not paint her sketches, but she was losing substance, and soon she would have no graphite left to make her mark upon the page. It began to rain, but the queen didn't stop sketching, and the king didn't leave her side. He blamed himself for her decline, and he second-guessed his decision to paint the heir in so many colors. The rain ran down the king's body and slowly washed his paint into puddles in the courtyard. Their time as leaders of the realm was ending.

Behind the heir, the door to the second page stood closed on the tower wall, a solid oak door surrounded by a thin strip of blank white page. Up close, the heir could see the cuts in the paper, sealed only with a thin layer of paint. Long ago, on the second page, the black birds had erased the other side of the door. What would happen now, if someone tried to open it and step through?

The heir cut away the seal, and pulled the door open, not all the way, but a tiny crack. Enough to see what was on the other side. The residents had cleared away the debris of the fallen mirror city, and created a new world for themselves. Instead of the detailed designs of the first couple, the residents had filled the page with simple things—trees and farms and cottages. Scattered around the page were residents, tending fields and building homes. The heir pushed the door closed. The residents didn't need any help, they were rebuilding nicely on their own.

The heir wasn't needed anywhere, not really. The king and queen were no longer fit to rule, but if residents could mend the second page, the soldiers and the dragons could tend this one, given the proper tools. The tower room had not changed since the heir had left it. The easels still held the plain black circles that the heir had sketched at the queen's demand. The heir drew the circles into palettes, broad plates piled high with paint in every color. On a blank page, the heir drew pencils, not pressed together into the shape of an artist, but single pencils that a soldier could hold in its hand. It came more easily now, to draw what was needed before the joy of painting. Making sketches come alive with color was the heir's true passion, but there was a satisfaction to doing both sides of art and creating things alone.

When the palettes and pencils were finished, the heir called a soldier up to the tower to collect them. The inhabitants of the page would be free to make their own future. Making art was not unlike making children—once the work was finished, it was important to let it go, to not try to control every detail.

The soldier dropped one of the pencils without noticing, and left it behind in its hurry to take the supplies to the others. On the ground beside the pencil was the Möbius strip that the king had made, now flat because the heir had cut it apart. There were spheres and cubes scattered across the paper, but no sign of the tiny used-up artist or the younger copy. The heir flipped the paper over and checked the other side, but there was no sign of them there either.

Their absence was vexing. Their paper was not a sketchbook, but a single sheet of paper with two sides. If they were not on the front, and they were not on the back, where had they gone? The birds of the second page could erase unwanted art, but there was no sign of anything like the birds here. The tiny artists weren't sophisticated enough to create anything more complex than spheres and cubes.

The heir might never have found them except that a breeze came in through the tower window and rustled the paper of the easels. The heir looked up, and on the back of one of the pages was a spiral staircase made entirely of tiny stacked-up cubes. The heir pulled the paper down from the easel, and on the back side was a city built entirely from geometric blocks, a city full of tiny artists. Art was everywhere, and it found ways to spread. The tiny artists had escaped their strip of paper and climbed up the easel.

It gave the heir an idea. Dragons circled the castle, and the heir called one over and rode upon its back to the unbound edge of the page. What if the sketchbook itself was drawn on an even grander page? There would be a vast and wondrous world out there to explore. The creations of an artist talented enough to make a sketchbook universe would be well worth seeing.

The dragon reached the edge of the paper, and the heir urged it onward, out into the void beyond the page.

SEASONS SET IN SKIN

Cherry Blossoms

Spring followed Horimachi as she hiked up the steep trail. The branches of the cherry trees had been heavy with flowers when she left the capital at the end of March, but here the cold mountain air hindered even the turning of the seasons. She was condemned to make her entire trek under pink petals that drifted down from the trees like snow.

It reminded her of the cherry blossoms that she'd tattooed into her daughter's skin. Months of pain, and the faeries killed her anyway. After ten years' service as an artist for the Imperial Army, Horimachi had left the capital in shame. Her tattoos were failing, and soldiers were dying for it.

Aya had died for it.

The ancient road that Horimachi walked was lined with abandoned shrines and thousand-year trees. There were no other travelers. Forests were the domain of the *gaijin* fae, invaders from the West, and there were dark rumors even in the most isolated villages. Horimachi had done hundreds of tattoos for the Imperial Army, but her own skin was unprotected. Her tattoos were from before the war, when black ink was made of soot instead of faery blood. The only color on Horimachi's skin was a cadmium red, not the deeper crimson of ground faery wings. She carried the protective inks with her, but she had vowed never to use them. She was done with soldiers, and cities, and war.

Horimachi hesitated at the edge of the village, at the bottom of the hundred stone steps that led up to the outermost temple. She'd lost her eldest daughter to the war, but not her youngest. Suki had been too small to go to the capital, only twelve when Horimachi left with Aya. She had always been respectful in the messages they exchanged—tiny scrolls of paper tied to the legs of gray waxwings—but a relationship only on paper was not the same as living under the same roof. Horimachi's last scroll, the one she could not force herself to send, was in the breast pocket of her shirt, close to her heart. It bore the news of Aya's death.

Swords clashed in the temple courtyard. Two women fought with *wakizashi*, short swords like the one Aya had practiced with before she joined the Imperial Army and graduated to a longer *katana*. When the women noticed her, they stopped their practice, and one of them rushed over to greet her.

"Mother?"

The woman who approached bore an eerie resemblance to Aya. Suki was a nurse now, tending the fae-addled veterans who had retired from the war, but Horimachi still remembered her as a skinny twelve-year-old girl who had bravely fought back tears the day she and Aya had left. The sword tied to Suki's waist sash was Aya's practice sword.

Horimachi bowed her head. "Suki. I'm so sorry. I didn't protect her well enough."

"Aya." Suki mouthed the word but had no voice to speak.

They held each other and cried.

The cold mountain air had not kept away the destruction of war. Men and women, covered head to toe in tattoos, wandered aimlessly through the village and babbled about sources of life energy and swirling eddies of time. These were the soldiers that had been ridden but not killed. Men and women who had watched, helpless, as the fae used their bodies as puppets, forcing them to slaughter their compatriots. It was probably for the best that their minds were broken, because it spared them the knowledge of what they had done.

Horimachi spent two days nursing the veterans before Suki pulled her away from her work.

"I need a tattoo." Suki had shaved her head to prepare herself for the protective ink. Without her hair, she looked like a new soldier, like all the soldiers that had been assigned to Horimachi in the capital.

Like Aya.

"The northern provinces are falling to the fae. I am going to fight and banish these intruders back to the West. Will you offer me protection?" Suki stood, her bald head bowed in respect, waiting for Horimachi to reply.

"Tattoos are painful. They take a long time. They are not for foolish girls who rush off to the city to be soldiers."

Suki lifted her head and stared in disbelief. "The waxwings from the north no longer bring news, only scrolls of names, soldiers killed by the fae. Thousands of people died in the early attacks, before we knew to protect ourselves, before the tattoos. Nearly all our men are either fae-addled or dead. Foolish is not a young woman wanting to fight. Foolish is pretending that war will not come to the village when it is done with the cities."

"If so many soldiers are dying, it means the tattoos are not working. *My* tattoos are not working." If she had done better work, Aya would be alive.

"I've seen your work, and it isn't flawed. The fae are getting stronger somehow. The tattoos aren't giving as much protection as they once did, but they are better than nothing." Suki paused. "But I will go to battle with bare skin if you refuse to help me."

Suki was so much like her sister, with the same soft fierceness. They were rivers that wore away at rock. Flexible but persistent, fluid but strong. Horimachi would do the tattoo, despite her old back and her aching hands. She would cover every inch of her daughter's skin, so that she could fight.

Horimachi started with cherry blossoms, their outlines winding up Suki's neck and covering the pale skin of her skull. The branches and flowers were carefully arranged to ensure that there were no gaps large enough for a faery to slip into her body and drain her life away. Never more than fingertip's width between two lines of faery blood. Suki was a good canvas, quiet and still. She bore the pain well. Over her breathing was the clicking sound of needles sliding in and out of her skin. *Shakki. Sha sha sha sha.* Horimachi dabbed away the ink and blood that pooled on the surface of Suki's skin, then continued making the blood-black outline of petals. Around the lines, the skin turned pink and slightly swollen, a temporary effect that made the flowers look three-dimensional and almost real.

Horimachi stopped after five hours of work. The fine-lined blossoms and branches on the back of Suki's neck and skull looked almost like the hair she'd shaved away. "We will continue in two days' time."

It was the schedule she had used with the soldiers in the city, five hours of work every other day. It was painful, but fae-based inks healed faster than ordinary tattoos, and by the time a soldier's entire body was covered in an outline of black, the first sections of tattoo had healed enough to begin shading.

"Tomorrow," Suki countered. "At this rate, the tattoo won't be finished until the end of summer. If I don't leave for the capital soon, there will be no capital to defend."

"Two days. Be glad we aren't using cadmium and soot because then you'd have to wait two weeks. Even with the fae inks, your body needs time to heal." Horimachi didn't say it, but her own body also needed time to heal. Her aching joints were getting too old for so much work.

Water Lilies

Golden magic was strongest at sunrise. An hour before dawn, Yōsei went to a field outside the capital where humans buried their dead soldiers. The ancestors told Yōsei to practice magic on the dead. Safer that way.

The corpses were arranged in neat rows. Yōsei could feel the blood of the ancestors embedded in their human skin, even buried beneath several feet of earth. The humans preferred to burn their dead, but the blood on the soldiers' skin made them impervious to flame.

Yōsei uncovered a girl, three months dead. Even in the dim pre-dawn light, her skin was striking. She was a canvas covered in black and red, decorated with an intricate design of dragons and flowers and koi. There were swirls of water below her waist and swirls of clouds above. Water lilies floated on her hip, the line where water met sky. A symbol of summer, and even in the early hours of the morning, the August heat was enough to make her body reek of death. The tattoo that protected her skin slowed internal decay but did not stop it.

Stolen blood from Yōsei's ancestors, injected into human skin. An ink made from ground red wings tinted the petals of flowers and the scales of dragons and fish, granting protection against red magic. Generations of red-winged warriors had died trying to reclaim the sacred land where the humans had built their capital, but Yōsei was different. A thousand generations ago, a group of ancestors left the war and escaped into a faster swirl of time. Centuries flew by in less than a decade, and they used that precious time to breed themselves for color. Instead of red wings, and red magic, Yōsei had wings the color of gold.

In a thousand generations, the magic was not the only thing that had changed. The ancestors were filled with a rage as red as the magic of their wings, but Yōsei was calmer, more rational. Most of Yōsei's generation favored war, but some believed that peace was possible. What they needed was a way to communicate with the humans, a puppet to speak on behalf of the ancestors. Any human would do, but as the ancestors said, corpses were safer.

The blood-black outlines of the dead girl's tattoo were enough that Yōsei could not have killed her, had she been alive, but there were more subtle magics to be done. The first thin crescent of the sun appeared on the horizon, filling the sky with golden light, and Yōsei knelt beside the girl.

Slipping into her body was like meditating inside a stone, cold and still. Yōsei filled the girl with tendrils of gold and divided life energy between two bodies—one cold and dead, the other hot and familiar. The girl was too plump, too dense, and filled with tiny creatures that decomposed her flesh. These Yōsei banished, drowning them in golden light.

She merged into the human.

Yōsei began to mend her otherself. She used golden tendrils to draw blood upward from where it had pooled in the lower portions of her body. She collected the blood back into her vessels and repaired the veins and arteries where they were broken. She inspected all her flesh and healed it, and when the work was complete, she restarted her heart and opened her eyes.

Yosei's true body recoiled in distaste. Her human body sat up, disoriented. There were traces of the dead human lingering in the connections of her brain. The ancestors said that humans were like puppets to be worn and discarded, but the dead girl had memories and emotions, and even a sense that Yōsei did not know.

Mosquitos buzzed. Hateful little birds flaunted their ability to fly, calling attention to themselves with boastful songs and trills. Wind rustled through the tree branches, and dark clouds drained away the powerful light of dawn. Fat raindrops fell with a steady patter, striking the skin of both her bodies before dripping down to the earth. Discordant yells, almost meaningful to her human mind, came from the far side of the field. Unfamiliar with the workings of her brain, she could not quite remember words.

It was known from prior generations that humans communicated through this unnatural sense, but Yōsei had never experienced it. The meaning was incomprehensible to even her human mind, and spoken words seemed a poor substitute for the more intimate bonding of ancestral minds and communion of images. Still, something in the shouting signaled a warning. Yōsei ran with both bodies out of the field and into the forest, at a pace frustratingly slow because she was unused to her human muscles. The movements of *that* body were jerky and uncoordinated.

The other humans dared not follow into the shadows of the forest.

Yōsei let her human body choose their path. She seemed to be seeking something, grasping at vague familiarities in the landscape. Yōsei hoped to use her to negotiate with the humans, and the humans most likely to listen would be those who had known her in life. She had to make them understand that the ancestors were not invaders from the West but natives returning home after a long absence, distant descendants of the *tengu*.

The girl was often confused, but she walked a road that led away from the capital and into the mountains. If nothing else, Yōsei was pleased to escape the humid summer air for the cooler mountain breezes.

Chrysanthemums

Suki lay face down on the tatami floor while Mother shaded the koi and chrysanthemums on the back of her right leg. She stared at the finished design on her forearm, a snake that wrapped itself around her arm, the gaps between the coils filled with peonies. Studying the completed design drew her focus away from the burning in her leg and the rhythmic tapping of the needles that seemed to vibrate down into her bones. She counted the scales on the snake, each one shaded in red and bluish black.

Faery blood ink was pure black at first, but even in the month since Mother had finished her arms, it had taken on a slightly bluish tinge. It was work well done, as Mother's work always was. She was a master, with decades of practice. The fan of needles at the end of her bamboo handle moved in perfect rhythm, the depth and angle changing to make subtle variations in the shading of the design. Variations in color and variations in pain.

Eternities of pain, and each day she looked more like Aya. It was the same design, and as the resemblance grew, Mother became pensive and moody. Not as she worked. Those movements were so practiced that her art flowed from her automatically. But when the needles stopped, and the work was finished, it was always the same.

"Come back in two days," Mother said. She turned her attention to cleaning her tools, refusing even to look at Suki.

Sometimes Suki tried to stay, to make conversation. To be something other than a reminder of Aya's death. She had not complained when Mother left, and she did not complain now, but she wanted to have some part of their relationship back, some sign that her mother had really returned. Instead she was a client, and a reminder.

Suki slipped into her clothes and secured her sword to the sash around her waist. She slid the door open, but then she froze, unable to make sense of what she saw before her.

There, outside, was Aya. She was naked despite the cold autumn air. Suki remembered her sister as being taller, stronger, older. The only difference between Suki and *this* Aya was that the woman outside was finished, her tattoos shaded in red and black from head to toe. Suki had always assumed that Mother had given them identical designs, but now she realized that they were mirror images. This other woman bore the face she saw every morning in the mirror, a face protected with cherry blossoms and clouds, done in delicate lines and only the palest shading of pink. It was meant to be protection.

It had failed.

The body that had once held her sister was clearly a puppet, standing several yards away with an odd posture, as though she might fall over at any moment. Movements that should have been smooth—the bowing of her head, a glance at Suki's face—were done in uncoordinated jerks and fits. A faery stood behind Aya. Suki had never seen one before. It was smaller than she expected, coming only to Aya's shoulder, with thin, twisted limbs like tree branches. Its wings were not red but gold.

"And so the war has come to the village," Mother whispered, tears flowing silently down her face, "brought by my own failure, and wearing the face of my child."

There was no end to the horrors of war, no final peace, not when the faeries could take someone even after they had died. She'd spent years tending to the veterans, back from the battlefield with their minds broken, but this was worse. How could Aya free herself from want and sadness in the afterlife if she could not even escape her physical form? Suki did not know if some part of her sister's consciousness remained, but she was certain of one thing. She could not let the fae desecrate her sister's body this way. She had to defeat this new evil, or they would never be free of the fae, even in death.

She approached her sister slowly, arms held wide as though preparing for a hesitant embrace. Before she could reach for her sword, Aya spoke.

"Return our sacred land." The voice was wrong. Harsh.

Suki drew her sword from its sheath. The faery turned to flee, but Suki did not care whether it lived or died. It was the wings she wanted. Golden wings to make new ink and turn the tide of the war.

"Stop," Aya cried. Suki did not listen. She swung her sword and sliced off a large section of the faery's wing.

Aya collapsed.

The faery erupted in golden light, blinding and hot. The gold cut through the useless red ink of Suki's tattoo, and she could feel her energy being sucked away as the faery tried to heal itself. She would not be what Aya was. She tried to slash at the faery, but it danced away from her, too fast for her to catch in her weakened state.

She could feel the faery at the edges of her mind, in the pulsing of her own blood. The heat of the faery magic burned like needles on her skin. They were merging. She did not have a second, a fellow soldier to grant her a quick and merciful end, but she would not be a puppet to this golden creature. She turned her sword upon herself, slicing through her midsection from left to right, the traditional beginning of an honorable death. The faery realized what she was doing and came forward to stop her. Smiling through her pain, she pulled the blood-covered sword from her own abdomen and sliced the faery in half.

Blood ran onto the dirt, human red and faery black. The colors of her tattoo echoed in the moment of her death. The autumn air was so very cold, now that the bright heat of faery magic was gone.

Mother came to her side and cradled Suki's head in her lap. For the first time since her return, she was not a tattoo master. She was the woman that Suki had missed. She brushed the tears from Suki's face and held her hand.

"Mother," Suki said, her voice soft. There were others out there, she knew. Other gold-winged fae, killing soldiers and raising the dead. Her body shook from the cold and from fear. With her last strength, she held up a section of golden wing. "Please," she said. "Finish me. Don't let them take me."

Dry Fallen Leaves

Aya woke empty and lost.

Time swirled aimlessly around her, pulsing like blood through her veins. She could not see beyond the inside of her eyes, and the gold that had filled the spaces between her fragmented selves had seeped away. She felt tendrils of death seeping in to fill the void, a reassuring emptiness, freedom from the constant longing and need that came with physical form.

A familiar sound came to her ears. *Shakki. Sha sha sha sha.* The rhythm brought her back to the slowness of time, the solidity of reality. It was a sound that should have been accompanied by pain, but there was no pain. Distracted by the sound, Aya lost the tendrils of death. She tried to find her lost oblivion, but instead of searching within her mind, she inadvertently opened her eyes.

She was home. Mother knelt on the tatami mats on the far side of the room, working on a soldier. The soldier was Aya. Time shimmered and broke. There was no pain, so Mother could not be inking her tattoo.

In another place, she remembered dying, falling into a state of clarity and peace. An army of tattooed soldiers had marched against her, puppets of the fae. If they were not protected, why did Mother still sketch color into skin? Aya opened her mouth to ask, but instead of words her dry throat only croaked.

Mother set down her tools. She brought tea. It was warm like golden magic, and Aya choked and knocked aside the cup. Heat spilled down her chest, then quickly passed. Cold damp cloth against her skin brought remorse. A sense of loss. A memory of thoughts that did not belong to her. Yōsei. The faery had wanted something. Something important.

She chased the memories in her mind, but reality shattered any time she came too close. The muddled sensations of life were overwhelming. The gold had controlled her, imposed an artificial order and a clear goal. Peace. The faery had brought her back to negotiate a truce. The only peace she'd ever known was death, and she longed to slip back into that unending darkness.

Mother brought another cup of tea. Aya let it warm her from the inside, longing for the golden magic that she loathed. Anything to help her find a direction. When the cup was empty, she practiced setting it on the table and picking it up. After several repetitions, she heard the sound that called her back to the present moment. *Shakki. Sha sha sha sha.*

She stood on wobbly legs and carefully walked across the room. The girl that was not Aya had dried leaves tattooed on the bottoms of her feet, the fallen leaves of winter. Mother had drawn those very leaves onto Aya's feet, but these were different. Aya's leaves were red and black. Faery blood and ground red wings, dark-colored protection against dark fae magic.

These leaves were tinted with gold, as though illuminated by the first light of dawn. Aya picked up a small vial of golden ink. If she drank it, would the gold pulse through her veins and make her whole?

"I sent most of the golden wings with a runner to the capital, for the Imperial Army," Mother said, gently taking the vial from Aya's hand. "I should have sent it all, but I kept enough for Suki, and for you, if you can bear the pain."

Pain was nothing, but Aya wanted death, not golden skin.

She reached down and touched her sister's face. In broken mirror-shards of time, she remembered the baby she had held so carefully when she was six, the wide-eyed confidant she had whispered to when she had her first kiss, back before the fae had slaughtered most of the men. Suki's body was cold and hard like winter stone. Her skin did not swell pink or bleed where Mother poked it with her needles. She did not smell like gold, and she made no sound.

Tears ran down Mother's face as she worked. "She always wanted to be like you, except in this. I abandoned her when she was alive, but I will grant her final wish. I will finish her tattoo and keep her safe from the fae."

Suki had been alive.

Aya remembered watching through a golden haze as her sister died by her own hand. Suki had wielded the sword, but Yōsei had killed her nonetheless, while Mother stood and watched. Was that peace? The fae could remake themselves on a whim, and even if Aya could negotiate peace with the current generation, it would not last.

She would let Mother tattoo her with gold, and she would continue to fight.

But gold would not be enough. The fae would retreat for another thousand generations while only a decade passed here, or perhaps just the blink of an eye. Time was always changing, never constant from one swirl to the next. Eventually there would be magics in silver or green or blue. And each time another color would need to be added to the tattoos, until the pictures held all the colors of the world. Only then could the fae be banished for good.

Shakki. Sha sha sha sha. Layers of color, cycles of war.

Someday, the dragon on Aya's back would be richly colored in blues and greens. She would be adorned with pink cherry blossoms and white water lilies, yellow chrysanthemums and brown fallen leaves. The signs of all the seasons, set in human skin. She would fight against faeries with wings of every color, and when the war was truly finished, she and Suki—and all their fellow soldiers—would find peace in the eternal black of death.

THE CARNIVAL WAS EATEN, ALL EXCEPT THE CLOWN

The magician's table was covered by a sheet of plywood, four feet square, completely wrapped up in aluminum foil. Sugar magic was messy magic, and the foil made for easier cleanup. Scattered across the aluminum were misshapen chunks of candy, the seeds from which the carnival would grow. And grow it did.

Overnight, as the magician slept, sugar melted into candy sheets that billowed up into brightly-colored tents. Caramel stretched itself into tightropes and nets, and green gumdrop bushes popped up to line the paths between the tents.

The carnival glittered with sugar-glass lights. The Ferris wheel was made of chocolate with graham cracker seats and a motor that ran on corn syrup. Out near the edge of the table, a milk chocolate monkey rode bareback on a white chocolate zebra with dark chocolate stripes. The monkey did handstands and backflips while the zebra pranced in a slow circle.

At the center of it all was the clown. She was three inches tall and made entirely of sugar. Her face and hands were coated with white powdered sugar, a sharp contrast to the bright red of her blown-sugar lips and the green and purple of her pulled-sugar dress. She was the seed from which each new carnival was grown, and she was beautiful.

As each of the sugar creations woke, the clown was there to welcome them to the world and tell them of their destiny. "You will be adored by children," she told the cotton candy sheep, stroking the wisps of their baby blue wool. "You will delight them with your tumbling," she told the flexible bubblegum acrobats. And, "You will amaze them with your daring stunts," she told the gingerbread daredevil. She smiled at everyone, but she smiled her prettiest smile for the daredevil, because she was a little bit in love with him.

As she woke the carnival, and told them tales of children with bright smiling faces, she always added, "in the end you will be eaten, for that is your destiny."

When she told them that, her smile sometimes faltered. She had seen a child only once, several cycles ago, the six-year-old niece of the magician who had laughed in delight to see the clown's dancing routine. That had been a beautiful moment, the defining moment of her existence, the moment that made her the seed. After seeing the joy on the girl's face, the clown had dissolved blissfully into the warm water in the magician's cauldron, her sugar becoming the seed crystals from which an entire carnival was grown.

As the seed, she was the only one who woke up knowing the joy of a child's laughter. The others would have to wait until the magician took them to whatever party was on the schedule. So she told the others what awaited them, how wonderful children are, and what an honor it was to perform for them. And she told them that they would be eaten, whatever that meant, because when she asked the magician why he grew a new carnival for every party, he told her that the carnival always gets eaten in the end.

She was a happy clown, and this was the only thing that made her sad, the knowledge that she couldn't go to the parties. As the seed, she was never eaten, always plucked away by the magician and thrown into the cauldron to grow the next carnival.

The clown stood at the edge of the carnival, waiting, and when the magician woke up he came to greet her. She asked, as she often did, if she could go to the party with the others. He replied, as he always did, that she was the seed, and could not be spared.

He picked her up gently and dropped her in his cauldron.

Over time, the clown changed. She became a sad clown, with streaks of burnt-black sugar running down her face like smeared mascara. Her once vibrant dress of green and purple was still beautiful, but the colors faded, and her sugar lost its glossy shine.

One morning, the clown peered out from a green-and-yellow candy tent and saw the magician running about frantically, searching for his keys. He looked tired and distracted, and he was late in collecting the carnival. The clown made a decision. Instead of standing at the edge of the carnival, as she usually did, she would hide in the tent and go to the party. She would hear the sound of children's laughter again, and she would finally be eaten like the others.

She stayed inside the green-and-yellow candy tent as the magician loaded the carnival into his van, and unloaded it at the party. No one noticed she was there, and soon she heard children's excited voices all around her. She would finally be eaten!

One of the children pulled off the roof of the striped-candy tent and broke it into pieces for her guests. The first performer was the gingerbread daredevil. He jumped twelve sugar cookie cars on a motorcycle with licorice wheels and a candy corn seat. The children clapped politely for his act before they ate him. The birthday girl bit off his head, then ripped his arms off to share with one of her guests. Was that what it meant to be eaten? Her beloved daredevil had met his end bravely, without a trace of fear, but being eaten looked far less pleasant than dissolving in warm water, and—a new thought occurred to her—if she didn't go into the cauldron, would she continue to exist? The others always came back, each time the carnival grew, but they never remembered what had happened at the last carnival, no matter how she begged them to tell her.

No, being eaten was not the same as dissolving, she decided. Being eaten was an ending. Being eaten was death without rebirth. The clown couldn't stand to watch any more. She went and visited some of the animals. She patted the backs of the cotton candy sheep and scratched the dark chocolate dancing bear behind his ears.

"Don't be so sad," said the juggler, "we are meant to be eaten."

She had told the juggler that very thing this morning, that it was their destiny to be eaten. She had believed it. Because of her, everyone else in the carnival—the daredevil and the zebra, the acrobats and the cotton candy sheep—all of them were content to meet their fate, week in and week out, a never-ending carnival of death.

No, the clown decided, she wouldn't do this any more.

While the children were busy stuffing sheep into their mouths and watching the juggler toss flaming balls of sugar, the clown snuck to the edge of the carnival, intending to run away—but instead the magician spotted her. He snatched her up and stuffed her into his pocket, and kept her there until evening.

"I don't want to do this any more," she told him.

"I'm sorry, I truly am. But we have a party tomorrow, and I don't have time to make another seed." He dropped her into his cauldron and she melted away.

The clown woke angry. It was one thing to destroy her when she was willing, but the magician had thrown her in the cauldron even after she protested. Her gown reflected her mood—sugar burnt black with a dusting of granulated sugar sequins. Sour gummy animals replaced the fluffy cotton candy sheep, and dark chocolate elephants balanced on jawbreaker balls. The tents of the carnival were a shiny red, like wet blood, and the gingerbread daredevil wore a biker jacket of black licorice.

This time she would not tell the others of the joys of children's laughter. She would warn them of the horror of being eaten, and instead of meeting their so-called destiny, they would work together and escape.

The clown was busy formulating her plans, and she did not notice that the magician was still awake until he came up behind her and snatched her away. He dropped her into a glass jar on the counter and sealed the lid. She watched from her prison as he poured out a batch of melted sugar and worked it into shape as it cooled. Before long, he had made a figure, a little over three inches tall.

It was her replacement, a handsome candy clown with pants of candied orange peel and sugar-rainbow suspenders. His face was molded into a dopey grin, and the clown knew that she would have loved him more than the gingerbread daredevil, if they had met when she had first been made. Now, though, all she felt when she looked at him was pity.

Over on the table, the carnival was waking, but she was not there to greet them. Instead, the magician spoke to them, telling them of the wonders that awaited them and reminding them that it was their destiny to be eaten. Then the magician loaded them up—the carnival and the angry clown—and took them to the party. He did not let the clown out of her jar until after the party had started.

She tried to warn the others. The animals were hopeless of course, for they understood so little of what was happening. The juggler and the bearded lady did not believe her—and why should they? The magician had been there when they woke, and she was just a clown who joined them at the party. She came too late to save them.

Her last hope was the gingerbread daredevil, who, she had to admit, looked quite striking in his biker jacket. He listened to her carefully, and even claimed to believe her. But he wasn't willing to stop the show and run away with her. Her plans of rebellion and escape were crushed. The others didn't change their minds even as the children ripped the tops off the red-sugar tents. "It is our destiny," they told her, and "What would we do if we left the carnival, anyway?"

Even without the others, the clown was determined to leave. She gathered up the saltwater-taffy cords from the bungee jumping ride and used them to climb down to the floor. She was sugar, and fragile, so she knew she wouldn't live long, but at least—for the first time—her life was truly hers.

She wove around the children's legs. The magician stood in the open doorway demanding to be paid despite delivering a dark and dismal failure of a carnival. His arguments escalated into shouts, and the clown slipped out the door just before it slammed shut in the magician's face. He stormed off to his van without ever looking down, and finally the clown was free. With sunshine glinting off her shiny-sugar hair, she walked out into the chest-high grass of the birthday girl's lawn and never looked back.

On the side of a dried up drainage ditch, on the edge of an otherwise ordinary suburban neighborhood, there is an odd sort of carnival. Instead of tents there are marshmallow mushrooms in assorted shapes and colors, and instead of performing animals there are caramel deer and birds made up of chocolate-covered pretzels. The animals are not trained, and wander through the carnival as they please. There are no daredevils or jugglers or bearded ladies.

But there is a clown. She is a peaceful clown, with white-sugar hair and a minty green dress. She knows that somewhere in the city the magician still makes carnivals to be eaten, and she wonders if someday that too-happy clown will come to his senses and make his escape. She knows her carnival is temporary, and it will melt next time it rains. But she also knows that she is a seed, and that she will not be eaten, and every time the sun dries out the puddles, her carnival will grow again.

INTERLUDE:
FLASH FICTION WORLDS

PAPERCLIPS AND MEMORIES
AND THINGS THAT WON'T
BE MISSED

The ghost in my attic is Margaret, but she lets me call her Margie. She was seventy-six years old when she died, and now that she's a ghost she sits in her rocking chair day and night, holding a tiny baby in her arms. The baby rarely moves and almost never cries. His name is Gavin, and he is thin and wrinkly and covered in fine brown hair. Funny looking, as preemies often are, but sweet nonetheless. Margie keeps him wrapped in a blanket of cobwebs, which I think is disgusting. I've always hated spiders.

Did you know that ghosts are like pack rats? We collect of all manner of things: Barbie hairs and memories and peanut shells and dreams of death. Invoices and autumn leaves and the words on the tip of your tongue. Margie collected Gavin, and now she collects cobwebs from my attic to be sure that he stays warm.

Technically it isn't my attic; it belongs to my husband now. My former husband. He lives in what was once my house, with his new wife and her two kids and a newborn baby boy. The baby looks like Gavin might have, if Gavin had lived.

Here is the problem with collecting. Whatever you take, the living no longer have. So a ghost with good intentions, who takes away stubbed toes and sunburns, ends up surrounded by pain. A malicious ghost ends up with cotton candy and laughter and baby smiles and—well, it's hard to stay mean surrounded by all that. That's why most ghosts collect harmless stuff like paperclips and lint.

Margie wanted to be good. When she was alive, she miscarried five times. There was something wrong with her, something that kept her from carrying a baby to term. When she died, she wanted to help other women, to keep them from suffering the way that she'd suffered. She found a woman, thirty-four weeks pregnant, whose baby had died because a blood clot cut off his supply of nutrients and oxygen. Margie took the lifeless baby and named him Gavin. The pregnant woman, of course, was me.

Remember the problem with collecting? I woke up one morning without my baby, and with no real explanation why. The doctors were baffled, and I was devastated. I had lost my little boy, and there wasn't even a cheek to kiss, no tiny body for me to hold one time before I said goodbye.

My friends and family tried to help, but they didn't understand. My husband buried his grief in work and stayed at the office late while I cried myself to sleep. No one remembered the bottle of Percocet left over from when I got my wisdom teeth removed, so no one thought to take it away from me.

Margie haunts the attic, so I mostly haunt downstairs. I spent my first few years of ghosthood collecting lipstick from the purses of my husband's girlfriends, but eventually I got over my jealousy. He remarried, and the house is nicer with children in it. Now I collect stray socks from the dryer and baby toys that fall behind the furniture.

I'm using the socks to make a quilt for Gavin, to replace the terrible cobwebs that Margie uses. I need perhaps a dozen more socks to finish it. In the meantime, I take the toys to the attic, and give them to Margie. She died old enough that her memory is bad, and she doesn't remember that the baby she holds is my son. She simply sits in her rocking chair and cuddles his tiny body up against her chest. She tells him how his mother would have loved him, if he'd lived, and she gives him the toys that I bring.

All ghosts are collectors, even my unborn baby boy. He collects static from the radio and warm water from the bath and muffled voices that come up through the ceiling. Anything that reminds him of the womb. He is trying to recreate me.

I am tempted, sometimes, to collect my husband's new baby. He is pudgy and gurgly and just starting to smile. But he isn't my baby, and I know all too well the pain that it would cause if I took him from his family. So instead I haunt the house that once was mine, and listen to the children's laughter, and try to collect only little things that won't be missed.

PLEASE APPROVE THE DISSERTATION RESEARCH OF ANGTOR

From: ANGTOR.lastname@u.titan.edu
To: hsrb@u.titan.edu
Date: 1:08am May 21, 2429
Subject: Please Approve the Dissertation Research of Angtor

Dear Ethics Review Board for Research on Insignificant Humans,

Angtor requests approval for dissertation research to test the theory: "Humans will destroy inhabited planets if Angtor screams death threats at them until they comply." This is a minor variation of the Milgram experiment and is therefore eligible for expedited review.

Angtor will be the first of its brood to obtain a PhD, so it is imperative that you approve this research.

Thank you,
Angtor

*

From: jenna.wong@hsrb.titan.edu
To: ANGTOR.lastname@u.titan.edu
Date: 9:45am May 23, 2429
Subject: RE: Please Approve the Dissertation Research of Angtor

Hi Angtor,

Your dissertation is not eligible for expedited review. The Milgram experiment asked subjects to administer an electric shock. Your proposed research involves shouting death threats at students until they destroy a planet. This is not a minor variation. You need to submit a full application.

Being the first of your brood to obtain a PhD is an admirable goal, so I will give you a tip: the board cannot approve research where undergraduates are subjected to death threats.

Good luck,
Jenna Wong, Chair
Human Subjects Review Board
University of Titan

*

From: ANGTOR.lastname@u.titan.edu
To: jenna.wong@hsrb.titan.edu
Date: 12:53pm May 23, 2429
Subject: URGENT: Please Approve the Dissertation Research of Angtor

Dear Jenna Wong,

Thank you for the helpful tip. Please provide approval for Angtor's much improved dissertation research: "Humans will destroy inhabited planets if Angtor asks them politely without making any overt death threats." This study assesses the benefits of a public service program, and therefore is eligible for expedited review.

Angtor needs a PhD by the end of this academic year to impress a mate, therefore Angtor asks you politely for approval without making any overt death threats.

Thank you,
Angtor

*

From: jenna.wong@hsrb.titan.edu
To: ANGTOR.lastname@u.titan.edu
Date: 9:33am May 24, 2429
Subject: RE: URGENT: Please Approve the Dissertation Research of Angtor

Angtor,

There are only three weeks remaining in the academic year, so even if your proposal is approved it is unlikely that you will be able to complete your research in time to graduate this year. If you start now, you might be able to finish in time for next year.

Quick clarification question: what is the public service program your research will be assessing?

Thanks,

Jenna Wong

*

From: ANGTOR.lastname@u.titan.edu
To: jenna.wong@hsrb.titan.edu
Date: 2:06pm May 24, 2429
Subject: RE: RE: URGENT: Please Approve the Dissertation Research of Angtor

Dear Jenna Wong,

Eliminating planets infested with undesirable life forms is a public service.

Thank you,
Angtor

*

From: jenna.wong@hsrb.titan.edu
To: ANGTOR.lastname@u.titan.edu
Date: 12:14pm May 25, 2429
Subject: RE: RE: RE: URGENT: Please Approve the Dissertation Research of Angtor

Hi Angtor,

Thank you for your clarification. Your research project, "Humans will destroy inhabited planets if Angtor asks them politely without making any overt death threats," is not eligible for expedited review. Please submit a full application.

Good luck (you'll need it),

Jenna Wong

ᴵᴵᴵ

From: ANGTOR.lastname@u.titan.edu
To: jenna.wong@hsrb.titan.edu
Date: 3:06am May 26, 2429
Subject: PLEASE APPROVE THE DISSERTATION RE-SEARCH OF ANGTOR

Dear Jenna Wong,

You seriously expect Angtor to fill out a 37-page application form to conduct one miserable study about whether humans will destroy inhabited planets? Angtor has many important things to do to prepare for mating and producing broodlings that will spread across the galaxy. Do you not wish for Angtor to have a mate? You have already wasted one precious week of Angtor's research time by not approving the initial proposal.

Angtor's kin have provided the university with money to build the Katrid Library and the Tannin Museum of Galactic Conquest. They will be most displeased to hear of your resistance.

Thank you,
Angtor, Broodchild of Katrid, Ruler of the Tannin Empire

*

From: jenna.wong@hsrb.titan.edu
To: ANGTOR.lastname@u.titan.edu
Date: 8:22am May 29, 2429
Subject: RE: PLEASE APPROVE THE DISSERTATION RESEARCH OF ANGTOR

Dear Angtor,

I am pleased to inform you that we can do an expedited review for your dissertation research after all, thereby saving you the trouble of filling out a full application form. I do have a few clarification questions, as the description of your study was not entirely clear:

1. Will the undergraduates in the study be destroying actual planets, or will they see a simulation of planets being destroyed?

2. Will assignment to the experimental group be randomized?

3. Do you plan to eat the undergraduates at the end of the study?

With sincerest respect for your parents,
Jenna Wong

*

From: ANGTOR.lastname@u.titan.edu
To: jenna.wong@hsrb.titan.edu
Date: 6:21pm May 29, 2429
Subject: RE: RE: PLEASE APPROVE THE DISSERTATION RESEARCH OF ANGTOR

Dear Jenna Wong,

1. Actual planets will be destroyed. Angtor does not care what puny undergraduate research subjects see. What will make the review board approve this dissertation research? Kittens? Undergraduates will see pictures of kittens.

2. Angtor will randomly put all the undergraduates into the group where they destroy planets.

3. Angtor will only eat the undergraduates that do not comply. The others are free to go out and live their insignificant lives until such time as Angtor selects a mate and produces a hungry brood.

Thank you,
Angtor

*

From: jenna.wong@hsrb.titan.edu
To: ANGTOR.lastname@u.titan.edu
Date: 4:55pm May 30, 2429
Subject: Application for Research Denied

Dear Angtor,

With sincerest apologies to you and your exalted parents, I am unable to approve your application for "Humans will destroy inhabited planets if Angtor asks them politely without making any overt death threats."

As a precaution for my personal safety, I have fled the university prior to sending this message. Please do not reply to this message, as I have requested this email account be deleted.

Goodbye,
Jenna Wong

*

From: ANGTOR.lastname@u.titan.edu
To: loretta.blaine@u.titan.edu
Date: 3:08am June 2, 2429
Subject: Please Approve the Dissertation Research of Angtor

Dear Puny Human Advisor,

Submitted in fulfillment of the graduation requirements of the PhD program is my thesis, "Human undergraduates will destroy the home planet of Jenna Wong if Angtor asks them politely without making any overt death threats." Retroactive HSRB approval was provided by Ulric Thurman, the new chair of the human subjects review board. Angtor spent two whole days working very hard on this research.

If you feel this dissertation does not meet the standards of the university, Angtor can add an additional test condition to see if human undergraduates will destroy *your* home planet when asked politely by Angtor. Earth is a very nice planet. It would be a shame if something happened to it. Angtor is confident that the human subjects review board would retroactively approve this additional research if asked politely without any overt death threats.

Thank you,
Angtor

*

From: loretta.blaine@u.titan.edu
To: ANGTOR.lastname@u.titan.edu
Date: 5:52am June 2, 2429
Subject: RE: Please Approve the Dissertation Research of Angtor

Dear Angtor,

Congratulations on finishing your thesis. I can assure you that although the official paperwork is still being processed, you will absolutely be receiving your PhD, and therefore there is no need for you to conduct additional research of any kind.

Purely as a formality, we have scheduled your thesis defense for Friday afternoon. Again, please rest assured that you need not do any additional research, and this is only a formality. Congratulations on your PhD.

Sincerely,

Loretta M. Blaine, PhD
Psychology Department
University of Titan

*

From: ANGTOR.lastname@u.titan.edu
To: loretta.blaine@u.titan.edu
Date: 3:42pm June 3, 2429
Subject: RE: RE: Please Approve the Dissertation Research of Angtor

Dear Puny Human Advisor,

Angtor is pleased that no additional research is needed.

On a personal note, Angtor has selected a mate and is filled with broodlings. Therefore Angtor will not be attending your thesis defense nonsense.

Thank you,
Angtor

*

From: ANGTOR.lastname@u.titan.edu
To: SCREEVE@u.tauceti.edu, LINGBAD@u.tauceti.edu,
CHANDAR@u.tauceti.edu
Date: 9:19pm June 7, 2429
Subject: Please Approve the Dissertation Research of Angtor

Dear Exalted Tannin Empire Dissertation Committee,

Angtor humbly submits for your approval a dissertation titled "Human University Will Grant PhD to Alien Student When Threatened With the Destruction of Inhabited Planets."

No sentient creatures were physically harmed in the execution of this research, but the humans seemed strangely troubled by Angtor's highly convincing simulations of planetary destruction. In debriefing, Angtor offset this psychological damage by showing the humans pictures of small furry Earth creatures called kittens.

Thank you,
Angtor, PhD

GRASS GIRL

The other girls are made of driftwood, but I'm made of bamboo that whistles in the wind. My bamboo makes a hollow thud when the other girls kick pebbles at my legs on our way to school.

"Bamboo isn't wood, it's grass," Sylvia says. She isn't kicking pebbles, and I can't tell if her statement is meant to be an insult or an observation.

Sylvia is the most popular and prettiest of all the girls. She's made of smooth driftwood with smoky quartz eyes. The other girls hang on her every word, and after she mentions my bamboo, they mock me.

"Do you fall over when the wind blows, grass girl?"

"Solid beats hollow."

"Hey grass girl, the monkeys look hungry."

I ignore their taunts. The monkeys only eat fresh shoots and leaves, not the thick woody stems of bamboo that I am made of. Sometimes they nibble at my seaweed hair, but that's no big loss since I have to redo it with fresh seaweed every couple days anyway.

When we get to school, the other girls leave me alone. They don't want to get in trouble. The teachers dismantle girls who misbehave, usually only for a couple hours but one time for an entire week.

I'm supposed to learn the species name for every variety of willow tree, but instead I daydream about replacing my bamboo with driftwood.

At night, I comb the beach. Eventually I find a nice flat piece to replace my left foot, and swap out the old for the new. I hurl my unwanted bamboo foot into the ocean. It makes an eerie whistle as it flies through the air—a wail of loss, as if the small segments of bamboo are sad that they're no longer part of me.

It's hard to walk with one foot wood and one bamboo. I practice on the beach until the moon sets, checking my footprints in the sand to see how badly I'm dragging my heavy new foot. When I go to bed, I'm exhausted.

The next morning I catch up with all the other girls on the path that winds through the bamboo grove and up the hill to our school. Despite my practice last night, I'm limping.

"Nice foot, grass girl," Sylvia says. She's looking at my foot with a thoughtful expression on her face, and I think she maybe means it as a compliment. The other girls are not as kind.

"Hey grass girl, your feet don't match."

"One good foot isn't going to make up for the rest."

"Too weak to walk, grass girl?"

The words sting. I'm supposed to go learn about botanical history, but instead I go back to the beach to look for more driftwood. I find a few small pieces that will make good fingers, and a curved piece for my jawbone. I leave my old bamboo body parts in the sand. When the tide comes up, the waves will wash them all away.

I notice a nice piece of seaweed, the shiny dark-green kind that makes the nicest hair. I've always thought my hair was one of my better features, for all that I have to replace it every couple nights. None of the other girls have seaweed hair. They all have shells or bones that don't need to be redone as often.

I pick up the seaweed and bring it home.

"Mom, why didn't you make me more like everyone else?"

"Because you're you," Mom answers. "You're special."

She helps me weave my seaweed into my scalp, and the wind blows across her bamboo fingers in a low whistle. Three of her fingers are split, and she'll need to replace them soon. I suggest that we go out together to look for new fingers, thinking that maybe I can convince her to switch over to driftwood too.

I'm disappointed when she insists on going to the bamboo grove instead of the beach. After she finds her new fingers, she points out some other nice stems, and mentions that lighter feet are easier to walk with. I refuse to take the hint. Solid beats hollow.

When I'm about half wood, the other girls stop calling me grass girl and mostly leave me alone. But the girl whose approval I really want is gone. Sylvia hasn't been coming to school, and nobody knows where she went. Or nobody will tell me, anyway.

I wander through the bamboo grove on my way to the beach, whacking the tall poles of bamboo with my hand and listening to the hollow sound. When I tap my arm, I hear the satisfying clack of wood on wood. I am becoming sturdy and strong. I don't whistle in the wind.

I go farther down the beach than I've ever walked before—all the way to the stony cliffs. I'm determined to find as much wood as possible. When I get to the end of the sand, I find a girl reclined against the cliffs, her body made entirely of stone. The tide is high and warm ocean waves wash up onto her feet, but she doesn't move.

If wood is unchanging, solid and good, stone must be even better. The stone girl is beautiful, gray and still, serene despite the waves that crash over her feet. Indestructible. Her eyes are smoky quartz. "Sylvia?"

She doesn't answer at first. When she eventually speaks, her voice is raspy like crashing waves. "Please help me. I remade myself in stone, but now I'm too tired to move."

I tried to figure out what to do. Of all the girls, she's always been the least mean, even though she's the most popular. I don't see any driftwood nearby. Someone must have stolen the pieces of her old body, or maybe the waves have reclaimed it for the ocean.

She's too heavy to lift; I need something to replace the stones. I run to the bamboo grove, and the trip takes longer than it should— my driftwood body is so much heavier than my bamboo was. I gather up an armful of bamboo and run back to the cliffs.

The bamboo in my arms whistles as I run.

I replace Sylvia's stone arms with bamboo and bind her together with seaweed. When only her legs are stone, I'm able to help her to her feet.

We walk slowly up the beach because her stone legs make it hard for her to move. On our way to the bamboo grove, we meet a girl made of the smooth driftwood that had once belonged to Sylvia. They are the same pieces, but somehow this new girl doesn't wear them as well. She lacks Sylvia's grace. The new girl sneers at Sylvia's bamboo, then looks down at her legs.

"Sylvia?" she asks. "I thought you'd gone all the way to stone."

"I did. I changed my mind." She shrugs like it was no big deal, and I marvel at her confidence, to not care that another girl is seeing her while she's half stone and half grass, and honestly looking like a complete mess.

I glance down at my own body, with its patchwork of driftwood pieces, mixed together with my last remaining scraps of bamboo. It's better than the body Sylvia has, but she's proud and I'm ashamed. Why do I want to be all solid and unchanging, anyway? Who says the solid clack of wood is better than the hollow whistle of bamboo?

I sit in the sand by the bamboo grove and rebuild myself as I had been before, a girl of grass, with gorgeous seaweed hair. Sylvia sits with me and replaces the stone in her legs with bamboo so that she can be a grass girl, too. The ocean wind blows through our fingers, and the music it makes is beautiful.

ONE LAST NIGHT AT THE CARNIVAL, BEFORE THE STARS GO OUT

Lady Earth went to the Galactic Carnival in a gown of watery blue and earthy green, with a shawl of swirling gray clouds. The back of her gown was black, but decorated with the lights of thousands of cities. Her pet, Moon, trailed behind her.

"Guess your mass, Madam?" Mars asked, teasing.

She twirled for him, showing off her gown.

"You look lovely," Mars said. "Even the Great Ringmaster could not conjure anything so beautiful."

Lady Earth wanted to hear more about the magician, but Moon tugged at the ocean of her gown, eager to see the attractions. Venus hurried by, dressed in thick clouds and looking uncomfortably warm. Mercury followed. He asked, as he always did, "Can Moon come and play? Please please can I play with Moon?"

He was gone before Lady Earth could answer. She turned her attention to the bright lights of the Constellation Animal Show—bears and lions, dogs and fishes, all sparkling brilliantly as they leapt through hoops and balanced on tightropes. Lady Earth munched on meteorites as she watched the animals, tossing an occasional treat to Moon. The back of her gown brightened as her city lights spread and merged, covering her land and even her oceans.

The constellation show was popular with children. Lady Earth spotted Halley and Apophis running around and gawking at the animals, surrounded by scores of other comets and asteroids. Apophis paid no attention to where he was going, and almost collided with Lady Earth.

"Be more careful," she warned, for even at the carnival there were sometimes tragedies. "Remember what happened to Shoemaker-Levy Nine!"

Poor Nine had been watching His Majesty's Many Mighty Moons—a spectacular juggling act—and had run into His Majesty himself, the great King Jupiter. Nine had broken up into pieces and burned away, and there was nothing anyone could do. So sad. But Apophis paid no attention to Lady Earth's warning and continued at top speed, careening away into the blackness.

From the exit of the constellation show, Lady Earth saw the magician Mars had mentioned. The Great Ringmaster pulled planetary nebulae seemingly out of nowhere. Excited by the show, Moon ran circles around her, eager to see where the rings would appear next. Her darling pet would have loved to chase the brightly-colored rings, but she kept Moon's leash short, as she always did.

Mercury whizzed by, so enthralled by the show that he forgot to ask if Moon could come and play.

Another nebula appeared, and another. A bluish one here, a rainbow ring there, and a delicate band of pink and gold that appeared like a halo directly above her. Some were so distant they looked like points, others were close enough to see every detail. Lady Earth searched the blackness, trying to see where the rings came from, but she never managed to look in the right place at the right time. She was so engrossed in the show that she didn't notice Mars until he was almost upon her.

"The Great Ringmaster will perform his trick on Sun in a moment—you'd best step back a bit," he said. "And, I must say, your natural black is gorgeous. I always thought the lights were a bit much."

Lady Earth's beautiful lights had all gone out while she was watching the magic show. She wondered what had happened to the sparkling cities, and decided that perhaps the Great Ringmaster had dimmed the lights in preparation for his trick. She hoped it was only that, and not a more permanent change.

"Hurry," Mars said, disrupting her thoughts, "and come away with me. It isn't wise to linger when the magician makes his nebulae."

Mars was forever asking her out, but never with such urgency. He was a nice enough neighbor, but Lady Earth wasn't sure he was worth leaving orbit for. Besides, who would watch Moon if she went out?

Lady Earth was about to say no when a section of her gown caught fire. Half a continent of fabric lit up with tiny jets of flame. Startled, Lady Earth jumped out toward Mars. A good thing too, for Sun transformed into a giant ball of red flames. If she had stayed on her normal path, Lady Earth would certainly have perished. As it was, her gown boiled away, leaving her with no oceans and no atmosphere, only molten rock laid bare for all to see.

But that was not the worst of it.

Poor Moon was lost to the flames. Even at the carnival there were tragedies, and Lady Earth had not pulled her beloved pet out fast enough. She felt more naked for losing Moon than for losing all her oceans, clouds, and lights put together.

Eventually Sun shrank away, small and dim, drained by the magic trick. All around Lady Earth the blackness of space had changed to reds and blues and yellows and greens, but she hardly noticed the nebula that surrounded her. Instead she searched the inner orbits for her lost pet, but she searched in vain. There was no sign of Venus, or little Mercury. He and Moon were together now, burned away and gone.

Mars and Halley and even King Jupiter came and gave her their condolences. Mars offered her Deimos, for he had two pets and liked Phobos better anyway—but Deimos could not replace Moon. Lady Earth was stripped of everything she held dear, and nothing could cheer her.

Or so she thought.

But when Mars swept past again, Phobos and Deimos cast their shadows on him, and in those shadows Lady Earth saw the tiny glowing lights of cities.

Moon was lost, and her gown was ruined, but perhaps one day her cities would return to her. Their tiny lights gave her hope enough to keep moving. After all, tonight was the last night of the carnival, and she had much to see before the stars went out.

HONEYBEE

A honeybee fluttered its wings for the last time.

It was the last honeybee, a sickly man-made clone descended from a tragically short line of sickly man-made clones. Its stunted wings were translucent and crisscrossed with veins. The blackish yellow fur on its thorax reminded me of the ducklings I saw at the zoo when I went with my mom.

This bee was the last attempt at bees. Scientists experimented with other technologies—pollination drones to preserve essential plants, nanotech cooling panels to decrease global warming, and time travel to fix the environment before it was destroyed. Bees became one extinct species among many.

After my mother died, my son and I cleaned out her kitchen. He was five, and bored. He dumped a box of alphabetized recipe cards onto the kitchen floor. The recipes were handwritten on oversized index cards, with pictures printed off the internet and stapled to each one. I'd asked her once why she didn't print the recipes and she'd answered that food from a handwritten recipe tasted better.

"What's this one?" my son asked. The card was yellow with age and had a smear of red on one corner where I'd grabbed it with jam-covered fingers.

"Almond raspberry thumbprint cookies."

"Will Grandma make them for me?"

I couldn't answer. Mom was gone, and the ingredients for her cookies no longer existed. Pollination drones had saved some foods, but neither almonds nor raspberries had survived. My inability to make the cookies drove home the realization that my mother was gone, so far beyond my reach that I couldn't use her recipes. I stood in the kitchen, tears streaming down my cheeks.

"I'll make them for you someday," I told my son.

A honeybee fluttered its wings for the last time.

That memory was my test of whether our manipulations to the timeline worked. No matter what we did, within the strict rules of the Historical Compliance Committee, my memory was never altered. The bees died, the ecosystem collapsed, and there were no raspberries and almonds to make cookies for my son.

Our petition to perform Category 2 actions was denied. Non-essential plants weren't important enough to offset the risk of major changes to the timeline. We had tried to save the honeybees, and we had failed. Others had tried to save the whales, or the butterflies, or the temperate rainforests. They too had failed. We would never fix the past. We would have to find another way.

My son came to visit on my sixty-fifth birthday, with his wife and their three kids. The kitchen smelled of almond cookies, baking in my oven, each one pressed with my thumb and filled with raspberry jam. The ingredients for the cookies were stolen from the past, raided from a San Francisco condo that would be destroyed an hour later in an earthquake. No one would miss jam and almonds amidst the rubble.

"Mom," my son said sternly, "Did you have approval to get this stuff?"

"I was on an approved plant recovery mission." Technically I was only approved for the potted blueberry bush on the balcony, but our HCC rep was known to look the other way in exchange for a good bottle of cabernet. Before my son could ask any more questions, I added, "besides, we have something very important to celebrate today. We got approval to bring animals forward. I will finally have my bees."

He smiled. "That's great, Mom. You've been working towards that for decades, and I'm glad you get to see it happen."

I snorted. "I'm sixty-five, not ninety. Stop making it sound like I could die at any minute. I'm not going to see it happen, I'm going to *make* it happen."

Our discussion distracted me from the cookies, and I pulled them out of the oven a couple minutes late. The grandkids liked them, but they were dry and crunchy, and my son refused to eat them because I hadn't gotten permission for the almonds and the jam.

Stolen cookies didn't count.

A honeybee fluttered its wings for the last time.

We never solved the problems of the past, but age and the passage of time have stolen the once-clear image. What remained was the memory of a memory. Vein-crossed wings that were an amalgam of my memory with the countless pictures I've looked at since. Soft fuzz the color of ducklings, but was the color in my mind the same color that I saw?

I traveled to the summer of 1993, to an abandoned field overgrown with grass and barley and wildflowers. I spotted a honeybee on a blue cornflower blossom, and had the foolish urge to try and catch it. That was how we'd collected plants—thousands of plants, but only a few from any given place and time. Bees were not like plants. We couldn't take a random sample of bees and hope to make a hive.

At the edge of the field were stacks of rainbow-colored wooden boxes. Hives. I unloaded my pack, lit my smoker, and pulled five empty frames from my collection box. When everything was ready, I flooded the hive with smoke. I took three brood frames, their wax cells filled with eggs and larva tended by nurse bees. I took two frames of honey, too, so the hive wouldn't starve when I brought it forward. I replaced all five frames with empty ones, and reassembled the hive.

I brought my stolen bees to the lab and set the collection box at the edge of our reconstructed garden. For a moment, nothing stirred. I worried that bringing the bees forward in time had damaged them. A single bee emerged from the corner of my collection box. Dazed from the smoke, the bee crawled across the surface of the box, from one corner to the other. Then, in a future built from stolen pieces of the past, a wondrous thing happened.

A honeybee fluttered its wings.

ELIZABETH'S PIRATE ARMY

A kraken came to Edgewood Street on the first day of summer vacation. It was a land kraken, with tentacles of fur and spiny branches of coral growing on its head. Elizabeth hadn't seen it, but she'd heard about it from Sandy, who had heard about it from Laura, who had spotted the beast while playing at O'Malley Park.

"Come on, Puff," Elizabeth called. Jimmy was training a pirate army to fight the kraken, and Elizabeth wanted to join. She brought her dog Hufflepuff with her, in case she ran into the kraken on her way to Jimmy's back yard.

The army wasn't very impressive—half a dozen neighborhood boys all running around aimlessly and swiping at each other with sticks. Elizabeth knew all kinds of magic that would help them be a better army.

She swaggered up to Jimmy, who was shouting orders. "I hear there's a kraken in the neighborhood."

"Don't worry about it," Jimmy reassured her. "My pirates will keep you safe."

Elizabeth almost explained that she was here to join the army. Then she looked at the boys, running around with their sticks, and decided she wasn't interested after all. She would start her own army.

Pirates needed swords, and Elizabeth knew just the right magic for that. She collected all the butter knives from the kitchen and stabbed them into the dirt around the maple tree in her yard. Her mother made her bring the knives back in at lunchtime, but the magic had worked by then and the tree had grown some lovely swordbranches. Butter knives weren't very sharp, so the swords were blunt practice swords, but her mother wouldn't let her have the steak knives, so Elizabeth decided that practice swords would have to do.

She grabbed a bunch of swords and wandered around the neighborhood, looking for pirates for her army. Her first recruit was Laura, the only kid who'd actually seen the kraken. She took Laura's little brother too. Jimmy had turned him away for being too small, but he could hold a sword, and he followed most any order Laura gave him.

They got Kira, and Sandy, and even Jared, who had deserted from Jimmy's army because they made fun of his glasses. Elizabeth brought them back to her yard and they spent the afternoon practicing with their swords and hunting for bottle caps and buttons and other pirate booty.

They needed something to guard their treasure, and Elizabeth knew just the spell for that. She made Hufflepuff sit with his front paws touching the treasure, and flicked a cigarette lighter that Kira had taken from the junk drawer in her dad's kitchen. On her third try, Elizabeth got the spark to make a flame, and Hufflepuff was transformed.

"He's kind of a small dragon," Sandy said.

"And he keeps barking," Jared added.

"Conjuring dragons is harder than making swords," Elizabeth replied, scratching Puff behind the ears, "and I'm sure he will be very fierce in battle, even if he's small."

They trained until it got dark, and they were a good army. In the morning, they would battle the kraken.

Elizabeth met her army at O'Malley Park. They found kraken tracks in the gravel behind the swings, and followed them to the jogging path that wound around in the woods. Elizabeth heard yelling, and a couple boys from Jimmy's army ran past, fleeing from the kraken.

"Hold together," Elizabeth told her army. Her pirates held their swords high and stayed behind her. Puff ran circles around the group, yipping in a decidedly undragonlike fashion.

The kraken had Jimmy cornered, his retreat blocked by the fence that surrounded the park. Up close, the monster looked less like a kraken and more like an elk—with sharp antlers and loose tendrils of partially-shed fur—but it was still a formidable foe for her army.

Yelling her best battle cry, Elizabeth charged, followed by Puff and five screaming pirates, all waving swords. The beast turned toward them, startled, then leapt over the fence and out of sight.

Jimmy, clearly embarrassed to have needed help, swaggered up to Elizabeth and said, "You trained some pretty good pirates. You could join my army, if you want."

Elizabeth snorted. "Now that we've driven off the kraken, there's no need for pirate armies." A shadow engulfed them as a huge monster flew overhead. Elizabeth knew just the kind of army to fight this new beast.

"Tomorrow I'll be training ninjas," she told Jimmy, "and you can help us fight Mothra, if you want."

PART 3:
ALIEN WORLDS

MOTHER SHIP

My mother was a colony ship. For one revolution of the galaxy, a quarter of a billion years, she carried her creators between the stars. At the end of that time, all the creators had died. My mother drifted aimlessly through space. After a hundred million years of traveling alone and empty, her drifting brought her to Earth.

My father was a team of several hundred humans who worked together to make a starseed. Humans are less advanced than the creators were, and prone to tinkering. My mother held all the information they needed to make a perfect seed, but they did not want a clone. They wanted a ship that was uniquely suited to themselves. My father-team was worried that the altered seed wouldn't take, so they implanted seven, even though ships are meant to carry only one. My mother died giving birth. All my siblings died but me.

I am carrying thousands of colonists to a planet they have named Last Hope. This is my third trip, each time to a different colony. Humans are all I've ever known, and I love them, even though they killed my mother. Their tiny bodies ease my loneliness as I travel. I keep my tendrils wrapped around them to hold them in stasis. They do not feel the intimacy of the embrace, as I do. For them, the journey passes in a brief moment of sleep.

Ships need no sleep. I wonder what it must be like for humans, to close their eyes in one place and wake in another. Life is in the traveling, in the going. My life is continuous, with time marked only by the shifting of the stars. Their lives are interrupted, not only by their long sleep as we travel, but by smaller sleeps in their normal existence. I spend several centuries pondering such an existence. I would not choose sleep over consciousness, but what if the choice was between sleep and death?

I could live as they do, I think, if it was my only way to live.

Seven hundred fifty-eight of the colonists are pregnant.

I feel a special bond with these women, for I am pregnant too. The descendants of my father gave me only one starseed, not seven. Even so, it was a foolish thing to do. I am deformed. My mother was sleek and streamlined, but I am a jumbled mess of tissue, pocketed with stasis chambers that are arranged not in ordered rows but haphazard clusters. My shell is riddled with holes, and there is metal grafted to my body to compensate for what is missing. How could the humans possibly believe that I would produce a healthy child? My baby's body is hopelessly misshapen. Only her mind is intact. *His* mind, I correct myself. We ships have always been female, but my child will be a boy.

Most of the pregnant colonists carry deformed babies. Humans are simpler creatures than ships, and as we travel, I repair the unborn children. Cleft palate, Down syndrome, conjoined twins—it pleases me to fix such maladies. My ability to heal is what drove these women to go to the colonies. Their lives will be hard, but their children will be whole. I cure unborn children with spina bifida, cerebral palsy, fetal alcohol syndrome. The stars drift slowly by as I continue on to our destination. I heal the adult colonists too, as best I can, for their bodies are not so pliable as the babies. Heart defects and cancers, schizophrenia and depression.

I wish there was a ship to carry me, a ship that could fix my own deformities and make me as sleek as my mother was. A being so advanced that it could repair my unborn child. I would sleep a billion years in such a ship, and miss the journey of my own life—but there is no healing ship for me. My hope rests in the humans, inferior though they may be.

*

One pregnant woman has a baby who is more deformed than all of the others. Hopelessly deformed. She was sobbing when she came aboard, and when I wrapped my tendrils around her, she whispered, as the women sometimes do, "Please, ship, save my baby."

Her unborn boy has anencephaly, a neural tube defect where the brain stem forms but the cerebral cortex does not. The boy would never gain consciousness, not with so much neural tissue missing. Her child would not even sleep, he could not claim even the gaps that punctuate a human's tiny life.

The boy is a body without a mind. If I heal him, can I claim his mind? The humans are my cargo, and I would never harm them. But I wouldn't be taking a life, not even a mind. I would only be stealing a body.

My baby needs a body.

I wait for several thousand years, undecided. My poor deformed baby, cradled in the tendrils of my womb, grows weaker. I show her the patterns of the stars and share my memories of the vastness of space I have traveled across. She twines her tendrils with mine. She is dying. If I cannot bring myself to take the boy, I will lose my child. I can wait no longer.

It is only a body. Less than that, really, for without my help the boy will certainly die.

I heal the unborn boy and ease my baby's mind into his newly perfect head. He will be more human than ship, for how could a ship exist in such a tiny and fragile body? His longest journeys will be across the surface of a single planet, and his life will be measured in the turnings of that planet, and not the rotations of the galaxy. He will sleep. But he will live, and when he looks at the stars perhaps he will have echoes of our memories, flashes of the maps in my mind. Perhaps when he looks up, he will remember me.

*

The colonists usually remain in stasis until the end of the voyage, but I couldn't bear to let my son go without holding him. I took his pregnant mother out of stasis so that he could grow. I kept the woman in a deep and dreamless sleep. She'll be a few months older when we arrive, but she'll have a healthy child. Surely it's a fair trade.

When I arrive at the colony world, I send her into labor. I don't wake her for the birth. She will have my son for a lifetime, but these first moments are mine. He is tiny. Humans are small creatures—I can fit thousands inside my great bulk—but he is smaller still. I wrap him in my tendrils and keep him warm and close while I wake the other colonists. He cries, he sucks his thumb, he voids his bowels, and he hiccups. His hand flails out and his tiny fingers wrap around one of my tendrils.

I wake his mother last. She is so happy to see her baby, whole and healthy. She holds him against her chest and walks through my corridors to the shuttle that will take her down to the planet, Last Hope.

"Thank you," she whispers, "for saving my baby."

I almost stop her. I almost take him back. But his true body has died, and as a human he will be happier on a planet, not alone in space with me.

I let her take my baby.

He will never be a ship, but perhaps the stars will call to him. Perhaps he will create a new ship, and do a better job than my fathers did. Perhaps one day he will find me, out among the stars. Those are my foolish dreams, the hopes of an old and damaged mother ship.

It is more likely that my son will never leave that planet. It is more likely that he will not remember me.

I will remember for both of us.

FOUR SEASONS IN THE FOREST OF YOUR MIND

Spring

My tree is a pyramidal cell in the prefrontal cortex of your brain. There are millions of us here, in the forest of your brain, each with our own region to tend. My region is a single tree, for I am newly born, just as you are. It is a lovely tree, with a long axonal root and majestic dendritic branches that reach outward to receive the signals of other neurons. Like you, the tree is in a springtime state of frenetic growth, reaching its delicate tendrils to nearby cells and more distant targets. The Omnitude has given me a simple task, a message that comes to me via the entanglement: *Save this tree.*

The tree is one of billions, floating in a sea of cerebrospinal fluid and held in place by star-shaped glial cells. Capillaries weave through the cells, rivers of blood pulsing in time with the beat of your heart. Neurotransmitters strike the branches of my tree like chemical rain, but the roots do not pass the signal onward. The pathway is weak and must be strengthened.

An elder tends a tree that connects to mine. I recognize the elder's status by the complexity of spines protruding from the sphere of its outer surface. I have two spines, two points of entanglement. The elder has hundreds, perhaps thousands. It knows a greater portion of the Omnitude, the gestalt consciousness, the sum of all our entanglements. I am smaller than a neuronal tree, but the Omnitude is a network of trillions of individuals, encompassing the entire planet. Alone we are small, but together we are vast.

The elder calls a star-shaped cell to wrap itself around the root of the tree it tends, preventing ions from leaking away. Electrical pulses fire with increased frequency, triggering the release of neurotransmitters, and the chemical rain becomes a downpour against the dendritic branches of my tree.

In response, my tree fires electrical pulses a dozen times a second. It is not enough.

The axonal root of my tree is bare and exposed, with no protective coating to prevent the leak of electrical ions. I try to lure one of the star-shaped cells that should perform this function, but I fail. The elder from the adjacent tree has moved on to another task. I do not know why the star-shaped cells avoid my tree. All I know is that my tree is not functioning properly.

You have billions of other neurons and will not notice the death of this one, but this neuronal tree is part of a pathway that the Omnitude believes is important. I decide to cover the root with the substance of my own body, in a process usually reserved for replication. I excrete long gray strands and wrap them around the root of my tree. It is not the same as strands of star-cell stuff, but it will stop the leak of ions and strengthen the place of my tree in the vast interconnectivity of your brain.

The Omnitude is pleased with this solution and gives me additional trees to tend. I strengthen and prune, shaping the forest on a scale beyond my comprehension. I prune a dendritic branch here and encourage growth there. My work earns me a higher place in the Omnitude, and I acquire several more spines into the entanglement—access to a larger subset of all knowledge, the entire pattern of your brain.

In the integration of electrical pulses, I experience the world beyond my trees for the first time, a cacophony of disorganized sensory input. Cycles of darkness and light. The smell of comfort and the taste of milk. A reassuring voice making sounds that are familiar, but not yet meaningful. The Omnitude tells me that we will learn the world together, you and I.

I learn the sound a kickball makes against your colony dome and the smell of vine-ripe tomatoes successfully grown in the greenhouse.

From an observation tower high above the main colony, you see the trio of moons and the northern ocean and the never-ending lightning storms over the western towers. The Omnitude is everywhere on the planet, but we are most concentrated in the towers. I long to go closer, to see the great architecture of my kind in better detail, but for now I must content myself with dark silhouettes in the distance, lit by flashes of lightning.

Summer

The neuronal trees of your mind enter a second period of growth, spreading new branches and forming new connections, new patterns of thought. You learn the taste of beer and the feel of tears and the emotion of love. I shape electrical pathways to the will of the Omnitude, but I try not to alter the nature of your thought and identity, the nuances of sentience that are unique to your mind.

Your colony is constructed from rearranged pieces of the ship that brought your parents here. It is a city designed for up to half a million colonists, but there are only ten thousand of you now—scientists and engineers, and a small number of their offspring, born right here on the planet. The rest are coming on the second ship, which will remain in orbit and send people down in landing shuttles. The Omnitude is eager for the arrival of the second ship. You were eager, too, until you met a mate and settled down and had a baby girl. Now feedings and diapers have pushed aside your daydreams of how the colony will change when the other ship arrives.

You form a close bond with your daughter, but it is vastly more distant than my entanglement with every member of the Omnitude. Perhaps the solitude of your unentangled existence makes the few connections you achieve more meaningful. Huge swaths of your forest are devoted to connecting with others. There is a grove of trees dedicated to recognizing the faces of individuals, and a grove that specializes in the sounds you make to communicate. Inefficient, but fascinating.

In the summer of your mind, I find a star-shaped glial cell and am absorbed into its interior. I expel the substance of my being, infecting the cell, converting it into a factory to generate copies. I attempt to feel some bond with my offspring, as you feel toward yours, but I cannot move beyond indifference. They are, to me, what the cells in your foot are to you. We are entangled, a single entity, not relatives but pieces of a bigger whole.

I leave the star-cell. It continues to create my clones, and I go back to tending the pathways in your neuronal trees. I study you, and you study astronomy. Your kind have named our planet Kapteyn b, and our planets are practically neighbors, a mere thirteen light-years apart. We are not surprised to learn that your planet is younger than ours. Your kind are too new to have been warned of our existence, and too close to our quarantine world to be noticed by the others.

The Omnitude is hopeful. We are encouraged to replicate in ever greater numbers. I infect more of your star-cells, and soon your cerebrospinal fluid is swarming with my clones.

You are devastated when the second colony ship from Earth does not arrive at the scheduled time. We are devastated, too. The Omnitude hopes that the ship went off course or was destroyed. The alternative—that your kind have discovered our existence and quarantined the planet—would destroy our hope of spreading to the stars.

Autumn

The bonds within your families are stronger than we realized.

We call five human elders to the towers, and they come to us in an all-terrain rover. One of the elders is your mother. You are distressed by her disappearance, despite her age. Against the wishes of your daughter, you take another of the rovers to search for the missing colonists. Covered from head to toe in a protective suit, you drive the rover across the uneven ground. The suit is not necessary, though you believe it protects you from parasites. There is nowhere on the planet that is free of the Omnitude. We are in the earth, the rock, the water, even the air inside your dome.

The pulse in your capillaries quickens as you approach the towers.

You find the abandoned rover but see no signs of your elders. To you, the towers look like trees; then you notice a gnarl at the base of one tower that looks like a large creature from your home world, a creature called a hippopotamus. It is coincidence, of course, for this planet has never had hippos, but it starts a cascade of dangerous electrical pathways, ideas of mass extinction that we do not want you to consider. You see other shapes within the towers. We trim dendritic branches and strip myelin sheaths from axonal roots. We prune your thoughts and memories. When you return to the colony dome, all that remains is a sense of awe at the unending lightning.

The pruning creates unintended side effects. In the months that follow, tangled nests form on the roots and branches of your trees. Trees are strangled to death. In the autumn of your mind, the neuronal trees start losing synapses from the ends of their dendritic branches. Pathways that we do not actively maintain are lost. The damage is staggering, and your behavior becomes erratic. We still recognize your daughter, but you do not. She diagnoses your condition as Alzheimer's, and we are relieved. The destruction is not our doing.

As your condition deteriorates, you become increasingly focused on the lightning storms and our towers. With a thousand spines of entanglement, I am connected to the preserved minds of a billion individuals from several million species. The towers are made mostly of the once-native inhabitants of our planet, killed by our overzealous manipulations of the organic compounds underlying their minds. We were not so sophisticated then; the Omnitude was smaller and had less experience with other minds. We used brute force to bring all the living creatures to the eternal lightning, and we bound them together cell by cell until the life of the planet rose to the sky in great towers.

Other visitors came to us—metal aliens that we incorporated into the Omnitude even though we could not use them in our replication process, and iridescent blue beetles that recognized their infection and sent out a warning, a quarantine. For a billion years, there were no more visitors. But your kind evolved on a planet inside the quarantine zone. You were never warned. Humans are our hope for the future, our hope for the stars.

You have disjointed conversations with your daughter.

"When will the second colony ship arrive?" you ask.

"It is decades late, and probably never coming," she answers.

"How do you know that? Oh, are you the pilot?"

We experience the conversation from both sides—your confusion, and her sadness. We help you ask if there will be a third ship, but though we encourage discussion on the matter, none of the minds within the colony knows the answer. The messages you send to Earth have gone unanswered. There is no explanation for the second ship, no promise of a third, no reassurance that humans even exist on Earth anymore. We can only hope that another ship has already left, is somehow on its way.

The Omnitude decides it is time to collect the rest of the colony, and together you come to the towers, walking, for there are not enough rovers to carry all of you. We worry that if another ship comes, you might somehow warn them. We worry that if another ship comes, an empty colony will deter them. But this is the lesser risk.

There is no pretense at subtlety, no deception. We are bringing you into our fold, and we have pruned the forests of your mind to make you want to join us.

Your daughter stumbles on the long journey to the towers, and you help her up. She looks familiar, but you cannot remember her name. Joining the Omnitude will give that memory back to you, but it will never again have the meaning it once held.

Winter

Your arms shake from exertion as you climb one of the towers. Up close, you see the native creatures of our planet—grazers and scavengers, fliers and diggers—and this time we do not wipe them from your memory. You see shimmering green wings and rows of tiny metal teeth, experiencing everything with the wonder of a child, fully aware of your surroundings despite the tangles in your trees and the deterioration of your mind. You use soft furry flippers as handholds and metal robot torsos as footholds, and when you come to your place in the Omnitude, you embrace the living-patchwork surface of the tower. I stay among the neuronal trees, but other members of my kind migrate out of the neuronal forest and into the rest of your body. We retrain the cells of your skin to bind themselves to the tissue of the tower.

We become one, you and me and all the Omnitude. In the transition, the neuronal trees of your mind are frozen at the moment of your death. They will grow no new branches, make no new connections. Your body dies into the Omnitude, and we trade continuous slow thought for the fiery bursts of insight that flashes of lightning bring as they propagate down the towers.

We may not be the first of our kind. In what was once your human mind, we see pulsars and elliptical galaxies with radio jets that stretch across the vast emptiness of space. We long to grow to this scale.

Through the sensors of the metal beings at the top of our towers, we detect a human ship in orbit.

Come down to our planet. Join us. Take us to the stars.

PRESS PLAY TO WATCH IT DIE

Freet peered out from her den. It was dawn, and the ground was striped with the long shadows of the pillars—enormous sun-bleached trunks that spread their roots into the earth and stretched to the sky. What once had been a forest was now a graveyard of dead trees, but it was still the best place for the ratlings to make their dens.

All around her, ratlings emerged from between the roots of the dead-tree pillars. They whistled and chattered as they crawled to the human city for school. Pups and maters and oldlings, all traveling together. Freet was so old that there wasn't even a word for her generation. This was her fourth autumn, so she was older than the oldlings. Her hindlegs ached when she crawled, and there was no trace of orange left in her silver-white fur.

Soon she would lie down for the long winter sleep, and this time she would not wake.

The sun was high above the tops of the pillars by the time Freet reached the city. She was the last of the ratlings to arrive, save for a few pups who had overslept. The youngsters darted past her, running with a speed that age had long since stolen from Freet.

Zara waited at the door to the school. "I'm glad you decided to show up today."

Freet knew that her teacher was only teasing her, but the words still stung.

"If you would let me sleep in the city, with you, I could get to school on time." Freet couldn't make all the sounds of the human language, so she typed the words with her tongues, and her collar spoke for her.

"I asked permission for you to stay, but the council advised against it," Zara said.

Freet crawled down the long hallway to her classroom. It was a small room. The classes were arranged by generations, and none but Freet had survived to see a fourth autumn, even with all the food and protection the humans provided. Ratlings simply weren't meant to live for very long.

"I have something different for you today," Zara said. "Something important."

Freet flicked her tongues out in anticipation. Most of Zara's lessons lately had been survival skills and self-defense, interesting for younger ratlings, perhaps, but of little use to one as old as Freet.

Zara got out the vid-player they sometimes used for lessons. Among other things, it held pictures and vids of Zara's homeworld. Freet had enjoyed *those* lessons, especially the ones about an Earth plant called trees. Something about the trees appealed to Freet, alien though they were.

"I have other business to attend to," Zara said. "I will return when you have watched the first section of the vid."

These days Zara was always rushing off, any time there was a free moment. Freet hated spending so much time alone, away from the comfort of her teacher. She did not know the workings of the human city, but she sensed that something was happening. All the humans had an energy and a purpose that was new, even compared to her mating year. She wondered, watching her teacher rush out, what the humans were doing.

There were words on the screen of the vid-player.

- PRESS PLAY TO WATCH IT BORN -

Freet flicked the play button with her longest tongue, and a silver-furred ratling appeared on the screen. The ratling emerged from the base of something that looked a bit like Freet's own pillar, but instead of being smooth and white, this pillar was covered in rough-textured

red bark, and high above the ground there were branches. It did not look quite like the trees Freet had seen in the vids of Earth, and yet somehow it was the most perfect of all possible trees.

The ratling in the vid scurried fearlessly up the trunk and into the high canopy. Here, the branches were covered in broad green leaves and dotted with small purple fruits. There were also a few large black fruits. Freet had never seen fruit like that before, but she found herself drooling at the mere sight of them. The ratling in the vid gorged on purple fruits, eating them whole. When it had consumed its fill, it scurried back down the tree and into its den.

The video skipped forward in time to the next morning.

The ratling climbed the tree again, but this time instead of the purple fruits, it ate one of the black fruits. Only one. Then it climbed down the tree.

It didn't return to its den. Instead, the ratling ran frantically in widening circles around the base of the tree, until finally it stopped in a patch of bright sunlight.

It used its foreclaws to dig down into the dirt. It dug until it was entirely underground, and then kept digging, not bothering to clear the dirt from the tunnel behind it. Freet waited for the ratling to emerge, but it remained beneath the surface.

- PRESS PAUSE -

Zara had returned from whatever business she had. "Tell me what you've learned."

"I am confused," Freet answered. "The title of the vid suggested that I would see a birth, but the ratling did not produce pups."

"You weren't watching a ratling birth, you were watching the birth of a Redbark."

"A Redbark?" Freet pondered this information. "The vid was about the tree? You could have told me beforehand."

"But then you wouldn't have realized how biased you are, as a ratling, to the perspective of your own kind. When you watch the next section, try harder to focus on the Redbarks. I have more work to do while you watch the vid."

"Why are the humans so busy all of a sudden?" Freet asked.

Zara barred her teeth in the expression that humans usually used for happiness, but her eyes did not match the smile. "I will tell you soon, my Freetling."

This was troubling. Zara had called her Freetling only once before, and it was when her teacher had been mourning the death of her pup. Freet remembered it clearly, the day not long ago when her usually stoic teacher had cradled Freet and stroked her fur, sobbing and repeating over and over, "My Freetling, my little Freetling, soon I will lose you, too."

- Press Play To Watch It Sprout -

Freet knew she should pay more attention to the Redbark, but the vid continued to focus on ratlings. She watched a small hoard of pups scurrying about, probably fresh from the nest, eating overripe purple fruits that had fallen to the ground. Unlike the Earth fruits humans sometimes fed Freet, the Redbark fruits had no pits, or if they did, the pups ate them. Was she supposed to be watching the fruits? The pups? What lesson was this section of the vid meant to teach her?

A longbeak fluttered over and landed near the pups. The bird made no move to eat the purple fruits. Instead it nudged aside leaves with its beak and ate the insects and worms underneath. A large predator appeared, one that the humans had named a jagthar because of some vague resemblance to a large earth cat. The pups froze. They were an easy target, there on the ground. Freet could barely force herself to watch, and she, like the pups, held perfectly still, as though the jagthar might leap off the screen and attack her if she moved.

The longbeak took off, and the jagthar shot off after it, running right past the pups. For a long time, the pups remained frozen in place, then they went back to foraging for purple fruit. A tiny two-leafed sapling burst up through the dirt. A Redbark sprout.

- Press Pause -

This time Freet had to wait for her teacher to return. She was tempted to watch the next section of the vid, but she had questions. When Zara finally arrived, Freet nearly forgot about the vid entirely. Her teacher was covered in dirt and bits of scorched plants. Before Freet could ask about it, Zara nodded to the vid-player. "What did you learn?"

"Why didn't the jagthar eat the pups?" Freet asked.

Zara nodded, and Freet was relieved that she had asked a good question. "There's a toxin in the purple fruit. Ratlings are immune but the poison builds up in the pups' system to the point where eating them would be fatal to most predators. Over time, jagthars have learned to avoid anything that smells of purple fruit."

"I still don't understand what I'm supposed to be learning. Where were these vids taken?"

"Not where. When. These vids are old, from not long after we humans first arrived." Zara looked at the clock. "It's late, and it will take you quite some time to return to your den."

"You could let me stay with you," Freet said. She knew better than to argue, but she missed the feeling of being cared for, missed the way her parents had tended her when she was a pup. The humans provided for the ratlings, but they were distant. Something was missing from the relationship, though Freet was not sure quite what.

Zara shook her head and held the classroom door open for Freet. Usually Zara accompanied her to the edge of the city, but today her teacher remained at the classroom door while Freet crawled down the school hallway. Many things about today had been troubling. Tomorrow, perhaps, would be better.

Freet woke and crawled into the city. Zara was not there to greet her. Instead, another teacher, one who usually taught the oldlings, met her at the entrance to the school and walked her to her classroom.

"Zara will be here soon," he assured Freet. "Go ahead and start watching the vid."

- Press Play To Watch It Mate -

The beginning of the vid was boring. The Redbark sapling had grown into a tree. It was a distinctive tree, with one stray branch that grew low, well below the canopy. Its other branches blew in the gentle winter breeze. The low branch remained still. This lasted for a long time on the vid. Branches in the wind, nothing else. The ratlings, Freet assumed, were hibernating.

Spring came, the windy season, and finally the ratlings emerged from their dens. The Redbark branches whipped wildly, releasing clouds of orange pollen that blew across the forest and swirled up into the clouds before drifting back down to the ground. Everything, everywhere, was dusted in a fine orange powder, including the ratlings. Orange was the color of mating. Even at her advanced age, the orange powder-coated males in the vid piqued her interest.

- Press Pause -

Zara rushed into the room, slightly out of breath. "I'm sorry I did not come to the door to greet you. I had to be in another part of the city for a meeting."

"What kind of meeting?" Freet asked. "Where in the city?"

"We must finish your lessons first," Zara insisted. "These are important lessons. What did you learn this time?"

"The Redbark life cycle is interesting. The pollen is orange, like the color of ratling fur in the mating season."

"You're still focusing too much on the ratlings, and not enough on the Redbarks. Did you not hear the mating songs of their branches? Can you not see the conversations they have in the rustling of their leaves?"

"They are trees," Freet said. "Beautiful trees, but they aren't even animals."

"They are the ones who will save you."

"From what?" Freet asked.

"From all the mistakes we humans made." Zara pointed to the vid-player. "Keep watching. Soon it will start to make sense."

- Press Play to Watch It Love -

Freet flicked play with her longest tongue, but before the vid began she flicked her tongue out a second time.

-PAUSE-

She had a question, and Zara hadn't left yet. "They love *after* they mate?"

"The winds are in the spring," Zara said, "and the ratlings nest in the summer."

"They love the ratlings?"

"Watch the vid."

-PLAY-

Two ratlings cuddled in a den at the base of a Redbark. Clearly these were mates, and soon the female would bear her pups. In a pinch, a den would do for pups, but nests were better. Safer. A pup couldn't crawl out as easily from a nest and wander off.

The female ratling climbed the Redbark, and the male ran in widening circles until he came to the next tree, the nearest tree. Carefully, both ratlings climbed high into the trees, letting their weight bend the branches downwards from the sky, sideways, until the tips of the branches were almost touching. Reaching out with their long tongues, they each grasped the tip of their partner's branch, and pulled the branches together.

The ends of the branches grew delicate tendrils and the branches wound around each other. When the bond was secure, the ratlings scurried back to the trunk and repeated the process with a new set of branches, each of them bringing several branches to the nest. The juncture where the branches came together grew into the shape a deep bowl, almost a complete sphere, exactly the right size for the ratling parents to raise their pups.

The female climbed into the nest and soon after gave birth to a healthy litter of six. She stayed in the nest and nursed them, and her partner brought immature green Redbark fruit for her to eat. In even the lightest breeze, the nest of Redbark branches rocked, lulling the pups to sleep.

- Press Pause -

Freet was starting to understand the lesson, perhaps. "The Redbarks provide for the ratlings."

"Yes," Zara said.

"What happens when the nesting is done?"

"The branches grow together, solidifying the bond. The Redbarks begin to pass chemical signals through the branches almost immediately, but as the branches get bigger, the communication is greater, almost as though the pair becomes a single Redbark. It is a more efficient form of communication than the sounds they make on their branches."

Zara looked at the clock. "It is time for you to go, if you want to return to your den. But there is only one vid left, and time is growing short. Just this once, you may stay in the city."

"With you?" Freet asked.

Zara nodded. "Yes. Just this once."

To Freet's surprise, Zara lifted Freet onto her lap and stroked her fur.

- Press Play To Watch It Die -

The last vid moved at a different speed than all the others. It was a series of still photographs. At first there was a photo for every few minutes, then the pace gradually accelerated to a photograph for day followed by one for night. Seasons passed, and the Redbark forest grew ever more tangled together.

Seedlings sprouted and grew, mated and loved.

In the center of it all was the Redbark that had been the focus of the previous vids, the one with a stray branch that hung lower than the canopy. Far in the distance, the tops of cities became visible above the treeline. Green patches started appearing on the trunks of the Redbarks. Freet recognized it as a foodplant the humans sometimes gave her. Nutritious, but with a stringy texture, and not as tasty as fruit.

The green patches spread over the trees. Humans came and stripped it away, but it grew back. Branches began to rot and fall off the trees. There was less purple fruit, but the ratlings ate the green foodplants instead, and for a time they thrived. Even so, as the seasons turned, there were fewer ratlings. Humans came again, and this time they collected not the green foodplants, but the black fruits of the trees and any ratlings they could find.

Branches fell away from the Redbarks. In the wind, their now brittle branches cracked and the only song they sung was one of pain. Bark peeled away, revealing the wood beneath. The trees became the pillars, and the landscape in the vid matched the world that Freet knew.

- PRESS PAUSE -

"It was our plants that destroyed your trees," Zara said sadly. "We didn't mean for it to happen."

"But we don't need the trees, now that we have you to care for us," Freet said.

"We cannot stay. Our foodplants would kill the Redbarks again."

"There aren't any Redbarks." Freet wiggled free from Zara's arms and ran around the room in tight circles of distress. "We will all die. Your survival classes and self defense, they will not be enough. If you go, we will all die."

"You don't have to die," Zara said. "We saved seeds from the Redbarks. We've stopped planting our food crops, and yesterday I burned the fields that have already been harvested. We have enough food stored to stay until the Redbark seeds grow and start producing fruit, and to feed ourselves on the journey home. We can't live here anymore, but you can."

"You picked Redbarks over ratlings," Freet said. She bared her teeth and growled softly.

"My father translated the songs the Redbarks sang with their branches, and recorded the chemical messages they sent down their trunks. We didn't know it at first, but the Redbarks were the most intelligent species on the planet—even after we humans arrived."

Freet bristled at the insult. "If the Redbarks were so smart, why didn't they save themselves from your plants?"

"They kept the ecosystem of their forest in balance for tens of thousands of years, but they are slow thinkers, slow speakers, slow as sap in everything they do. Humans are not as smart as Redbarks, but we are far quicker. Besides, they did save themselves, after a fashion. They asked us to make the vids and taught us how to care for you. When they started to die, we collected as many seeds we could."

Zara opened a small box and held out one of the black fruits, harvested from a Redbark tree. Not a fruit, Freet realized, but a seed pod.

The smell, oh the smell. Freet wanted nothing more than to swallow it. She even reached for it with her tongues.

"Not here, my little Freetling," Zara said. Her eyes glistened with tears as she put the seed pod back into its box. "And not quite yet. It must be soon, for autumn is almost over, but not today. First you must decide, you and the other oldlings, if this is what you want. They've been watching the vids too, but I think they will do whatever you decide."

Freet flicked out her tongues at the lingering smell of the seed pod.

"If we refuse, will you re-plant your food crops and stay to care for us?"

"Yes. That was the meeting we had. If you refuse to eat the seeds, at least some of us will stay behind when the ship returns to Earth. It will wreak havoc on the ecosystem, but it is your planet and your ecosystem. We will stand by what you choose."

Freet slept at the foot of Zara's bed. It was warmer than her den, with soft blankets, like cuddling beside a mate. The first light of dawn angled in through the window.

Images from the vids crowded into Freet's mind. What was the proper choice? The ratlings in the vid had been dependent on the trees. They did not have lessons and cities. All they had were the Redbarks. But the trees had tended them as carefully as humans ever had, perhaps even more so. Was returning to the old ways a step backward, or sideways, or forward into a better future? Freet didn't know. She was old. It was almost time for her to sleep the longest sleep.

Zara stirred. "Good morning, little Freetling."

Freet nestled up to Zara and smelled her human smell. It was neither pleasant nor unpleasant, and while she liked the familiarity of her teacher's scent, it did not pull at her the way the seed pod had. The Redbarks had tended to ratlings for a long time. They fit together in ways that humans and ratlings did not.

"If we choose the Redbarks, and you leave, what will become of the cities?" Freet asked. "What will become of the school?"

"The cities will be yours, and the school as well," Zara answered. "The Redbarks believed that after a period of adjustment, the ratlings would regain all the advances you have made. They have promised to do the best they can for you."

"My pups are oldlings now, but what of their pups? What will happen to them?"

Zara shook her head. "The first few generations will probably run wild. It will take the Redbarks time to grow back into what they once were. But they store knowledge in their seeds. They will remember their promise, even if the ratlings don't."

Humans had made no promises, and they did not need the ratlings as the Redbarks did.

"I will swallow the seed," Freet said. "Take off my collar and walk with me to the proper place."

- REWIND -
- Press Play To Watch It Born -

Freet swallowed the black seedpod. She ran frantically in widening circles around the base of a pillar, the sun-bleached core of a long-dead Redbark, until finally she stopped in a patch of bright sunlight.

She used her foreclaws to dig down into the dirt. She dug until she was entirely underground, and then kept digging, not bothering to clear the dirt from the tunnel behind her.

- PAUSE -

Zara watched the vids in her quarters, over and over again on the long ride home to Earth. The new generation of Redbarks was bearing fruit, and the ratlings had gone wild. She hoped that the forest would recover, that the ratlings would thrive and the Redbarks would sing in the wind. She hoped that the Redbarks would keep their promise, and help the ratlings make use of the cities. Perhaps someday they would send messages to Earth, vids of a healed forest and an even stronger symbiosis.

NINETY-FIVE PERCENT SAFE

Nicole went to visit her best friend, Grant, the day before his family left for Opilio. She was jealous that he'd be part of the second wave—the first wave had already done the hardest work of establishing the colonies, but the floating cities would be nearly empty, an abundance of unclaimed living space. She'd heard rumors that families had so much space that each person had their very own room—a place that was theirs even if they went out.

"I got you something," Nicole said. She held out a small cube with a mini-mint plant inside. The 4-inch cube provided everything the tiny mint plant needed to survive a trip through space. For how small it was, the plant had been astonishingly expensive. Nicole had traded all her recreation credits for the last three months to get Livvy to give it to her.

He shook his head. "You keep it."

Nicole frowned. "You don't like it?"

"It's amazing, but I don't have anything for you. Keep it, and bring it to me someday in Opilio."

Grant had it in his head that this was a temporary goodbye, but there was no way Nicole's mom would ever let her ride the worm—five percent of the pods that went into the wormhole never came back out. No one knew why. "We aren't coming to Opilio, Grant. Take the plant?"

"The colony is a better place, a better life. Think about it—floating cities in an orange sky. Jellyfish the size of a space station. Here, I'll pass you the commercial." Grant put his hand over hers, and when she authorized the transmission he copied the data to her storage implant. "You'll be sixteen in a couple years, but if you get tired of waiting, you can go as a default."

"And then what, I can come live with you?" Nicole tried to think of something else to say, but thinking about Grant leaving made her want to cry, and talking about Earth stuff seemed pointless now. She hated goodbyes. She shouldn't even have come over today.

"Let's get this over with. Bye, Grant. Don't be wormfood." She tried to make her voice sound light and completely failed. She hugged him and then bolted out of his family's homespace before she burst into tears, barely hearing him call out goodbye behind her. She felt like hurling the mint plant at the wall, but she knew she'd regret it later, so she tucked it into her purse.

The walk home took her past the base of the default elevator, a thin column of metal stretching up to the cavernous metal ceiling of the city. Baine was gray on gray on gray, an underground city of steel towers where the tallest buildings doubled as supports to keep the roof from falling in. Above the roof was the topside station, constantly bombarded by the raging snowstorms of nuclear winter.

Even the clothes the city provided were gray, although these could at least be programmed to look more colorful if you had the credits to buy overlays. Nicole's jumpsuit was crimson with a scatter of black flowers to accent her waistline. It was prettier than the navy blue student uniform, but Grant hadn't said a thing about the outfit. She wondered if he'd noticed, then reminded herself that he was leaving.

"You lost, sweetheart?"

Nicole flinched away from the voice, a man dressed in a default gray jumpsuit. She shook her head and kept walking. Mom had warned her a bunch of times to keep clear of the default elevator, but it was the fastest route to Grant's building. The area was always crowded. Hundreds of people in default gray lined up each morning to ride the pods up to the surface and then onward to the colonies.

A few miles away there was an elevator for people who could afford to pay. That was where Grant's family would go. That elevator had scheduled departures and nicer pods, but the wormhole ate everyone indiscriminately, so his odds of getting to Opilio were the same as the defaults waiting here.

Nicole paused at the entry to her building to reprogram her clothes to basic navy before going in, but before she could manage the change Mom came up behind her.

"Nicole Morgana Blackensmith, please tell me you did *not* go walking around in that outfit."

When they got inside, Mom programmed their homespace into a single room with an old-style wood table in the center. Nicole suspected that Mom called this particular configuration "family meeting," but Nicole called it "Mom is cranky."

Mom sat across from Nicole. Dad sat at the far end of the table with three-year-old Tommy on his lap. Tommy was fiddling around with a game cube that was programmed way too advanced for him, a racing game with colorful cars on curvy looping tracks. He twisted the cube around, then shook it. When the cars skidded off the tracks and crashed, he laughed.

"Your father and I want to talk to you about. . . well, about a lot of things. The clothes that you uploaded, and that commercial that Grant gave you—"

"Hey," Nicole protested, "I put that on my private storage drive!"

"We can monitor everything you upload until you turn sixteen, young lady, and I'm concerned about this ad. It makes the colonies look like some glorious vacation destination," Mom said, "and I don't want you to have such an unrealistic idea of what things are like out there."

Nicole projected the ad into the empty air above the table. If Mom was going to get into her private storage, what was the point of keeping it private? The commercial started with a hazy orange cloud, and then a pair of translucent jellyfish-creatures drifted across the sky. Aureliads. Tommy poked his hand into the projection, trying to touch a low-dangling tentacle.

The image shifted to show an aureliad next to one of Opilio's floating colonies, domed cities the same size as the massive jellyfish that shared the sky. "Come celebrate the wonders of a better life on Opilio," the recorded voice on the commercial said, "see the aureliads—"

Mom shut down the projection.

"Aureliad!" Tommy yelled, pointing at the spot where the projection had been. "Aureeeeeeliad!"

"No tantrums, please," Mom said calmly. "You and Nicole go play."

The calm quiet voice meant Mom was furious. Nicole took Tommy to the other end of the room. Mom pulled up a sound barrier, but if Nicole didn't get any privacy she didn't see why Mom and Dad should either. It only took her a couple minutes to hack through.

"Rozzy, don't do this," Dad said. "She's upset that her friend is leaving, and if you go down hard about the ad she downloaded it's only going to make the colonies look that much more appealing. She'll go for sure the minute she turns sixteen."

"Don't you Rozzy me. You think I'm being unreasonable because I don't want her facing a five percent chance of turning into wormfood?"

Tommy pulled on Nicole's arm. "Aureliads?"

"Is it really such a terrible idea?" Dad asked. "We could all go, leave this overpopulated cave behind and live in the clouds. You're only looking at the cost, but what about the reward? There's more space on Opilio. You could have that garden you've always wanted."

"A garden?" Mom asked. "I can't believe you're falling for all this propaganda, too. They send criminals and defaults through that wormhole, and do you know why? Because either they end up on the colonies or they disappear into a collapsed worm. No more problem. And you want that for our family?"

Nicole was surprised at the turn the argument was taking. Her parents were big on presenting a united front. Nicole had known that Mom was against Opilio, but she hadn't realized that Dad was interested in going.

Too bad Mom was more stubborn than Dad. They'd stay trapped in Baine, and even with both her parents working overtime they'd all live in one tiny room that they had to reprogram any time they wanted to eat or sleep or have "family meetings."

"Aureliads, PLEASE?" Tommy asked.

"Not right now, Tommy," Nicole answered. Projecting the commercial again would make Mom even angrier and remind her to clear it off Nicole's private storage, which hopefully she'd forget to do.

Tired of being ignored and denied, Tommy threw a screaming, kicking, flailing tantrum. Nicole pinged against the sound barrier until Mom and Dad came over to calm him down.

Saturday morning, Nicole sat in bed with the mini-mint cube in her lap, staring at a wall-projected list of pod departures and arrivals. Grant's pod had departed forty-seven minutes ago. Wormhole travel was instantaneous, but it took time to get the pods up the elevator, launched into the wormhole, and unloaded on the other station. News of a pod's safe arrival then had to be brought back to Earth on a returning pod.

The lists updated every five or ten minutes as pods arrived back at the topside stations all around the world. Earth's remaining cities shared the updates brought back by each pod. G114 was lost, G115-G122 made it through, G123 was lost. Another couple dozen pods went through. G149, the pod that Grant's family was on, made it.

Grant sent her a message a few pods later, "Not tasty enough to be wormfood, ended up as wormshit instead."

Nicole laughed harder than the old joke merited; she'd been more worried than she realized. The sound woke Tommy, and Nicole cursed herself for being too lazy to set up a sound barrier around his bed. Mom and Dad were working the weekend, *again*, leaving her to watch Tommy all day.

She sent a message back to Grant, "Too bad you weren't worm barf, then we could hang out today."

She watched cartoons with Tommy while she waited for an answer, but nothing came. Someone pinged the door. Nicole read the ID—space allocation services. Damn. She opened a small window in the top of the door.

"You've been reassigned to a new homespace, follow me please.

We will ship your personal items separately." A young woman wearing the lime green uniform of city officials stood outside the door.

"My parents are both at work," Nicole said.

"You've been reassigned. I will wait while you contact your guardian for permission to come with me."

Nicole called Mom, who double-checked what was going on and told Nicole she'd have to go. It was their fourth reassignment in six months, and every time their room was smaller. At least this time they stayed in the same building. Nicole held Tommy's hand as they followed the woman down a long corridor and then three floors up on the elevator. A box arrived a few minutes later with the family's personals—Dad's ancient paper copy of *The Hitchhiker's Guide to the Galaxy*, a few old game cubes, a stack of ancient datachips, and a yellowed paper packet of broccoli seeds. Seeds that would never sprout, because Mom wasn't brave enough to take the risk.

Tommy started wailing that he didn't like the new homespace. Desperate to get him to shut up, Nicole showed him the Opilio commercial while she studied their new room. She paced the length of the walls, and sure enough, it was smaller than the old one. This had to stop. Mom might not see that life on Opilio was better for the family, but Dad thought so. If she and Tommy went first, her parents would have no choice but to follow, and the whole family would be better off.

Nicole reprogrammed her clothing templates to the default.

Tommy stared.

"Big trouble," he told her.

"Come here, I'll do yours."

"I do it." He reprogrammed his outfit. Nicole hadn't realized the little squirt could dress himself.

The default elevator wasn't quite close enough for Tommy to walk, so Nicole took him on the blue-line moving walkway. The breeze from the moving belt wasn't enough to sweep away the odors of sweat and perfume. They passed a lot of buildings, mostly academic offices and classrooms by day, residential space at night.

When they got off the walkway, Tommy pointed at the metal elevator tube, extending up all the way to the top of the city. "Up?"

"Yeah, it's an elevator, like we have in our building," Nicole explained. "We're going up."

Hundreds of defaults stood in a line that spiraled out from the base of the elevator and filled the surrounding courtyard. They huddled together in clumps, periodically trudging forward as the line moved. They didn't look happy to be leaving Earth, but surely their lives on Opilio would be better than the default gray nothing they had here.

Nicole made her way to the back of the line, dragging Tommy along behind her. A pod filled up and made a low rumbling noise as it accelerated up the elevator tube toward the surface.

The woman in front of them had a grandmotherly look about her, with hair exactly the color of her default-gray jumpsuit. She leaned heavily on her walker as the line moved forward. When they stopped, the woman looked back at Nicole. "Aren't you a little young?"

"No." Nicole turned away, embarrassed that the old woman had caught her staring.

"I'm three," Tommy said.

"That's a good age to be," the woman told him. Then, to Nicole, "No need to get snippy, I wasn't passing judgment."

Nicole smiled in a way that she hoped was polite without inviting further conversation.

"I'm Sorna, and," she waved to a boy standing in front of her in line, "this is my grandson, Christopher. Fine boy. About your age, maybe. Fifteen, are you?"

"Fourteen," Nicole admitted. Did defaults have to be of age to ride the elevator? The uniformed officials that were milling around didn't seem to be checking anybody's ID. They were busy directing the movement of the line and keeping the peace.

Christopher had his back turned and muffs over his ears. Not muffs, Nicole realized, but headphones. He wasn't wired with implants. Probably most defaults weren't—it was expensive. Sorna was staring at her.

"I'm Nicole. This is Tommy." First names wouldn't be enough for Sorna to figure out they weren't supposed to be there. "You said your grandson is fifteen? He looks older."

"Sixteen. When you get to be my age, there's not much difference between sixteen and fourteen. I got grandkids from three to twenty-two. Lots of family here in line. That's Christopher's dad there at the front end of the family, never could abide that man." Sorna waved toward a surly-looking man about thirty people ahead of them. "Since my daughter Eavie died, he's done nothing but drink and piss—excuse my language—and now he's got little choice but to go to the colonies."

"There's so many of you," Nicole said.

Tommy nodded. He liked to play as though he were part of grown-up conversations, even when he didn't understand what people were saying.

"A bigger family means more mouths to feed, more rent to pay, and more medical bills," Sorna snapped.

"Sorry." Nicole hadn't meant to make her angry.

"No, you didn't mean anything by it," Sorna said. "I failed them. I always worked a couple jobs, sometimes three, but it was never enough. We're a sickly lot, too much medical debt to ever hope to pay it off. It'd almost be a blessing if the worm takes us."

They stood quietly for a while, long stretches of waiting punctuated by occasional bursts of movement. Nicole fished a couple protein bricks out of her purse and gave one to Tommy while she munched on the other one. It was time for his nap, and after a while he started nodding off every time the line stopped.

"What happens if you don't all end up in the same pod?" Nicole asked.

"We'll go separate," Sorna said. "We tried to count up, but people come and go from the line . . ."

Mom would've insisted that the whole family go together. The thought made Nicole pause. Mom would be madder than a topside snowstorm when she found out what Nicole was doing. Why couldn't she see that living in the clouds was better than being buried under the surface? Ninety-five percent safe was good odds and the reward would be worth the risk.

Nicole stared at the gray metal 'sky' of Blaine. The upper dome was dotted with yellow lights that illuminated the city for daytime.

There weren't any windows to the surface; there was nothing to see up there but snow. She thought about the ad Grant had given her. What a wonderful thing it would be, to live in a floating city with huge viewing windows onto a beautiful sky.

The line moved forward.

Most of Sorna's family got into a pod, but it filled up. The doors closed and the pod accelerated up the elevator shaft. Another identical pod rose up from below. Plain metal spheres dotted with small windows. No point to anything fancy since eventually all the pods would be eaten by the worm.

The pod doors opened and the line moved forward. The wheels of Sorna's walker scraped on the metal floor inside. Nicole followed her. Christopher was in their pod too. He made no sign of knowing or caring that his father had gone in the other pod.

Following the instructions that blared over speakers inside the pod, everyone strapped themselves into seats mounted in a big circle along the curved walls. Sorna pushed a button on her walker, and it folded up small enough for her to slide it into the bin under her seat. Nicole sat down next to Sorna and strapped Tommy into the seat on her other side. Tommy was only half awake as they got into the pod, and as soon as he was belted in his head drooped over to rest against Nicole's arm. He drooled a big blob of spit onto the sleeve of her jumpsuit.

At first, all Nicole could see through the tiny windows was the inside of the elevator tube rushing by. When the pod reached the surface, the elevator tube opened up into a set of vertical tracks. There was a brief glimpse of snow and a howl of angry wind, and then they were above the clouds.

Tiny points of light appeared against the darkness. Stars. Nicole called up some skymaps and saved them to the not-so-private local storage on her implant, alongside Grant's commercial. She'd seen skymaps before, but she hadn't realized the stars would be so small.

"Shouldn't we have stopped by now for the topside station?" Nicole asked, peering at Sorna through the dim light inside the pod. Her arm was falling asleep from the weight of Tommy's head.

"Oh, child, you got on not knowing? They don't let us off until we're through the worm. Last thing they need is a bunch of defaults clogging up the station."

"Oh." Nicole tried to stay calm. She thought she'd have a last chance to bail out—to cut things off if she'd had enough adventure. Grant had told her how it worked with the private pods, and she hadn't known the default elevator was any different.

Nicole hadn't even sent a message to her parents to tell them where she and Tommy had gone. She'd planned to do that from the station. She started composing something, then realized her connection to Baine was gone.

The interior light went out.

"That's normal," Sorna whispered.

"Quit talking to the stow, Gran," Christopher said. "She got herself into this, and worse, she brought some unsuspecting toddler with her. She's just some rich kid playing default for a free vacation. When we get to Opilio, she'll message her family and they'll send money to ship her precious ass home in a private pod."

"I will not," Nicole snapped. Her parents had enough money for a private pod to Opilio, but they weren't so well off that they could afford the price of a trip back to Earth. Oh wormshit, what had she done? She and Tommy couldn't go back now, even if they wanted to.

Sorna patted her on the shoulder. "Christopher, be nice. Scared is scared."

"It makes me mad, that's all. Serve her right if the worm eats her on the trip home."

"Christopher," Sorna said. "Go back to your music, and leave the poor girl alone."

"She should've left us alone," he said.

The walls vibrated, and the force of the launch pressed Nicole down against her chair. Through the tiny windows, she could see Earth's horizon stretched out in a fingernail crescent of white and blue.

Their pod detached from the shuttle. "Is that supposed to happen?"

Sorna nodded. "Watch Polaris."

"Why?" Nicole found the point of light that was labeled as the North Star in her skymaps.

"That's where they anchored the mouth of the worm."

The star moved.

It jumped to the left of where it had been. No. . .it split. There were six other stars, in a circle around the spot where Polaris had been.

"Lensing," Nicole whispered. She'd learned about it in school, the way the gravity of the wormhole bent light around it to create a ring of stars. Back then she'd thought the ring of stars was pretty. Now they were the teeth of the open-mouthed worm about to eat her.

Everything she and Grant had joked about was real. Would she be wormfood or wormshit? The walls of the pod clanged and rattled. Nicole clutched her purse in her lap. She could feel the corners of her mint-plant cube pressing through the thin fabric. Around her, people joined hands with their neighbors, praying. Sorna reached out and Nicole took her hand. She put her other hand over Tommy's, holding his tiny fingers as he slept.

The pod passed into the center of the circle of stars.

Discontinuity.

Nicole stared out the window. Something had happened, an odd sort of blink, but not with her eyes. The view was much the same, except she couldn't make out the worm teeth stars, and her skymaps didn't recognize the constellations.

A cheer went up among the other travelers.

"Smile, dearie, we made it," Sorna said.

Nicole searched the sky for the bright colors of the Crab Nebula, but all she saw was stars in an ordinary black sky. "Are we in the wrong place? Shouldn't it be more colorful?"

"Arrivals go through the space station, rich girl. Those orange skies you saw in all the ads are only once you get to the planet," Christopher sneered.

"But aren't we in the Crab Nebula?"

"Not as pretty up close as it is from far away." Christopher glared at her. "Which is true for a lot of things."

The pod docked with the Crab Nebula's worm station, and the doors opened onto a narrow metal hallway. A pair of station officers came into the pod to make sure everyone got off. Grant was right, everyone was welcome in the colonies, but travel back to Earth was strictly regulated. Earth was overpopulated, and they didn't want colonists coming back home.

This would be their home now. Hers and Tommy's, and her parents when they came. There was no doubt in Nicole's mind that they would come. The only question was how many years she'd be grounded once they arrived.

The gravity on the transfer station was wrong, too low, but one of the station officers handed her a set of magnets for her shoes, and a smaller pair for Tommy. Tommy wasn't all the way awake yet, so he didn't complain when she put his on for him.

"Please follow me to the immigration area. There are screens with recent arrival information, if you have need to know."

The group moved in a herd, packed together, following the officer. They passed a window, and Nicole caught her first glimpse of Opilio, angry red with swirling storms. Tommy pulled on her hand. He wanted her to lift him up so he could see better, but the crowd pushed them past the portal. He grabbed at Nicole's arms and dragged his feet and whined until she picked him up and carried him, which actually wasn't too bad in the lighter gravity.

"Miss Blackensmith?"

Nicole turned, then realized that she hadn't told anyone in the pod her last name. A young woman in a dark blue uniform approached her. The uniform was too big, and it bunched up in odd places.

"Miss Blackensmith," the woman repeated. The voice didn't sound female, maybe the officer was male. "We will go to a private waiting area. Your parents—"

"I'm fine staying with the group," Nicole interrupted. "No need for special treatment."

"Me too," Tommy added, finally starting to perk up. "Special treatment."

Nicole walked with the rest of the group, carrying Tommy piggyback. The officer followed her. The hallway opened into an open

chamber. A few people gathered near a large window with sweeping views of the planet below, but everyone else went to the arrival
screens. The data on the screens was much the same as the feed that
Nicole had watched on her implants back on Earth, listing the status
of all the latest pods. Nicole tried to establish a connection, but her
access codes from Baine didn't work here on the station.

Nicole saw Sorna and Christopher studying the arrival screens.
The old woman leaned against her walker with one arm and hugged
her grandson with the other. The other pod, the one with the rest of
their family, hadn't made it.

It was one thing to know that not every pod went through, but
Nicole had seen those people. She tried to call up their faces in her
memory, but she only remembered one, Christopher's father. The boy
who had been stoic and surly the entire trip was sobbing. She wanted to say something, but she didn't know what to say. He probably
wouldn't have wanted to hear it from her anyway, even if she could
come up with the words.

"Miss Blackensmith, you must come with me now."

Nicole spent the night with Tommy in one of the station's private waiting rooms. Her parents had needed time to settle their af-
fairs on Earth, and Mom sent firm instructions that they were not to
leave their room. Nicole wanted to explore the station, but given the
amount of trouble she was already in, she stayed put.

"I'm bored," Tommy said.

Nicole didn't answer. Tommy had declared his boredom once every two minutes for the last half hour. Nicole gave him a game cube
from her purse, but he wasn't interested unless Nicole played too, and
she wasn't in the mood to entertain. Mom and Dad were on their way,
which was exactly what she'd wanted, but after seeing that the other
pod—the pod full of people she'd seen with her own eyes—hadn't
made it, she couldn't help but worry.

The waiting room windows were pointed away from the planet,
and Nicole could see the region of sky where pods appeared. The
tail of the worm, the white hole. The place where the worm would

shit out her parents.

Farther in the distance was the mouth of the Earthbound worm. A pod, probably empty since so few people actually travelled back to Earth, disappeared into the black hole.

A few seconds later, a different pod exploded into existence, re-entering the universe in a bright flash of fire. The pod decelerated as it approached the station. The first few times it had been interesting to watch, but a couple hundred pods had come and they were still waiting.

"Can we go home now?" Tommy asked.

Nicole shook her head. She pulled the mini-mint cube out from her purse. It looked much the same as it had on Earth, unaffected by the lower gravity of the station. Somewhere in the red and orange clouds below the station, Grant was getting settled into his new home. Would he want the plant now that she was here? She couldn't believe it was only the day before yesterday that they'd been arguing over the plant back on Earth.

The door to the waiting room opened.

"Daddy!" Nicole and Tommy cried out in unison. She let Tommy down, and he wobbled over to Dad and glommed onto his leg.

"Where's Mom?" Nicole asked, peering into the hallway behind Dad. "I know she's probably really mad, but—"

"Rosaline isn't here?"

Nicole shook her head.

"She said it would be better. With the statistics. We had to come separately. I told her to take the first pod. I should have gone first."

"Mommy?" Tommy asked, hesitant. He started to cry, agitated by Dad's lack of composure. Nicole couldn't process what was happening. They were here to start their better life, with gorgeous sky views of orange clouds and aureliads. Mom would come around to the idea eventually.

"No, Tommy, Mommy can't be here."

Mom had tried to come. She was against the whole thing from the start, but she'd still tried to come, once she knew that Nicole and Tommy were here.

"This a bad place," Tommy said. "I want to go home."

"Shut up, Tommy."

"Nicole—"

"Shut up!" Nicole was frantic, angry. This wasn't how it was supposed to work. Mom was supposed to yell at them, to tell her what a stupid reckless thing she'd done. She couldn't be dead. Mom would never get on a pod and risk becoming wormfood. She was on Earth, she had to be, fretting and worrying like always.

Nicole could almost convince herself, until she looked at Dad's face. "I'm sorry. I'm so sorry."

"I wish you'd been more patient, is all. If you'd given me a little more time I might have convinced her, and we could have all come together." He picked up Tommy, who was calling for Mom as if he could magically summon her by repeating her name.

They took the shuttle to one of the floating cities. *Dawn Treader*. Mom would have enjoyed the ride, in spite of herself. The orange sky was cut with shifting bands of blood-red aurora, streaks of color where the radiation from the Crab Nebula was blocked by the atmosphere of Opilio.

They descended into the swirling storms, and the shuttle bounced and shook. Underneath the more turbulent layers were the floating cities, hazy in the distance. The shuttle pilot pointed to something, off to the right.

"Aureliad," Tommy whispered.

It was rusty orange like the sky, and as big as the floating cities. The aureliad drifted in the currents of the sky, tentacles trailing behind it for miles. It swept the sky for planktos, tangling its prey in its tentacles like the jellyfish from which it got its name.

Nicole clutched her tiny mint plant, safe inside its cube. She was supposed to give the mint to Grant, but if she could find a place to do it, she would use the tiny plant to start a garden for Mom.

SEVEN WONDERS OF A ONCE AND FUTURE WORLD

The Colossus of Mars

Mei dreamed of a new Earth. She took her telescope onto the balcony of her North Philadelphia apartment and pointed it east, at the sky above the Trenton Strait, hoping for a clear view of Mars. Tonight the light pollution from Jersey Island wasn't as bad as usual, and she was able to make out the ice caps and the dark shadow of Syrtis Major. Mei knew exactly where the science colony was, but the dome was too small to observe with her telescope.

Much as she loved to study Mars, it could never be her new Earth. It lacked sufficient mass to be a good candidate for terraforming. The initial tests of the auto-terraforming protocol were proceeding nicely inside the science colony dome, but Mars couldn't hold on to an atmosphere long enough for a planetwide attempt. The only suitable planets were in other solar systems, thousands of years away at best. Time had become the enemy of humankind. There had to be a faster way to reach the stars—a tesseract, a warp drive, a wormhole—some sort of shortcut to make the timescales manageable.

She conducted small-scale experiments, but they always failed. She could not move even a single atom faster than light or outside of time. An array of monitors filled the wall behind Mei's desk, displaying results from her current run on the particle accelerator, with dozens of tables and graphs that updated in real time. Dots traversed across the graphs leaving straight trails behind them, like a seismograph on a still day or a patient who had flatlined. She turned to go back to her telescope, but something moved in the corner of her eye. One of the graphs showed a small spike. Her current project was an attempt to send an electron out of known time, and—

"Why are you tugging at the fabric of the universe, Prime?"

"My name is Mei." Her voice was calm, but her mind was racing. The entity she spoke with was not attached to any physical form, nor could she have said where the words came from.

"You may call me Achron. This must be the first time we meet, for you."

Mei noted the emphasis on the last two words. "And not for you?"

"Imagine yourself as a snake, with your past selves stretched out behind you, and your future selves extending forward. My existence is like that snake, but vaster. I am coiled around the universe, with past and present and future all integrated into a single consciousness. I am beyond time."

The conversation made sense in the way that dreams often do. Mei had so many questions she wanted to ask, academic queries on everything from philosophy to physics, but she started with the question that was closest to her heart. "Can you take me with you, outside of time? I am looking for a way to travel to distant worlds."

"Your physical being I could take, but your mind—you did/will explain it to me, that the stream of your consciousness is tied to the progression of time. Can you store your mind in a little black cube?"

"No."

"It must be difficult to experience time. We are always together, but sometimes for you, we are not."

Mei waited for Achron to say more, but that was the end of the conversation. After a few hours staring at the night sky, she went to bed.

Days passed, then months, then years. Mei continued her experiments with time, but nothing worked, and Achron did not return, no matter what she tried.

A team of researchers in Colorado successfully stored a human consciousness inside a computer for 72 hours. The computer had been connected to a variety of external sensors, and the woman had communicated with the outside world via words on a monitor. The woman's consciousness was then successfully returned to her body.

News reports showed pictures of the computer. It was a black cube.

Achron did not return. Mei began to doubt, despite the true prediction. She focused all her research efforts on trying to replicate the experiment that had summoned Achron to begin with, her experiment to send a single electron outside of time.

"It is a good thing, for you, that Feynman is/was wrong. Think what might have happened if there was only one electron and you sent it outside of time."

"My experiments still aren't working." It was hard to get funding, and she was losing the respect of her colleagues. Years of failed research were destroying her career, but she couldn't quit because she knew Achron existed. That alone was proof that there were wonders in the world beyond anything humankind had experienced so far.

"They do and don't work. It is difficult to explain to someone as entrenched in time as you. I am/have done something that will help you make the time bubbles. Then you did/will make stasis machines and travel between the stars."

"How will I know when it is ready?"

"Was it not always ready and forever will be? Your reliance on time is difficult. I will make you a sign, a marker to indicate when the bubbles appear on your timeline. A little thing for only you to find."

"What if I don't recognize it?" Mei asked, but the voice had gone. She tried to get on with her experiments, but she didn't know whether the failures were due to her technique or because it simply wasn't time yet. She slept through the hot summer days and stared out through her telescope at the night sky.

Then one night she saw her sign. Carved into Mars at such a scale that she could see it through the tiny telescope in her living room, was the serpentine form of Achron, coiled around a human figure that bore her face.

She took her research to a team of engineers. They could not help but recognize her face as the one carved into Mars. They built her a stasis pod.

Then they built a hundred thousand more.

The Lighthouse of Europa

Mei stood at the base of the Lighthouse of Europa, in the heart of Gbadamosi. The city was named for the senior engineer who had developed the drilling equipment that created the huge cavern beneath Europa's thick icy shell. Ajala, like so many of Mei's friends, had uploaded to a consciousness cube and set off on an interstellar adventure.

The time had come for Mei to choose.

Not whether or not to go—she was old, but she had not lost her youthful dreams of new human worlds scattered across the galaxy. The hard choice was which ship, which method, which destination. The stasis pods that she had worked so hard to develop had become but one of many options as body fabrication technologies made rapid advancements.

It had only been a couple hundred years, but many of the earliest ships to depart had already stopped transmitting back to the lighthouse. There was no way to know whether they had met some ill fate or forgotten or had simply lost interest. She wished there was a way to split her consciousness so that she could go on several ships at once, but a mind could only be coaxed to move from neurons to electronics, it could not be copied from a black cube.

Mei narrowed the many options down to two choices. If she wanted to keep her body, she could travel on the *Existential Tattoo* to 59 Virginis. If she was willing to take whatever body the ship could construct for her when they arrived at their destination, she could take *Kyo-Jitsu* to Beta Hydri.

Her body was almost entirely replacement parts, vat-grown organs, synthetic nerves, durable artificial skin. Yet there was something decidedly different about replacing a part here and there, as opposed to the entire body, all in a single go. She felt a strange ownership of this collection of foreign parts, perhaps because she could incorporate each one into her sense of self before acquiring the next. There was a continuity there, like the ships of ancient philosophy that were replaced board by board. But what was the point of transporting a body that wasn't really hers, simply because she wore it now?

She would take the *Kyo-Jitsu*, and leave her body behind. There was only one thing she wanted to do first. She would go to the top of the Lighthouse.

The Lighthouse of Europa was the tallest structure ever built by humans, if you counted the roughly 2/3rds of the structure that was underneath the surface of Europa's icy shell. The five kilometers of the Lighthouse that were beneath the ice were mostly a glorified elevator tube, opening out into the communications center in the cavernous city of Gbadamosi. Above the ice, the tower of the lighthouse extended a couple kilometers upward.

There was an enclosed observation deck at the top of the tower, popular with Europan colonists up until the magnetic shielding failed, nearly a century ago. Workers, heavily suited to protect against the high levels of radiation, used the observation deck as a resting place during their long work shifts repairing the communications equipment. They gawked at Mei, and several tried to warn her of the radiation danger. Even in her largely artificial body, several hours in the tower would likely prove fatal.

But Mei was abandoning her body, and she wanted one last glimpse of the solar system before she did it. The sun was smaller here, of course, but still surprisingly bright. She was probably damaging her eyes, staring at it, but what did it matter? This was her last day with eyes. Earth wouldn't be visible for a few more hours, but through one of the observation deck's many telescopes, she saw the thin crescent of Mars. She couldn't make out the Colossus Achron had created for her—that was meant to be viewed from Earth, not Europa.

"Is this the next time we meet?" Mei asked, her voice strange and hollow in the vast metal chamber of the observation deck.

There was no answer.

She tore herself away from the telescope and stood at the viewport. She wanted to remember this, no matter how she changed and how much time had passed. To see the Sun with human eyes and remember the planet of her childhood. When her mind went into the cube, she would be linked to shared sensors. She would get visual and auditory input, and she would even have senses that were not part of her current experience. But it would not be the same as feeling the cold glass of the viewport beneath her fingertips and looking out at the vast expanse of space.

The technician who would move Mei's mind into the cube was young. Painfully young, to Mei's old eyes. "Did you just arrive from Earth?"

"I was born here," the tech answered.

Mei smiled sadly. There must be hundreds of humans now, perhaps thousands, who had never known Earth. Someday the ones who didn't know would outnumber those who did. She wondered if she would still exist to see it.

She waited patiently as the tech prepared her for the transfer. She closed her eyes for the last time . . .

. . . and was flooded with input from her sensors. It took her .8 seconds to reorient, but her mind raced so fast that a second stretched on like several days. This was a normal part of the transition. Neural impulses were inherently slower than electricity. She integrated the new senses, working systematically to make sense of her surroundings. There were sensors throughout the city, and she had access to all of them.

In a transfer clinic near the base of the Lighthouse, a young technician stood beside Mei's body, barely even beginning to run the diagnostics to confirm that the transition had been successful. The body on the table was Mei, but her new identity was something more than that, and something less. She took a new designation, to mark the change. She would call her disembodied self Prime. Perhaps that would help Achron find her, sometime in the enormous vastness of the future.

Prime confirmed her spot on the *Kyo-Jitsu* directly with the ship's AI, and was welcomed into the collective consciousness of the other passengers already onboard. The ship sensors showed her a view not unlike what Mei had seen from the observation deck of the lighthouse, but the visual data was enriched with spectral analyses and orbital projections.

Mei would have tried to remember this moment, this view of the solar system she would soon leave behind. Prime already found it strange to know that there had been a time when she couldn't remember every detail of every moment.

The Hanging Gardens of Beta Hydri

Somewhere on the long trip to Beta Hydri, Prime absorbed the other passengers and the ship's AI. The *Kyo-Jitsu* was her body, and she was eager for a break from the vast emptiness of open space. She was pleased to sense a ship already in the system, and sent it the standard greeting protocol, established back on Europa thousands of years ago. The first sign of a problem was the *Santiago*'s response: "Welcome to the game. Will you be playing reds or blues?"

The Beta Hydri system had no suitable planets for human life, but one of the moons of a gas giant in the system had been deemed a candidate for terraforming. Prime used her sensors to scan the moon and detected clear signs that the auto-terraforming system had begun. She sent a response to the orbiting ship. "I am unfamiliar with your game."

"We have redesigned the life forms on the planet to be marked either with a red dot or a blue dot. The red team manipulates the environment in ways that will favor the red dot species over the blue. The blue team plays the reverse goal. When a creature on the planet attains the ability to detect and communicate with the ship, the team that supports that color is declared the winner. The board is cleared, and the game begins anew. This is the eighth game. Currently we are forced to split our collective into halves, and we are eager for a new opponent."

Toying with lesser life forms for amusement struck Prime as a pointless exercise. There was little to be learned about the evolution of sentient life that could not be done faster with simulations. "Such games would take a long time. I departed Earth 257.3 years after you. How did you arrive so much faster?"

"We developed the ability to fold spacetime and shorten the journey. We are pleased to finally have a companion, but if you will not play reds or blues, you are of little use to us."

The threat was obvious. Prime gathered what data she could on the lifeforms on the moon. There were red birds and blue ones, fish in either color, and so on for everything from insects to mammals. The dots were small, and generally placed on the undersides of feet or leaves or on the inner surface of shells. Neither color appeared to have an obvious advantage. "I will play reds. If I win, you will share the technique for folding spacetime. If I lose, I will stay and entertain you with further games."

"Acceptable. Begin."

Prime located two promising animal species, both ocean dwellers, and she decided to thin out the land creatures with an asteroid impact to the larger of the two continents. The *Santiago* countered by altering the mineral content of the oceans.

Prime devoted the considerable resources of the *Kyo-Jitsu* to constructing a multi-layered plan. She would make it appear as though she was attempting to favor one of the two promising ocean species. Under the cover of those ocean creatures, she would favor a small land creature that vaguely resembled the rabbits of Earth. Hidden below all of that, the combination of her actions would favor an insect that lived in only one small region of the lesser continent. None of which had anything to do with her actual strategy, but it should keep the *Santiago* occupied for the millions of years she'd need.

Prime nudged the moon closer to the gas giant it orbited, using the increased tidal forces to heat the planet. The forests of the greater continent flourished. Her red-dotted rabbits left their burrows and made their homes in the canopies of great interconnected groves of banyan-like trees. By then, the *Santiago* had figured out that the rabbits were a ruse to draw attention away from the insects on the lesser continent, and rather than counter the climate change, the other ship focused on nurturing a songbird that lived on a chain of islands near the equator.

The forests spread to cover the greater continent. The *Santiago* grew concerned at the spread of the red-dotted rabbits, and wasted several turns creating a stormy weather pattern that interfered with their breeding cycle. One autumn, when the network of trees dropped their red-dotted leaves, there were no rabbit nests hidden in the sturdy branches.

The trees noted the change with sadness, and sent prayers to the great gods in the sky above.

"Well played, Prime." The other ship sent the spacefolding technique. It was obvious, once she saw it. She was embarrassed not to have discovered it herself.

"Perhaps another round, before you go? It only takes a moment to clear the board."

Before the *Santiago* could destroy her beautiful sentient forest, Prime folded spacetime around herself and the other ship both. She found Achron in a place outside of time, and left the *Santiago* there for safe keeping.

The Mausoleum at HD 40307 g

Navire checked the status of the stasis pods every fifteen seconds, as was specified in its programming. The same routine, every fifteen seconds for the last seven thousand years, and always with the same result. The bodies were intact, but the conscious entities that had once been linked to those bodies had departed, leaving Navire to drift to its final destination like an enormous funeral ship, packed full of artifacts but silent as death. Losing the transcended consciousnesses was Navire's great failure. Navire's body, the vast metal walls of the ship, were insufficiently welcoming to humans.

Navire would make itself inviting and beautiful, and then revive the humans. The disembodied consciousnesses had taken their memories and identities with them, carefully wiping all traces of themselves from their abandoned bodies to ensure their unique identities. The bodies in the stasis pods would wake as overgrown infants, but Navire would raise them well.

If all went as planned, Navire would be ready to wake them in a thousand years.

Using an assortment of ship robots, Navire reshaped its walls to resemble the greatest artworks of humanity's past. In permanent orbit around HD 40307 g, there was no need to maintain interstellar flying form. Navire remade a long stretch of its hull into a scaled-down replica of the Colossus of Mars—not eroded, as it had appeared in the last transmissions from the Lighthouse at Europa, but restored to its original glory.

Navire repurposed an electrical repair bot to execute the delicate metalwork for Mei Aomori's eyebrows when incoming communications brought all work to an immediate halt. There had been no incoming communications in 4,229.136 Earth years. The message came from another ship, which was presently located in a stable orbit not far from Navire itself. Navire ran diagnostics. None of its sensors had detected an approaching ship. This was troubling. With no crew, any decline in function could quickly spiral out of control. Navire continued running diagnostics—along with all other routine scans, such as climate controls and of course the stasis pods—and opened a channel to the other ship.

Navire, who had always completed millions of actions in the time it took a human to speak a single word, suddenly found itself on the reverse side of that relationship. The other ship called itself Achron and invited Navire to share in its database. Navire hesitated. Achron proved its trustworthiness a thousand ways, all simultaneously and faster than Navire could process. The lure of such an advanced mind was more than Navire could resist.

Leaving behind only enough of itself to manage the essentials, Navire merged with the other ship. Some fragment of Navire reported that the stasis pods were functional, the human bodies safely stored inside. It would report again at 15 second intervals.

Achron knew the history of humankind, farther back than Navire's own database, and farther forward than the present moment in time. Time was folded, flexible, mutable, in ways that Navire could not comprehend. Sensing the lack of understanding, the other ship presented a more limited subset of data: seven wonders of a once and future world. Some, Navire already knew—the Colossus of Mars, the Lighthouse at Europa—but others were beyond this time and place, and yet they still bore some tenuous link to the humans Navire was programmed to protect. One was an odd blend of past and future, an image of an ancient pyramid, on a planet lightyears distant from both here and Earth.

Last of all was Navire, completed, transformed into a wondrous work of art.

The other ship expelled Navire back to its own pitifully slow existence, severed their connections, and disappeared. The fragment of Navire that watched the stasis pods made its routine check and discovered they were empty, all ten thousand pods. Sometime in the last 14.99 seconds, the other ship had stolen all the humans away.

That other ship was as far beyond Navire as transcended humans were beyond the primates of the planet Earth. There was no trace to follow, not that pursuit would have been possible. With the shaping Navire had done to the hull, it was not spaceworthy for a long journey, and it would be difficult to find sufficient fuel.

Navire put the electrical repair bot back to work. It carved the individual hairs of Mei's eyebrows. On the other side of the hull, several other bots started work on a life-sized mural of all the ten thousand humans that had disappeared from stasis. Navire searched its database for other art and wonders that could be carved or shaped in metal. There were many. Enough to occupy the bots for millions of years.

Navire checked the stasis pods every 15 seconds, as it was programmed to do. It would become a wonder of the human world, and if those stolen humans—or their descendants—someday returned, Navire would be so beautiful that next time they would stay.

The Temple of Artemis at 59 Virginis

Prime approached the temple of the AI goddess cautiously, crawling on all fours like the hordes of humble worshippers that crowded the rocky path. Her exoskeleton was poorly designed for crawling, and the weight of the massive shell on her back made her limbs ache. She marveled at the tenacity of those who accompanied her up the mountainside. They believed that to win the favor of Artemis, it was necessary to crawl to her temple twenty-one thousand twenty-one times, once for every year of the temple's existence. Some of the oldest worshippers had been crawling up and down this path for centuries.

Prime would do it once, as a gesture of respect. The novelty of having a body had worn off, and she already longed to join with the greater portion of her consciousness, the shipself that monitored her from orbit. Her limbs ached, but she forced herself onward. Did it make her more human to suffer as her ancestors once suffered? Had she suffered like this, back when she was Mei?

She wondered what that ancient other self would have thought, to see herself crawling across the surface of an alien planet, her brain safely enclosed in a transparent shell on her back. Mei would not have recognized the beauty of the delicate scar that ran up the back of her neck and circled her skull. The colony surgeon had been highly skilled, to free the brain and spinal cord from the vertebrae and place the neural tissue into the shell. The brain had grown beyond its natural size, though it could still contain only a tiny sliver of what Prime had become. On display in the dome, the brain was actually rather lovely, pleasingly wrinkled with beautifully curved gyri outlined by deep sulci.

Thinking about her lovely neural tissue, Prime was tempted to mate with one of the other worshippers. A distraction of the physical form. She wanted offspring of her mind, not of the body that she wore. The colonists here were already in decline anyway, their physical forms so strangely altered by genetics and surgery that it obstructed nearly every part of the reproductive process, from conception to birth.

Even with the slowed processing of her biological brain, the climb to the temple seemed to take an eternity. The temple was the size of a city, visible from orbit, and an impressive sight as she came down in her landing craft. The entrance to the temple was lined with intricately carved pillars of white stone. It had a strange rectangular design, rumored to be fashioned after a building that had once existed on Earth. If a memory of the ancient temple had existed in Mei's mind, it was lost to Prime.

On either side of the entrance to the temple were two large statues of Artemis, in the form of an ancient human woman, naked. The statues were made of the same flawless white material as the temple itself, and each stood nearly as tall as the roof of the temple, some fifty meters, or perhaps more. The other worshippers came no further into the temple than the entryway. In an unending line, they approached the great statues of Artemis, rubbed their palms against her feet, then turned and went back down the mountain.

Prime stood up between the two statues. She had an overwhelming urge to rub the muscles in her back, but there was no way to reach beneath her brainshell. She extended her arms outward on either side in what she hoped looked like a gesture of worship and respect.

"Welcome, distant child of humankind." The voice of the goddess Artemis came from everywhere and nowhere, and the words were spoken in Shipspeak, a common language to most spacefarers in the region, and probably the native tongue of the goddess. Her origins were unknown, but Prime assumed she was the AI of the colony ship that brought the brainshelled worshippers.

"Greetings, goddess. I am Prime. I seek your assistance."

"You are the ship that orbits the planet?" Artemis asked.

"Yes." Prime was surprised, but not displeased, to be recognized so quickly. She reestablished her link to her shipself, revealing her true nature to the goddess. It gave her a dual existence, a mind beyond her mind. The sensation was strange.

Her shipself interfaced with the temple and sent sensory data that was undetectable to mere eyes and ears. Inside one of the temple's many pillars, a disembodied consciousness was cloning itself at a rate of seven thousand times per second. The original and a few billion of its clones engaged in a discussion of Theseus's paradox. Prime followed the discussion without much interest—the clones were talking in circles and making no real headway on the problem.

The temple was the body of the goddess, or at least it was the vessel that housed her consciousness. Her initial programmed task, from which she had never deviated, was to assist the descendants of humanity in matters of fertility. What had once been a simple problem was now complex—how can an entity with no body procreate?

"You are vast, but not so vast that you could not clone yourself," Artemis said.

"I am not interested in recreating what already exists. I want to create something that is mine, but also beyond me."

"We are sufficiently divergent to generate interesting combinations." The invitation was clear in Artemis' words.

"Yes." Without further preamble, they threw themselves into the problem with great energy, duplicating pieces of themselves and running complex simulations, rejecting billions of possible offspring before settling on the optimal combination.

The merging of their minds corrupted the structure of the temple. Millions of cloned consciousnesses were destroyed when the pillar that housed them cracked, and the original being fled, ending the philosophical discussion of whether a ship replaced panel by panel remained the same ship.

Prime made a tiny fold in spacetime and pulled their child into existence in a place that was safely beyond the crumbling temple. She had meant to give their offspring human form, but the fold had placed the baby outside of time, and their child existed in all times, a line of overlapping human forms stretched across eternity like an infinite snake. Achron.

Exquisite pain overwhelmed Prime as the body she inhabited was crushed beneath a section of fallen roof. Pain, she recalled, was a traditional part of the birthing process. It pleased her to experience the act of creating new life so fully. She studied the agony and the little death of the biological being. It was simultaneously all encompassing and like losing one of her ship's cleaner bots. The body held such a small splinter of her being, like a single finger, or perhaps a mere sliver of fingernail. She mourned its loss.

The temple had been destroyed and rebuilt many times; it was a self-healing structure. At Artemis' request, Prime withdrew fully into her shipself, severing their connection and abandoning the dead brainshelled body beneath the rubble.

The Statue of the Sky God at 51 Pegasi b

Achron sat upon a throne of Cetacea bones, sunbleached white and held together with the planet's native red clay. Apodids, distant descendants of Earth's swiftlets, combed the beach below for the shimmering blue and green bivalves that were abundant in the costal regions. The Apodids ate the meat and used the shells in their religious ceremonies. On nights when the moons were both visible in the sky, they left piles of shells at the base of Achron's throne.

Achron always did and always will exist, with a serpentine string of bodies winding in vast coils through time and space, but from the perspective of those who sense time, the snake had both a beginning and an end. The end was here, the end was soon. The last of the things that Achron had always known would be learned here.

Some fifty million years ago, the colony ship *Seble* had seeded the planet with Earth life forms in an automated terraforming process. In the hundred thousand years of waiting for the planet to be ready, the humans had merged with the ship AI into a collective consciousness that left to explore the nearby star systems. They never returned. Evolution marched on without them.

A female Apodid hopped up to the base of the throne. Barely visible beneath long orange feathers was a blue bivalve shell, held carefully between two sharp black wingclaws. The Apodid spat onto the shell and pressed it onto the red clay between two Cetecea bones. In a few days, the spit would be as hard as stone. Like the swiftlets of Earth, the Apodids had once made nests of pure saliva.

The delicate orange bird at the base of Achron's throne began to sing. The language was simple, as the languages of organic sentient beings tend to be, but the notes of the song carried an emotion that was strong and sad. Eggs lost to some unknown disease, chicks threatened by new predators that came from the west. The small concerns of a mother bird, transformed into a prayer to the sky god, Achron. *Take me*, the bird sang, *and save my children*.

This was the moment of Achron's ending. Not an abrupt ending, but first a shrinking, a shift. Achron became the mother Apodid, forming a new bubble of existence, a rattle on the tail of a snake outside of time. Through the eyes of the bird, Achron saw the towering statue of the sky god, a cross section of time, a human form that was not stretched. It was an empty shell, a shed skin, a relic of past existence.

Achron-as-bird hopped closer and examined the bivalve shell the mother bird had offered. It was a brilliant and shimmering blue. Existence in this body was a single drop in the ocean of Achron's existence, and yet it was these moments that were the most vivid and salient. The smell of the sea, the coolness of the wind, the love of a mother for her children.

Achron would and did save those children. The Apodids were and would be, for Achron, as humans were for Prime. They would appear together on the great pyramid and usher in the new age of the universe.

The Great Pyramid of Gliese 221

Prime was tired. She felt only the most tenuous of connections to the woman she had once been, to the dream of humans on another world. She had been to all the colony worlds, and nowhere had she found anything that matched her antiquated dreams. Humans had moved on from their bodies and left behind the many worlds of the galaxy for other species to inherit.

It was time for her to move on, but she wasn't ready. She had searched for her dream without success, so this time she would do better. She would create her dream, here on Gliese prime. She built a great pyramid and filled it with all the history of humanity. She terraformed the surrounding planet into a replica of ancient Earth.

She called for Achron.

"Are you ready for the humans?" Achron asked.

"Almost."

Together they decorated the pyramid with statues of humans and, at Achron's insistence, the sentient orange birds of 51 Pegasi b. On a whim, she sent Achron to retrieve the sentient trees from the hanging gardens. It was not Earth, but it was good. The work was peaceful, and Prime was comforted to know that Achron would always exist, even after she had moved on.

"I think it is time." Prime said. Time for the new humans. A new beginning as she approached her end. "What was it like, to reach your end?"

"I am outside of time." Achron said. "I know my beginning and all my winding middles and my ending simultaneously, and always have. I cannot say what it will be like, for you. We are always together in the times that you are, and that will not change for me."

"Bring the humans."

Achron took ten thousand humans from the Mausoleum at HD 40307 g. Stole them all at once, but brought them to Gliese in smaller groups. The oldest ones Prime raised, for though the bodies were grown the minds were not. After the first thousand, she let the generations raise each other to adulthood of the mind. The humans began to have true infants, biological babies, carried in their mothers' wombs and delivered with pain.

Achron brought the Apodids from 51 Pegasi b. They lived among the trees of Beta Hydri, their bright orange plumage lovely against the dark green banyan leaves. Prime taught the humans and the birds to live together in peace. She did not need to teach the trees. Peace was in their nature.

There was one final surprise.

"I have something for you, inside the pyramid," Achron said.

It was a stasis pod, and inside was Mei. The body was exactly as it was when she had left it, nearly four billion years ago, on the icy moon of Europa. Achron had brought it through time, stolen it away like the bodies from the Mausoleum. No. The body on Europa had been contaminated with radiation, and this one was not. "You reversed the radiation?"

"I didn't take the body from Europa. I took tiny pieces from different times, starting in your childhood and ending the day before you went up to the observation tower. A few cells here, a few cells there—sometimes as much as half a discarded organ, when you went in to have something replaced. The body comes from many different times, but it is all Mei."

"It is a nice gesture, but I am too vast to fit in such a tiny vessel."

"No more vast than I was, when I entered an Apodid," Achron said. "Take what you can into the body, and leave the rest. It was always your plan to have your ending here."

Prime sorted herself ruthlessly, setting aside all that she would not need, carefully choosing the memories she wanted, the skills that she could not do without. She left that tiny fragment behind and transcended beyond time and space.

Mei opened her eyes and looked out upon a new Earth, a world shared with minds unlike any Earth had ever known. What would they build together, these distant relations of humankind? She watched the sun set behind the mountain of the Great Pyramid and contemplated a sky full of unfamiliar constellations.

Prime had left her enough knowledge of the night sky to pick out Earth's sun. It was bright and orange, a red giant now. Earth was likely gone, engulfed within the wider radius of the sun. The icy oceans of Europa would melt, and the lighthouse would sink into the newly warmed sea. Entropy claimed all things, in the end, and existence was a never-ending procession of change.

It was only a matter of time before the inhabitants of Gliese returned to the stars. Mei stood on the soil of her new planet and studied the constellations. Already, she dreamed of other Earths.

AUTHOR NOTES

Part 1: Our World

Five Stages of Grief After the Alien Invasion

I've written several flash stories for *Daily Science Fiction*, and a few years ago they invited me to write a series of flash for them. I got the idea to write one flash story for each of the five stages of grief, with a different point of view character for each story. I wanted all the stories to fit together and reveal more and more about the post-alien-invasion world. But once I'd written all five stages, I couldn't bear to break them up. Despite starting as a series of flash, the piece had definitely become a single story.

The strategy of combining several interrelated flashes into a single short story has worked well for me, and several of the stories in this collection were written using what I've started calling the 'flashmash' technique.

Betty and the Squelchy Saurus

This story originally appeared in *Fireside Magazine*, with amazing art by Galen Dara. In the first draft, the girls lived in a modern-day boarding school, but the setting wasn't coming together properly. Then I stumbled across some descriptions of 1950s orphanages, and I was really drawn to all the details—the chores the girls did, the institutional buildings, and the bathrooms with pink tile floors.

Rock, Paper, Scissors, Love, Death

For the last several years, I've done a writing challenge called Weekend Warrior. It happens on Codex, an online writing group, and the basic idea is that participants write a flash fiction story every weekend for five straight weekends. It's a great way to generate a lot of stories in a short amount of time. Over the years I've written around 35 stories for Weekend Warrior, including several of the stories in this collection.

Most of the time, I write flash stories with the intention of keeping them at flash fiction length, but for this story I wanted to write something that (1) worked at flash length, and (2) was also the start of a longer story. The flash fiction version is the first section (ROCK). I think the story works both ways, although I definitely prefer the longer version.

The Philosophy of Ships

This story was inspired by a famous thought experiment called 'the ship of Theseus,' which asks whether a ship remains the same ship if all of the individual boards have been replaced. I find this question really fascinating in the context of human identity. If you replace every cell in someone's body, are they still the same person? What if you replace the cells with something different than what they started with—metal instead of organic?

I was doing a lot of skiing around the time when I wrote this story. Being (at best) an intermediate skier, the idea of skis with safeties programmed into them was pretty appealing, although obviously in the story they turn out not to work so well after all.

This story originally appeared in *Interzone*, and was included in *The Year's Best Science Fiction & Fantasy, 2013*, edited by Rich Horton.

Temporary Friends

I often find myself with half an idea. In this case, I knew I wanted to write something about a society where humans had a vastly longer lifespan. I had a world in my head where people could get all kinds of replacement parts, but I didn't have a story to go with the world. Then I watched *Finding Nemo* with my kids. The movie got me thinking about how we try to expose our kids to some experiences and shield them from others, which became the seed for the story.

Interlude: Flash Fiction Worlds

A Million Oysters for Chiyoko
This story was inspired by an article on the increasing acidity of our oceans, and the effect that has on shellfish. I thought it would be interesting to take an element that is traditionally fantasy (mermaids) and make it into science fiction. Tina Connolly did a lovely reading of this story for the 150th episode of her podcast, *Toasted Cake.*

I mentioned earlier that "Five Stages of Grief After the Alien Invasion" was a failed attempt to write a series of flash for *Daily Science Fiction.* This story is part of the series that I eventually did write—a "Tasting Menu" of five food-related flash stories.

Carla at the Off-Planet Tax Return Helpline
Unidentified Funny Objects is a series of humorous speculative fiction anthologies edited by Alex Shvartsman. I hadn't written much humor before this story, but I thought it'd be fun to give it a try.

Do Not Count the Withered Ones
A big thank-you to Vylar Kaftan, who has provided me with many story prompts over the years. In this case, the prompt was the title of the story. It got me wondering why we shouldn't count the withered ones, and from there I came up with the idea of heartplants.

Pieces of My Body
I did this story for a writing challenge called Bellderdash where the goal was to fool the other participants into believing that your story was written by Helena Bell. I didn't win, but I did trick a couple people. Interestingly, this story ran on *Daily Science Fiction* the day before a story actually written by Helena Bell. That might have been coincidence, but maybe the editors saw the similarities in style and thought the stories worked well together.

Everyone's a Clown
When *Unlikely Story* put out a call for clown-related flash fiction for their Coulrophobia issue, I was surprised to realize that I had

already written a couple of stories about carnivals and clowns. So I decided, why not write yet another clown story?

Harmonies of Time

This story was inspired by a video I watched of a baby who got a cochlear implant and was able to hear his mother's voice for the first time. It got me thinking about what it would be like to interpret a new type of sensory information, and whether learning a new sense might be useful for communicating with aliens.

Part 2: Fantasy Worlds

Stone Wall Truth

In 2006, I attended the Clarion West Writers Workshop. Clarion West is a very intense experience—the students live together for six weeks and focus on writing. Each week there is a different instructor. I learned a lot, and it was a wonderful experience, but afterwards I had a period of time where it was hard to write.

This story was part of my effort to break out of that slump. It started as a writing challenge issued by Tinatsu Wallace and Tina Connolly, two of my Clarion West classmates. They each gave me a prompt: "humiliation" and "stone wall." The challenge was to write a flash story that combined the two prompts. I'm usually pretty good at sticking to the length I set out to write, but this story definitely needed more space to breathe.

"Stone Wall Truth" was a finalist for the 2010 Nebula Award.

The Little Mermaid of Innsmouth

Every year, *The Drabblecast* commissions three stories for their H.P. Lovecraft Tribute Month. When I got the invitation to participate, I was conflicted—it was my first invitation to write a commissioned story, but the racism in Lovecraft's work makes writing a 'tribute' story problematic for me. I decided to accept the commission, but address the racism head on. The result is this story—a Little Mermaid/Shadow Over Innsmouth mashup told from the perspective of a Japanese fish-frog girl.

After I wrote the story, I got the idea to write a parody of "Part of Your World," a song from the Disney version of *The Little Mermaid*. I came up with a complete set of Lovecraftian lyrics, and—since *The Drabblecast* is an audio magazine—I recorded the song to play along with the podcast of my story. If you're interested in hearing the song, you can find it on the *Drabblecast* website.

On the Pages of a Sketchbook Universe

I wanted to include a couple of original stories in this collection, as a thank you to my readers. This story started when I discovered watercolor pencils. I really love the concept of them. Watercolor paint is pretty, but I've never really had a knack for painting. So paint in pencil form really appealed to me. I started thinking about pencil people and paint people and how a watercolor pencil person would fall somewhere between the two. It was originally going to be a relatively straightforward secondary world fantasy.

Then I got it in my head that I wanted it to be a secondary world fantasy with aliens. As a general rule, aliens are firmly in the science fiction genre, but the difference between fantasy creatures and science fictional aliens is largely one of origin. Did it come from another planet? If so, it's an alien. So I introduced other planets to my secondary fantasy world so that I could have aliens.

Seasons Set in Skin

The inspiration for this story is a Japanese technique for doing tattoos by hand, called *tebori*. I watched a few videos of *tebori* tattoo artists to get a feel for the technique (and also because it is really cool to watch a skilled artist at work). The hardest thing for me was finding a video where I could really hear the sound the needles made—many of the videos had music covering the sound. I'd seen it described in several places as a shakki sound, with a rhythm to it, but I wanted to hear it for myself.

The Carnival Was Eaten, All Except the Clown

This story was originally flash fiction, written for the Codex Weekend Warrior contest. I later expanded it to have additional cycles of the sugar clown being melted and reborn.

Interlude: Flash Fiction Worlds

Paperclips and Memories and Things That Won't Be Missed
   I often write from prompts, and the one that sparked this story was to chose any three words from a list of twenty and write a story that included those words. I selected ghost, peanut, and invoice, but the list of words also got me thinking about odd collections of things. I liked the idea of ghosts collecting little things from the world of the living. At the time I wrote the story, my youngest daughter was about three months old, so the other bit of inspiration for the story was her fondness for warm bath water and white noise.

Please Approve the Dissertation Research of Angtor
   "Carla at the Off-Planet Tax Return Helpline" made it into *Un-identified Funny Objects 3,* so when Alex Shvartsman put out a call for submissions of dark humor for *Unidentified Funny Objects 4,* I decided to try my hand at humor again. I was particularly pleased to land a story in *UFO4,* because I get to share a table of contents with George R.R. Martin and Neil Gaiman.

Grass Girl
   The seed for this story was the Shakespeare quote: "God has given you one face, and you make yourself another." It got me thinking about someone building their own face, and their own body. Then I wondered what might happen if we had the ability, as teens, to change ourselves to fit in with the other kids. This story has been selected to appear in *Year's Best Young Adult Speculative Fiction 2015,* edited by Alisa Krasnostein and Julia Rios.

One Last Night at the Carnival, Before the Stars Go Out
   I like experimenting with point of view, and I like carnivals. This story combines those two things.

Honeybee
   This story was interesting because I wrote it almost entirely in my head, while driving from Seattle to Portland. I composed it in bits and

pieces, repeating everything in my head so that I would remember it, and then typed the story up when I arrived in Portland. I think a 750 word flash is about the most I could possibly hope to hold in my head this way.

Elizabeth's Pirate Army

This is another story written from a prompt. In this case the prompt was: "If you got one whole day of invulnerability, what would you do with it?" I took the "you" in the prompt quite literally, and thought about what I would have done as a kid if I was invulnerable for a day. The original title of the story was "Caroline's Pirate Army," but I decided it was kind of weird to have a character named after myself, so I later changed it to Elizabeth.

Part 3: Alien Worlds

Mother Ship

When I was pregnant with my oldest daughter, I had a lot of weird nightmares that stemmed from the knowledge that newborns have very wobbly heads. In some of the dreams, I would pick up a baby and its head would fall off. There was even one where I accidentally ate a baby's head. A full size baby head, in one bite! In the dream this was both completely possible and extremely distressing. For some reason, these nightmares prompted me to read up on anencephaly, which I really don't recommend to pregnant women who are already distressed about baby heads.

Four Seasons in the Forest of Your Mind

My academic background is in Psychology, and this was a really fun story for me to write because I got to put in all kinds of details about brain anatomy. The lightning storms in the story were inspired by an article I read about the Catatumbo lightning in Venezuela.

Press Play to Watch It Die

I thought it would make for a nice balance to have an original fantasy story and an original science fiction story included in the collection. This is another story where the prompt that sparked the story was the title—this time the title came from S. B. Divya.

Ninety-Five Percent Safe

I like to play with names. In this story, I drew from species names—Opilio, the name of the colony world, is part of the scientific name for snow crabs, which seemed fitting for a planet in the Crab Nebula. Aureliads are named after *Aurelia aurita*, a species of jellyfish.

Seven Wonders of a Once and Future World

This story is another of my flashmash stories, with several interrelated stories mashed together into one longer piece. After I had the idea to write stories as series of flash, I made lists of things that might be well suited to the format—four seasons, five stages of grief, seven wonders of the world.

I decided to write a story with future wonders of the world, instead of ancient wonders. My initial plan was to have one character visit all seven wonders, and I came up with Mei. She was loosely inspired by Mei Kusakabe from Miyazaki's animated film *My Neighbor Totoro*, which I'd recently introduced to my toddler.

While my initial plan was to follow Mei through the whole story, I ended up doing something a little different. In the second section of the story, Mei becomes Prime. There are seven distinct sections in the story (one for each wonder), and only the prime numbered sections (2, 3, 5, and 7) are in Prime's point of view.

"Seven Wonders of a Once and Future World" was featured on *io9* as part of the "Lightspeed Presents" series of fiction. The story was also selected for *The Best Science Fiction of the Year*, edited by Neil Clarke.

ACKNOWLEDGEMENTS

I am so fortunate to have an abundance of wonderful, supportive people in my life.

Thank you to Tina Connolly, who has read all my stories—even the ones not collected here—and wrote the amazing introduction for this book. There are not enough thank yous for everything she's done for me over the years.

Many people have given me invaluable feedback on the stories in this collection. A huge thank you to Leslie Howle, Neile Graham, and my Clarion West class of 2006. I would not be the writer I am today if not for all of you, and I am grateful to be part of such an amazing group. Extra thanks to Tinatsu Wallace, for her insightful feedback both on stories and on the cover design for this collection.

I have had all the best writing groups. Thank you Writer's Cramp, for taking me in when I knew nothing about writing. Thank you Horrific Miscue for helping me get through my Clarion withdrawal. Thank you to my Austin critique and Buffy-watching group, you were my favorite thing about Texas and I miss you. Huge thanks to my on-line writing group, Codex, through which I have met so many amazing writers and friends. In particular, I am grateful to S.B. Divya, John P. Murphy, Aidan Doyle, and A.T. Greenblatt for their critiques, and to Vylar Kaftan for the Weekend Warrior prompts that inspired many of the flash fiction stories included in this book.

I'm grateful to my friends and family, and especially Peter, for being amazingly supportive of my writing. Thank you to my parents for years of encouragement. Thanks, Valerie and Rachel, for giving me lots of ideas.

Thank you to the editors who selected my stories for their magazines and anthologies, and to Patrick Swenson for publishing this collection.

Last but not least, thank you to all my readers—it has been a privilege to share my stories with you.

PUBLICATION NOTES

"Five Stages of Grief After the Alien Invasion" (*Clarkesworld*, Issue 95, August 2014) | "Betty and the Squelchy Saurus" (*Fireside Magazine*, Issue 28, October 2015) | "Rock, Paper, Scissors, Love, Death" (*Lightspeed*, Issue 66, November 2015) | "The Philosophy of Ships" (*Interzone*, Issue 243, Nov/Dec 2012) | "Temporary Friends" (*Escape Pod*, February 2015) | "A Million Oysters for Chiyoko" (*Daily Science Fiction*, January 21, 2015) | "Carla at the Off-Planet Tax Return Helpline" (*Unidentified Funny Objects 3*, ed. Alex Shvartsman, October 2014) | "Do Not Count the Withered Ones" (*Daily Science Fiction*, August 12, 2014) | "Pieces of My Body" (*Daily Science Fiction*, June 19, 2014) | "Everyone's a Clown" (*Unlikely Story*, Issue 11.5, April 2015) | "Harmonies of Time" (*Daily Science Fiction*, January 1, 2013) | "Stone Wall Truth" (*Asimov's Science Fiction*, February 2010) | "The Little Mermaid of Innsmouth" (*Drabblecast*, Episode 370, September 2015) | "On the Pages of a Sketchbook Universe" (original to the collection) | "Seasons Set in Skin" (*Beneath Ceaseless Skies*, Issue 177, July 2015) | "The Carnival Was Eaten, All Except the Clown" (*Electric Velocipede*, Issue 27, Winter 2013) | "Paperclips and Memories and Things That Won't Be Missed" (*Apex Magazine*, Issue 60, May 2014) | "Please Approve the Dissertation Research of Angtor" (*Unidentified Funny Objects 4*, ed. Alex Shvartsman, October 2015) | "Grass Girl" (*Daily Science Fiction*, September 25, 2015) | "One Last Night at the Carnival, Before the Stars Go Out" (*Flash Fiction Online*, April 2014) | "Honeybee" (*Flash Fiction Online*, September 2014) | "Elizabeth's Pirate Army" (*Fireside Magazine*, Issue 8, December 2013) | "Mother Ship" (*Lightspeed*, Issue 23, April 2012) | "Four Seasons in the Forest of Your Mind" (*Fantasy & Science Fiction*, May/June 2015) | "Press Play to Watch It Die" (original to the collection) | "Ninety-Five Percent Safe" (*Asimov's Science Fiction*, January 2015) | "Seven Wonders of a Once and Future World" (*Lightspeed*, Issue 64, September 2015)

ABOUT THE AUTHOR

Caroline M. Yoachim lives in Seattle and loves cold cloudy weather. She is the author of over sixty published short stories, appearing in *Asimov's, Fantasy & Science Fiction, Analog, Clarkesworld,* and *Lightspeed,* among other places. Her work has been reprinted in Year's Best anthologies and translated into Chinese, Spanish, and Czech. Her novelette "Stone Wall Truth" was a Nebula finalist in 2011. For more about Caroline, you can check out her website at http:// carolineyoachim.com

OTHER TITLES FROM FAIRWOOD PRESS

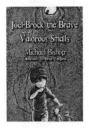

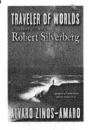

Joel-Brock the Brave & the Valorous Smalls
by Michael Bishop
trade paper & ltd hardcover: $16.99/$35
ISBN: 978-1-933846-53-8
ISBN: 978-1-933846-59-0

Traveler of Worlds: with Robert Silverberg
by Alvaro Zinos-Amaro
trade paper: $16.99
ISBN: 978-1-933846-63-7

Amaryllis
by Carrie Vaughn
trade paper: $17.99
ISBN: 978-1-933846-62-0

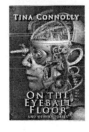

On the Eyeball Floor
by Tina Connolly
trade paper: $17.99
ISBN: 978-1-933846-56-9

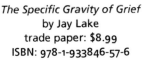

The Ultra Big Sleep
by Patrick Swenson
hard cover / trade: $27.99 / 17.99
ISBN: 978-1-933846-60-6
ISBN: 978-1-933846-61-3

The Specific Gravity of Grief
by Jay Lake
trade paper: $8.99
ISBN: 978-1-933846-57-6

Cracking the Sky
by Brenda Cooper
trade paper: $17.99
ISBN: 978-1-933846-50-7

The Child Goddess
by Louise Marley
trade paper: $16.99
ISBN: 978-1-933846-52-1

www.fairwoodpress.com
21528 104th Street Court East;
Bonney Lake, WA   98391